Praise for #1 *New York Times* bestselling author Stephanie Laurens

"Stephanie Laurens never fails to entertain and charm her readers with vibrant plots, snappy dialogue and unforgettable characters."
—*Historical Romance Reviews*

"One of the most talented authors on the scene today… Laurens has a real talent for writing sensuous and compelling love scenes."
—*Romance Reviews*

"Stephanie Laurens plays into readers' fantasies like a master and claims their hearts time and again."
—*RT Book Reviews*

Praise for bestselling author Michelle Willingham

"Michelle Willingham writes characters that feel all too real… A truly emotional read."
—*Publishers Weekly* on *Her Warrior Slave*

"The story is emotionally charged, with smoldering sensuality, memorable characters and sexy Vikings."
—*RT Book Reviews* on *To Tempt a Viking*

#1 *New York Times* bestselling author **Stephanie Laurens** began writing romances as an escape from the dry world of professional science, and her hobby quickly became a career. Her novels set in Regency England have captivated readers around the globe, making her one of the romance world's most beloved and popular authors. Stephanie has published fifty-nine works of historical romance, all of which remain in print and are readily available.

Stephanie lives with her husband and two cats in the hills outside Melbourne, Australia. When she isn't writing, she's reading, and if she isn't reading, she's tending her garden.

For information on all published novels and upcoming releases, and to sign up for her newsletter, visit Stephanie's website, stephanielaurens.com.

RITA® Award finalist **Michelle Willingham** has written over twenty historical romances, novellas and short stories. Currently she lives in southeastern Virginia with her husband and children. When she's not writing, Michelle enjoys reading, baking and avoiding exercise at all costs.

Visit her website at michellewillingham.com.

#1 *New York Times* **Bestselling Author**

STEPHANIE LAURENS

IMPETUOUS INNOCENT

HARLEQUIN® BESTSELLING AUTHOR COLLECTION

ISBN-13: 978-0-373-01026-4

This edition published by arrangement with Harlequin Books S.A.

For questions and comments about the quality of this book, please contact us at CustomerService@Harlequin.com.

Printed in U.S.A.

CONTENTS

Also available from Stephanie Laurens and MIRA

By Winter's Light
The Tempting of Thomas Carrick
A Match for Marcus Cynster

And coming soon

The Lady's Command

IMPETUOUS INNOCENT

Stephanie Laurens

CHAPTER ONE

"GEORGIE? GEORGIE! OPEN this door! Aw—c'mon, Georgie. Jus' a bit of a kiss an' cuddle. D'you hear me, Georgie? Lemme in!"

Georgiana Hartley sat cross-legged in the middle of her bed, fully clothed, a small, slight figure in the huge four-poster. The flickering light of a single candle gleamed on her guinea-gold curls, still dressed in an elegant knot. Her large hazel eyes, fixed on the door of her chamber, held an expression of annoyance; her soft lips were compressed into a disapproving line. Charles was becoming a definite boor.

It was her seventh night in England, her fourth at the Place, seat of her forefathers and home of her cousin Charles. And it was the third night she had had to seek the safety of her bedchamber at a ridiculously early hour, to avoid Charles's drink-driven importunities.

She had done it again.

Pulling a pillow across her lap, and wrinkling her nose at the musty smell that arose when she settled her elbows on it, Georgiana berated herself, for what was certainly not the first time and would undoubtedly not be the last, for her apparently innate impulsiveness. It had been that alone which had driven her to leave the sunny climes of the Italian coast and return to the land of her birth. Still, on her father's death, it had seemed the most sensible course. With a deep sigh she dropped her chin on to her hands, keeping her eyes trained on the door. All was quiet, but she knew

Charles was still there, just outside, hoping she might be silly enough to try to slip out.

James Hartley, painter and vivant, had left his only child to the guardianship of his only brother, her uncle Ernest. Uncle Ernest had lived at the Place. Unfortunately, he had died one month before his brother. Georgiana sniffed. Doubtless she should feel something for her uncle, but it was hard to feel grief on the death of someone you had never met—particularly when still coping with a far more shattering loss. And particularly when circumstances had conspired to land her in Charles's lap. For the news of her uncle's death had not reached James Hartley's Italian solicitors in time to stop her instinctive flight from the beauties of Ravello, her home for the last twelve years, now filled with too many painful memories. She had arrived at the Place to find Charles—Uncle Ernest's son, and a stranger to her—in possession.

The solid oak door rattled and jumped in its frame. Georgiana eyed it with increasing concern. The worn lock and the old iron hinges were all that stood between her and her drink-sodden cousin.

"Aw, Georgie, don' be a prude. You'll like't, I promise. Just a bit o' fun." A loud hiccup reached Georgiana's ears. "It's all right. You know I'll marry you. Lemme in and we'll be married tomorrow. You hear me, Georgie? C'mon, Georgie, open this door, I say!"

Georgiana sternly repressed a shiver of pure revulsion. Marry Charles? Feeling panic stir, she determinedly pushed the horrifying thought aside. Now was no time to go to pieces.

The door bounced, reverberating on its hinges as Charles made a determined assault on the thick panels. Georgiana's eyes grew round. As the thumping continued, she scanned the room for some implement, some weapon. But there was nothing, not even a candelabrum. With a grimace of resignation, she returned her gaze to the heavy oak door, philosophically waiting for whatever came next, confident that, one way or another, she would deal with it.

But the door stood firm. With one last defeated thump, Charles stopped his hammering.

"Damn you, Georgie! You won't get away! You can't escape me. You'll see—you'll have to give in, soon or late." A jeering, drunken laugh crept into the room. "You'll see."

Unsteady footsteps retreated down the passage as Charles took himself off to bed, giggling crazily.

Slowly Georgiana raised her brows. She remained perched on the bed, listening. When five minutes had passed with no sound from beyond her door, she hurled aside the pillow and slipped from the bed. A determined frown settled across her heart-shaped face. She fell to pacing the room. Can't escape?

For five minutes she walked the unpolished boards. The wind whistled and moaned, little blasts worming their way through the ill-fitting shutters to send the curtains skittering. Absent-mindedly Georgiana dragged the patched quilt from the bed and flung it about her shoulders. She reviewed her options. There weren't many. She knew no one in England, had no one to turn to. But one thing was certain—she could not stay here. If she did, Charles would force her to marry him—by hook or by crook. She couldn't hide behind locked doors forever.

With the dogged and purposeful air which had carried her across an unstable Continent unharmed, she threw off the quilt and crossed to the wardrobe. Setting the door wide, she struggled to pull her trunk free. Once she got it to the floor, she tugged the cumbersome corded box to the side of the bed. She opened the heavy lid and propped it against the bed.

A scratching at the door startled her.

Slowly Georgiana straightened and eyed the scarred oak panels with misgiving.

The noise came again.

"Miss Georgie? It's me, Cruickshank."

Georgiana let out the breath she had been holding and went to the door. It was a fight to turn the heavy key. After much tugging, the bolt fell back and she eased the heavy door open. "Cruckers! Thank goodness you've come. I was racking my brains to think of how to get hold of you."

Maria Cruickshank, a thin, weedy woman, tall and lanky, with iron-grey hair tightly confined, sniffed loudly. Originally maid to Georgiana's mother, she was the closest thing to a family retainer Georgiana had.

"As if I'd not come running with all that racket. He may be your cousin, but that Charles is no good. I told you so. *Now* do you believe me?"

Together they pushed the door shut. Cruickshank wrestled the lock home and turned to face the child-cum-lovely young woman she adored. She placed her hands on her hips and frowned grimly. "Now, Miss Georgie, I hope you're convinced. We've got to leave this house. It's no place for the likes of you, what with Master Charles as he is. It's not what your father intended, dear me, no!"

Georgiana smiled and turned back to the bed.

Cruickshank's eyes widened. She drew full breath, girding her loins for battle. Then she saw the trunk. Her breath came out with a soft whistle. "Ah."

Georgiana's smile grew. "Precisely. We're leaving. Come and help."

Cruickshank needed no further urging. Ten minutes later, all of Georgiana's possessions were back in her trunk. While Cruickshank tightened the straps, Georgiana sat on the lid, biting the tip of one rosy finger and plotting her escape.

"Now, Cruckers, there's no point in setting out before dawn, so we may as well get some sleep. I'll stay here, and you go back downstairs and warn Ben. Charles must be dead to the world by now. I'm sure I'll be safe enough."

Georgiana waited for the inevitable protest. Instead, Cruickshank merely snorted and clambered to her feet.

"True enough. A whole decanter of brandy he poured down his gullet. I doubt he'll be up betimes."

Georgiana's hazel eyes widened in awe. "Truly? Heavens!" She wriggled her toes, then jumped to the ground. "Well, that's all the better. The longer he sleeps, the farther we'll get before he finds out."

Cruickshank sniffed disparagingly. "D'you think he'll follow?"

A worried frown drew down Georgiana's fine brows. "I really don't know. He says he's my guardian, but I don't see how that can be." She sank on to the bed, one hand brushing gold curls from her forehead in a gesture of bewilderment. "It's all so confusing."

Her tone brought Cruickshank to her side, one large hand coming up to pat Georgiana's shoulder comfortingly. "Never you worry, Miss Georgie. Ben and me, we'll see you safe."

Fleetingly, Georgiana smiled, her hand rising to grip that of her maid. "Yes, of course. I don't know what I'd have done without my two watchdogs."

Bright hazel eyes met faded blue, and Cruickshank's stern features softened. "Now, lovey, do you have any notion where you should go?"

It was the question Georgiana had spent the last three days pondering. To no avail. But her tone was determined and decisive when she said, "I've thought and thought, but

I can't think of anyone. As far as I can see, the best thing I can do is throw myself on the mercy of one of the ladies of the neighbourhood. There must be someone about who remembers Uncle Ernest or Papa and will at least advise me."

Cruickshank grimaced, but did not argue the point. "I'll be back before first light. I'll bring Ben for the trunk. You get some rest now. Enough excitement for one night, you've had."

Obediently Georgiana allowed Cruickshank to help her into her nightgown, then clambered into the big bed. Cruickshank resettled the quilt and tucked the sheets under the lumpy mattress. Again the maid sniffed disparagingly.

"Even if 'twas your grandpa's house, miss, all I can say is the accommodation leaves much to be desired." With a haughty glance at the aged bedclothes, Cruickshank clumped to the door. "Just to be on the safe side, I'll lock you in."

With the problem of Charles already behind her, and her immediate actions decided, Georgiana's mind slowed. With a sigh, she snuggled deeper into the mattress and curled up tight against the cold. Her lids were already drooping as she watched the door close behind the faithful Cruickshank. The lock fell heavily into place. Georgiana yawned widely and blew out her candle.

"SHHH!" CRUICKSHANK HELD a finger to her lips and with her other hand indicated a door giving off the dimly lit passage.

Georgiana nodded her understanding and slipped silently past the room where Charles's slatternly housekeeper and her equally slovenly spouse snored in drunken unison. The Pringates were new to the Place, and Georgiana could not conceive how Charles had come to hire them. They seemed to know little to nothing of managing a household. None of the old servants had remained after her uncle's death. Presumably it was hard to get good help in the country. And, even to her untutored eyes, the Place was in sorry condition, hardly an attractive proposition to experienced staff.

Mentally shrugging, she hurried on. The dank corridor ended in a huge stone-flagged kitchen. Cruickshank was struggling with the heavy back door. As she eased it open, the tell-tale sound of a horse whickering drifted in with the wet mist. Galvanised, Georgiana hurried out into the yard, Cruickshank close behind.

Her own travelling carriage, battered and worn after the long journey from Italy, but thankfully still serviceable, stood in the muddy yard, her two powerful carriage horses hitched in their harness. She spared the time to bestow a fond pat on each great grey head before allowing Ben to help her into the coach.

As the door shut, sealing her within, with Cruickshank on the seat opposite, Georgiana settled herself on the padded leather with a weary sigh. She had hoped to enjoy a rest after the jolting roads of the Continent. True, the English roads were in much better condition, but she had looked forward to keeping her feet on firm ground and her bottom on softer seats for some time. Fate, however, had clearly decided otherwise.

The carriage rocked as Ben climbed to his perch. Without his customary whistle, he set the team moving. The coach rumbled quietly out of the yard and turned into the lane.

As the miles fell slowly behind them, Georgiana wondered anew at the oddity of the Place. The old house stood in its own extensive grounds, overgrown and choked with weeds, amid fields and meadows, all lying fallow as far as she had seen. She lifted the window flap and peered through the early morning gloom. There was no sign of livestock anywhere. Fences were broken and gates hung crazily on ruptured hinges. An air of decay hung like a pall across the estate. Heaven knew, it wasn't all that large as estates went. But the Place had hit hard times, and neglect had taken its toll. She was sure her father had not known the state of his family's property. If he had, he would never have suggested she seek refuge there. Or, alternatively, he would have made some provision to restore the Place to its former glory.

As the carriage drew to the crest of a hill which marked the limit of the estate, Georgiana, leaning past the leather flap, caught a last glimpse of the grey roofs of the Place. Then the horses started on the downward slope and trees blocked her view. In truth, from what she had seen in her three days there, she doubted the Place was worth saving.

Her only regret in leaving was that she had failed to unearth the set of paintings her father had told her he had left there. Close to twenty finished canvases, he had said. The only one she was really interested in was a portrait of her mother which he had painted shortly after their marriage. He had always maintained it was the best of the handful of portraits he had done of his wife. Georgiana had looked forward to seeing again the face of her gentle mother, otherwise no more than a misty memory. But Charles had denied all knowledge of the paintings, and her surreptitious searches had failed to find any trace of them. Now, as she didn't fancy staying within Charles's reach, the paintings would remain lost to her. Philosophically, she sighed. She knew she'd made the right choice. But she had so wanted that portrait of her mother.

The lane which led to the Place was long and winding. It followed a strange line, around the boundaries of the holdings of a neighbouring estate, eventually joining a road which ultimately led to Steeple Claydon. The morning mists were lifting by the time the coach trundled into the small village of Alton Rise, no more than a cluster of cottages nestling at the first crossroads. Ben pulled the horses up before the tiny inn. He jumped down from his perch and came to the carriage window.

Georgiana pushed aside the window flap and leant out. "Can you ask where the nearest magistrate lives? If that sounds too far, ask for the nearest big landowner."

Ben nodded and disappeared into the inn. Ten minutes later he was back. "They said best to go on up to Candlewick Hall. It's owned by a London swell, name of Lord Alton. His family's been hereabouts for generations, so it seems a safe bet. The innkeeper's missus thought you'd be safe enough asking for help there."

"Heavens, Ben!" Georgiana looked at her faithful henchman in horror. "You didn't tell them about…?"

Ben shrugged his old shoulders. "'Tweren't no news to them. By all accounts, that cousin of yourn's not much liked."

Georgiana considered this view. It was not hard to believe. Charles, in three days, had proved his colours beyond question. "How far is it to Candlewick Hall?"

"No more'n a couple of miles," said Ben, hauling himself up.

As the coach lumbered forward, Georgiana sat back and rehearsed her explanation. Doubtless she would have to be frank with Lady Alton. She was not sure what she expected her ladyship to do for her. Still, at the very least, surely Lady Alton would be able to recommend a hotel in London where she could safely stay?

The coach had picked up speed on the better-surfaced road. Georgiana's wandering attention was reclaimed by the slowing of the vehicle as Ben turned the horses sharply to the left. Drawing closer to the window, she rolled up the flap and fastened it above the frame so she could gaze unimpeded at the landscape. And a very different landscape it was. In just a few miles, all evidence of rot had vanished. The fields they now passed were well tended; sheep and cattle dotted the pastures. All was neat and pleasant perfection. As if to give its blessing, the sun struck through the clouds, bathing the scene in warmth and brightness.

Georgiana was even more impressed when they reached the park of Candlewick Hall. Two stone eagles, perched atop tall gateposts, stood guard. Between them, massive wrought-iron gates hung wide. A neat gravelled drive led onwards, curving away between two lines of beech trees. The horses appreciated the even surface and trotted easily onward. Georgiana looked about her and was pleased to approve. This was how she had imagined an English gentleman's country residence would look, with trimmed shrubberies and manicured lawns falling away on one side to an ornamental lake, a white summer-house perched on an island in the middle. The vista had about it an air of peace and tranquillity. As the coach swept around a bend, she caught a glimpse of colour through the green of the trees—presumably the gardens, which meant the house was near. She scooted to the other side of the coach and looked out.

Her eyes grew round and her lips formed an "Oh" of delight.

Candlewick Hall rose before her, its cream stone walls touched here and there with bright creeper. Three storeys of square-paned windows looked down on the gravel court before the front steps. In the morning light, the house was cloaked in a still serenity, a peaceful solidity, which tugged oddly at her. Candlewick Hall embodied everything she had come back to England to find.

The pace of the coach was checked, and they rocked to a stop before the white steps leading up to two massive front doors. Ben swung down and came to assist her to alight. He escorted her up the steps and plied the heavy knocker.

Georgiana faced the heavy wooden doors. It had seemed much easier to claim help from an unknown lady when she had been sitting in her bed last night. But the memory of Charles's ravings stiffened her resolve. As the sound of footsteps drew nearer, she took a deep breath and fixed a confident smile on her lips.

"Yes?"

A stately butler looked majestically down upon her.

"Good morning. My name is Georgiana Hartley. I wonder if I might have a word with Lady Alton?"

Georgiana was pleased with her tone. She sounded confident and in control, despite the fact she was inwardly quaking. If the butler was this starchy, what was his mistress like? She kept her chin up and waited.

The butler did not move. Georgiana felt her confidence draining, dissipating like the morning mist under the intensity of his scrutiny. She wondered if the man was hard of hearing, and was gathering her courage to repeat her request in more strident tones when he smiled, quite kindly, and bowed. "If you will step into the drawing-room, Miss Hartley, I will inform Lord Alton immediately."

Buoyed by her success, Georgiana was across the threshold before she analysed his words. She came to an abrupt halt. "Oh! But it was Lady Alton I wished to see."

"Yes, of course, miss. If you would take a seat?"

Unable to resist the deferential and strangely compelling courtesy of the impeccable butler, Georgiana found herself ushered into a beautifully appointed room and made comfortable in a wing-chair. Having ascertained that she was not in need of any refreshment this early in the day, the dignified personage withdrew.

Feeling slightly dazed, Georgiana looked about her. The interior of Candlewick Hall did justice to its exterior. Exquisite taste and a judicious eye had chosen and arranged all the furnishings, creating and enhancing a mood of peace and serenity to match that of the gardens. Her hazel gaze wandered over the room, coming to rest on the large painting in pride of place above the mantelpiece. As a painter's daughter, she could not do otherwise than admire Fragonard. She was intrigued, nevertheless, to find a picture incorporating numerous naked female forms so publicly displayed. A more private room would, she thought, have been more appropriate. But then, she reminded herself, she knew nothing of the latest whims of English social taste. And there was no doubt the Fragonard was an exquisite work of art.

The subtle colours of the room slowly eased her tension, seeping into her sight and mind. Georgiana smiled to herself and settled back in the chair. Candlewick Hall seemed designed to calm the senses. With a grateful sigh, she relaxed.

The effects of three late nights dragged at her eyelids. She would close them. Just for a moment.

"THERE'S A YOUNG lady to see you, m'lord."

Dominic Ridgeley, fifth Viscount Alton, lifted his blue eyes to his butler's face. Around him, on the polished mahogany table, the remains of a substantial breakfast bore mute testimony to his recent occupation. But the dishes had been pushed aside to make way for a pile of letters, one of which his lordship clasped in one long-fingered hand.

"I beg your pardon?"

"A young lady has called, m'lord." Not a quiver of emotion showed on the butler's lined face.

Lord Alton's black brows rose. His features became perceptibly harder, his blue gaze perceptibly chillier. "Have you taken leave of your senses, Duckett?"

Such a question, in such a tone, would have reduced most servants to incoherent gibbering. But Duckett was a butler of the highest standing. And he had known the present Lord Alton from the cradle. He answered the question with an infinitesimal smile. "Naturally not, m'lord."

His answer appeared to appease his master. Lord Alton regarded his henchman with a puzzled and slightly wary frown. "Oh?"

At the prompt, Duckett explained. "It seems the young lady requires assistance with some difficulty, m'lord. She asked to see Lady Alton. She appears to be in some distress. I thought it wise not to turn her away. Her name is Miss Hartley."

"Hartley?" The black brows drew down. "But there aren't any Miss Hartleys at the Place, are there?"

In response to his master's quizzical look, Duckett graciously informed him, "I have heard that Mr James Hartley's daughter has been visiting the Place for the past few days. From the Continent, I believe."

"Staying with frightful Charles? Poor girl."

"Exactly so, m'lord."

Lord Alton fixed Duckett with a suspicious look. "You said she was distressed. She's not weeping and having the vapours, is she?"

"Oh, no, m'lord. Miss Hartley is perfectly composed."

Lord Alton frowned again. "Then how do you know she's distressed?"

Duckett coloured slightly. "It was her hands, m'lord. She was clutching her reticule so tightly, her knuckles were quite white."

Suitably impressed by his butler's astuteness, Lord Alton leant back in his chair, absent-mindedly laying the letter he had been reading on the pile before him. Then he glanced up. "You think I should see her?"

Duckett met his master's eye and did not misunderstand his question. No one who was acquainted with Lord Alton could fail to comprehend the delicacy of the matter. For a young lady to meet a gentleman alone, particularly in the gentleman's house, with no other lady anywhere about, was hardly the sort of behaviour someone as conservative as Duckett would normally encourage. And when the gentleman in question was Lord Dominic Alton, the situation took on an even more questionable hue. But Duckett's perception was acute. Miss Hartley was in trouble and out of her depth. His master could be relied upon to provide the answer to her troubles. And, regardless of his reputation, she stood in no danger from him. She was too young and too green, not his type at all. So, Duckett cleared his throat and said, "Despite the—er—conventions, yes, m'lord, I think you should see her."

With a sigh, Lord Alton rose, stretching to his full six feet. Relaxing, he shook out his cuffs and settled his dark blue coat over his broad shoulders. Then he looked up and wagged an admonitory finger at Duckett. "If this lands me in scandal, old friend, it'll be all your fault."

Duckett grinned and opened the door for his master. "As you wish, m'lord. She's in the drawing-room."

With one last warning glance, Lord Alton passed through the door and crossed the hall.

GEORGIANA'S DREAM WAS distinctly disturbing. In it, she had transformed into one of the nymphs depicted in the Fragonard canvas. Together with her unknown sisters, she cavorted freely through a sylvan glade, blushing at the cool drift of the breeze across her naked skin. Abruptly, she halted. Someone was watching her. She glanced around, blushing even more rosily. But there was no one in sight. The sensation of being watched grew. She opened her eyes.

And gazed bemusedly into eyes of cerulean blue.

Her gaze widened, and she saw the man behind the eyes.

She stopped breathing, no longer sure which was reality and which the dream. For the man watching her, a gleam of undisguised appreciation in the depths of those beautiful blue eyes, was undoubtedly a god. And even more disturbing than her erotic dream. His shoulders were broad, filling her sight, his body long and lean and muscular. His face was strongly featured, yet held the clean lines painters adored. Thick dark hair cloaked his head in elegant waves, softening the effect of his determinedly squared chin. Finely drawn lips held the hint of a disturbing smile. And his eyes, glorious blue, set under strongly arched brows and framed by lashes too long and thick for a man, seemed to hold all the promise of a summer's afternoon.

"Oh!" It was the most coherent response she could muster.

The vision smiled. Georgiana's heart lurched.

"You were sleeping so peacefully I was loath to disturb you."

The deep tones of his voice enclosed Georgiana in a warmth reminiscent of fine velvet. With an effort, she straightened, forcing her body to behave and her mind to function. "I… I'm so sorry. I must have drifted off. I was waiting for Lady Alton."

The gentleman retreated slightly to lean one elegant arm along the mantelpiece, one booted foot resting on the hearth. The blue eyes, disconcertingly, remained trained on her face.

"I'm desolated to disappoint you." The smile that went with the words said otherwise. "Allow me to introduce myself. Lord Dominic Alton, entirely at your service."

He swept her an elegant bow, blue eyes gleaming.

"But alas, I've yet to marry. There is, therefore, no Lady Alton."

"Oh, *how* unfortunate!"

The anguished assessment surprised Dominic. He was not used to such a response from personable young women. His lips twitched and his eyes came alight with unholy amusement. "Quite!"

His tone brought the hazel gaze to his face. But she showed no consciousness of her phrasing. Seeing real consternation in the warm hazel eyes, Dominic rejected the appealing idea of explaining it to her. Clearly, Duckett's assessment of her state was accurate. She might be sitting calmly, rather than indulging in hysterics, as females were so lamentably prone to do, but he had no doubt she was seriously adrift and knew not which way to turn. The expression in her wide hazel eyes said so. In response, he smiled beguilingly. "But I gather you have some problem. Perhaps I could be of help?"

His polite query flustered Georgiana. How could she explain…? To a man…?

"Er—I don't think…" She rose, clutching her reticule tightly. As she did so, her gaze went beyond Lord Alton to the Fragonard. Georgiana froze. What sort of man, with no wife, hung a scandalous masterpiece in his drawing-room? The answer threatened to scuttle what wits she still possessed.

Unknown to Georgiana, her thoughts passed clearly across her face, perfectly readable to the accomplished gentleman watching her. All Dominic's experience told him to accept her withdrawal as the blessed release it doubtless was. But some whimsical and unexpected impulse pushed him to learn what strange story, what quirk of fate, was responsible for depositing such a very delightful morsel on his doorstep. Besides, he didn't entirely like her assumption that he was powerless to help her. He drew himself to his full height and fixed her with a stern eye. "My dear Miss Hartley, I do hope you're not about to say you '—doubt that I can be of assistance—' before you've even told me the problem."

Georgiana blinked. She had, of course, been about to say just that. With the ground cut from under her feet, she struggled to find some acceptable way out.

Lord Alton was smiling again. Strange, she had never before encountered a smile that warmed her as his did.

"Please sit down, Miss Hartley. Can I get you some refreshment? No? Well, then, why don't you just tell me what your problem is? I promise you, I don't shock easily."

Georgiana glanced up, but the blue eyes were innocent. Sinking once more into the wing-chair, she considered her choices. If she insisted on leaving Lord Alton without asking for his advice, where would she go? And, more importantly, how far behind her was Charles? That thought, more than any other, drove her to speak. "I really wanted to ask for some advice…on what I should do, finding myself in the situation I… I now find myself in." She paused, wondering how detailed her explanation need be.

"Which is?" came the soft prompt.

The need to confide in someone was strong. Mentally shrugging, Georgiana threw caution to the winds. "I recently returned to England from the Continent. I've lived for the last twelve years in Italy with my father, James Hartley. He died a few months ago, leaving me to the guardianship of my uncle, Ernest Hartley."

She looked up. Lord Alton's expression was sympathetic. He nodded encouragingly. Drawing a deep breath, she continued. "I returned to England immediately. I…didn't wish to remain in Italy. On my arrival at Hartley Place, I learnt that my uncle had died a month or so before my father. My cousin Charles owns the Place now." Georgiana hesitated.

"I'm slightly acquainted with Charles Hartley, if that's

any help. I might add that I would not consider him a fit person for a young lady such as yourself to share a roof with."

His cool, impersonal tone brought a blush to Georgiana's cheek.

Seeing it, Dominic knew he had struck close to the truth.

Keeping her eyes fixed on the empty fireplace, Georgiana struggled on. "I'm afraid...that is to say, Charles seems to have developed a fixation. In short," she continued, desperation lending her words, "he has been trying to force me to marry him. I left the house this morning, very early."

She glanced up and, to her surprise, found no difficulty in meeting his lordship's blue gaze. "I've no one in England I can turn to, my lord. I was hoping to ask your wife for advice as to what I should do."

Dominic's gaze rested on the heart-shaped face and large honey-gold eyes turned so trustingly towards him. For some perverse reason, he knew he was going to help her. Ignoring the inner voice which whispered he was mad even to contemplate such a thing, he asked, "Have you any particular course of action in mind?"

"Well, I did think of going to London. I thought perhaps I could become a companion to some lady."

Dominic forcibly repressed a shudder. Such a glorious creature would have no luck in finding that sort of employment. She was flexing her fingers, her attention momentarily distracted. His eyes slid gently over her figure. The grey dress she wore fitted well, outlining a pair of enticingly sweet breasts, young and firm and high. Her skin was perfect—peaches and cream. As she was seated, he had no way of judging her legs, although, by the evidence of her slender feet, he suspected they would prove to be long and slim. Her waist was hidden by the fall of her dress, but the swell of her hips was unmistakable. If Georgiana Hartley became stranded in London, he could guess where she'd end. Which, all things considered, would be a great shame. Her candid gaze returned to his face.

"I have my own maid and coachman. I thought that might help."

Help? A companion with her own maid and coachman? Dominic managed to keep his face impassive. There was no point in telling her how ludicrous her ideas were, for she wasn't going to hire out as a companion. Not if he had anything to say in the matter. The wretched life most paid companions led, neither servant nor family, stranded in limbo between stairs, was not for Miss Hartley.

"I will have to think of what's best to be done. Instant solutions are likely to come unstuck. I've always found it much more useful to consider carefully before committing any irrevocable act."

Listen to yourself! screamed his inner voice.

Dominic smiled sweetly. "I suggest you spend an hour or so with my housekeeper, while I consider the alternatives." The smile broadened. "Believe me, there are alternatives."

Georgiana blinked. She wasn't sure what to make of that. She hoped she hadn't jumped from the frying-pan into the fire. But he was turning her over to the care of his housekeeper, which hardly fitted with the image revolving in her mind. There was another problem. "Charles might follow me."

"I can assure you this is one place Charles will never look. And I doubt he'd pursue you to London. You're perfectly safe here." Dominic turned and tugged the bell-pull. Then he swung back to face Georgiana and smiled reassuringly. "Charles and I don't exactly get on, you see."

A pause ensued. While Miss Hartley studied her hands, Dominic studied Miss Hartley. She was a sweetly turned piece, but too gentle and demure for his taste. A damsel in distress—Duckett had been right there. Clearly, it behooved him to help her. The cost would be negligible; it would hardly take up much of his time and might even afford him some amusement. Aside from anything else, it would presumably annoy Charles Hartley, and that was a good enough reason in itself. He determinedly quashed his inner voice, that advocate of self-protection at all costs, and returned to his agreeable contemplation of Miss Hartley.

The door opened, and Georgiana came slowly to her feet.

"My lord?"

Dominic turned. "Duckett, please ask Mrs Landy to attend us."

"Yes, m'lord." Duckett bowed himself from the room, a smile of quiet satisfaction on his face.

AFTER A PLEASANT and reassuring hour spent with Mrs Landy, Georgiana was conducted back to the drawing-room. The motherly housekeeper had been shocked to learn of Georgiana's plight and even more moved when she discovered she had missed her breakfast. Now, fortified with muffins and jam and steaming coffee, and having been assured her two servants had been similarly supplied, Georgiana faced the prospect of her interview with Lord Alton with renewed confidence. No gentleman who possessed a housekeeper like Mrs Landy could be a villain.

She smiled sweetly at the butler, who seemed much less intimidating now, and passed through the door he held open for her. Lord Alton was standing by the fireplace. He looked up as she entered, and smiled. Georgiana was struck anew by his handsomeness and the subtle aura of a deeper attractiveness that owed nothing to his elegant attire, but derived more from the quality of his smile and the lights that danced in those wonderful eyes.

He inclined his head politely in response to her curtsy and, still smiling, waved her to the wing-chair. Georgiana seated herself and settled her skirts, thankful she had this morning donned one of her more modish gowns, a grey kerseymere with a fine white linen fichu, edged with expensive Italian lace. Comfortable, she raised expectant eyes to his lordship's dark-browed face.

For a full minute, he seemed to be looking at her and thinking of something else. Then, abruptly, he cleared his throat.

"How old are you, Miss Hartley?"

Georgiana answered readily, assuming him to be considering what employment might best suit her years. "Eighteen, my lord."

Eighteen. Good. He was thirty-two. She was too young, thank God. It must just be his gentlemanly instincts that were driving him to help her. At thirty-two, one was surely beyond the stage of lusting after schoolroom chits. Dominic smiled his practised smile.

"In light of your years, I think you'll find it will take some time to discover a suitable position. Such opportunities don't grow on trees, you know." He kept his manner determinedly avuncular. "I've been thinking of what lady of my acquaintance would be most useful in helping you. My sister, Lady Winsmere, is often telling me she pines for distraction." That, at least, was the truth. If he knew Bella, she would leap at the opportunity for untold distraction that he intended to offer her in the charming person of Miss Georgiana Hartley.

Georgiana watched Lord Alton's face intently. Thus far, his measured statements made perfect sense, but his patronising tone niggled. She was hardly a child.

"I have written a letter to her," Dominic continued, pausing to draw a folded parchment from his coat, "in which I've explained your predicament." His lips involuntarily twitched as he imagined what Bella would make of his disclosures. "I suggest you take it and deliver it in person to Lady Winsmere in Green Street." He smiled into Miss Hartley's warmed honey eyes. "Bella, despite her occasional flights of fancy, is quite remarkably sane and will know precisely how you should go on. I've asked her to supervise you in your search for employment, for you will be sadly out of touch with the way things are done. You may place complete confidence in her judgement."

Relief swept over Georgiana. She rose and took the letter. Holding it carefully, she studied the strong black script boldly inscribed across the parchment. Her fingers moved across the thick, finely textured paper. She felt oddly reassured, as if a confidence placed had proved to be well founded. After her problems with Charles, the world seemed to be righting itself. "My lord, I don't know how to thank you. You've been more help than I expected, certainly more than I deserve." Her soft voice sounded so small in that elegant room. She raised her eyes to his, smiling in sincere gratitude.

Unaccountably irritated, Dominic waved one fine hand dismissively. "It was nothing, I assure you. It's entirely my pleasure to be able to help you. Now one more point." He hurried on, strangely unwilling to bear more of Miss Hartley's gratitude. "It seems to me that if Charles is out there scouting about he'll be looking for your carriage, with your coachman atop. I've therefore given orders for you to be conveyed to London in one of my carriages, together with your maid. One of my coachmen will drive you and will return with the carriage. After a few days, when Charles has given up, your coachman will follow you with your coach. I trust such an arrangement is satisfactory?"

Georgiana felt slightly stunned. He seemed to have thought of everything. Efficiently, smoothly, in just one short hour he had cleared the obstacles from her path and made all seem easy. "My lord, you overwhelm me. But surely—you might need your carriage?"

"I assure you my carriage will be...better used conveying you to London than it otherwise would be," Dominic responded suavely, only just managing to avoid a more subtly flattering selection of words. God! Dealing with an innocent was trying his wits. A long time had passed since he had engaged in social discourse with a virtuous young lady of only eighteen summers. It was too abominably easy to slip into the more sophisticated and seductive modes of conversation he used almost exclusively to females these days. Which, he ruefully reminded himself, was a definite reflection on the types of ladies whose company he currently kept.

With another dazzling smile, Georgiana Hartley inclined her head in acceptance. At his intimation, she fell into step beside him, gliding towards the door on tiny, grey-slippered feet.

Still bemused, and with the feeling that events were suddenly moving rather faster than she could cope with, Georgiana could nevertheless find no fault with his arrangements.

Duckett met them in the hall with the information that the coach stood ready.

Dominic could not resist offering her his arm. With gentlemanly courtesy he conducted her to the coach, pausing while she exchanged farewells with Ben, surprising everyone, Ben included, by breaking off her words to give him a quick hug. Then Dominic handed her into the luxuriously appointed coach, wherein her maid was already installed, and stood back. Duckett shut the door firmly. The coachman, Jiggs, gave the horses the office. The coach pulled smoothly away.

Dominic Ridgeley stood on the steps of his manor house,

his hands sunk in his pockets, and watched his coach roll out of sight. Then, when he could no longer see the swaying carriage roof, he turned to go inside, pausing to kick at a piece of gravel inadvertently, inexcusably resident on the steps. With a sigh and a pensive smile, as if some pleasant interlude had come to its inevitable conclusion, he went inside and shut the door.

CHAPTER TWO

NIGHT HAD DESCENDED by the time Lord Alton's travelling carriage drew to a halt on the cobbles before the elegant town house of Lord and Lady Winsmere. Georgiana glanced up at the tiers of lamplit windows reaching high above the street. Beside her, Cruickshank sat silent, her lips set in a severe line. The groom swung down and trotted up the steps to jangle the doorbell before returning to help them to the pavement.

A portly butler appeared. One glance at the groom's livery was apparently enough to effect instant entrance for Georgiana and Cruickshank.

Georgiana allowed the butler to remove her pelisse. Then she turned and, in a voice tinged with nervousness, said, "I wish to speak with Lady Winsmere, if you please. I have a letter of introduction from Lord Alton."

Despite the butler's gracious bow and solemn face, Georgiana was instantly aware of his avid interest.

"I will convey your letter to Lady Winsmere, miss. If you would care to wait in the drawing-room?"

Shown into a reception-room of pleasing proportions, Georgiana stopped and blinked. The door shut behind her. Cruickshank had dutifully remained in the hall. Georgiana scanned the room, then, finding nothing of greater moment to consider, gave her attention to a careful appraisal of the white and gilt décor. The room was well stocked with furniture, and every available flat surface sprouted at least one ornament. The rule seemed to be that if it wasn't white it had to be gilded. Not even the ornate cornices had escaped. The effect was overpowering. With a sigh and a shrug for English fashions, Georgiana chose a stiff-backed, spindle-legged chair, heavily gilded and upholstered in white damask, and gingerly sat down.

Her gaze roamed the walls once more, but there was no Fragonard to provide distraction.

She folded her hands in her lap and tried to subdue the uncomfortable feeling of encroaching upon those whom she had no right to call on. But Lord Alton had seemed unperturbed by her request for help. Maybe, despite her misgivings, there was nothing so very peculiar about her predicament. At least, not to an English mind. Determined to be optimistic, she endeavoured to compose herself to meet Lady Winsmere's questions. Doubtless, she would have a good few. What was she making of her brother's letter?

Only then did Georgiana realise she had no idea in what light Lord Alton had presented her to his sister. The thick parchment had been fixed with a heavy lump of red wax, on which the seal of the Viscounts Alton had been imprinted. Georgiana frowned. A wave of tiredness rose up to envelop her. Not for the first time since leaving the comfort of Candlewick Hall, she wondered at the wisdom of her actions. She was too impulsive. Often she had landed herself in the suds by rushing headlong on her fate—witness her flight from Ravello. But it was too late to draw back now. She grimaced. The more she thought of it, the more clearly she perceived her inability to influence the course of events Lord Alton had charted for her. These, presumably, would determine her immediate future. Somehow she had placed herself in Lord Alton's hands.

Georgiana stifled a despondent sigh. She hoped she looked more confident than she felt.

ON THE FLOOR above, Bella, Lady Winsmere, was in the middle of her toilette, preparatory to attending the theatre. A knock on the door of her boudoir was followed by a whispered conference between her dresser, Hills, and her butler, Johnson.

Distracted from the delicate task of improving on nature, Bella frowned. "What is it, Hills?"

Her black-garbed dresser produced a folded parchment, inscribed to herself in her brother's unmistakable scrawl. Intrigued, Bella immediately laid down her haresfoot. Bits of red wax scattered in all directions as she broke open the seal.

Five short minutes later, she was crossing her front hall in a froth of lacy peignoir, rendered barely respectable by a silk wrapper. Johnson, having anticipated her impetuous descent, stood ready to open the drawing-room door for her.

As the door shut, bringing her guest to her feet, Bella's bright blue eyes, very like her brother's, surveyed her unexpected visitor.

Unconsciously clutching her reticule, once again in a tell-tale grip, Georgiana beheld an enchanting vision, fashionably slender and no taller than she herself was. But there the resemblance ended. Lady Winsmere was dark-haired, her fine skin was alabaster-white. Her blue eyes Georgiana had seen before. And the elegance of her lacy gown made Georgiana feel awkward and abominably young.

For her part, Bella saw a girl on the threshold of womanhood. Her innocence shone beacon-clear. She was all honey and cream, from the top of her curls, tinged with the sun's kiss, to her delicately tinted complexion. Her golden eyes contained a quality of unusual candour. And she had no more inches than Bella herself. Bella's face brightened. A little sigh escaped her. With a generous and genuine smile, she floated forward, both hands outstretched to capture Georgiana's cold fingers in a warm clasp.

"My dear! So you are Georgiana Hartley! Dominic has written me all about you. You poor dear! What a dreadful thing to happen, and you newly returned to England. You must let me help you."

At Georgiana's murmured, "My lady," Bella broke her stride. But when Georgiana attempted to curtsy, Bella held on tightly to her hands, preventing it.

"No, no, my dear. You're among friends here. You must call me Bella, and I hope you won't think me terribly forward if I call you Georgiana." She tilted her small head to one side, blue eyes twinkling.

Georgiana found her engaging manners difficult to resist. "Why, of course not, my… Bella. But truly, I feel as if I'm imposing dreadfully upon you."

"Oh, pooh!" Bella pulled a face. "I'm always bored; there's so little to do in London these days. I'm positively thrilled Dominic thought to send you to me! Why—" she paused, struck by a wayward thought "—just think. If you'd grown up at the Place, we would have been neighbours." Bella waved Georgiana to the chaise and sank to the white damask beside her. "So, you see, there's no need for you to feel at all bothered about staying with me."

Georgiana's head reeled. "Oh! But I wouldn't dream of imposing—"

"Not at all! It's the very thing. You have nowhere to go and we have plenty of room." Bella gazed intently at Georgiana. "Truly, it's no trouble at all."

"But—"

Bella shook her head. "No buts. Just consider it as doing me a favour. We'll have such fun. I'll take you about and introduce you to all the right people."

Despite a sudden tug of impetuosity, urging acceptance

of the exciting offer, Georgiana, grappling with the flow of Bella's burgeoning plans, felt constrained to protest. "But my la… Bella. I don't think Lord Alton can have properly explained. I need to find a post as a companion."

Recalling the specific instructions contained in her brother's letter, Bella assured Georgiana that he had, indeed, explained fully. "But my dear, in order to find the right post for you, particularly considering your age, you must first become established in society."

Bella watched the frown gathering in Georgiana's fine eyes. Before her guest could raise any further objection, she raised one slim, restraining hand. "Now before you start arguing—and I do so hate people who must forever be sniping and finding fault—I must tell you that you will be doing me the biggest favour imaginable in allowing me to help you. You can have no idea how boring it is to pass the Season with no real purpose. The Little Season is coming up in a few weeks. I implore you to relieve my frustrations and stay with me and allow me to present you. Surely that's not too much to ask?" Bella's big blue eyes pleaded eloquently.

Bemused by the sudden twist the situation seemed to have taken, with Lady Winsmere now begging the favour of her company, and feeling too drained by the day's events to fight a fate so apparently desirable, Georgiana found herself weakly acquiescing. "If it's really not too much trouble… Just until I can find a position."

"Splendid!" Bella grinned in delight. "Now the first thing we must do is get you settled in a bedchamber. A hot bath is just what you need. Always so soothing after travelling."

With a magic wave of one small bejewelled hand, Bella took charge. In short order, Georgiana, her luggage, Cruickshank, dinner on a tray and a large tub together with steaming hot water to fill it had been conveyed to the best guest chamber on the floor above.

An hour later, after she had closed the door of Georgiana's room behind her, having seen her young guest settled in bed, Bella Winsmere's face took on a pensive frown. Slowly she descended the stairs, so deep in thought that she was halfway across the hall towards the front door before she recalled her intended destination. Swinging about, she turned her steps towards the library at the back of the house.

At the sound of the door opening, Lord Winsmere looked up from the pile of documents he was working on. His lean face lit with a smile of great warmth. He laid aside his pen to reach out a welcoming arm to his wife.

With a quick smile, Bella went to him, returning his embrace and dropping a quick kiss on his greying hair.

"I thought you were bound for Drury Lane tonight?" Lord Winsmere was more than twenty years older than his beautiful wife. His staid, sometimes regal demeanour contrasted sharply with her effervescent charm. Many had wondered why, from among her myriad suitors, Bella Ridgeley had chosen to bestow her dainty hand on a man almost old enough to be her father. But over the years society had been forced to accept the fact that the beautiful Bella was sincerely and most earnestly in love with her eminently respectable lord.

"I was, but we have an unexpected guest."

"Oh?"

His lordship pushed his papers aside, consigning them to the morrow. If his Bella had sought him out, then she had some problem to discuss. He rose and, Bella's hand still in his, led her to the two armchairs stationed before the fireplace.

Bella sat, chewing the tip of one rosy finger, a habit when thinking profoundly.

Smiling, Lord Winsmere seated himself opposite her and waited for her to begin.

"It's really most intriguing."

Inured to his spouse's methods of explanation, Lord Winsmere made no response.

Eventually Bella gathered her wandering mind and embarked on her story. "Dominic's sent a girl to stay."

At that, Lord Winsmere's brows rose sharply. But the knowledge that, despite his apparent lack of moral concern, Dominic Ridgeley had never permitted the slightest breath of scandal to touch his sister's fair name held him silent.

"She's a would-have-been-neighbour. Her name's Georgiana Hartley. Her father was a painter, one James Hartley. He died in Italy some months ago and Georgiana was left to her uncle's care. Most unfortunately, her uncle, who lived at the Place—you know, it's that funny estate that was made by selling off a piece of Candlewick—well, he died too. Just before her father, only she didn't know that, being in Italy. The long and the short of it is, Georgiana travelled all the way from Italy, only to find her uncle dead and her cousin Charles in charge. It only needs to add that Charles is an out-and-out bounder and you have the picture." Bella spread her hands and glanced at her husband.

"How did Dominic come to be involved?"

"It seems Georgiana was forced to flee the Place at dawn this morning. She doesn't know anyone—no one at all. She asked at the Three Bells, thinking to find a sympathetic lady in residence at a neighbouring estate. Of course, the Tadlows sent her to Candlewick. You know how all our people are about Dominic."

Lord Winsmere nodded sagely, a thin smile hovering about his lips at the thought of the godlike status his far from godly brother-in-law enjoyed on his own lands.

"Well, she went to the Hall and met Duckett. And then

Dominic came and persuaded her to tell him all." Bella suddenly broke off. "Oh—are you imagining she must be some encroaching mushroom?" Her ladyship leant forward slightly and fixed her big eyes on her husband. "Truly, Arthur, it is not so. She's the most engaging little thing. So innocent and green and so…so trusting."

Lord Winsmere's fine brows rose slightly.

Abruptly Bella dropped to her knees, draping her silk-clad arms over her husband's knees. She smiled, impish and seductive all at once. "Please, Arthur. Please say she may stay. You know how bored I am. She's perfectly presentable, I give you my word. I could take her about and present her to the *ton*… Oh—I'd have such fun! The balls and parties are so tame, if one's not part of the game. Please, my love. Say she may stay."

Lord Winsmere smiled down into his wife's upturned face while his mind canvassed the possibilities presented by her unknown guest. Their son and only child was ensconced in the country, happily growing out of short coats. Jonathon's constitution was not sickly but did not cope well with the stale air of the capital. But his own work necessitated his presence in London. Bella, torn between the two men in her life, had chosen to remain by his side. As he doubted he could live without her, he would willingly make any sacrifice to alleviate the boredom he knew she found in the predictable rounds of tonnish entertainment. But an unknown girl? And, if he knew his Bella, she meant to fire the chit off with all flags flying. Not that the expense worried him. But was the girl truly as innocent as Bella, herself not much more experienced for all her matronliness, believed?

He reached out a finger to trace the graceful curve of his wife's brow. Impulsively, she caught his hand and kissed it, then continued to hold it in a warm clasp, her eyes on his face.

"You needn't worry about the cost. Dominic said to charge everything to him."

"Did he, indeed? How very magnanimous, to be sure." Lord Winsmere's mobile lips twitched. Dominic Ridgeley had inherited a fortune of sizeable proportions and could easily afford to underwrite the launching of an unknown damsel into the *ton.* The question that exercised Lord Winsmere's mind was *why* his hedonistic brother-in-law should wish to do such a peculiar thing.

"I think perhaps I should meet this paragon before I allow you to take her under your wing."

Bella's eyes grew round. "Are you thinking she is one of Dominic's paramours? I must admit, I did, too, at first. Well, whoever would imagine him having any contact with an innocent young girl? But I assure you she's just what Dominic says—young and innocent and…and hopelessly lost. I dare say she'll have no idea how to go on, having lived in Italy all this time."

Lord Winsmere's face remained impassive. The possibility that his brother-in-law had sent Bella a lady needing help to cover some lapse of acceptable conduct had certainly occurred, only to be immediately dismissed. Few knew better than himself that, despite Viscount Alton's reputation as a well heeled, insidiously charming and potentially dangerous rake, underneath, Dominic Ridgeley adhered most assiduously to a code of conduct that, if it were more widely recognised, would see him hailed as a pillar of society. But it was the veneer society saw—a façade erected to hide the boredom of a man who had never had to exert himself to win any prize. Born with the proverbial silver spoon tightly clamped between his jaws, and with the compounding assets of a handsome face and an athletic frame, there was little Dominic Ridgeley needed in life. And what he did want came easily. Society adored him. His well born mistresses fell at his feet. With ready charm, Dominic moved through it all, and with the years his boredom grew.

"What, exactly, did Dominic say?"

Bella smiled and shifted to sit at his feet, her hand still holding his, her shining blue eyes turned lovingly on him. "Well…"

Fifteen minutes later, Lord Winsmere felt he was in possession of all the salient facts. The only puzzle remaining was his brother-in-law's motives. A whimsical start? Dominic was hardly in his dotage. Nevertheless, young and girlish and innocent was assuredly not his style. The spectre of Elaine, Lady Changley, drifted into Lord Winsmere's mind. Involuntarily, his face assumed an expression of distaste. Lady Changley was definitely not young and girlish, and not by the remotest stretch of the most pliable imagination could she be described as innocent.

Bella saw the disapprobation in her husband's face. Her own face fell. "You don't like the idea?"

Recalled, Lord Winsmere smiled and confessed, "I was thinking of something else." At his wife's fond smile, he continued, "If the girl is all you and Dominic seem to think, I have no objections to your taking her under your wing. Aside from anything else, she'll have to be terribly innocent to swallow this yarn of yours about the way to securing a position being to make a splash in society."

Bella met his sceptical look with a bright grin. "Oh, I'll manage it—you'll see."

Five minutes later Lord Winsmere returned to his desk to tidy his papers away for the night. The memory of Bella's bright eyes remained with him. She was more animated than she had been in months. Perhaps Dominic's damsel in distress was an angel in disguise. He smiled fondly. All in all, he was looking forward to meeting his wife's protégée.

THE SHARP CALL of the orange sellers woke Georgiana. Bemused, she stared about her, then remembered where she was and how she came to be there. Despite the evidence of her eyes, reality retained the aura of a dream. She was lying propped in her pillows, still wondering, when Cruickshank came bustling through the door with her early-morning chocolate.

Georgiana waited silently for her maid's comment. No one could size up an establishment faster or more accurately than Cruickshank.

No sniffs were forthcoming. Not even a snort.

As she accepted the tray across her knees, Georgiana was taken aback to hear the dour maid humming.

Catching sight of her mistress's startled look, Cruickshank smiled. "A right proper place they keep here, Miss Georgie. No need to teach them anything. Mrs Biggins, the housekeeper, is a tight old bird, but fair, mark my words. Runs the place just as she should. And Johnson—he's the butler—and her ladyship's dresser, Hills, are everything they ought to be. A relief, it is, after the Place."

"So you're comfortable here?"

At the wardrobe, Cruickshank nodded emphatically. She drew out a violet morning gown trimmed with fine lace and laid it ready across a chair, then went to search for the accessories.

Georgiana sipped her chocolate. As the sweet warmth slid down her throat and heat seeped through her body, she sighed. So wonderful—to have real chocolate again. She closed her eyes and was immediately back on the terrace at Ravello, her father opposite, across the breakfast-table. Abruptly she opened her eyes, blinking rapidly. Enough of that! She had shed all the tears she possessed long ago. Her father had wanted her to get on with her life. He had warned her not to grieve for him. He had had a good life, so he had said, and wanted his daughter to have the same. That was why she was to return to England and the bosom of her family. Some bosom Charles had turned out to be. At the thought, Georgiana wriggled her toes. The idea of Charles scouring the countryside for her, only to return, dusty and beaten, to the damp and musty Place, brought a glow of satisfaction to her honey-gold eyes. Serve him right.

"How long are we staying here?"

Cruickshank came to draw back the covers. Georgiana slid from the bed, busying herself with washing and dressing while she considered how best to answer. She had not discussed her plan to get a position with either of her servants, sure they would veto the idea as soon as they heard it. Come what may, she was determined to keep them with her. They were all that remained of her parents' happy household.

So, standing patiently as Cruickshank laced her gown, she answered airily, "I'll have to discuss the matter with Lady Wins… Bella. She seems to wish us to stay for a while."

Cruickshank snorted. "So I gathered. Still, she seems a real lady; none of your hoity-toity airs about that one."

Georgiana grinned, remembering Bella's fussing the night before. It had been a long time since anyone other than Cruickshank had fussed over her.

After Cruickshank had settled her curls in a knot on the top of her head, Georgiana tentatively made her way downstairs. Johnson found her in the front hall and, gracious as ever, directed her to the breakfast parlour overlooking the rear gardens.

"There you are, my dear!"

Georgiana had the feeling Bella had been waiting for her to appear. Her hostess surged across the Turkey carpet in a cloud of fine-figured muslin. Georgiana returned her smile.

"Are you sure you've recovered from your ordeal?"

Georgiana flushed slightly and nodded. A man, somewhat older than Bella, had risen from the table to watch them, an affectionate smile on his thin lips. She felt forced to disclaim, "It was hardly an ordeal, ma'am."

"*Ma'am?* I thought I told you to call me Bella." Bella smiled mischievously. "And of course it was an ordeal. Fleeing from horrible Charles was always an ordeal."

Georgiana stopped and stared. "You know Charles?"

Bella's big blue eyes opened wide. "But of course. Didn't I mention it last night?"

When Georgiana shook her head, Bella tucked her arm in hers and drew her guest to the table.

"But we were neighbours; you know that. Of course, Charles came over to play sometimes. But he never got on with Dominic and the other boys, mainly because he was younger and always tried to show off. He used to tease me unmercifully. At least, he did if Dominic wasn't around. So, you see, I know just what it feels like to run away from your cousin Charles. And I can't think he's improved with age."

Standing by the chair beside her new friend, Georgiana shook her head. "I expect you're right." She looked expectantly at the man. He smiled and bowed slightly.

"Permit me to introduce myself, my dear. I'm afraid, if we wait for Bella to remember my existence, we might not be introduced until dinner."

"Oh, fustian!" said Bella, catching his hand and giving it a little shake. "My dear Georgiana, allow me to present my husband, Arthur."

Georgiana dropped a demure curtsy, hiding her surprise. She had not thought about Bella's husband at all, but would never have imagined the youthful Bella married to a man so much older. As she straightened, her eyes met his, grey and kindly, and she had the feeling of being read like a book. But then he smiled, such a sweet smile, and suddenly it no longer seemed so odd that Bella should be his wife.

"Miss Hartley. Might I say how pleased we are to welcome you to our home?"

Georgiana murmured her thanks.

Over breakfast, Lord Winsmere made little comment, but contented himself with listening as Bella and she discussed feminine interests.

"I see you are out of blacks," said Bella. "So fortunate."

Georgiana hesitated, then explained, "Actually, it's only four months since my father died, but he made me promise that I wouldn't go into mourning for him. But—" she shrugged slightly "—I thought greys and lilacs were a reasonable compromise."

Bella's candid gaze assessed her dispassionately. "I must say, if your father was a painter, I can understand why he was so insistent you stay out of black. With your skin, it would certainly not suit."

Georgiana grinned. "I'm not certain that wasn't at the back of his mind when he made his request."

As she turned her attention to her piece of toast, she was conscious of his lordship's grey eyes resting on her with approval.

In fact, Lord Winsmere was pleased to approve of his wife's prospective protégée. Georgiana Hartley, he decided, was a neat little thing. His eye had seen too many beauties to class her as one, but her features were pure and, with the gloss of a little animation, presently lacking, she could lay claim to the appellation of attractive with ease. She was petite, but her figure was full and delicately curved, not unlike Bella's curvaceous form. And, more important than any other quality, the girl from Italy was not missish. Which was just as well, if she was to deal with his forthright Bella. All in all, Bella's assessment had been accurate. Miss Georgiana Hartley was eminently acceptable.

When the ladies left him to his coffee and the morning's news-sheet, he spent some time in a blank study of the parlour door. Undoubtedly, Dominic had done right in sending Georgiana to Winsmere House. There was little hope such an attractive miss could find decent employment without subjecting herself to dangers he, for one, did not wish to contemplate. Dominic's plan to introduce her into society was a wise one. Thus far, the young lady seemed of a most amenable disposition. And, although not highly born, her lineage was not beneath consideration. He had checked for himself in the Register of Landowners. The Hartleys had been an unremarkable family for generations, but they were nevertheless of good stock. She would make some young squire an unexceptionable wife.

However, more importantly from his point of view, her presence would ease Bella's boredom. His darling had talked non-stop since rising this morning, a sure sign of happiness.

With a smile at his own susceptibilities, Lord Winsmere rose and, taking up his unread news-sheet, retired to the library. For once, Dominic seemed to have bestirred himself for purely philanthropic reasons. His scheme was in the girl's best interests and would keep Bella amused. There was no reason to interfere. Bella could entangle herself in the chit's life to her heart's content. Neither would take any ill. As his shrewd brain began to sort through the potential ramifications of his brother-in-law's plan, Lord Winsmere's brows rose. His lips curved slightly. In the end, who knew what might come of it?

"NOW, GEORGIE, PROMISE me you won't put me to the blush," said Bella, firmly drawing on her gloves as the carriage drew to a standstill. "I couldn't endure it in front of Fancon. The woman's a terror. Lord only knows what damage she could do to your chances if she heard you asking about the price of a gown."

Georgiana blushed. The slight frown on her friend's face told her Bella was not yet convinced she had won their last battle. Georgiana simply couldn't see the necessity for new gowns for herself. Surely it was not a requirement for a companion to be fashionably dressed? But Bella had been adamant.

"Just wait until you *are* a companion before you start dressing like a dowd."

At Georgiana's instinctive and forlorn glance at her demure grey gown, Bella had been instantly contrite. "Oh, I don't mean that! Your gowns are perfectly acceptable, you know they are. It's just that for going out into society you need more…well, more society clothes. This is London, after all."

Finally, worn down by Bella's arguments, strengthened by the defection of Cruickshank, who had deciphered enough of their conversation to give her a hard stare, Georgiana had consented to accompany Bella to the salon of the modiste known as Fancon. It was her third day in London, and she was beginning to feel at home in the large mansion on Green Street. Lord Winsmere was all that was kind. And Bella, of course, was Bella. Georgiana was overwhelmed by their kindness. But not so overwhelmed that she would consent to Bella's buying her new gowns.

"If I must have new gowns to go about and become known, then of course I'll pay for them." Her calm statement had caused Bella to look at her in concern.

"But, my dear Georgie, gowns, you know…well, they're not all that… I mean to say…" The garrulous Bella had flustered to a halt.

The drift of her thoughts had reached Georgiana. "Oh! Did you think I have no money?"

Bella's eyes widened. "Well, I thought you might not be exactly flush, what with your trip and expecting your uncle to be there to help at the end of it."

Georgiana smiled affectionately. They had thought her a pauper but had still wanted to help. She knew enough of the world to appreciate such sentiments. "Not a bit of it. My father left me reasonably well to do—or at least, that's how my Italian solicitors described it. I don't know what exactly that means, but I have funds deposited here on which I may draw."

To her relief, Lord Winsmere had insisted on accompanying her to the bank her father had patronised. She had little doubt it was his lordship's standing that had resulted in such prompt and polite service. There had been no difficulty in establishing her *bona fides* through papers she had carried from Italy.

While waiting for the carriage to stop rocking, Georgiana glanced at Bella's profile. They had taken to each other as if each were the sister the other had never had. "Only two gowns, mind."

Bella turned, her eyes narrowing. "Two *day* gowns *and* an evening gown." She stared uncompromisingly at Georgiana.

With a wry grimace, Georgiana acquiesced. "All right. *And* an evening gown. But nothing too elaborate," she added, as the groom opened the door.

Together they entered the discreet establishment of Fancon. A woman dressed in severe black glided forward to greet them. Her black hair was pulled back and, it appeared to Georgiana, forcibly restrained in a tight bun. Black eyes, like gimlets, sharp and shuttered, assessed her. This, she soon learned, was the great Fancon herself. Imbued with suitable awe, Georgiana noted a certain restraint in the woman's manner and was careful to give no cause for offence.

Half an hour passed in the most pleasant of occupations. Fancon had numerous gowns to choose from. Georgiana tried on a great many. There were fabrics, too, which could be fashioned to any style she wished. Georgiana found Bella's interest infectious. And she could not resist the temptation to indulge in Fancon's elegant creations. However, true to her word, she chose only two day dresses, one in softest lilac, the other a deep mauve. Both suited her well, their high waists outlining her youthful figure. She feared that Fancon would be irritated by her meagre order, particularly after the woman had been so insistent she try on such a great number of gowns. Yet nothing but the most complete equanimity showed on the modiste's stern face.

Much discussion went into the creation of an evening gown. The styles which favoured her were easy enough to decide. Yet there was nothing suitable made up.

"Your colouring, Miss Hartley, is less pale than the norm. It is no matter. We will decide on the fabric, and I will have my seamstresses work up the gown by tomorrow." With a calm wave of her hand, Fancon summoned her underlings. They brought bolts of fine cloth, in mauves and lilacs. While Georgiana stood, wreathed in fabric, Bella and Fancon studied her critically. Georgiana, too, watched proceedings in the mirror.

"It must show you off to your greatest advantage," declared Bella.

Georgiana seriously doubted that companions were chosen for the picture they made in the ballroom.

Fancon turned and murmured a command. A minute later, a fresh selection of materials arrived. Sea-green gauze, spangled and shimmering, was draped around Georgiana. The assistant stood back, and Georgiana raised her eyes to the mirror. She gasped. Was the slim, slender mermaid she saw there really herself? The green brought out the lights in her hair and eyes, and emphasised the creaminess of her skin. She stood and stared. Then, slowly, she shook her head sadly.

"Not yet. I'm still in mourning, remember?"

Another murmur from Fancon saw a deep topaz silk replace the sea-green gauze. Again, Georgiana stared. This time she looked almost as worldly as Bella. The silk added an air of allure, of mystery. She looked…enticing. But again she refused.

Apparently resigned to using the purplish hues, Fancon next produced a pale amethyst silk. Georgiana regarded it critically. The colour suited her well enough, making her appear soft and feminine. But the amethyst simply did not do for her what the previous two shades had. In this, she simply looked passably pretty. She turned and looked longingly at the topaz and the sea-green, lying discarded beside her. Still, she couldn't allow herself to be distracted from her purpose. Doubtless ladies who needed companions would approve of the amethyst silk.

"Yes. I'll take this fabric. And the pattern we agreed on."

Georgiana turned in time to catch the look that passed between Bella and Fancon. It was a look that bespoke an understanding, but she got no further clue to assist in its interpretation.

While they waited for the two day dresses to be packed, Georgiana reflected that Madame Fancon had not seemed anywhere near as dragon-like as Bella had led her to believe.

Settled in the barouche, with Fancon's boxes on the opposite seat, Bella leant forward and spoke to her coachman. "Once around the park for luck. Then back to Green Street."

The carriage moved off. Georgiana sat quietly, wondering a little at the revelations of the sumptuous sea-green and topaz silks. Could she really appear like that? Her? Little Georgiana?

Bella also sat quietly, smugly satisfied with the outcome of her scheming. She had been to see Fancon the day before, while Arthur had taken Georgiana to see her banker. The modiste knew her well; she was, after all, one of her best customers. Fancon had been most helpful, particularly after she had let fall the information that a certain peer was most desirous that Georgiana should be well presented, and hence money was no option. Dominic could hardly take exception to that. Bella grinned. She had little doubt Fancon would guess who the gentleman was. Who other than her brother would be likely to leave a young girl in her care?

"Bella, there's been some mistake. We have six boxes instead of two."

Georgiana's words reclaimed Bella's attention. She turned and found Georgiana frowning at the offending extra boxes. "No, no," said Bella. "It's all right. I bought some gowns, too. I couldn't resist after seeing you in them, and we're much of a size." All of which, Bella told her conscience, was perfectly true.

Georgiana raised her brows but said no more.

Bella returned to her absent-minded contemplation of the pavements. Undoubtedly she'd have to argue hard and fast to get Georgiana to accept the gowns she had bought. But none of them were in colours she, so much darker of hair and fairer of skin, could wear. The sea-green gauze and topaz silk would look hideous on her. They were to be delivered tomorrow, along with the amethyst silk. Surely Georgie would see what a waste it would be simply to throw them away?

As the barouche turned into the park, Bella sat up straighter. She looked across at Georgiana, sitting quietly beside her. Demure she might look, but Georgiana Hartley had a mind of her own. Stubborn to a fault, she was sure to balk at accepting what she would probably class as charity. Still, Bella was perfectly certain Dominic would have wanted her to spend his money as she had. She was sure he would approve, when he saw Georgiana in the topaz silk. And, after all, Georgiana should be grateful enough to want to please her brother. She made a mental note to remember Dominic, if she had need of further ammunition to force Georgiana to accept the gowns.

"IT'S MY 'AT HOME' this afternoon." Bella came bustling into the downstairs parlour.

Georgiana looked up from the magazine she was idly leafing through. She felt supremely confident this morning, arrayed in one of her new gowns, a soft bluey lilac cambric. Bella's elegance seemed less daunting now. She caught Bella's eye as it rested pensively upon her. Georgiana raised one fine brow in invitation.

"About the story we should tell about you. To account for your being here."

"What about the truth?" asked Georgiana, not quite sure what her friend meant.

"Well, yes. The truth, of course. But...do you think the whole truth's wise?"

When Georgiana looked her confusion, Bella continued, "You see, if you tell about how you met Dominic, people might get the wrong idea. To support your story, you'd have to explain about Charles. And, my dear, if you're looking for a position, the last person you would want to claim kinship with is Charles."

Bella had put a great deal of thought into how best to broach this most delicate of subjects. Now she watched Georgiana carefully to see how the younger girl took her suggestion. Georgiana was frowning, her thoughts clouding her big eyes.

"You mean…?"

"What I mean," said Bella, candid to a fault, "is that Charles is hardly a gold-plated reference. But there's really no need to mention him at all. All we have to do is decide how you came to stay with me. I think the most sensible thing to say is that we had met, years ago, at Candlewick, before you went to Italy. We became such friends that we've been corresponding ever since. Naturally, when you returned to England and found your uncle dead, you came back to London to stay with me. That should be believable enough, don't you think?" When Georgiana made no reply, Bella pressed her final argument. "And you wouldn't want to put Dominic in a difficult position, would you?"

Put Lord Alton in a difficult position? For a minute, Georgiana could make no sense of her friend's allusion. Then the Fragonard materialised in her mind's eye…and the image of his lordship as she had last seen him, a vision that had not yet faded from her memory.

"Oh."

Of course. Georgiana gave herself a mental shake. She wasn't so innocent that she couldn't follow Bella's drift. While her visit with Lord Alton had been utterly without consequence, society, if it heard of it, might view it otherwise. She raised her gaze to Bella's face. "I'll do whatever you think best. I wouldn't want to cause your brother any trouble."

Bella grinned, entirely satisfied.

"Oh, and one last thing. It will be better, at this stage, if we make no mention of your wish for a position. Such things are better negotiated after you're known."

Georgiana nodded her acceptance, Lord Alton's assurance that his sister knew what was best echoing in her mind.

That afternoon three matrons came to tea, bringing with them a gaggle of unmarried daughters. Georgiana did not succeed in fixing which young ladies belonged to which mama. In the end, it made little difference. To a woman, they accepted Bella's charmingly phrased explanation of her presence. Quick eyes surveyed the latest entrant in the marriage game. The ladies found no reason not to be gracious. Miss Hartley was no beauty.

Miss Hartley had difficulty subduing her mirth. They were really so blatant in their pursuit of well heeled and preferably titled son-in-laws.

To her surprise, Georgiana found conversing with the younger ladies almost beyond her. Used to dealing with the gracious conversation of the Italian aristocracy, among whom she had spent much of her life, used to the subtle ebb and flow of polished discourse, she found it hard to relate to the titters and smirks and girlish giggles of the four very proper English maids. However, she did not make the mistake of attempting to join the matrons. Stoically, she bore her ordeal as best she could.

Bella, watching her, was pleased by her confidence and innate poise. Innocent and trusting Georgiana might be, but she was no mindless ninny, scared to open her mouth in company. Her manners were assured, unusually so for a girl of her age.

When the guests had departed, Bella grimaced at Georgiana. "Witless, aren't they?" She smiled at Georgiana's emphatic nod. "They're not all like that, of course. Still, there are a lot of unbelievably silly girls about." Bella paused, considering her words. "Just as well, I suppose. There are an awful lot of silly men, too."

They shared a grin of complete understanding.

Five minutes later, just as they had settled comfortably

to their embroidery, Johnson entered. "Lady Winterspoon, m'lady."

Bella rose. Georgiana was disconcerted to see perturbation in her friend's blue eyes. Then Lady Winterspoon was in the room.

"Bella! Haven't seen you in ages! Where've you been hiding yourself?"

Lady Winterspoon's trenchant accents reverberated through the room. Bella suffered a hug and a hearty kiss and, looking slightly shaken, settled her ageing guest in an armchair. Lady Winterspoon was, Georgiana guessed, quite old enough to be Bella's mother. Who was she?

"Amelia, I'd like you to meet Georgiana Hartley. She's an old friend of mine from the country. Georgiana, this is my sister-in-law."

Georgiana met the clear grey gaze and found herself smiling warmly in response. Lord Winsmere's sister, of course.

"Hartley, hmm? Well, I probably knew your father, if he's the one I'm thinking of. Painter fellow. Jimmy? James? Married Lorien Putledge."

Georgiana nodded, eager to hear more of her parents. She had never before met anyone who had known them in their younger days.

Reading her interest in her eyes, Lady Winterspoon waved one hand in a negative gesture. "No, my dear. I can't tell you much about them; I didn't know them that well. I take it they've passed on?"

Disappointed, Georgiana nodded. Bella promptly stepped in with their agreed explanation for her presence in Green Street. Lady Winterspoon's shrewd eyes remained on Georgiana throughout Bella's speech. Whether she accepted the story, neither young woman felt qualified to say.

"Hmph!" was all the response she made.

After a moment of silence, during which both Bella and Georgiana racked their brains to think of something to say, Lady Winterspoon commented, "Dare say you'll make quite a hit. Not just in the common way. In the circumstances, not a bad thing to be."

Georgiana decided that was meant as a compliment. She smiled.

Lady Winterspoon's lips twitched. She turned purposefully to Bella. "But that's not why I came. Bella, you've got to have a word with that brother of yours. Elaine Changley's becoming entirely too much, with her airs and graces and subtle suggestions she'll be the next Viscountess Alton." Lady Winterspoon snorted.

Bella frowned and bit her lip. She cast a slightly scandalised look Georgiana's way. But Georgiana was too engrossed in Lady Winterspoon's disclosures to notice.

"If I thought there was any chance of it coming to pass, I'd insist Arthur break the connection. Elaine Changley! Why, she's..." Amelia Winterspoon became aware of Georgiana's clear hazel gaze. She broke off. "Well, you know what I mean," she amended, glaring at Bella.

Relieved at the opportune halt to her sister-in-law's tirade, Bella gracefully seated herself on the sofa. "Amelia, you know I have no influence whatever with Dominic."

"Pshaw! You'd have influence enough if you chose to use it!"

Bella coloured slightly. "I assure you I share your concern about Lady Changley, but mentioning her to Dominic is entirely beyond me."

"Well, Elaine Changley is beyond the pale! Just bear that in mind. You'll look no-how if you wake up one morning to find her your sister-in-law."

Lady Winterspoon heaved herself up. "Must go. Just

wanted to let you know things need a bit of push from you." She fixed her grey gaze firmly on Bella.

Despite her annoyance, Bella could not help grinning back. She rose.

Lady Winterspoon paused to nod to Georgiana. "I'll see you at Almack's, my dear." She turned to Bella. "I'll get Emily to send you vouchers."

"Thank you," said Bella, taken aback. She had forgotten Amelia had the ear of several of the patronesses of Almack's. She went out with Lady Winterspoon.

Minutes later, returning to the back parlour, Bella found Georgiana staring into space. She shut the door with a click, jolting her guest to attention. "Well!" she said, with determined brightness. "Vouchers for Almack's without even having to charm one of the patronesses. We'll go just as soon as Lady Cowper sends them."

"Yes, of course," said Georgiana. But it was plain to Bella that her friend was absorbed in distant thoughts… thoughts she made no move to share.

CHAPTER THREE

BELLA HEARD THE door of her boudoir open and shut, but, absorbed in brushing the haresfoot delicately over her cheekbones, she did not turn around. In her mirror, she saw Hills obediently drop a curtsy and leave. Finally, satisfied with her appearance, she swung about. "Arthur— Oh! Dominic!"

She was out of her chair and across the room on the word.

Half laughing, half frowning, Dominic held her off. "No! Compose yourself, you hoyden. What will staid Arthur think? And I can't have you ruining my cravat as you did the last time."

So Bella had to make do with clasping his hands. "Oh, thank you, dearest Dominic, for sending Georgie to me! We're having such a wonderful time!" She drew him down to plant a sisterly kiss on one lean cheek.

Dominic suffered the embrace, using the moment to cast a knowledgeable eye over his sister. "So you and Miss Hartley have hit it off?"

"Famously!" Bella sat with a swirl of her satin skirts. "But whoever would have thought you'd…?" She broke off, biting her lip.

Dominic's black brows rose. There was a disconcerting glint in his eye, but his voice was gentle when he softly prompted, "I'd…?"

Bella flushed and turned back to her dressing-table,

skirts rustling, and busied herself with a pot of rouge. She refused to meet his eye. "That you'd behave so uncommonly sensible, if you must know. From everything I've heard, it must be the first time in weeks!"

"Weeks?" The arrogant black brows rose again. Dominic considered the point for all of ten seconds. "Feels more like years."

Bella, surprised by his weary tone, chanced a glance at him in the mirror. He raised his head at that moment, and she was caught in his chilly blue gaze. "That aside, dear sister mine, you would be well advised not to listen to gossip—about myself, or anyone else, for that matter."

Eyes wide, Bella knew better than to remonstrate. Dominic was ten years her senior and had been the strictest of guardians in the years preceding her marriage. She half expected some more pointed rebuke, but he turned aside, a far-away look settling over his handsome face. To her, that pensive look was far more frightening than Amelia's bluster. Surely he wasn't serious about Elaine Changley?

She waited, but he made no further remark. Finally she asked, "Will you stay for dinner?"

He looked up.

Bella fidgeted with her hairbrush. "Georgie and I are going on to Almack's later, so you needn't fear you'll have to kick your heels in my drawing-room."

Her tone brought a smile to her brother's face, dispelling the withdrawn look which had so concerned her. Still, she was sure he would refuse.

Instead, after a moment's hesitation, she heard him murmur, "Why not?"

As it seemed a purely rhetorical question, Bella made no attempt to answer it.

Dominic shrugged, then turned his sweetest smile full

on her. "Since you ask, dear sister, I'll stay. It might be interesting to meet my...*your* protégée."

As Bella reached for the bell-pull to summon Hills, Dominic surveyed a nearby chair through his quizzing-glass. Reassured, he carefully disposed his long limbs in the delicate piece.

"So how came you to get vouchers for the Marriage Mart so soon?"

"Well! It was the most fortunate thing!" Bella seized on the question to lead the conversation on to lighter ground, hoping her intrusion into her brother's private life would be the quicker forgotten. Dominic had never allowed her any speculation on the possible candidates for the position of Viscountess Alton. And she had long ago learned that any mention of his mistresses, past, present or potential, was sure to invite one of his more painful set-downs. Still, after Amelia's warning, and her own unfortunate gaffe, she had felt justified in at least trying to broach the subject.

While Hills informed Johnson of the necessity of setting an extra place and returned to twist her hair into an elegant knot, Bella described the recent history of Georgiana Hartley. As she prattled, she watched her brother's face in the mirror. He sat quietly studying his nails, paying scant attention to her words. His lack of interest worried her. She had hardly expected him to be seriously concerned with Georgiana. After all, he had barely met her and she was certainly not the sort of woman to hold his attention. But his introspection was unusual and disquieting, suggesting as it did the existence of some weightier matter dragging on his mind. Like matrimony. But surely, *surely,* he wouldn't choose Elaine Changley?

It was with relief that Bella finally rose from her dressing-table. What with the distraction of Dominic's arrival, the hour was well advanced. He accompanied her down the wide staircase and entered the drawing-room by her side.

Georgiana was talking to Arthur. Warned by his face that someone unexpected had entered, she turned and was trapped, once again without warning, in the blue of Lord Alton's eyes.

The same eyes that haunted her dreams.

For Georgiana, it was a definite case of *déjà vu*. Her breathing stopped; her heart contracted. Her gaze was oddly restricted, the rest of the room fading away, leaving one strong face to impress itself on her mind. Her stare widened to take in his immaculate evening clothes, and the way his dark hair sat in elegant waves about his head. A cornflower-blue sapphire winked in his cravat, its colour no more intense than his eyes.

Then, thankfully, Arthur moved forward to greet his guest.

The worst was past. Georgiana's natural poise reasserted itself and she could function again. Then Lord Alton turned to take her hand. His clasp was cool and gentle. He smiled and bowed elegantly.

"Miss Hartley. So we meet again. I do hope Bella hasn't been tiring you out with her gadding."

To Georgiana's intense chagrin, her tongue promptly tied itself in knots and her voice deserted her. She managed to force out a weak, "Of course not, my lord," around the constriction in her throat. What on earth was the matter with her?

Luckily, Johnson entered to announce dinner. Inwardly, Georgiana heaved a sigh of relief. But relief died a sudden death when she discovered Lord Alton was dining at his sister's board. Naturally, he sat opposite her. Throughout the meal, which could have been the meanest fare for all she noticed, Georgiana struggled to avoid looking directly at the gentleman opposite, with mixed success. Arthur unwittingly came to her rescue, turning the conversation into political waters. He engaged his brother-in-law in a detailed discussion of the Corn Laws, leaving the ladies to their own interests.

As Bella seemed abstracted, Georgiana confined her gaze, if not her attention, to her plate. As course followed course, and the gentlemen's discourse continued unabated, she was conscious of a growing irritation. Admittedly her awkwardness in the drawing-room had hardly been encouraging, but Lord Alton could at least make the effort to address some remark to her. Perhaps, in England, it was not done to talk across the table, even at family meals.

When the sweets appeared before her, Bella shook herself and glanced about. Only then did she notice that her husband and brother had embarked on a most tedious discussion, leaving poor Georgie to herself. It was on the tip of her tongue to call attention to their lapse of manners, when she recalled that neither gentleman would feel the least inhibited about alluding to her own brown study of the past hour, nor in asking the subject of said study. As she had no intention of once again drawing her brother's fire, she turned instead to Georgiana.

"You see what it is to dine *en famille* in Winsmere House? Pearls before swine, my dear. Here we sit, only too willing to be enthralled, and all they can think of is their political problems." Her eyes twinkled at her husband, sitting opposite her at the head of the table.

Unperturbed by her attack, he smiled back. "In truth, I'm surprised to see you still here. I had thought you were off to Almack's tonight."

Bella's eyes swung to the clock, peacefully ticking away on the sideboard. "Heavens! I'd no idea. Georgie, we'll have to bustle. Come. We'll leave our two fine gentlemen to their port."

Both men stood as she rose.

Georgiana perforce rose too. She could not resist throwing one last glance at the tall figure opposite her. To her confusion, she found he was watching her. But his face bore nothing more than a remotely polite expression. He returned her nod with genial but distant civility.

As the ladies departed the room, Arthur turned to his brother-in-law. "If you have the time, I'd value your opinions on how best to go about this business."

Dominic started slightly, as if his mind had wandered from the matter they had been discussing for the past hour. "Yes. Of course." His usual, sleepily bored smile appeared. "I'd be only too delighted, naturally."

Arthur, not deceived, laughed. "Which means you'd much rather be elsewhere, discussing more enthralling subjects, but you will, of course, humour your host. You, Dominic, are a complete hand. Why you must belittle your efforts in this I know not."

By unspoken agreement, they moved to the door. Dominic waved one languid hand, and a priceless sapphire caught the light. "Perhaps because my—er—efforts, as you term them, are so undemanding as to be positively valueless."

Arthur was surprised into a snort. "Valueless? Who else, pray tell, has succeeded in even introducing the subject in Prinny's presence?"

They entered the library and made for the two large armchairs by the hearth.

"Introducing the subject's hardly the same as gaining His Highness's support." Dominic sank into one chair, stretching his long legs before him and emitting a weary sigh.

Arthur glanced sharply at him. "You know that's not necessary. Just as long as His Highness is aware of how things stand. That'll be more than enough." He handed Dominic a cut-crystal glass filled with his oldest port, then settled comfortably in the chair opposite.

Silence fell, broken only by the ticking of the long case clock in the corner and a sudden crackle as a log settled in the grate. Arthur, who had had plenty of opportunity to observe his brother-in-law over dinner, and to note the arrested expression in those startlingly blue eyes whenever they rested on Georgiana Hartley, continued to watch the younger man, waiting patiently for whatever came next, confident that something, indeed, would be forthcoming.

Finally, Dominic's gaze sought his face. "This Miss Hartley I've foisted on you… I assume you approve?"

Arthur nodded. "Georgiana is exactly the sort of company Bella needs. You have my heartfelt thanks for sending her to us."

The black brows rose. "Seemed the least I could do." Dominic's face showed evidence of distraction, as it frequently had that night. Arthur's lips twitched. He sternly repressed the impulse to smile.

Eventually Dominic shook off his abstraction sufficiently to comment, "Bella was saying she's becoming rather stubbornly taken with this idea of hiring out as a companion. She seemed to think that she, Miss Hartley, might take things into her own hands. That, I need hardly say, will simply not do."

Arthur nodded gravely. "I entirely agree. Also, I have to concur with Bella on her reading of Georgiana's character." He paused to steeple his fingers, and stared into the fire over the top of the structure. "Georgiana is clearly unused to relying on the bounty of others. It irks her, I think, to be living, as it were, on our charity. She has some money of her own, but not, I suspect, the requisite fortune. She has spoken to me about the best way to go about hiring herself out. I returned an evasive and, I hope, restraining answer. Luckily, the fact that she has been out of England for so long makes it relatively easy to make excuses which on the face of it are reasonable, without going into over-many details. However—" he smiled at Dominic "—beneath that demure exterior lies a great deal of strength and not a little courage. From what I gather, she made her way to England virtually unaided—not an inconsiderable feat. I seriously doubt she'll accept our vague answers for much longer."

A black frown of quite dramatic proportions dominated the Viscount's face.

Arthur suppressed a grin. Finally he asked, "Do you have any ideas?"

Still frowning, Dominic slowly shook his head. Then he glanced at Arthur. "Do you?"

"As a matter of fact, I do." Arthur straightened his shoulders and prepared to explain. His grey gaze rested thoughtfully on Dominic's face. "Bella, of course, needs distraction. Essentially, that means a companion. But can you imagine how she would feel if I insisted she hire one?"

Dominic's frown lightened.

"Bella has been most assiduous in helping Georgiana and, from what I've seen, Georgiana is truly grateful. I plan to suggest to Georgiana, in confidence, that she become Bella's companion in truth. However, in order to spare Bella's quite natural feelings, the arrangement will be a secret between the two of us. To all outward appearances, which of course must include the servants, she will continue as a guest in this house." Arthur's brows rose interrogatively. "Do you think that'll pass?"

Dominic grinned. "I'm sure it will. How useful to be able to turn your talents to something other than politics." His grin broadened into a smile. "And no wonder you're so invaluable in your present capacity."

Arthur smiled and inclined his head. "As you say." For a moment he regarded the younger man intently. Then, almost imperceptibly, he shrugged. "I'll speak to Georgiana in the morning. It would be wise, I suspect, to ensure she has no opportunity to take the bit between her teeth."

"THANK YOU, MY LORD." Georgiana curtsied and watched young Lord Mortlake mince away across the floor. Still, at least he had danced well.

She flicked open her fan and plied it ruthlessly. The large, sparsely furnished rooms which were Almack's were crammed with bodies dressed in silks and satins of every conceivable hue. The day had been unseasonably warm, and the evening, initially balmy, had turned sultry. The air in the rooms hung oppressively. Ostrich feathers wilted. As a particularly limp pair, dyed puce, bobbed by, attached to the head-dress of an extremely conscious beauty, Georgiana hid her smirk behind her fan.

Her eyes scanned the company. Other than Bella, standing by her side, engaged in a low-voiced conversation with an elderly matron, Georgiana knew only those few people Bella had thus far introduced her to. And, she reflected, none of them needed a companion.

As her eyes feasted on the spectrum of colours mingling before her, she spared a smile for her sartorial elegance. By comparison with many about her, she was underdressed. The pattern of Fancon's amethyst silk robe was simple and plain, with long, clean lines uncluttered by frills and furbelows. Her single strand of pearls, inherited from her mother, shone warmly about her neck. Originally uncertain, she now felt smugly satisfied with her appearance.

Thoughts of dresses brought her earlier discovery to mind, together with the subsequent argument with Bella. How on earth could she accept the sea-green gauze and topaz silk dresses from Bella, to whom she was already so deeply indebted? Yet it was undeniable that Bella could not wear them. Both dresses were presently hanging in the wardrobe in her chamber. She had been quite unable to persuade Bella to repack and return them. What was she to do about them?

The idea that, if she had been wearing the topaz silk gown that evening, Lord Alton would have paid more attention to her flitted through her mind. Ruthlessly, she stamped on the errant thought. She was here to find employment, not ogle lords. And what possible interest could Lord Alton have in her—an unremarkable country lass, not even at home in England?

Depressed, by that thought and the lowering fact she had not yet made any headway in finding a position, Georgiana determinedly looked over the sea of heads, pausing on the occasional powdered wig that belonged to a previous generation. Maybe, beneath one, she would find someone to hire her?

"Here, girl! Georgiana, ain't it? Come and help me to that chair."

Georgiana whirled to find Lady Winterspoon beside her. The old lady was leaning on a cane.

Seeing her glance, Amelia Winterspoon chuckled. "I only use it at night. Helps me get the best seats."

Georgiana smiled and obediently took her ladyship's arm. Once settled in a gilt chair by the wall, Lady Winterspoon waved Georgiana to its partner beside her.

"I can only take so much of this place. Too much mindless talk addles the brain."

Georgiana felt the sharp grey eyes assessing her. She wondered whether she would pass muster.

A wry smile twisted Amelia Winterspoon's thin lips. "Just as I thought. *Not* in the common style."

The old lady paused. Georgiana had the impression she was reliving long-ago evenings spent under the candlelight of ballroom chandeliers. Then, abruptly, the grey gaze sharpened and swung to her face.

"If you're old enough to heed advice, here's one piece you should take to heart. You ain't a beauty, but you're no antidote either. You're different—and not just because you're fair when the current craze is for dark. The most successful women who've ever trod these boards were those who were brave enough to be themselves."

"Themselves?"

"Themselves," came the forceful answer. "Don't put on airs, nor pretend to be what you ain't. Thankfully, you seem in no danger of doing that. Don't try to ape the English misses. Don't try to lose your foreignness—use it instead. All you need to make a go of it is to smile and enjoy yourself. The rest'll come easy."

"But—" Georgiana wondered whether she should explain her situation to Arthur's sister. Maybe she could help her find a position?

"No buts, girl! Just do it! There's no point in wasting your life away being a wallflower. Get out and enjoy yourself." Lady Winterspoon used her cane to gesture at the dance-floor. "Now go on—off you go!"

Despite the conviction that she should feel piqued at such forthright meddling, Georgiana found herself grinning, then laughing as Lady Winterspoon nodded encouragingly. Rising, Georgiana swept a curtsy to her ladyship, now comfortably ensconced, and, a smile lingering on her lips, returned to the throng. She made her way to where she had left Bella.

But Bella was no longer in sight.

Perturbed, Georgiana stood still and wondered what to do. She could go back and sit with Lady Winterspoon, only she would probably drive her off again. English social strictures were not Georgiana's strong suit. Still, she rather suspected she should not wander about the rooms alone. Suddenly she realised she was frowning.

Lady Winterspoon's strong voice still echoed in her mind. "Enjoy yourself!"

Georgiana lifted her head. She had been introduced to Italian society at the age of sixteen. Surely, at the ripe old age of eighteen, she could manage such a simple social occasion as this? Consciously drawing about herself the cloak of social calm her father's female patrons had impressed on her was the hallmark of a lady, she stepped out more confidently to search for Bella—not hurriedly, in a frenzy, but in a calm and dignified way, smiling as she went.

As she moved slowly down the room, truly looking about her for the first time that evening, she heard snatches of conversation wafting from the groups she passed.

"Did you see that Emma Michinford? Making such sheep's eyes at…"

"Well, we all know what *he's* after!"

"She's really rather pathetic, don't you agree?"

"Not that it'll come to anything, mark my words. The likes of him…"

Waspish, biting, cutting gibes… The comments blurred into a melody typical, Georgiana suspected, of the place. Her smile grew.

"Oh!" Her elbow jogged that of another stroller. "I'm so sorry. Pray excuse me."

"Gladly, my dear, if you'll tell me what could possibly be so amusing in Almack's."

The languid tones of the gentleman bowing before her were, Georgiana judged, devoid of menace. He was very neatly and correctly attired, soberly so. His blue coat was well cut, his satin breeches without a crease. Brown hair, stylishly but not rakishly cut, framed a pleasant face. There was nothing one could put a finger on to account for the air of elegance which clung to him.

As he continued to look at her with mild curiosity, Georgiana, Lady Winterspoon's dictum still fresh in her mind, answered him truthfully. "It was merely the conversation, caught in snippets as I walked about. It's—" she put her head on one side as she considered her words "—rather single-minded, if you know what I mean."

A quirky grin twisted the gentleman's lips. "I do indeed know what you mean, Miss…?"

Having embarked on her course, Georgiana dispensed with caution, "Hartley. Georgiana Hartley. I'm staying with Lady Winsmere. I seem to have lost her in the crush."

"Ah, the lovely Bella. I think I saw her over by the door, in earnest conversation with Lady Duckworth. Permit me to escort you to her."

With only a single blink, Georgiana laid her gloved hand on the proffered sleeve. If she was going to be escorted by any gentleman tonight, she was quite content that it should be this one. He hadn't told her his name, but he seemed thoroughly at home.

"From your comment, you seem almost to laugh at the purpose of this great institution. Yet surely you propose to avail yourself of its services?"

This was the sort of conversation Georgiana had cut her social eye-teeth on. "I most certainly intend to avail myself of its services, but not, I think, as you might assume."

Her companion digested this riposte, before countering, "If that means you are not here to snare a title, or a fortune, what possible other use for this place can you have found?"

"Why, that to which I was putting it when you met me."

A pause developed, followed by a great sigh. "Very well.

I confess myself stumped. What is it you've discovered within these faded grey walls?"

Georgiana smiled, eyes dancing. "Why, enjoyment, of course. I was enjoying myself." To her surprise, she realised this was true. She turned to glance into her companion's grey eyes. In them, she saw thunderstruck amazement.

"*Enjoyment?* In Almack's?"

Georgiana laughed. "Of course. I'm enjoying myself now. Aren't you?"

Her gentleman stopped stock-still, a ludicrous mixture of horror and humour in his face. "Dreadful! I'll never live this down." Then his face cleared and he smiled, quite genuinely, at Georgiana. "Come, Miss Hartley. Let me restore you to Lady Winsmere. You're clearly too potent a force to be let loose for long."

Perfectly content, Georgiana strolled by his side through the crowd, who, she now noticed, seemed to part before them. Even before she caught sight of Bella's surprised face, she had started to question the identity of her escort. But she was determined not to worry. And, thankfully, whoever he was, her escort seemed to find nothing amiss.

Bella curtsied and chatted animatedly, but Georgiana still heard no name. With a final, *sotto voce,* "Enjoying oneself in Almack's. Whatever next?" the very correct gentleman withdrew.

Georgiana turned to Bella, but, before she could utter her question, Bella was exclaiming, albeit in delighted whispers, "Georgie! However did you do it?"

"Do what? Who is he?" Instinctively, Georgiana whispered too.

"Who? But…don't you know?" Bella stared in disbelief, first at her, then at the elegant retreating back.

"No. No one introduced us. I bumped into him and apologised."

Bella fanned herself frantically. "Heavens! He might have cut you!"

"Cut…? But who on earth is he?"

"Brummel! George Brummel. He's one of society's most powerful arbiters of taste." Bella turned to survey Georgiana appraisingly. "Well! Obviously he's taken to you. What a relief! I didn't know what to think when I saw you with him. He can be quite diabolical, you know."

Georgiana, conscious now of the envious eyes upon her, smiled confidently. "You needn't have worried. We were just enjoying ourselves."

Bella looked incredulous.

Georgiana laughed.

"GOODNIGHT, JOHNSON."

"Goodnight, my lord."

The door of Winsmere House shut softly behind Dominic. The night continued mild, but the low rumble of distant thunder heralded the end of the unseasonal warmth. Still, Alton House in Grosvenor Square was only five minutes away. Dominic set off, swinging his slim ebony cane, his long strides unhurried as he headed for North Audley Street.

The evening had left him with a sense of dissatisfaction which he was hard put to explain. He had broken his journey to Brighton to check on Miss Hartley, although, to be precise, it was more to relieve his mind over whether Arthur and Bella had been put out over her descent on them. Thankfully, all had turned out for the best. Arthur's scheme would undoubtedly pave the way for Georgiana Hartley to spend the upcoming Little Season with Bella, after which it would be wonderful if she had not received at least one acceptable proposal. The girl was not a brilliant match, but a perfectly suitable connection for any of the lesser nobility who made up the bulk of the *ton.* He had checked on her antecedents and knew them to be above reproach. Yes, Georgiana Hartley would very likely soon be betrothed. Which was far more appropriate than being a companion.

As he swung south into North Audley Street, Dominic grinned. How typical of Arthur to concoct such a perfect solution to the girl's troubles. And Bella's. Everything seemed set to fall smoothly into place. Which, all things considered, should leave him feeling smugly satisfied. Instead, he was feeling uncommonly irritated. The grin faded. A frown settled over his features.

A watchman passed by unobtrusively, unwilling to draw the attention of such a well set up and clearly out-of-sorts gentleman to his activities. Dominic heard him but gave no sign.

Why should he be feeling so disillusioned, so disheartened? He'd been living this life for the past twelve years. Why had it suddenly palled? The circumstances that had driven him to seek the peace of Candlewick drifted into his mind. All the glamour and glitter and laughter associated with the doings of the Carlton House set. And the underlying vice, the predictability, the sheer falsity of most of it—these were what had sent him scurrying for sanctuary. But even Candlewick had failed to lift his mood. While its serenity had been comforting, the huge house had seemed lonely, empty. He had never noticed it before; now its silence was oppressive.

The corner of Grosvenor Square loomed ahead. Dominic swung left and crossed the road to the railed garden. The gates were locked at sunset, but that had never stopped him strolling the well tended lawns by night. He vaulted the wrought-iron railings with accustomed ease, then turned his steps across the lawns in the direction of his town house on the south side of the Square. Tucking his cane under his arm, he thrust his hands into his coat pockets and sank his chin into the soft folds of his cravat. Doubtless, if he were still in the care of his old nurse, she would tell him to take one of Dr James's Powders. The blue devils, that was what he had.

A vision of honey-gold eyes crystallised in his brain. Why on earth Georgiana Hartley's eyes, together with the rest of her, should so plague him he could not understand. He was not a callow youth, to be so besotted with a female's finer points. He had hardly exchanged two words with the chit, yet, throughout the evening, had been aware of her every movement, every inflexion, every expression.

Leaves from the beech trees had piled in drifts and softly scrunched underfoot. Dominic paused to regard his feet, lightly covered with golden leaves. Then he shook his head, trying to rid it of the memory of curls sheening guinea-gold under candlelight. God! What was this? The onset of senility?

Determined to force his mind to sanity, he removed his hands from his pockets and straightened his shoulders. Ten long strides brought him to the fence, and he vaulted over to the pavement beyond. A few days, not to mention nights, of Elaine Changley's company would cure him of this idiotic fancy. As his feet crossed the cobbles, he commanded his memory to supply a vision of Lady Changley as he had last seen her, reclining amid the much rumpled sheets of the bed he had just vacated. Of course, Elaine's ambitions were on a par with her charms. But as he was as well acquainted with the former as he was with the latter he felt justified in ignoring them. A smile played at the corners of his fine lips as he trod the steps to his front door.

In the instant he raised his cane to beat a tattoo on the solid oak door, an unnerving vision in which Georgiana Hartley was substituted for Elaine Changley flooded his brain. So breathtaking was the sight that Dominic froze. The gold top of his cane, yet to touch the door, remained suspended before him.

The door opened and Dominic found himself facing his butler, Timms.

"My lord?"

Feeling decidedly foolish, Dominic lowered his cane. He sauntered past Timms, one of Duckett's protégés, as if it were perfectly normal for him to stand rooted to his own doorstep. He paused in the hallway to draw off his gloves, then handed the offending cane to Timms.

"I'll be leaving for Brighton early tomorrow, Timms. Tell Maitland to be ready about nine."

"Very good, m'lord."

Frowning, Dominic slowly ascended the gently curving staircase, pausing, as was his habit, to check his fob watch against the long case clock on the landing. Restoring his watch to his pocket, he reflected that, if nothing else could cure him of his disturbing affliction, the decadent amusements to be found within the Prince Regent's pavilion at Brighton would.

BY THE TIME the Winsmere House ladies were handed into their coach for the drive home from King Street, Georgiana had had proved to her, over and over again, the truth of Lady Winterspoon's dictum. If she enjoyed herself, then her partners seemed to enjoy her company. If she laughed, then they laughed, too. And, while such overt behaviour did not sit well with one brought up to the self-effacing manners expected of young Italian girls, it was a great deal better, to Georgiana's way of thinking, than simpering and giggling. Her upbringing clearly had not conditioned her for English social life. Nevertheless, the unrufflable calm she had been instructed was a lady's greatest asset certainly helped, allowing her to cloak her instinctive responses to some of those she had met—like Lord Ormskirk and his leering glances, and Mr Morecombe, with his penchant for touching her bare arms.

"The Sotherbys are holding a ball next week. Lady Margaret said she'd send cards." Bella's voice came out of the gloom of the seat opposite. "After tonight, I've no doubts we'll be kept busy. So fortunate, your meeting with Brummel."

The unmistakable sound of a smothered yawn came to Georgiana's ears. She smiled into the darkness. Despite her tiredness, Bella seemed even more excited by her success than she was. She had originally found her hostess's claim of boredom difficult to believe. Now she could find it in her to understand that, without any special interest, the balls and parties could indeed turn flat. Still, to her, everything was too new for there to be any danger of her own interest flagging before Bella's did. Hopefully Bella would not feel too let down when she found a position and moved away. Into obscurity. Georgiana frowned.

If she had been asked, five days previously, whether she had any ambition to enter the *ton,* she would unhesitatingly have disclaimed all such desire. However, having now had a small sample of the diverse entertainments to be found amid the social whirl, she rather thought she might enjoy being able to savour these, in moderation, by way of a change from the quieter lifestyle she considered her milieu. A saying of her father's drifted past her mind's ear. "Experience, girl! There's nothing quite like it and no substitute known.'

As the clop of the horses' hoofs echoed back from the tiered façades of the houses they passed, Georgiana puzzled over her change of heart. Still, nothing could alter the fact that she would need to earn her way, at least to some extent. That being so, perhaps she should take this opportunity of experiencing the *ton,* of enjoying herself amid the glittering throng? According to Bella, she needed to be known to find a position. So, until she secured one, she could, and perhaps should, follow her father's and Lady Winterspoon's advice.

Bella yawned. "Oh, dear. I'd forgotten what it was like." Another yawn was stifled behind one slim white-gloved hand. Then, "I wonder if Dominic has managed to convince Charles to sell the Place yet?"

The question jolted Georgiana out of her reverie. "Lord Alton wishes to buy the Place?"

"Why, yes. Didn't I mention it?"

Her friend's voice was sleepy, but Georgiana's curiosity was aroused. "No. Why does he want it? From what I saw, it's terribly run down."

"Oh, it is. Run down, I mean. Even when Charles's father was alive… And now…"

Georgiana waited, but Bella's mind had clearly drifted. "But why does he want it?" she prompted.

"The Place? Oh, I keep forgetting you don't know all that much about it." Bella's skirts rustled as she sat up. "Well, you see, the Place didn't exist a hundred years ago. It used to be part of Candlewick. But one of my ancestors was something of a loose screw. He gambled heavily. One of his creditors was one of your ancestors. He agreed to take part of the Candlewick lands in payment. So that was how the Place came about. My spendthrift ancestor didn't live long, much to the family's relief. Ever since then, the family has tried to buy back the Place and make Candlewick complete again. But your family have always refused. I don't know how long it's been going on, but, generally, both families have always dealt amicably despite all. That is…" Bella paused dramatically; Georgiana sat enthralled "—until my father's death. Although he had always talked of rejoining the Place to Candlewick, my father hadn't, as far as Dominic could discover, done much about it. So when he inherited, Dominic wrote to your uncle to discuss the matter. But your uncle never replied. He was, by that time, something of a recluse. Dominic could never get to see him. After a while, Dominic gave up. When he heard of your uncle's death, he wrote to Charles. Charles didn't reply either. Mind you," Bella added on a reflective note, "as Charles dislikes Dominic as much as Dominic dislikes him, I can't say I was surprised at that. Still, from what you've said, the Place is falling down about Charles's ears. I really can't see why he won't sell. Dominic's prepared to pay above the odds, and Charles must know that."

"Perhaps it's mere stubbornness?"

"Maybe," Bella conceded, tiring of her brother's problems. She lapsed into silence, the better to consider the doors the evening had opened for her protégée.

Georgiana puzzled over Charles's behaviour. In the few days she'd had to observe him, her cousin had given the impression of being addicted to the good things in life, or rather, that he had a liking for the finer things but had little of the wherewithal required to pay for them. Which made his refusal to sell the Place, in which he demonstrably took no interest, stranger still.

From consideration of Charles, it was a short step to thoughts of the man so inextricably linked in her mind with her escape from her cousin. The demands of her début at Almack's had precluded her thinking of her earlier meeting with Lord Alton, beyond the wish that she had made a better impression. Undoubtedly she had appeared as a gawky, tongue-tied, awkward child. Where on earth had two years of experience gone? Certainly, nothing in her previous existence had prepared her for the odd effect he had on her. She had never reacted to a man in such a way before. It was both puzzling and unnerving. When it came to Bella's brother, her carefully nurtured Italian calm deserted her. Hopefully, by the time they next met, the peculiar effect would have worn off. She did not wish to be forever appearing as a graceless schoolgirl to the gentleman before whom, more than all others, she wished to shine. Still, no doubt she was refining too much on their meeting. Lord Alton would have seen her merely as a child he had assisted in her time of trouble. She could be nothing more than that to him. The thought that she would like to be a great deal more than that to Lord Alton she ruthlessly decapitated at birth. He was a noted Corinthian and, from what she had heard at the dinner-table, one of the Carlton House set. She had nothing to recommend her to his notice—not beauty, nor fortune, nor birth. To him, she would be no more than a passing acquaintance, one he had perhaps already forgotten.

Besides, it seemed he was on the verge of contracting an alliance, although Lady Winterspoon certainly seemed to think the lady in question was rather less than suitable. But she had heard more than enough in Italy to distrust the conclusions of society. Who knew? Maybe Lord Alton was genuinely fond of Lady Changley. She tried to imagine what the lady Lord Alton was in love with would look like, but soon gave up. She knew so little of him that it was impossible to guess his preferences.

As she ruminated on the twist of fate that had caused them to meet, Georgiana reflected that it was perhaps as well she would get few chances to be in Viscount Alton's company. He was the stuff schoolgirl dreams were made of. Unfortunately, she was no longer a schoolgirl. And she did not have the capital to indulge in dreams.

CHAPTER FOUR

"MY LORD, I'M most truly sensible of the honour you do me, but, indeed, I cannot consent to becoming your wife."

Georgiana watched as Viscount Molesworth, an earnest young man more at home on his ancestral acres than in a London ballroom, rose awkwardly from his knees.

Dusting off his satin breeches, he sighed. "Thought you might say that."

Georgiana swallowed a giggle and managed to look politely interested.

Seeing this, the Viscount obligingly continued, "Told m'mother so. But you know what women are. Wouldn't listen. Said you'd be bound to accept me. Said you were just the thing I needed. Must say, I agree with her there." He glanced once more at Georgiana. "Sure you won't change your mind?"

Shaking her head, Georgiana rose and put her hand on the Viscount's sleeve. "Truly, my lord, I don't think we would suit."

"Ah, well. That's it, then." Lord Molesworth, heir to an earldom of generous proportions, lifted his head as music drifted from the ballroom down the hall. "Best get back to the dancing, then, what?"

Unable to command her voice, Georgiana nodded. Strolling back into the ballroom on his lordship's arm, she could not keep a happily satisfied smile from her face. She had known the Viscount was bordering on a declaration, had been teetering on the brink for the past week. And, as with her two previous proposals, Georgiana had dreaded having to hurt his feelings. But it had all passed off easily, even more easily than the others. Her first proposal had been from young Lord Danby, who had been truly smitten but so very young that she had felt she were dealing with a younger brother, not a potential lover. Her second offer had come from Mr Havelock, a quiet man of thirty-five summers. She was sincerely fond of him, but in a friendly way, and doubted she could ever think of him other than as a friend. He had accepted her refusal philosophically, and they continued friends, but he had impressed on her that, should she have need of support or even something more, he was forever at her disposal.

Relieved at having weathered yet another proposal with no bones broken, Georgiana gave silent thanks that she had attracted only true gentlemen. Some of the more dangerous Corinthians had certainly looked her over—almost, she had felt, as if she were a succulent morsel they were planning to gobble up. But when they learned she was staying with the Winsmeres they usually smiled and passed on.

However, there were a few who had remained long enough to enjoy a light flirtation, a moment of dalliance. Such a one was Lord Edgcombe, who now approached to claim her for the waltz.

Georgiana smiled and curtsied. "My lord."

His lordship, resplendent in a dark green coat which leant a deeper tinge to his golden locks, bowed easily over her hand. "My lovely." His cool grey eyes flicked to the Viscount, still hovering by her elbow.

Georgiana realised he must have seen them re-enter the room, and wondered how much he guessed. She was now too experienced to take umbrage at his outrageous but calculated greeting. Instead, she spoke confidently, succeeding in distracting his lordship from his contemplation of the hapless Viscount. "I take it that means you approve of my gown?"

Lord Edgcombe's grey gaze swung slowly to her face. His lips twitched. Then, to pay her back for her temerity, he raised his quizzing-glass and embarked on a minute inspection of her person. "Mmm," he murmured. "The style, of course, is superb. Fancon, I trust?"

Georgiana, far from blushing and dissolving into a twittering heap, the prescribed reaction to his behaviour, could not restrain her smile. She understood his lordship's tactics only too well.

Far from being put out by her refusal to succumb, Lord Edgcombe responded with a smile of genuine enjoyment and offered his arm. "Come, sweet torment, the dance-floor awaits and the musicians will soon grow weary."

As she twirled down the room in Lord Edgcombe's arms, Georgiana wondered again at the success, for her part unexpected but none the less flattering, which had resulted in her receiving the attentions of one such as his lordship. He was well born, with a comfortable estate, and could be pleasant enough when it suited him. However, as it only suited him to behave so with a select circle of acquaintances, he was generally thought to be beyond the reach of the matchmaking mamas. Georgiana did not entirely understand his interest in her, but instinctively knew she was in no immediate danger of receiving a proposal from Lord Edgcombe. At least, she amended, as she looked into his smiling grey eyes and correctly divined the thoughts behind them, not a proposal of marriage.

"Relieve my curiosity, my dear. What could possibly be so interesting that you needs must be alone with the noble Viscount?"

Georgiana opened her eyes wide. "Why, we were merely strolling, my lord."

The grey gaze remained on her face for a full minute. Then his lips curved once more. "I see." After a moment he added, his voice low, "I don't suppose you feel like taking a stroll with me."

Georgiana's eyes danced. Keeping her face straight, she shook her head primly. "Oh, no, my lord. I don't think that would be at all wise."

They executed a complicated turn at the end of the room, pausing to allow two younger and more enthusiastic couples to pass by. When they were once more proceeding up the long room, his lordship's attention refocused. "Now why is that, I wonder? Surely you don't mean to say that you fear my company would be less…scintillating than the Viscount's?"

Georgiana laughed lightly, her eyes still holding his. "Oh, no—far from it. My fear is more that your company might prove rather *too* scintillating, my lord."

Lord Edgcombe was no more immune to the flattery of a beautiful young woman than the next man, even if he fully understood her machinations. So he smiled again, sharing in her laughter. "My dear, you're a minx. But a delightful minx, so I'll let you escape the set-down you undoubtedly deserve."

Schooling her features to reflect a suitable gratitude, and reducing her voice to a breathless whisper, Georgiana replied, "Oh, thank you, my lord."

"Gammon!" said Lord Edgcombe.

Returning three dances later to Bella's side, Georgiana was given no time to draw breath. Her mentor immediately demanded to be told what Viscount Molesworth had had to say.

Georgiana regarded Bella warily. "He proposed."

"And?" Bella's face was alight.

Georgiana knew it was her friend's dearest wish that she contract a suitable alliance, and Viscount Molesworth was certainly that. But she had no real ambition to marry where she did not love, not even for her best friend. So she drew a deep breath and confessed. "I refused him."

"Oh." Bella's face fell. "But why?"

Seeing the real consternation in Bella's big eyes—eyes that constantly reminded her of another—Georgiana was tempted to make a clean breast of it. But the approach of the gentleman to whom she was promised for the next dance reminded her of their surroundings. "I'll explain later. Not now. Please, Bella?"

Now Bella saw Mr Millikens and smiled and nodded, adding in an undertone for Georgiana's ears only, "Yes, of course. Later. But Georgie, we really must talk of this."

Georgiana nodded her agreement and moved forward to take Mr Millikens's arm.

The rest of the evening passed in a blur before Georgiana's eyes. She spent much of her time examining and assessing the changes the past two weeks had wrought in her life. Arthur's quietly worded request that she remain in Green Street, theoretically a guest, but in truth as a companion for Bella, had been a turning point. His explanation of Bella's need for purpose in an otherwise frivolous existence had struck a chord of sympathy. After that, she had no longer pursued the idea of finding employment with an older lady. Bella, of course, was kept in ignorance of the arrangement, for it was generally only much older women who had companions.

That first night at Almack's had set the seal on her success. From that evening, a steady flow of invitations had poured into Green Street, and she and Bella had been immersed in a tide of balls and parties, routs and breakfasts.

Her popularity, both with the gentlemen and the ladies of society, had made Bella crow. For her part, Georgiana wryly thanked her less than perfect looks. Because she was no beauty, she was not a challenge to the reigning *incomparables*. Thus she was accepted without any great fuss, nor was she the butt of any jealousies. Her natural vivacity, which, thanks to Lady Winterspoon and Beau Brummel, she had discovered, carried her through. In her heart, she strongly suspected it was this, together with her unconventionally un-missish behaviour, which made her so attractive to the gentlemen. Certainly, they flocked about her. And, if she were to be truthful, she could not deny a happy little glow of self-satisfaction whenever she thought of her court. She might not be a hit, or a beauty, but she had her own little niche, her own place in the scheme of things. As Lady Winterspoon had suggested, there were many roads to success.

They were among the last to leave the ball. As she had anticipated, Bella returned to the subject of Viscount Molesworth as soon as the carriage door was shut upon them.

"Why, Georgie? I thought you liked him."

Georgiana leant back against the fine leather upholstery and resigned herself to the inevitable. "Viscount Molesworth is all that is amiable. But truly, Bella, do you think that's enough?"

"Enough? But, my dear, many girls marry with far less than—er—liking for their husbands."

Georgiana stifled a sigh. She would have to try to make Bella understand. "Bella, did you marry like that?"

Bella shifted in her seat, her satin skirts shushing. "Well, no. But...well, you know it's not the done thing, to marry for love. And," she hurried on, "you've no idea the trouble I had, in marrying Arthur. No one could understand it. Oh, it's accepted now. But if Dominic had opposed the match everyone would have agreed with him. Love is simply not a…a determining factor in marriage in the *ton*."

Hearing the sincere note in Bella's voice, Georgiana debated whether to tell her the truth. But, even as the idea formed, she shied away from it. Instead she tried another tack. "But you see, dearest Bella, I didn't come to London to marry. I've given no thought to marrying into the *ton*. I'm not at all sure it would suit me."

To this, Bella returned a decidedly unladylike snort. "Not marry? Pray tell, what else are you going to do with your life? Oh—don't tell me you'll be a companion to some old lady. You'll never convince me you would rather be that than married to some nice, considerate gentleman who'll shower you with everything you desire."

Under cover of the dark, Georgiana grinned. Well, she was a companion, although Bella didn't know it and the lady wasn't old. But would she really prefer to be married, regardless of the man, to have to tend to the comfort and consequence of some faceless gentleman? Georgiana sighed. "You make it all sound so straightforward."

"It is straightforward. It's simply a matter of making up your mind to it and then, when a suitable gentleman comes along, saying yes instead of no."

Georgiana gave a weary giggle. "Well, if the right gentleman comes along, I'll promise to consider it."

Bella wisely refrained from further pushing, hopeful that she had at least made her errant protégée think more deeply on her future position within the *ton*. For Bella was quite determined her Georgie should marry well. She was attractive, which was more to the purpose than beautiful. And the gentlemen liked her—as evidenced by three proposals within two weeks. She had held great hopes of Mr Havelock, but Georgie had refused him without a blink. All she could do now was to hope Georgie's elusive right gentleman came along before her protégée got the reputation of being difficult to please.

A GENTLE BREEZE cooled Georgiana's warm cheeks as she accompanied Lord Ellsmere back to his phaeton. She deployed her sunshade to deflect the glances of any curious passers-by as they left the secluded walk and crossed the lawns to the carriageway. Her hand resting gently on his sleeve, she cast a tentative glance up into his lordship's handsome face. He was watching her and, catching her gaze, smiled ruefully.

"Forgive me, my dear, if my actions seem somewhat importunate. You'll have to make allowances for my—er—strong feelings in this matter."

For the first time since that night at Almack's, now more than three weeks ago, Georgiana felt flustered. Only this morning she had been congratulating herself on having managed to keep her earnest suitors from making any further declarations. How could she have guessed what his lordship had planned in the guise of a perfectly decorous drive in the park?

"Oh, yes, of course," she muttered incoherently. She noticed his lordship's slightly smug expression, and her temper, usually dormant, stirred. As she allowed him to help her up to the high seat of the phaeton, she made a heroic effort to pull herself together.

She could hardly claim that no gentleman had tried to kiss her before. But, in Italy, the flowery speeches and extravagant gestures that usually preceded such an attempt gave any lady all the warning she could need, should she wish to avoid the outcome. But Lord Ellsmere had given no indication of his intent. One minute they had been strolling comfortably along a secluded walk, screened by the lush growths of a long summer from the more populated carriageway and lawns, and the next she had been trapped in his arms, quite unable to free herself—not that she had struggled, stunned as she had been. Lord Ellsmere had, unfortunately, taken her lack of reaction for acquiescence and acted accordingly. Then she had struggled.

To give him his due, Lord Ellsmere had immediately released her, only to capture her hand. He had then proceeded to declare his undying love for her, to Georgiana's utter confusion. Her mind had been miles distant before he had acted, and she had struggled to manage even the most feeble disclaimer.

And now, of course, he merely felt he had acted precipitately and swept her off her feet. He had made it clear he did not accept her refusal of his suit. He would, he had said, live in the hope she would, with time, see its advantages.

As he climbed to the seat beside her, Georgiana turned impulsively towards him. "My lord..."

Lord Ellsmere's eyes followed his diminutive tiger as the boy left the horses' heads to swing up behind them. Then he turned and smiled at Georgiana. "I'll see you at the ball tonight, my dear. We'll continue our discussion then, when you've had more time to consider."

His words were kindly, and Georgiana inwardly groaned. This was precisely the sort of situation she had been trying to avoid. But with the tiger behind, she could do nothing other than acquiesce to his lordship's plan.

In truth, as she felt the cooling breeze ripple past, she welcomed the time to marshal her arguments better. Lord Ellsmere was not Mr Havelock, nor Viscount Molesworth. He had every right to expect her serious consideration of his suit. He was eminently eligible—title, fortune, property and connections. Oh, heavens! What would Bella say this time?

Any thoughts Georgiana might have entertained of keeping her latest offer from her friend died a swift death when, re-entering Winsmere House, she made her way to the back parlour. Bella was there, reclining on the sofa, flicking through the pages of the latest *Ladies' Journal*. She looked up as Georgiana entered. And frowned.

"I thought you were driving with Lord Ellsmere."

Georgiana turned aside to lay her bonnet on a chair. "I was."

Bella's frown deepened. "Didn't he come in?"

"No." Georgiana would have liked to add an excuse which would explain this lapse of good manners on his lordship's part, but could think of nothing to the point. Under Bella's close scrutiny, she coloured.

"Georgie! *Never* say it! He's *offered?*" Bella sat up abruptly, the magazine sliding unheeded from her lap.

Bright cheeks made it unnecessary for Georgiana to answer.

"Oh, my dear! *Ellsmere!* Whoever would have thought it? Why, he's..." Georgiana's lack of response suddenly struck Bella. She stopped in mid-exclamation, disbelief chasing elation from her face. "Oh, no!" she moaned, falling back against the cushions. "You've *refused* him!"

Georgiana smiled weakly, almost apologetically. But she wasn't to be let off lightly. Not this time.

Half an hour later, Bella threw her hands up in the air in defeat. "But I *still* don't understand! Danby was one thing; even Mr Havelock I could sympathise with. But Molesworth...and now, of all men, Ellsmere. Georgie, you'll never live it down. No one will believe you're turning Ellsmere down for the ridiculous reason that you aren't in love with him. They'll start saying there's something wrong with you, I know they will." Bella's voice quavered on the edge of tears.

Georgiana wasn't entirely composed herself. But she endeavoured to keep her tone even as she replied, "But I don't mean to make them propose. I do everything I can think of to avoid it."

Bella frowned, aware this was so. She had watched her protégée like a hen with one chick, and had puzzled over Georgiana's apparent uninterest in her suitors as suitors, rather than acquaintances. To her mind, the offers were coming in thick and fast precisely because, in comparison with most of the other débutantes, the gentlemen found Georgie so comfortable to be with. Then the oddity in Georgiana's declaration struck her. Her head came up. "*Why* don't you wish them to become attached? You can't possibly have decided you can't love any of them. You can't expect me to believe you truly consider the single state preferable to being married."

There was no possibility of avoiding Bella's stern gaze. Georgiana had, in fact, spent the last weeks fantasising on marriage, albeit marriage to one particular gentleman. She felt her cheeks warm as she blushed guiltily.

And Bella, being Bella, and every bit as impulsive as Georgiana herself, immediately leapt to the correct conclusion. "Oh, Georgie!" she wailed. "You haven't formed a…a *tendre* for some unsuitable gentleman, have you?"

Driven to the truth, Georgiana nodded dully.

"But who?" Bella was nonplussed. She had conscientiously vetted those to whom she introduced Georgiana. There had been no one unsuitable. None of the truly dangerous blades had approached her, and, in the circles they frequented, there was precious little chance for any outsider to gain access to her charge. So who was this mysterious man?

"He's not actually unsuitable, exactly," put in Georgiana, anticipating Bella's train of thought. At her friend's interrogative glance, she looked down at her hands, clasped tightly together in her lap, and continued, "It's more a case of…of unrequited love. I fell in love with him, but he doesn't love me."

"Well, then," said Bella, perking up at this, "we'll just have to see to it that he changes his mind."

"No!" squeaked Georgiana. She drew a deep breath and went on more calmly, "You don't understand. He doesn't know I love him."

Bella looked thunderstruck. Then, after a moment, she ventured, "Well, why not tell him? Oh, not in words. But there are ways to these things, you know."

But Georgiana was adamantly shaking her head. "He's in love with someone else. In fact," she added, hoping to shut off the terrifying prospect Bella seemed set on exploring, "he's about to offer for another."

"Oh." Bella digested this unwelcome news, a frown settling over her delicate face. For the life of her, she still could not fathom who Georgie's mystery man could be. In the end, she looked again at Georgiana where she sat on a chair, twisting the ribbons of her bonnet in her fingers, an uncharacteristically desolate look in her eyes.

Bella's kind heart was touched. She had been thrilled at Arthur's scheme to hire Georgiana as her companion and truly grateful for the way Georgie had tactfully gone along with the charade. Inwardly, she vowed she would do everything possible to learn who it was who had stolen Georgie's heart and, if possible, change his mind. Unlike Georgiana, she did not imagine a man about to contract an alliance was necessarily in love with his prospective bride. Hence, she did not consider Georgie's case lost. But, if it was, she must look to protect her friend's best interests. She now knew enough of Georgiana to know she would never consider alternatives until, perhaps, it was too late. So, in a gentle way, Bella asked, "I don't mean to pry, my dear. But do you not feel you could tell me who the gentleman is?"

Georgiana hung her head. Her feelings of guilt were increasing by the minute. How could she repay Bella's kindness in this way? How could she tell Bella she was in love with her brother? Slowly she shook her head. Then, feeling some explanation was due, she said, "You know him, you see. And, as I said, he doesn't know I love him. I... think it would be unfair to tell you—unfair to you and unfair to him."

Bella nodded understandingly. "I won't push you, then. But perhaps, in the circumstances, it would be best if I spoke to Lord Ellsmere this evening." Georgiana's startled look had Bella hurrying on. "Oh, I won't tell him what you've told me. But there are ways and means. I'll just hint him away. It would be best, I think, for all concerned if I had a word with him."

Georgiana thought over this offer. Perhaps, in this case, she would be wise to accept Bella's superior knowledge of how things were done. She raised her eyes to her friend's blue gaze, wishing, for the umpteenth time, that Bella and her brother had taken after different parents in that respect. "If you don't mind speaking to him..."

"Not at all." Bella rose and impulsively hugged Georgiana. "Now! I'm going to ring for tea, and we'll talk about something quite different."

Georgiana summoned a smile and tried to tell herself that the peculiar emptiness within was only hunger.

TWO HOURS LATER Georgiana escaped to the sanctuary of her chamber. She did not ring for Cruickshank, wishing only to lie down and rest her aching head.

Quite when it was that she had finally realised she was in love with Lord Alton she could not be sure. Certainly, her social success and the proposals of Lord Danby and Mr Havelock had precipitated her thoughts on marriage. Only then had her feelings crystallised and gained substance. But, given that Lord Alton was so much older than she, and was shortly to marry Lady Changley, aside from having no inkling of her attachment and certainly no reciprocal emotions, she had originally decided her infatuation, for surely that was all it could be, was bound to pass. In such circumstances, and knowing Lord Alton was unlikely to spend much time in his sister's house, or dancing attendance on them, she had not seen her position as Bella's companion to be in any way compromised.

That had been before the shock of this afternoon had opened her eyes. Lord Ellsmere was all any young lady could desire. He was handsome, considerate, worldly and charming. And rich and titled… The list went on. But he was very definitely not the man she desired. When his lordship had taken her in his arms, she had been deep in a daydream in which she was walking with Bella's brother. The disappointment she had felt on realising that it was not Lord Alton kissing her had been acute.

She could no longer delude herself. What she felt for Viscount Alton was what her mother had felt for her father. She had seen them together often enough, laughing happily in a world of their own, to have an innate sense of the emotion. Love. That was what it was, plain and simple.

How had it happened?

Ridiculous it might be. Impossible it might be. But it was real.

With a great sigh, Georgiana burrowed her head into the soft pillow. How she was going to cope when next they met, as it seemed certain they would, she did not know. But cope she would. She had no intention of letting Bella guess the truth, nor of running away and leaving Bella alone. Arthur had offered her a way out of her troubles, and she had accepted in good faith. She would not let him down. Somehow she would manage.

Worn out, she closed her eyes. She needed to rest her troubled mind. And her troubled heart.

THE DUCHESS OF Lewes was holding her Grand Ball three nights later.

"One has to be a Duchess to call your ball 'Grand,'" Bella acidly remarked. "Still, one has to be seen there. It's one of the compulsory gatherings, you might say."

She had arrived in Georgiana's chamber just as that damsel emerged from her bath. Drifting to the bed, Bella fingered the lilac silk gown laid out there. Then, as if making up her mind, she turned to Georgiana. "Georgie, I know your feelings on this, but I really think you should consider wearing the sea-green gauze. You know I can never wear it. Please, wear it to please me."

Georgiana looked up, arrested in the act of towelling herself dry. Golden curls, dampened with steam, wreathed her head. For one moment she hesitated, considering Bella's plea.

"Wouldn't it cause comment, being so soon after my father's death?"

"But your father said you weren't to go into mourning, remember? And although it's common knowledge that your father has recently died, I haven't told anyone how recently. Have you?"

Georgiana shook her head. She considered the sea-green gauze. Stubbornly, she had bought three more evening gowns from Fancon, all in lilac shades, rather than wear the two gowns Bella had surreptitiously bought. But really, what right had she to refuse? It was a simple request and, after all Bella's help, it was a small price to pay. In reality, it was only her pride that forbade her to wear the delicate creations hanging ownerless in her wardrobe. So she smiled, fleetingly. “If it would please you.”

Bella grinned happily. “Immensely.” Her objective gained, she did not dally but whisked off to place herself in the hands of Hills.

Some three hours later, when they had finally gained the ballroom of Lewes House, Georgiana stood beside Bella and wondered why she had not overturned her stubborn pride weeks ago. The approbation in Arthur’s eyes when she had entered the drawing-room that evening had assured her that her decision to wear the gown had been the right one. And the unusually intent attention of her court, and of numerous other gentlemen she had not previously encountered, bore testimony to their approval of her change in style.

As she accepted Lord Mowbray’s arm for the first waltz, she smiled happily, laughingly returning his lordship’s pretty compliments. To her surprise, she had discovered she could preserve the façade of a young lady enjoying her first London Season, free of care and the tangles of love, despite her empty heart. She had never been encouraged to think her own troubles of particular note. Hence, she continued to observe the lives and foibles of those about her with interest. She treated all her court in the same friendly style she had always affected. True, there were few among the débutantes she could yet call friend, but Bella was there to supply that need, for which she would always be thankful.

Georgiana had no idea what exactly Bella had said to Lord Ellsmere. Whatever it was, he had gracefully withdrawn his suit, simultaneously assuring Georgiana of his lifelong devotion. For a whole evening, she had speculated on what Bella could have said. In the end, she decided she didn’t need to know.

Despite Bella’s fears, her refractory behaviour in the matter of her suitors had not given rise to any adverse effects. She was still "that most suitable Miss Hartley" to the hostesses, and the cards and invitations continued to flood in. She could hardly claim she did not enjoy the balls and parties. Yet, somewhere, some part of her was detached from it all, aloof and unfulfilled, empty and void, waiting. But, as she sternly lectured herself in the long watches of the night, what she was waiting for had no chance of arriving. Lady Winterspoon's dictum had come to her rescue. There was nothing she could do but enjoy herself, thereby pleasing Bella and, as her father would have told her, extending her own experience. So, with typical abandon, she did.

By the end of the third dance, a cotillion, the rooms were starting to fill. Georgiana was escorted back to Bella's side by her partner, Mr Havelock, and he remained beside them, chatting amiably of social happenings. When he finally made his bow and left them, Georgiana turned an impishly animated face to Bella. But what she had intended to say regarding Mr Havelock remained unsaid. In fact the words melted from her mind. Her lips parted slightly in surprise as her gaze locked with Viscount Alton's.

Dominic had made his way to Bella's side through the crush, intending to learn what had become of the golden girl he had left in her care. Only when she turned to face him did he recognise in the exquisite woodland nymph, standing slim and straight in silver-green gauze beside his sister, the same young girl whose heart-shaped face and warmed-honey eyes inhabited his dreams. The realisation left him momentarily bereft of words.

It was Bella who came, unwittingly, to their rescue. She uttered a small squeal of delight and, remembering to restrain her impulsive habit of throwing her arms about his neck, grabbed both of Dominic's hands instead. He looked down at her, and the spell was broken. Smoothly, suavely, he raised her hands, first one, then the other, to his lips. "Dear Bella. Clearly in fine fettle."

"But I thought you were fixed in Brighton." Bella received her hands back, but had eyes only for her brother. She saw his gaze had moved past her to Georgiana. When he made no reply but continued to stare at Georgiana, she felt constrained to add, "But you remember Georgiana?"

"Assuredly." Dominic couldn't help himself. His voice had automatically dropped to a deeper register. He smiled into those huge honey-coloured orbs in a manner perfected by years of practice and, taking her small hand, raised it fleetingly to his lips.

Barely able to breathe, Georgiana blushed vividly and sank into the regulation curtsy.

Her blush recalled Dominic to his senses. When she straightened, his face had assumed its usual, faintly bored mien. He turned slightly to address Bella. "As you see, I've decided to exchange the extravagant but questionably tasteful entertainments of His Highness for the more mundane but distinctly more enjoyable pursuits of the *ton*."

"Shhh!" said Bella, scandalised. "Someone might hear you!"

Dominic smiled sleepily. "My dear, it's only what half of the Carlton House set are saying. Hardly fodder for treason."

Bella still looked dubious.

But Dominic's attention had wandered. "Perhaps, Miss Hartley, I can steal a waltz. Judging by the hordes of gentlemen hovering, you have few to spare."

By this time, Georgiana had regained her composure and was determined not to lose it again. "The fruits of your sister's hard work, my lord," she responded readily. She placed her hand on his lordship's sleeve, suppressing by force the shiver that ran through her at that simple contact. How on earth was she to survive a waltz?

Thankfully, Lord Alton seemed unaware of her difficulties. One strong arm encircled her waist, and she was swept effortlessly into the dance. As her feet automatically followed his lead, she relaxed sufficiently to glance up into the dark-browed face above hers.

He intercepted her glance and smiled. "So you've been filling in time with all manner of social gadding?"

Georgiana shrugged lightly. "The pleasures of the *ton* have yet to pall, though I make no doubt they eventually will."

The dark brows rose. "What a very novel point of view." Dominic's lips twitched. "Surely my sister has taught you that all débutantes must, of necessity, profess addiction to all *tonnish* pursuits?"

A small and intriguing smile lifted Georgiana's lips. "Indeed, Bella has tried to convince me of the irreparable harm my lack of long-term enthusiasm might do to my chances. Still, I prefer to hold my own views." Georgiana paused while they twirled elegantly around the end of the room, before continuing, "I find it difficult to imagine being satisfied with a routine composed entirely of balls and parties and such affairs. Surely, somewhere, there must be some greater purpose in life?"

She glanced up to find an arrested expression on the Viscount's face. Suddenly worried she had inadvertently said more than she intended, Georgiana made haste to recover. "Of course, there may be a hidden purpose in such affairs—"

"No. Don't recant." His voice was low and betrayed no hint of mirth. His eyes held hers, unexpectedly serious, strangely intent. "Your views do you credit. Far be it from me to disparage them."

Georgiana was left wondering whether there was, underlying his seriousness, some fine vein of sarcasm she had failed to detect. But she got no chance to pursue the matter; the music ceased and Lord Alton returned her to his sister's side. With a smile and a lazy flick of one finger to Bella's cheek, and a polite inclination of his head in Georgiana's direction, he withdrew.

On the other side of the ballroom, Elaine Changley shut her ivory fan with a snap. Her cold blue eyes remained fixed upon a head of gold curls just visible through the throng. Surely Dominic hadn't left her for a schoolgirl? Impossible!

The intervening bodies shifted, and Lady Changley was afforded a full view of Georgiana Hartley, slim and elegant at Bella Winsmere's side. The blue eyes narrowed. Her ladyship had not reached her present position without learning to sum up the opposition's good points. There was no doubt the girl had a certain something. But the idea of the charms of a delicate and virginal schoolgirl competing with her own experienced voluptuousness was too ridiculous to contemplate.

Lady Changley's rouged lips set in a hard line. The thought of what her so-called friends would say if, after all her crowing, she was to lose a prize like Dominic Ridgeley to a chit of a girl fresh from the schoolroom was entirely too galling to bear. Perhaps a little reminder of what she could offer was due.

IT WAS PAST midnight when Georgiana slipped on to the terrace outside the ballroom. The last dance before supper was in progress, and the terrace was vacant except for the moonbeams that danced along its length. As the chill of the evening bit through her thin gown, she wrapped her arms about her and fell to pacing the stone flags, drawing in deep breaths of the refreshing night air.

She had yet to become fully acclimatised to the stuffy atmosphere of *tonnish* ballrooms. Feeling the heat closing in on her, she had very nearly suggested to her cavalier of the moment, Lord Wishpoole, that they retire to the terrace. Luckily, a mental vision of his lordship's face expressing his likely reaction to such an invitation had stopped her from uttering the words, and doubtless saved her from the embarrassment of extricating herself from his lordship's unnecessary and very likely scandalous company. Wary of giving Bella any further reason to view her with concern, she had pleaded a slight headache to Lord Wishpoole and headed for the withdrawing-room. Once out of his lordship's sight, she had changed direction. The long windows of the ballroom had been left ajar, but the weather had turned and few guests had availed themselves of the opportunity to stroll on the long terrace.

Georgiana leant against the low balustrade and wished she was not alone. The idea of strolling beside Lord Alton, conversing easily while they took the air, was enticing. Only, of course, there was no possibility of Lord Alton wishing to stroll with her. Unfortunately, reality and dreams did not merge in that way.

The sound of footsteps approaching one of the doors at the far end of the terrace brought her upright. Someone pulled a set of doors wide, and light spilled forth. Startled, Georgiana looked around for a hiding-place. A tall cypress in a tub stood against the wall. Without further thought, she squeezed herself between the balustrade and the tree.

Through the scraggly branches of the tree she watched as a tall woman glided on to the terrace. The moonlight, resurrected now the doors were again shut, silvered her blonde hair. As she turned and looked towards the cypress, Georgiana caught a glimpse of diamonds glittering around an alabaster throat. The lady's silk dress clung revealingly to a ripe figure; her long, graceful arms were quite bare.

Again light flooded the terrace and was abruptly cut off. Georgiana's eyes grew round.

Dominic Ridgeley's blue eyes were hard as they rested on Elaine Changley. His brows rose. "To what do I owe the pleasure of this meeting, my lady?"

Inwardly, Elaine Changley winced at his tone. *My lady?* Clearly she had lost more than a little ground. But not a suspicion of her emotions showed on her sculpted face as she moved forward to place one slim hand on the Viscount's lapel. "Dominic, darling. Why so cold?" she purred.

To her surprise and real consternation, Lady Changley sensed an instinctive rejection, immediately suppressed, but undeniable. Shock drove her to make a grab, however unwise, for her dreams. Allowing her lids to veil her eyes, she moved seductively closer. "Surely, my love, what lies between us cannot be ended with a simple 'Goodbye'?"

Lady Changley was a tall woman. In one smooth movement, she pressed herself to Dominic's chest, reaching up to place her lips against his.

Automatically, Dominic's hands came to her waist, initially to hold her from him. But as he felt her silken form between his hands he stopped and quite coldly considered the situation.

He had come to the terrace in response to Elaine's note, intending to make it quite clear that his "Goodbye" had meant just that. The problem he was having with Georgiana Hartley, or, rather, with making sense of his feelings towards a schoolroom chit, was his major and only concern. He had almost succeeded in convincing himself that it was merely a passing aberration, that the reason he no longer desired the company, let alone the favours, of the delectable Lady Changley was no more than a function of the natural passage of time and had nothing whatever to do with a slim form in green silk gauze. Almost, but not quite.

And now here was Elaine, providing him with a perfect chance to test the veracity of his conclusions. The acid test. Surely, if he were to kiss her now, a woman he had recently known so well, he would feel something?

On the thought, his hands moved to draw her more firmly against him. Then his arms closed around her and his head angled over hers as he took possession of her lips and then her mouth. He felt the ripple of relief that travelled through her long limbs. Warning bells sounded in his brain. He felt nothing—no glimmer of desire, no flicker of flame. The coals were long dead.

Abruptly he brought the kiss to an end and, lifting his head, put Elaine Changley from him. "And that, my dear, is very definitely the end. Adieu and goodbye." With a terse bow, he spun on his heel.

Before he could leave, Elaine, desperate, stretched out one white hand to his sleeve. "You can't just walk away from me, Dominic. There's too much between us."

The chill of his very blue eyes as they turned on her froze Elaine Changley's blood. But, when he spoke, Dominic's voice was soft—soft and, to Elaine Changley, quite deadly. "I suspect, my dear, that you'll find you're mistaken. I should perhaps point out that any embarrassment you might suffer upon our separation will be entirely your own fault. And, furthermore, any attempt on your part to talk more into the relationship than was ever present will only result in your further embarrassment. So—" Dominic smiled—a singularly humourless smile—and lifted her hand from his sleeve, and thence, mockingly, to his lips "—I will, for the last time, bid you adieu."

Elaine Changley made no attempt to detain him as he strode from the terrace. She was shivering, though not from the cold. Far too experienced to run after her ex-lover, Lady Changley forced herself to stand still until her composure returned. Only then did she follow Lord Alton back into the ballroom.

Georgiana let out a long breath. She emerged from behind the tub, automatically brushing her skirt free of small sticks and needles. She felt as if she had hardly breathed since scuttling behind the tree. That, of course, was the reason she was feeling light-headed. Nothing to do with the revelation that Bella's brother was quite clearly and indisputably in love with Lady Changley. Why else would he have kissed her like that? She had been too far away to overhear their conversation, or to see their expressions, but the evidence of her eyes had been plain enough. Lady Changley had melted into Lord Alton's arms. And he had welcomed her and kissed her as if he intended to passionately devour her.

She knew her love for him was hopeless. Had always known it.

Georgiana shivered. Slowly she looked around the terrace. Her innocent daydream seemed more distant than ever, elusive as the mist which wreathed the treetops. With a deep sigh, she pulled open one of the ballroom doors and re-entered the heated room. She finally located Bella amid a knot of their friends. Pushing through the throng, she made her way to her side, rehearsing her request to leave early on the grounds of a headache which she could now quite truthfully claim.

CHAPTER FIVE

DURING THE NEXT WEEK, Georgiana had plenty of opportunity to develop her tactics for dealing socially with Viscount Alton. Contrary to her expectations, his lordship graced all the functions she and Bella attended. He was politely attentive. There was nothing in his behaviour to feed the flame she was valiantly trying to dampen. To her irritation, she found that fact depressing. More than ever aware of the disparity of their stations, she doggedly reminded herself that a thick skin could only be obtained through exposure. Consequently, she did not shrink from contact with Lord Alton. Instead, whenever he asked her to dance—which he invariably did at least once, and, on one memorable occasion, twice—she endeavoured to amuse him with her observations on life in the *ton*. To her surprise, he seemed genuinely entertained by her comments. Indeed, he went out of his way to encourage her to air her opinions. Doubtless, she thought, it ensured he was not overcome with boredom in her otherwise unenlivening company.

Her own motive in maintaining a steady flow of conversation lay in distracting his lordship from the other peculiar responses he awoke in her. Breathlessness, often occurring with a unnerving sense of exhilaration, was the least of these. Sometimes she believed the thudding of her heart would be plainly audible if she weren't covering the noise with her chatter. Thankfully, he had not yet noticed the tremors that ran through her at his slightest touch. She had hoped these would ease with time, with familiarity, as it were. Unfortunately, they were becoming more acute with each passing day; she went in dread of his remarking them.

Absorbed as she was with dealing with his lordship, by the time they climbed into their carriage each night to return to Green Street she was thoroughly worn out. Gradually, the strain grew, until, in order to preserve her defences for the evenings, she found herself forced to forgo the pleasures of the day. When she excused herself from the afternoon's promenade for the second day in a row, Bella's concern became overt.

"Georgie, I simply cannot bear to see you so pulled down." Bella plumped herself down on the *chaise-longue* beside her friend. Georgiana was listlessly plying her needle, setting the occasional stitch in a piece of fine embroidery. Bella glanced anxiously into her face. "You aren't going into a decline, are you?"

Despite her tiredness, Georgiana grinned. "Of course not." After a moment she added, "I assure you I've no intention of pining away. It's just that I find the…the tension of the evening entertainments draining."

Born and bred to such things, Bella could not readily imagine being drained by a ball. However, she was not without sympathy. She frowned as she mulled over the matter. "We could cut down a trifle, perhaps. The Minchintons' ball is on Friday—we need not go to that, I suppose."

But curtailing Bella's activities because of her own weakness was further than Georgiana was prepared to go. She was supposed to be Bella's companion, not an inhibiting influence. "Don't be a goose," she replied, her tone affectionate but firm. "I'm only feeling a bit low, that's all. I dare say if I make a special effort I'll be fine by this evening." She paused. "On second thoughts, perhaps some fresh air would help. If you'll wait, I'll get my bonnet and come with you."

"Of course." Bella smiled encouragingly.

But as soon as Georgiana disappeared through the door, the frown returned to Bella's face. Far from reassuring her, Georgiana's rapid about-face convinced her that her friend was endeavouring, however unsuccessfully, to conceal the true effect of her hopeless love. Who knew to what depths of misery Georgie descended when no one was by? Bella fretted over the problem, rendered more acute by the restraint she felt in confiding in anyone. Arthur was her long-time mentor, but in this case Bella felt she would need Georgiana's permission before revealing her friend's state to him.

Georgiana's footsteps sounded in the hall. With a sigh, Bella rose and picked up her discarded bonnet, absent-mindedly swinging it by its long aqua ribbons. She sorely needed advice. Then, in one instant of blinding clarity, she saw the answer. Dominic. He knew all of Georgiana's background. And, after all, Georgiana herself had seen fit, at the very outset, to confide in him.

When Georgiana stuck her head around the door, Bella grinned widely. "Yes, I'm coming," she called and, feeling much more light-hearted, all but tripped from the room.

"PLEASE, DOMINIC. I really *must* talk to you. Privately." Bella put every ounce of sisterly need into her gaze as it rested on her brother's handsome face. But his habitually bored mask showed no evidence of lifting. In fact, she noted, he regarded her even more dubiously than he had before her plea.

"I warn you, Bella, I need no lectures from you."

Far from striking fear into her heart and stifling her request as intended, his precise tones made her relax and give a dismissive smile.

"Not about that! I want to talk to you about Georgiana."

"Oh!" Dominic followed her gaze to the object of their discussion, twirling gaily about the dance-floor in Harry Edgcombe's arms. Then the piercingly blue eyes swung back to Bella. "What about Miss Hartley?"

Bella looked at the knots of people surrounding them. "Not here." She glanced impishly up at him. "Don't you know of an alcove where we might be alone?"

The blue eyes glinted down at her. "Don't be impudent." He caught her hand and drew it through his arm. "As it happens," he said, leading her through the crowd, "I do. But I can't spare too many minutes. I'm engaged to dance with Miss Hartley myself, two dances hence."

"It won't take long," Bella promised.

The small ante-room Dominic led her to was thankfully empty. She sank on to a well padded sofa. Dominic elected to stand, leaning one blue-silk-clad arm along the mantelpiece. "Perceive me all ears, dear sister."

Bella eyed him suspiciously, but could detect no hint of the sarcasm he frequently employed when irritated. "As I said, it's about Georgiana." Now she came to it, she found herself short of the necessary words.

"Has she discovered Arthur's little deception and become difficult?"

"No, no. Nothing like that." Bella frowned, then, sensing Dominic's growing impatience, she abandoned her efforts to find the best phrasing and blurted out, "She's fallen in love."

For a moment, she wondered whether he had heard. His face showed no reaction to her words; he seemed frozen, petrified. Then his black brows rose. "I see." He turned aside, resettling the fine lace on his cuff. "It is, after all, not an uncommon happening. Who is the lucky man?"

"That's just it. She won't say."

Dominic's eyes rested thoughtfully on his sister's dark head. "And you imagine, as she won't divulge his name, he must therefore be in some way unsuitable."

"No, that's not it either." Bella glanced up to find her brother's eyes full on her, irritation fermenting in their blue depths. She hastened to explain. "He's not unsuitable in the way you mean. But it seems she's fallen *irrevocably* in love with a man who's about to offer for another. She says he doesn't know she's in love with him. I've tried to get her to confide in me, but she won't. She says I know him so it wouldn't be fair."

Dominic digested this information in silence. Then, abruptly, he pushed away from the mantelpiece and paced across the room. Returning, he looked again at his sister. "How, then, am I supposed to help? I do take it I'm supposed to help?"

Bella smiled, a trifle warily. "Yes, of course. I wouldn't have told you if I didn't think you could help. I want you to find out who Georgie's gentleman is."

Dominic's brows flew. "That all?"

At his tone, Bella's face fell. "But you must be able to guess. Who is it whom I know is about to marry? Or at least offer for someone. You men always know such titbits before it's common knowledge."

Pacing once more, Dominic considered his acquaintance. He knew all the gentlemen his sister was on speaking terms with, and would very likely know if any were contemplating matrimony. "Unfortunately, to my knowledge, no one fits the bill."

Twisting her fingers anxiously, Bella ventured, "I had wondered whether it was Lord Edgcombe."

"Harry?" Dominic paused, then shook his head. "Not likely. He does have to marry in the not overly distant future or risk his family hauling him to the altar themselves.

But he must marry money, and I doubt Miss Hartley's prospects fit his bill."

"But couldn't she have fallen in love with him anyway? He's certainly personable enough."

Again, Dominic gave the matter his consideration. Again, he shook his head. "Harry has no plans to marry yet awhile. I doubt he'd even mention the possibility to a young lady circumstanced as Miss Hartley is. And, certainly, he would not have suggested he's about to do the deed." He uttered a short laugh. "Not even to escape a snare would Harry bring up the subject of marriage."

Bella sighed. "So you can't guess either." Disheartened, she stood and shook out her skirts.

Dominic hadn't moved from his stance in the middle of the floor. Now he looked shrewdly at Bella. "What prompted you to ask for help?"

Bella shrugged. "It's just that Georgie's so wan and listless nowadays."

"Listless?" her brother echoed, the vision of Miss Hartley as he had last seen her vivid in his mind. "I've rarely seen anyone *less* listless."

"Oh, not in the evenings. She seems quite lively then. But during the day she's drawn and quiet. Her looks will suffer if she goes on as she is. If *only* she would accept Mr Havelock."

"Havelock? Has he offered for her?"

Bella frowned at the odd note in her brother's voice. It was not like Dominic to be so insultingly disbelieving. "Yes," she averred. "Not only Mr Havelock, but Lord Danby and Viscount Molesworth. *And* Lord Ellsmere, too!"

For once, she had the satisfaction of knowing she had stunned her brother. Dominic's brows rose to astronomical heights. "Good lord!"

After a moment, his puzzled gaze swung back to her face. "And she refused them all? Even Julian?"

Bella nodded decisively. "Even Lord Ellsmere." She looked down at her hands, clasped schoolgirl fashion before her. "I don't know what I'm to do, for there's bound to be more offers. They can't seem to help themselves."

She looked up to see her brother's shoulders shaking. Bella glared. "It's not funny!"

Dominic waved one white hand placatingly. "Oh, Bella! Would that all women had a sense of humour like Miss Hartley's. I assure you she would see the oddity in such a situation."

Bella was puzzled by her brother's far-away smile. But before she drummed up enough courage to ask what prospect it was that so fascinated him, he came back to earth. "And, speaking of Miss Hartley, we must, I'm afraid, return to the ballroom."

Falling into step beside him, Bella tucked her hand in his arm. "You will try to discover who he is, won't you?"

Dominic's eyes glinted steely blue. "Fear not, Bella mine. I'll give it my most earnest consideration."

And with that Bella had perforce to be content.

IT WAS WELL after midnight when Dominic returned to Grosvenor Square. He let himself in with his latchkey. In the large tiled hall, shadows danced about a single candle burning in a brass holder on the central table. He had long ago broken his staff of their preferred habit of lying in wait for him to return from his evening entertainments. Picking up the candle, he stood at the foot of the stairs, contemplating the broad upward sweep. Then he turned aside and made for a polished door to one side of the hall.

The fire in the library was a glowing mass of coals. He lit the candles in the large candelabrum on the mantelpiece before crouching to carefully balance a fresh log on the embers. After a little encouragement, the flames started to lick along the dry wood.

Standing, he stretched, then crossed to the sideboard. A balloon of fine brandy in one hand, he returned to the wing-chair by the fireplace and settled his cold feet on the fender.

Georgiana Hartley. Undoubtedly the most beguiling female he had met in over a decade on the town. And she was in love with another man. Furthermore, she was in love with a man who didn't even have the good sense to love her. Ridiculous!

Dominic stared into the flames. For what felt like the six hundredth time, he tried to make himself believe that his interest in Miss Hartley didn't exist. But he had travelled that road before and had given up weeks ago. What he had yet to discover was what his interest in Georgiana Hartley portended.

He couldn't believe it was love. Not after all these years. His experience of the opposite sex was as extensive as hers was negligible. And he had never felt the slightest inclination to succumb to any of the proffered lures. Why on earth should he suddenly wish to entangle himself with a young woman barely free of the schoolroom?

Yet he could not get her out of his mind. Her heart-shaped face and honey-gold eyes inhabited his thoughts to the exclusion of almost everything else. He had underestimated the strength of his distraction when he had returned from Candlewick to Brighton. The chit had unexpected depths. Her eyes, like a siren's song, beckoned with a promise he found difficult to resist. Luckily he had realised his state before Elaine had precipitated any renewal of their intimacy. She had, predictably, reacted badly to his withdrawal.

Light from the flames gilded the spines of the leather-covered tomes on the shelves which stretched away into darkness on either side of the fireplace. Dominic took a sip of his brandy, then sank his chin into his cravat, cradling the glass between his hands. He had no regrets about Elaine. In truth, his desire for her had waned before the advent of Georgiana Hartley had banished all thought of illicit dalliance from his mind. A smile of gentle malice touched his lips. Doubtless Elaine would suffer due embarrassment as a result of her posturing. It had been her plan to use public knowledge of their relationship to pressure him into making her aspirations come true. She had been most indiscreet. Lionel, Lord Worthington, his guardian prior to his attaining his majority, had even been moved to post to Candlewick to dissuade him from contracting a *mésalliance,* on account of the bluster of a trollop's long tongue. No, he had no sympathy for such as Elaine Changley.

The fire crackled and hissed as the fresh log settled. With a sensation akin to relief, he turned his mind from the past to contemplate the nebulous future. What did his feelings for Georgiana Hartley mean? Did they amount to anything more than infatuation, regrettable but harmless and, most importantly, transient? Would the lovely Georgiana fade from his mind in six months' time, as Elaine Changley had? These were the questions that tormented him. They had forced him to return to London, to assuage a need he did not wish to acknowledge. Yet, after a week in the capital, he was no nearer the answers.

The only truth he had uncovered was that his normally even temperament was now somehow dependent on Miss Georgiana Hartley's smile.

He dropped his head back against the deeply padded leather. He had tried to tell himself she was too young, little more than a schoolgirl. Any liaison between them would be virtually cradle-snatching. But, whenever he thought along such lines, Arthur's and Bella's happiness would rise up to mock him. And, even worse, Georgiana no longer *looked* like a schoolgirl. Every time they met, Fancon's gowns, or, rather, the delectable shape they displayed, shredded his well rehearsed rationalisations.

But enough was enough. According to Bella, Georgiana was making herself ill over some no-hoper. He had no right to intervene. Not, that was, unless he wished to take their interaction further, to make some positive move in her direction. And that, he was not yet prepared to do.

If Bella, or anyone else, got a whiff of his possible intentions, there would be no chance of wooing her in private. Their every meeting would be watched over by dozens of gimlet eyes. Every word, every expression would be duly noted and analysed. He couldn't subject her to that, not when he wasn't sure what he wanted of her.

Experience, however, was on his side. If he wished, he did not doubt he could create the necessary opportunities to advance his cause, without alerting every gossip-monger in the *ton.* He smiled. There was an undeniable challenge in such an enterprise. The snag was, he was not yet sure. Not sure of what he felt for her. Not sure of what he would do once he was certain the odd feeling in his chest was more than infatuation.

It had taken him three weeks to reach his present state of acknowledged indecision. He had no intention of enduring the situation for much longer, particularly if Georgiana threatened to pine away before his very eyes. Still, how did one test an infatuation? Never having suffered such an emotion before, he had no real idea how to proceed.

The clock in the corner ticked ponderously, marking his heartbeats. His eyes grew unfocused as he stared at the flames slowly dying around the charred log. Finally he stirred. He drained his glass, then rose to return it to the tray. He relighted his bedroom candle at the candelabrum, then snuffed the five long candles it held. In the soft flickering light of the single flame, he made his way to the door.

If he wanted to burn out his obsession with Georgiana Hartley, there was only one way to go about it. He needed to meet with her often, in every possible context, to see all her faults and blemishes, the little incompatibilities which would reduce her status in his mind to one of a mere acquaintance. That was the only way forward.

And, if it proved to be more than infatuation, it was high time he faced up to the truth. And acted.

"I TOLD YOU everyone would be here." Bella stopped on the lawn below the terrace. Tucking her furled parasol under one arm, she retied the strings of her new bonnet in a jaunty bow beneath one ear. "Lady Jersey's entertainments are always well attended, particularly when they're held here."

"Here" was Osterley Park, and the entertainment in question was an alfresco luncheon. To Georgiana, standing patiently by her friend's side, it seemed as if the entire *ton* was gathered on the manicured lawns sloping gently away from the Palladian mansion to the shrubberies and parkland beyond. "Lady Lyncombe is nodding to us. Over there on the left."

Bella turned and bowed politely to the portly matron, who had three gangling girls in tow. "Poor dear. Freckle-faced, the lot of them. She'll never get them off her hands."

Georgiana stifled a giggle. "Surely it can't be that bad. They might be quite nice young girls."

"They can be as nice as they please, but they'll need something more to recommend them to the eligible gentlemen." Bella sighed, in keeping with her worldly-wise pose.

Strolling by her side, Georgiana wondered what it was that recommended her to the gentlemen. Certainly not her looks, for, in her estimation, these were only passing fair.

And her fortune was, she suspected, so small as to be negligible. Yet she had received four offers. Despite the fact that she had wished to avoid each one, the very existence of four eligible offers was no small fillip to her confidence.

Smiling and bowing to acquaintances, they strolled the length of the lawn to where three gaily striped marquees had been erected. One housed the beverages; one protected the food. The third was a withdrawing-room of sorts, where ladies feeling the effects of the sun could rest before rejoining the crush.

And it certainly was a crush. The broad expanses were filled with swirling muslins and starchy cambrics, parasols and elegantly cut morning coats dotting the colourful scene. It was difficult to see more than ten feet in any direction. Registering this fact, Georgiana turned to Bella to point out the advisability of staying close together. Too late.

"If you're looking for Bella, she's fallen victim to Lady Molesworth."

Georgiana looked up into Viscount Alton's blue eyes. He was smiling, and she noted the set of small lines radiating from the corners of his eyes. Such a handsome face. Entranced, she forgot her role of sister's companion and smiled warmly back.

Dominic expertly captured her hand and conveyed it to his lips. He caught his breath when she smiled with such guileless joy. For one instant, he could almost believe…

A sudden intentness in Lord Alton's gaze brought Georgiana to her senses. "Oh! Er—where exactly?" She flustered and blushed, and turned away as if looking for Bella, to cover her confusion.

"No, no. This way." Dominic's voice was gentle, softened by an emotion he couldn't quite define.

Georgiana looked where he indicated—to the right—and found Bella deep in discussion with Lord Molesworth's mother—she who had decreed Georgiana could not do other than marry her son.

Dominic recalled Bella's mention of the luckless Viscount. His grin grew. "Perhaps," he said, "as Bella is so absorbed, I could escort you on a ramble by the lake. It's really much more pleasant than being packed amid all this crowd. Unless you're famished?" One black brow rose interrogatively.

"Oh, no," Georgiana disclaimed. She bit her lip. The prospect of a stroll in less cramped surroundings was very tempting. But could she weather such an excursion with Lord Alton? Were her nerves up to it? She glanced up at him and found him regarding her quizzically, as if trying to read her mind. As she watched, a faintly satirical gleam entered the very blue eyes, and his brows rose slightly, as if in challenge. Puzzled, she put aside her misgivings. "If it wouldn't be too boring for you."

With a laugh, Dominic offered her his arm. When she laid one small hand on his sleeve, he covered it with his other hand. "My dear Miss Hartley—or can I call you Georgiana?" He felt the hand under his quiver. His brows rose again. He looked down into her golden eyes. "Oh, yes. Surely, in the circumstances, I can claim that privilege?"

Georgiana had no idea how she should answer. But her nerves were already a-tingle, and she didn't have the capacity to cope with distractions. So she merely inclined her head in assent. "If it pleases you, my lord."

Oh, it pleased him. In fact Dominic felt inordinately pleased with that small success. "As I was saying, my dear Georgiana," he continued, deftly steering her clear of Lord Harrow, another of her present encumbrances, "your company is forever entertaining. Tell me, which of your suitors do you favour?"

Now what on earth was she to answer to that? Georgiana

thought quickly, then assumed a bored air. "Why, in truth, I'd not given the matter much thought, my lord." She heard a deep chuckle. "It's all so fatiguing, this marriage game." Lassitude dripped from her every syllable.

Laughing, he countered, "Very neat, my dear. But don't let any of the *grandes dames* hear you espousing such controversial standards. You'll be driven forth, cast out from the bosom of the *ton*."

Georgiana smiled, dropping her pose. "In all honesty, I'm not sure I'm suited to this life."

To mock her words would be the easy way out. Instead Dominic answered seriously. "My dear, it's such as you who keep the *ton* alive."

Her eyes flew to his face.

Reading the question in the golden-lit depths, he explained, "If we did not have people with different ideas, people brought up to different ideas, such as yourself, join us now and then, to refresh our tired fashions, then the *ton* would be an excessively boring and stale society. Instead, if you look about you carefully, you'll see the *ton* encompasses a wide spectrum of tastes and types." He smiled down at her. "Don't worry. You'll fit in. You'll eventually find your place, that niche that has your name engraved on it."

Shyly Georgiana returned his smile.

They strolled on in companionable silence, around the shrubberies and on to the shore of the lake. A cool breeze lifted off the expanse of grey-green water, flicking little wavelets across the surface. Beeches lined an avenue that followed the bank, golden leaves a carpet beneath the still canopied crowns. There were other guests enjoying the peace, but none intruded on their privacy.

While enjoying the early autumn colours, Georgiana pondered the cause of his earlier satirical look. As she noted the giggling and sighing of more than one damsel they passed, it suddenly occurred to her that Lord Alton might have thought she was questioning the propriety of walking alone with him. Inwardly, she sighed. If only that were her trouble. But she was abysmally aware she was in no danger of receiving any amorous attentions from Bella's brother. Rather, she was more afraid of boring him witless. She cast about in her mind for a suitable topic of conversation.

Far from being bored, Dominic was revelling in the unusual pleasure of strolling in relative peace in a glorious setting with a beautiful woman who was blessedly silent. The only itch to his contentment was the realisation of how deeply contented he in fact was. That, and the strength of his desire to preserve the moment at whatever cost. That unnerved him.

"Do you spend much time with the Prince Regent? What's he like?"

Georgiana's questions broke his train of thought. Dominic paused, considering, before he answered. "My family have for the past few generations been close to the throne." He smiled down at her. "In the present case, the Regent."

"But..." Georgie hesitated. She had taken in enough of the discussion between Lord Alton and Arthur over Bella's dinner-table to realise the Viscount was more deeply involved in politicking than one might suppose from his pose of arrogantly bored aristocrat. Carefully choosing her words, she ventured, "You discuss politics with His Highness, don't you? Not just...well, social matters."

Inwardly cursing Arthur for his lapse from their normal secretiveness, Dominic attempted to turn her far too perceptive query aside. He laughed lightly. "I assure you, my dear, that—er—social matters are generally dominant with the Regent."

The teasing look he sent her along with his words should

have had her blushing. Instead, he saw her beautiful eyes narrow slightly, and knew his diversion had failed. Damn it! She was younger than Bella. She should accept his word without question. And since when did young ladies institute probing inquisitions into a man's politics? She deserved a set-down. Instead, Dominic heard himself say, "However, you're quite right. I do act as a sort of…conduit—a channel of communication, if you like—between certain factions of the Parliament and the Regent." He paused to help her step over a large tree root distorting the even surface of the path. Settling her hand once more in the crook of his arm, he continued, "Despite appearances, Prinny is not entirely insensitive to the problems of the realm. And, while he has limited powers as far as actual law-making goes, his influence can go a long way to seeing changes made where they are desperately needed."

"And you explain these things to him?"

Dominic laughed. "Oh, no! I merely act as a form of Greek messenger."

Georgiana looked her question. Smiling, he explained. "My task is merely to bring up the subject, to introduce the problem, whatever it might be, to His Highness's notice." He grinned. "That's why I'm back from Brighton with leisure to enjoy your company."

Georgiana frowned, puzzling this out. "He didn't like your last problem?"

Her companion's gaze had shifted to the distance, but he was still smiling.

"Not in the least. I'm presently in disgrace, although, of course, that's not general knowledge."

It seemed to Georgiana that there was quite a deal about the fascinating Viscount that was not general knowledge. But before she could frame any further questions, they emerged from the beech walk and were joined by a gaggle of young ladies and their escorts. Viscount Molesworth was there; so too was Lord Ellsmere. Georgiana caught a look of surprise on Lord Ellsmere's handsome face, followed swiftly by an expression she could only interpret as consideration. However, he said nothing to her, beyond a polite greeting, and fell into step on the other side of Lord Alton, engaging the Viscount in a low-voiced conversation which seemed to have a distinctly pugilistic flavour. In a laughing, chattering group, they made their way back to the marquees. Bella met them there. To Georgiana's disappointment, she got no further chance to converse alone with Lord Alton.

TWO NIGHTS LATER, a masked ball was to be held at Hattringham House. Bella was thrilled. "It's quite fun, really. Most people know who you are, of course, but the masks allow everyone to pretend they don't."

It was the afternoon of the big event, and Bella was lolling on Georgiana's bed.

Georgiana was frowningly considering her wardrobe. The one evening dress she had yet to wear was the topaz silk. For some reason, she had resisted temptation, saving it for some undefined purpose. She rather thought the time for wearing it had come. Why she should feel so she had no idea. She simply did. She drew it forth and held it to her.

"Oooh, yes!" said Bella. "I'd forgotten about that one. It's perfect."

"You don't think it's a little too…?" Georgiana gestured vaguely.

"Heavens, no! A 'little too…' is exactly what one wants for a masked ball."

"Do you have a mask I can borrow?"

"Heaps! They're in a drawer in my room." Bella sat up

and jumped off the bed. "Come, let's go and look. Bring the dress."

Five minutes later they had found the mask. A bronzed affair with elaborate upswept wings, it fitted snugly across Georgiana's upper face from forehead to upper cheeks. Her hazel eyes glittered from the darkened depths of the slanted eye holes. There was no debate on the matter; it was perfect.

When they descended the stairs that evening to twirl joyfully about Arthur in the hall, his face told them they were both visions of delight. "You won't be able to move for all the beaux at your feet," he said, taking one hand of each fair maid and gallantly bestowing a kiss on them both.

As he escorted his two charges to their carriage, Arthur smiled in fond anticipation. He was accompanying them ostensibly because the Hattringham House ball was one of the major events of the Season. In reality, he cared little for the social swim but intended to keep a watchful eye on his youthful wife. Bella too often forgot that what she intended as innocent play might be reciprocated by actions far from innocent. As he rarely had time to devote solely to his wife, Arthur was looking forward to enjoying the evening. He knew Dominic would be there and was quite sure he could leave his brother-in-law to look after Georgiana. In fact, he thought, as his gaze rested on the alluring figure clad in topaz silk seated opposite, he doubted his brother-in-law, in his present state, would have eyes for anyone else.

Georgiana travelled the miles to Hattringham House in an unusual state of nervous anticipation. Nervous anticipation of itself was no surprise—she was accustomed to feeling it grow every time she appraoched the moment she would meet Bella's brother. But tonight the tension was heightened. It was the fault of the dress. If she had known how it would affect her, she would never have worn it. Far from decreasing her anxiety, the realisation tightened the knots in her stomach. Inwardly quivering with trepidation, she accepted Arthur's hand to descend from the carriage to the torchlit steps of Hattringham House. With assumed calm, she glided beside Bella as they made their way through the hall and into the ballroom beyond.

There was no footman to announce anyone, of course. The guests merely entered and joined the shifting throng. Already the rooms were crowded. Glittering jewels winked under the chandeliers. Gay silks and satins swirled, fans fluttered in flirtation, curls bobbed teasingly about artful faces. A hubbub of conversation rose to swamp them; warm air redolent with a heady mix of perfumes and flower scents wrapped them about.

"Phew! What a crush!" exclaimed Bella. "And it's not even ten."

A tall, dark-haired gentleman materialised at Georgiana's side. He bowed elegantly over her hand. "Could I beg the favour of this dance, fair maid?"

Behind the dark mask, Georgiana descried the features of Lord Ellsmere. "I would be honoured, my lord," she replied, rising from her curtsy.

"Now how do you know if I'm a lord or not?" her partner asked as he whirled them on to the floor.

"Given that at least half the gentlemen present must be titled, it seemed a reasonable assumption," Georgiana glibly explained. "And besides, even if wrong, the mistake could only flatter, whereas, if it were the other way about, I could be stepping on toes."

His lordship laughed. "You never step on my toes, my dear."

Abruptly Georgiana wondered whether he had accepted her dismissal of his suit or was, in reality, merely waiting in the expectation that she would change her mind. Held easily within his arm, she was loweringly conscious that she felt nothing—no ripple of excitement, no increase in her heartbeat to betray her emotions. His nearness touched her not at all.

The dance ended and they whirled to a halt. Immediately they were mobbed by a crowd of gentlemen, all wishful of securing a dance with the exciting newcomer. Not everyone recognised her; of that Georgiana was certain. But before she could make sense of all their requests and determine whom it was safe for her to accept, a deep voice spoke from just beside her.

"My claim is first, I think."

Georgiana glanced up, her breath trapped, as usual, somewhere between her lungs and her throat. Her eyes took in the tall, broad-shouldered form at her side, exquisitely garbed, dark hair falling in waves about a dark mask. Blue, blue eyes watched her from the depths of the mask. Even if his eyes and voice hadn't informed her clearly who he was, her senses were screaming it.

"Of course, my lord," she said, drawing again on her inner strength, the only way she could weather the storm of emotions his nearness always unleashed within her. She placed her hand on his proffered arm and allowed him to lead her on to the floor, entirely forgetting the rest of her court.

"Well!" expostulated Viscount Molesworth, left standing by Lord Ellsmere. "If that don't beat the Dutch!" He glared at the broad shoulders of the gentleman whose arms now held the lady in topaz silk. His glare turned to a petulant frown. "Who is he, anyway?"

Lord Ellsmere was watching the couple on the dance-floor, a slight smile on his face. He looked down at the Viscount. "Don't you know?"

Lord Molesworth puffed indignantly. "Wouldn't ask if I did. Stands to reason."

Julian Ellsmere continued to watch the dancers, then,

shaking his head in wonderment, left Lord Molesworth without his answer.

Georgiana was struggling to subdue her senses, running riot as usual. As they reached the end of their first circuit, she felt almost in control again. If Lord Ellsmere left her cold, Lord Alton did exactly the opposite. She felt flushed—all over. And the peculiar sensation of weakness she had suffered during their more recent meetings seemed tonight to be intensified. Perhaps it was because he was holding her rather more closely than was the norm. Still, at least her brain seemed to be functioning again.

If she had been more experienced, Georgiana might have wondered at her partner's silence. But, engrossed in her inner struggle, she did not question what it was that kept Lord Alton speechless for the better part of the waltz. Dominic was, in fact, dealing with a revelation of his own. When he had seen Georgiana enter the ballroom at Bella's side her beauty had stunned him to immobility. In his eyes, she was the most ravishing female in the room. A goddess, all gold and bronze. A golden angel, from the topmost gold curl to the tip of her tiny gold slippers. A prize beyond price. He had watched as she circled the floor in Julian's arms, dazedly waiting until he could approach her. He no longer questioned the effect she had on him; it was now too marked to ignore. But, as he had deftly extricated her from her other admirers, for the first time his full attention had been focused on her. What he saw had effectively knocked him back on his heels. He was far too experienced not to recognise the signs. In all their previous meetings, his mind had been fully occupied in analysing his responses to her, not her responses to him. Now, all his well honed expertise on alert, he let his senses feel for her, and convey back to him her state. Every little move she made was now registered—every indrawn breath, every flicker of an eyelid.

The information came in and was automatically assessed, allowing him to respond to her smoothly, easily, encouraging her, heightening her awareness of him, learning her reactions to his attentions. His instinctive conclusions hammered at his conscious mind. When had it happened? In truth, he didn't care. All that now concerned him was how to capture what was there, how to foster and nurture her feelings, to make them grow to what he desired them to be. And all his experience told him that wouldn't be difficult.

So, with gentle patience, he waited until she had herself in hand once more and could cope with his, "And what might your name be, fair one?"

Georgiana blinked. Surely he recognised her? But then, she reflected, she wasn't sure the others had either. Maybe it wasn't that obvious. She thought quickly, then replied, "I really don't think the purpose of her ladyship's entertainment would be furthered if I answered that question, my lord."

Inwardly, Dominic grinned, but outwardly he was all dejection. "But what, then, should I call you, sweetheart?"

It was a struggle to keep her tone even. "'Sweetheart' will do very nicely, my lord."

Great heavens! Had she really said that? Georgiana glanced up from under her long lashes and blushed when she encountered her partner's blue gaze. But he merely smiled, slowly, and said, "Sweetheart it is, then, my dear."

His deep voice sent tingling shivers down her spine. What on earth was she doing? What on earth was he doing?

The music ceased, and Georgiana turned towards the other end of the ballroom, where she had left Bella. Her partner detained her by the simple expedient of tightening the arm that still lay about her waist. "Oh, no, sweetheart," he said on a soft laugh. "Hasn't anyone told you?" At her enquiring look, he explained, "One of the main—if not the primary—purposes of a *balle masquée* is to permit those who wish to…further their acquaintance to do so without attracting the notice of the tattle-mongers." His voice had dropped to a mesmerising tone. His breath wafted the curls about her ear as he bent closer to add, "And I find I very definitely want to further my acquaintance with you."

Georgiana gasped. There was no doubting the subtle invitation couched in those otherwise innocuous words. Involuntarily, her eyes sought his in the darkened recesses of his mask. The glow she saw in the blue depths merely served to tighten the iron band that had clamped around her chest, threating to suspend her breathing. "My lord!"

Despite her panic, her words came out in a seductive whisper, quite contrary to her intention. It was as if something stronger than her will was impelling her to accept the challenge she saw in his eyes.

He laughed, softly, his eyes on hers, and Georgiana's bones felt weak. Then he put the challenge into words. "Surely, sweetheart, you're not afraid of what you might learn?"

His head was bent close to hers, his large body overwhelmingly near. His breath felt warm against her cheek; his hands came up to surreptitiously stroke her arms where they were bare above her elbow-length gloves. Georgiana could not repress the shiver of pure delight that coursed through her at his touch.

What on earth was he doing? Dominic mentally sat at a distance and marvelled at himself. He knew—none better—that this was no way to behave towards a gently reared young lady. To experienced courtesans, to the likes of Elaine Changley, his attentions would be perfectly in order. But delicate virgins were apt to flee for cover, to faint or screech if treated to such subtle but strong tactics. Certainly, they wouldn't know how to respond to them. The trouble was, Georgiana Hartley's responses had more in common with those of a courtesan than of the virgin he knew her to be. Fascinated, he waited for her reaction.

Georgiana had no thought of fleeing, fainting or screeching. Her conscious mind was entirely taken up with a fight against her desire to learn what it was his lordship proposed to teach her. Desire won, hands down. She'd deal with reality later.

"Afraid?" she echoed, buying time. "Hardly that. But I do wonder at the wisdom of being seen too much together. Surely our friends, if no one else, will recognise us and think it odd?"

Dominic understood the hidden meaning in her words, but chose to ignore it. He was in no hurry to confirm or deny his recognition of her. "In this mêlée? I doubt any of our friends can even see us. Can you see any of your party?"

He had already seen Bella and Arthur move into one of the adjoining salons, so was not surprised when, after a quick survey of the room, Georgiana shook her head. "I can't see anyone I know."

Smiling, Dominic tucked her hand into his arm. "You see? A *balle masquée* is a time to have fun. So come and enjoy yourself with me." As he steered her in the direction of the terrace, he added for her ears only, "I assure you I have every intention of enjoying myself with you."

To Georgiana's delight, the evening proved to be one of unalloyed pleasure. Initially, she was wary, convinced Lord Alton had not recognised her, and on tenterhooks lest he, not knowing who she was, overstepped the line. Instead, while he certainly drifted very close to the invisible limit of acceptable conduct, he never once gave her cause to rue her deception. For deception it certainly was. What on earth would he think if he ever learnt it was his sister's little protégée on whom he was lavishing his attentions?

To be the object of his attentions was a most sinful pleasure. Georgiana sparkled, animated as she had not been since her father's death. For one blissful evening she forgot her situation, forgot her cousin, forgot everything beyond the dancing lights in a pair of cerulean blue eyes. They walked through the salons and he pointed out numerous well known identities hidden behind their masks, elaborating on their idiosyncrasies, regaling her with gossip and the latest *on dits,* making her laugh, making her blush. When she confessed to hunger, they found the supper-room and helped themselves to heaps of lobster patties. She had her first taste of champagne, and giggled as it fizzled down her throat. They danced again, waltzing with effortless grace. Georgiana felt as if she were floating, held to earth by the strong clasp of his arm about her waist, drawn to heaven by the warmth in his eyes. Later they strolled on the terrace. She stood at the balustrade and he stood behind her, pointing out the features of the famous topiary gardens, thrown into silvered relief by the moonlight. His breath wafted the curls by her ear; his lips gently grazed her temple. Gently, so gently that she had no strength to resist, his hands lifted to her bare shoulders in a practised caress, skimming down over her bare arms. Ripples of delight shivered through her. He drew her around to face him, lifting one gloved hand and raising it to his lips.

"The evening is gone, sweetheart." His eyes lingered on hers, then dropped to her lips. For one instant, Georgiana wondered if he would kiss her. She hovered, poised on the brink of returning such an embrace, and felt oddly deflated when, in a voice curiously devoid of emotion, he remarked, "Come. Let me take you to find your party."

It was some minutes before Georgiana spied Arthur, Bella by his side, just inside the door to the main salon. She turned to the gentleman beside her, only to find he had disappeared, melting into the still considerable crowd.

Suppressing a smile at his tactics, Georgiana went forward to Bella's side.

"Good heavens, Georgie! I was starting to wonder if you'd been spirited away." Bella looked closely at Georgiana, then asked, "Where have you been?"

"Oh, just here and there," replied Georgiana, smiling beatifically. She couldn't help her smile, even though it was making Bella suspicious. Still, with Arthur present, she doubted her friend would seek to interrogate her tonight. And she would handle tomorrow's queries when they came.

Ten minutes later, the Winsmere carriage rolled out along the road back to London.

Dominic Ridgeley watched it go. Pulling on his gloves, he nodded to a waiting footman, who promptly departed to summon the Viscount's carriage. Once comfortably ensconced in soft leather, the excellent springs ironing out the inevitable bumps and jolts, Dominic allowed his mind to coolly assess his involvement with Georgiana Hartley. He placed due emphasis on the "cool"; there had been more than one moment during the evening just past when, for all his experience, he had felt anything but cool. She was an enigma, his golden angel, an innocent who responded with delicious abandon to every practised caress he bestowed on her, who promised to respond with even greater passion to those caresses he had yet to expose her to. A golden angel who had already captured his hardened rake's heart, but, unless he mistook the matter, had yet to realise that fact. A fascinating proposition.

He treated the darkness to a smile of pure delight. Who would ever have believed it?

As the miles fell beneath his horses' hoofs, he relived the evening in his mind. She had accepted at face value his intimation that he hadn't recognised her. Would she still believe that tomorrow? And, if she did, what would she then make of his attentions to an unknown lady? Dominic grimaced. He would have to take the earliest opportunity to disabuse her mind of the idea he had not known who she was. Silly child. He would have known her instantly even if she had worn a full domino. Still, she did not have the experience to know she affected him as much as he affected her. More, if anything. The memory of how hard he had had to fight to refrain from kissing her on the terrace made him groan.

No more anonymous wooing. From now on, he resolved, he would openly court her. Doubtless, eyebrows would be raised. Too bad. His friends were sure to have recognised him tonight anyway. Julian Ellsmere certainly had. And Julian had known which lady he had spent the evening with. Thank heavens she had already refused Julian. The last thing he needed was to have a resurgence of the old story. God knew why the gossip-mongers had never realised that Julian himself bore him no ill will over the affair of Miss Amelia Kerslake. His black brows rose cynically. Truth, of course, was never of great interest to the gossips.

With a deep sigh, Dominic leant back against the squabs and shut his eyes. Without the slightest difficulty, he conjured up the vision of a pair of big hazel eyes, so brilliant that they seemed to flash with gold fire. His doubts were gone. All considerations of age and station had long since fallen away, discarded as irrelevant in the face of his desire. He wanted Georgiana Hartley. And he intended to have her.

CHAPTER SIX

THE HATTRINGHAM HOUSE masked ball proved a revelation to others as well. While Georgiana waltzed and laughed on the arm of her cavalier, faded blue eyes, pale and washed out, watched her from the anonymity of the side of the room. Under his breath, Charles Hartley cursed. It didn't look promising.

Two weeks he had spent, searching the countryside for his little cousin. Finally he had been forced to conclude that the minx had somehow found her way to London. He had closed up the Place—had been forced to do so. Dismissing the Pringates had been an ugly affair, from which he was thankful to have escaped with a whole skin. But paying them off had severely depleted his reserves. He had hastened to town, reduced to finding lodgings in a mean and dingy street beyond the fashionable areas. Once installed, he had suddenly found himself at *point non plus.* Where would Georgie have gone?

That question had worried him until he was nearly crazed. Luckily, the recollection that her servants had disappeared with her surfaced to lead him from the brink of despair. From what he had seen of them, they would never have countenanced Georgiana doing anything that would bring her into danger. Or ill repute. Hence, they must have found lodgings in an acceptable quarter.

Days of trudging the streets had followed, calling surreptitiously at the fashionable hotels, hours of drinking in the taverns favoured by the servants of the gentry. Gradually he had been forced to consider the more *tonnish* areas. Finally, his luck had turned. He had seen her in Bond Street.

She had been dressed in the height of fashion, a parasol shading her delicate features, and he had almost missed her. The effect her appearance had had on him, leaving him gaping, had, by sheer luck, saved him from prematurely revealing his presence.

Before he had gathered his wits, she was joined by another female, likewise fashionably elegant. A nagging sense of the familiar had finally crystallised. Little Bella Ridgeley! He had barely made her out, rigged up to the nines as she was, but she was still the little girl he had teased so unmercifully whenever her big brother had not been around.

His eyes had narrowed. So Georgiana had sought refuge at Candlewick Hall—the one place he had not considered looking. Smart of her—or was it pure luck? He had decided on luck, for there was no way Georgiana could have known, and was about to step forward and accost the fair pair, when they were helped into a waiting carriage by a burly footman.

Balked of his prey, the wisdom of reconnoitring the lie of the land was brought home to him. Bella had married a Lord Winsmere. A powerful man. If the Winsmeres were Georgiana's friends, he had better be sure of his strategy before he approached her.

He had followed the carriage through the bustling streets and had seen the ladies set down outside the house in Green Street. They had entered, and he had found an alley close by, from which he could keep the door in view. Georgiana had not re-emerged until the evening, when she had left in the carriage with Bella, both gorgeously arrayed in evening gowns. The sight of those gowns had sent a spasm of sheer fury through him. They had swanned off to a ball while he, half perished with cold, was forced to slink off to his miserable lodgings, with no prospect of a decent meal in sight. He had consoled himself with the thought that at least he now knew where his pigeon had come to roost.

But how to best approach the matter of getting his hands on her once more? With his limited resources, joining the social whirl was a near impossibility. His clothes alone would mark him as pecuniarily embarrassed. The cent per centers were too fly to be taken in by a glib tale; they would advance him nothing. Thanks to the restrictions his father's failings had placed on him, he had no friends among the swells. How to break into the glittering circle?

He had cudgelled his brains for hours. Eventually he had found a young tailor operating on the outskirts of the fashionable districts, one too inexperienced to quibble about his offer of a small down payment with the remainder of the costs to be sent on account. With his most immediate need assuaged, he had turned his mind to gaining an entrée to the balls and parties his cousin frequented.

The Hattringham House masked ball had presented itself, ready-made for his needs. For the cost of a mask and a deal of studied self-confidence, he had been able to enter the ballroom as a guest, to wander slowly through the salons, carefully studying the female forms present. He had not even had to be covert about this enterprise; most of the young bucks were similarly engaged.

As it transpired, he had not recognised her. It was her voice, gaily answering some sally, which had identified her for him.

Now, as he watched her dance for the third time with the handsome dark-haired man who had monopolised her company for the entire evening, he ground his teeth. He stood no chance of competing honourably with the likes of her present cavalier. And, even from the obscurity of the sidelines, he could sense the rapport which existed between the pair. Damn her! She'd escaped him, only to fall victim to some other aspiring scoundrel. He brushed aside the thought that none but he knew her worth.

Seething, muttering imprecations beneath his breath, he watched helplessly as the dashing cavalier waltzed past, his cousin held securely in strong arms, mesmerised by a smile too experienced for any young damsel to resist.

"Soon," said Charles, entirely to himself. "I'll have to move soon." Having seen quite enough of his cousin and her consort to despair of parting them that night, he left Hattringham House, his brain awash with half-formed schemes.

IT WAS THE next afternoon before Georgiana had leisure to thoroughly examine the events of the Hattringham House ball. Viewed in the calm light of day, she wasn't entirely sure what to make of them. Had he really not recognised her?

Over the weeks, by dint of subtle questioning, she had learnt a great deal more of Bella's brother. For instance, a quiet afternoon spent in the back parlour the previous week had yielded the tale of the initial incident that had given rise to Lord Alton's reputation of being dangerous company for young ladies.

"It happened during the Season immediately following Papa's death. Dominic had missed the beginning of the Season, still tied up with settling the estate." Bella had laid aside her embroidery and stared in concentration at the opposite wall. "I wasn't there, of course, but I've heard the tale umpteen times. Apparently Lord Ellsmere—he's a particular friend of Dominic's, you know—fell desperately in love with a scheming miss from somewhere up north. I forget her name—something like Kertlake. She and her mama had come to town determined to catch the biggest matrimonial prize." Bella turned to Georgiana. "Well, you know how eligible Julian Ellsmere is."

Georgiana had had the grace to look sheepish.

"Well," her preceptress had continued, "Julian fell very heavily, and no one could make him see what she was really like. Apparently she was an out-and-out schemer, flirting with every man, but carefully checking their assets at the same time. Lots of people tried to dissuade him, but he went ahead and proposed and was accepted. Then Dominic returned to town. He saw through Miss Whatever-her-name-was and decided something had to be done. It was too late for Julian to draw back with honour, so the lady had to be made to withdraw." Bella had paused, eyeing Georgiana carefully. Georgiana had raised her brows in question. Bella had grimaced.

"You know what men are. And you've seen what Dominic's like. So I don't suppose you'll find it hard to believe that he swept the lady off her feet. He's a bigger catch than Julian. So the lady broke off her engagement with Julian, who by now had his eyes well open. Dominic had managed it so she did it in the expectation of him offering for her, but he never made any formal declaration or anything like that. And, of course, as soon as Julian was publicly free, Dominic just dumped the girl. The trouble was, not everyone was in the know. A lot of gossips just saw Dominic entrapping a beautiful girl and then ruthlessly discarding her. That's what started it all. And, needless to say, Dominic doesn't give a damn what people think of him. Naturally, all his friends know the truth."

At this point, Bella had picked up her embroidery again. Then she had paused, to add matter-of-factly, "Of course, later, when he went around seducing all the bored wives and beautiful widows—the Lady Changleys of the world, you understand—they simply painted his reputation blacker."

Smothering a choking laugh, Georgiana had bent her head once more over her own embroidery, her thoughts far removed from *petit point*.

"Mind you," Bella had added, waving her needle in the air to give her point emphasis, "despite all, he's never particularly enamoured of them—the women he seduces, I mean." She had frowned, totally absorbed in her subject and no longer conscious of her audience. "I suspect it's because it's all so easy." She had shrugged. "Just like me, getting bored with the Season—it's all too easy without some purpose behind it."

They had fallen silent after that, each busy with their own thoughts.

Now Georgiana sat alone in the back parlour, having seen Bella off on a visit to her old nurse. Her thoughts revolved incessantly, driven by an unnerving juxtaposition of longing and uncertainty. The breathtaking thrill of basking in the warmth of his smouldering blue gaze... All the subtle attentions he had paid her throughout the long night of the masked ball... She'd already lost her heart to Lord Alton. Now he seemed intent on leading her on to more dangerous ground. But had he known it was her he was leading? Surely not. Her mind rebelled at the thought. If he had known, then that would mean... No. He couldn't be seriously pursuing her. What on earth could he mean by it, if he was? And what on earth was she to do about it?

She puzzled and worried at her questions, but when Johnson knocked and entered the room two hours later she had still not found any answer.

"There's a gentleman to see you, miss. A Mr Charles Hartley."

The butler's words effectively banished Georgiana's

dreams. Charles? Here? How on earth had he traced her? And why?

The soft clearing of Johnson's throat recalled her scattered wits. She had enough unanswerable questions without Charles adding to the score. And, secure and safe in Winsmere House, she had no reason to fear her cousin. Johnson, she felt sure, would hover protectively near the door. "My cousin?" It was hard to believe.

Johnson bowed. "The gentleman did mention the connection, miss."

From the butler's stiff tone, Georgiana surmised her cousin had failed to find favour in his shrewd eyes. The observation gave her confidence. "I'll see him in here."

"Very good, miss." Johnson made for the door, but paused with his hand on the knob. "I'll be just outside the door, miss, in case you should need anything."

Georgiana smiled her gratitude as Johnson withdrew.

A minute later, the door opened once more to allow Charles Hartley to enter. In the light streaming in through the long windows, Georgiana studied her cousin as he crossed the room towards her. His appearance had improved considerably since last they had met. She suppressed a grin at the memory. He had been drunk. Now he was clearly quite sober. His clothes were not as elegant as those she had grown used to seeing, but were clean and, unless she much mistook the matter, new. His cravat was tied neatly, if not with flair. A great improvement over the stained and ill-fitting togs he had worn at the Place. He was neither tall nor short, neither corpulent nor lanky. Yet his figure was unimpressive compared to the other in her mind. His colouring was much paler and less vibrant than her own. Lank fair hair hung across pallid skin; pale reptilian eyes regarded her with little evidence of emotion. Repressing her instinctive shrinking, she extended her hand as he drew near. "Charles."

As he took her hand and bowed over it, Charles was

conscious that his little cousin had somehow changed. The young girl who had fled to her chamber to escape his love-making had grown even more lovely. And more confident. But she would never be a match for him. He smiled, struggling to keep his thoughts from showing. She had blossomed into a more delectable piece than he would have predicted. The figure outlined by the bronze silk dress she had worn at the ball was quite real, albeit now garbed in sober grey. Perhaps he would enjoy the role of her husband rather more than he had anticipated.

At his continued scrutiny, Georgiana allowed her brows to rise haughtily.

Recalled to his purpose, Charles assumed a serious face. "Georgiana, I've come to beg your pardon."

Now Georgiana's brows flew upwards in surprise.

Charles smiled tentatively and pressed his advantage. "For my boorish behaviour at the Place. I… Well—" he shrugged and smiled self-deprecatingly "—I was swept away with desire, my dear. I should have told you, of course, of the arrangements that had been made. But I had a hope you would love me for myself and it would not be necessary. I see now I should have explained it to you at the start. You see, my father and your father wanted us to marry." At her instinctive recoil, Charles raised a placating hand. "Oh, at first I felt as you. You can imagine my dismay, a young man being told his marriage was already arranged. I ranted and raved, but in the end I agreed to do my duty to the family. So I waited for the day your father would send you home. As things fell out, he died before he had brought himself to tell you and send you away from him." Pale eyes carefully scrutinised Georgiana's face. "I can imagine how attached he was to you, and doubtless he sought to keep you by him for as long as possible." Charles smiled meaningfully into Georgiana's eyes. "I can understand his feelings."

To his consternation, Charles could detect no response

to his revelations, other than a slight widening of the huge hazel eyes.

"In the circumstances, you can imagine my surprise when I first saw you, first learned of your beauty."

Another smile accompanied this piece of flattery, but evoked no hint of feminine preening.

Charles frowned. Was the child paying attention? He turned the frown to good effect as he continued, "I'm afraid my behaviour was rather wild. I can only ask you to excuse my excesses on the grounds of my incredible relief that, now you were finally here, everything was going to be all right."

Still Georgiana gave no sign of reaction to his tale.

Mentally groping in the dark, Charles put on a humble face and asked, "Georgiana, can you possibly forgive me?"

At the start of her cousin's tale, Georgiana had schooled her features to impassivity. As his story unfurled, she was thankful for the iron control, polished over the weeks of social gadding, that held her silent. She had no doubt that the existence of a long-standing, family-arranged betrothal between them was a fabrication. Her father had always shown particular concern for her eventual state. He had not expected to die suddenly, it was true. But that he had died forgetting to tell her she was formally betrothed was impossible. She resisted the impulse to laugh scornfully, and forced her voice to a cool and even tone. "I suggest your behaviour at the Place is best forgotten."

At his too ready smile, she assumed her most regal manner and forged on. "However, as to this other matter you have raised, of us being betrothed, I'm afraid I must insist that such a betrothal never occurred. Certainly my father never told me of it. Nor were there any documents among his effects to support such a notion. I'm afraid, if your father led you to suppose there was an agreement, then he misled you."

Charles's frown was quite genuine. So much for that idea. He would have to try his second string. He turned slightly and moved away from his cousin, taking a few steps away, then pacing back. His features obediently fell into a look of downcast dismay. He looked straight at Georgiana, an expression of wordless misery on his face. Then he gestured eloquently and turned aside. "Georgiana. My dear, what can I say to convince you?"

If she had not been so sensitive on the subject, Georgiana would have found his histrionics quite entertaining. As it was, she felt no inclination to smile, let alone laugh.

From the corner of his eye, Charles watched her stony countenance. Intuition told him an avowal of love would fall on barren soil. Instead, he opted for a more avuncular line. "I would do everything possible to make you happy. Your father's death has left you alone in the world. Please, I beg you, allow me to take on the task of caring for you."

Georgiana barely managed to keep from laughing in his face. He, to talk of caring for her! He had threatened her—more than threatened her—and under his own roof! She could manage quite well, she felt, without his sort of protection. With perfect composure she replied, "Please say no more. My mind is quite unalterable on this point. I will not marry you, Charles."

Yet another proposal, she thought with a wry inward grin. Even less welcome than the others.

Charles sighed dramatically and turned so she could no longer see his face. All in all, he was just as well suited with her decision. It was hardly a great surprise. At least now he had a clear path to follow. After a pained moment, he turned back to her and smiled bravely. "I knew it was no use. But, you see, I felt I had to try. If I could just ask that we remain friends?"

Georgiana blinked. Friends? Well, it couldn't hurt to

make that concession. It meant so little. She smiled gently, somewhat relieved that the episode seemed set to conclude on a much more reasonable note than she had anticipated. She held out her hand, a friendly enough gesture, but still a clear dismissal. "Friends, then, if you wish it."

Charles took her hand and bowed over it. As he straightened, his face cleared as if reminded of a pleasant event. "Ah, I nearly forgot." His eyes sought Georgiana's. "Those paintings you were looking for. At the Place."

Georgiana's heart leapt.

Sensing her response, Charles inwardly smirked. So much for her impenetrable shell.

"Yes?" Georgiana prompted, not bothering to conceal her eagerness.

Charles smiled. "I don't want to get your hopes up, but the Pringates were clearing out the attics when I left. They sent me a message two days ago that they had found some pictures, among other things. I wrote back to ask who had painted them. If they are the ones you seek..." He let his voice trail away.

Breathlessly Georgiana seized the proffered moment to issue the invitation Charles was angling for. "You'll let me know at once? Please, Charles?"

Genuinely pleased, he allowed his smile to broaden. "I'll let you know at once."

Deeming it wise to leave well enough alone, he merely bowed over her hand and smiled encouragingly as she crossed to the bell-pull to summon the butler.

NATURALLY, AFTER SHE had considered the matter from all angles, Georgiana sought Bella's opinion of Charles's visit and his declaration.

"Friends?" The incredulity in Bella's voice left lit-

tle doubt of her opinion of Charles. She snorted. "He's a bounder. Always was, always will be."

Georgiana shrugged. "Well, that's neither here nor there." She bent her head over her stitchery. It was the day after Charles's visit and they were in the back parlour, as was their habit of a morning.

Bella stifled a yawn. "Ye gods! I declare I'm infected with your illness."

Georgiana raised an enquiring eyebrow.

"Finding the evenings over-tiring," Bella explained. "I would never have thought a musical supper would be so positively exhausting."

"I rather think that depends on the music," put in Georgiana, with a smile for her hostess. "Besides, from what I saw, you were half asleep through most of the recital."

Bella waved a hand airily. "It's fashionable to nod off. All the best people do it."

With a gurgle of laughter, Georgiana set her work aside. "Seriously, though, do you think Charles will give me my father's paintings back?"

"Don't get too carried away. They might not be your father's at all."

A discreet knock heralded Johnson's entry. "A note for you, miss. There's a messenger waiting for your reply."

Georgiana lifted the simple note from Johnson's salver. It was sealed with a nondescript lump of wax.

Dismissing her butler with a nod, Bella turned to find her friend regarding the missive in her hand with some nervousness. "Well? Open it!"

With a small sigh, Georgiana broke the seal and spread out the single sheet. "It's from Charles," she told the waiting Bella. After a moment, her face brightened. "He's found them! Oh, Bella! They were there after all!"

Seeing the sunshine in Georgiana's face, Bella relaxed

and grinned back. "How lovely for you. Is he sending them over?"

Georgiana was reading on. A small frown clouded her brow, then lifted. "Yes and no. He hasn't actually got them yet. He says he's sent to Pringate to bring them to the Hart and Hounds—that's the posting inn, the last before London on the road to Candlewick. I remember stopping there on our way here."

Bella nodded absent-mindedly. "Yes, but why? Why not just bring them to London?"

Georgiana, engrossed in deciphering Charles's scrawl, shrugged aside the quibble. "Charles says he's going to meet Pringate this afternoon to pick up the pictures, and asks if I would like to come too. Oh, Bella! Just think! By this afternoon I'll have them."

"Mmm." Bella eyed her friend with a frown. It would be of no use to tell Georgiana that Charles was not to be trusted. From her face it was clear nothing on earth would stop her from going to fetch her paintings. With a definite feeling of misgiving, Bella held her peace.

While Georgiana penned an enthusiastic reply to Charles's invitation, Bella sat and worriedly chewed her lip. But, by the time Johnson departed to give Georgiana's note to the messenger, she had perked up and was able to listen to Georgiana's excited ramblings with an indulgent smile. It was obvious really. To protect Georgiana from Charles's machinations, all she had to do was precisely what she had always done whenever Charles had threatened. She would tell Dominic.

When Charles called for Georgiana at three, Bella played least in sight. Charles was high on her list of unfavourite people. She had already surreptitiously dispatched a note to her brother, summoning him to her instant aid. As she watched Charles's small phaeton carry Georgiana away, she struggled to subdue a disturbing sense of disquiet.

Impatiently, she waited for Dominic to call.

ENSCONCED IN THE comfort of well padded leather, Dominic Ridgeley, Lord Ridgeley, Viscount Alton, man of the world and political intriguer, was deep in consideration of the beauties of nature. Or, more specifically, one particular golden-haired, golden-eyed beauty. The silence of the reading room of White's was punctuated by the occasional snore and snuffle and the crackle of turning pages. Otherwise, there was no sound to distract him from his reverie. The daily news-sheet was held open before his face, but he would have been hard pressed to recall the headlines, let alone the substance of any of the articles. This morning Georgiana Hartley occupied his mind to the exclusion of all else.

He had not seen her for over twenty-four hours. Which fact, he felt, was more than ample excuse for his preoccupation. A political dinner had prevented him from attending Lady Overington's musical supper—a mixed blessing, he was sure. Hence, he had to be content with reliving the events of the masked ball. A slow grin twisted his lips as he recalled his angel's response to some of his more outrageous sallies. He would have to make certain he disabused her mind of her apparent belief that he had not known her identity. The point niggled, like a burr caught under his collar. It had been a strategic error, to allow her to leave him still thinking he was showering his attentions on a damsel unknown to him. An error he was more than experienced enough to recognise. Still, he would ensure the matter was rectified at their next meeting—tonight, at the Pevenseys' gala. Consideration of her likely reactions to his revelations kept him entertained for some minutes. The sight of her face when the penny finally dropped, her innocent confusion, all unknowingly reflected in her glorious eyes, would afford him untold pleasure.

A soft smile of pure anticipation curved his fine lips.

Seeing it, Lord Ellsmere paused, before clearing his throat meaningfully.

At the sound so close by his ear, Dominic jumped. His eyes met those of his friend in pained surprise.

Julian Ellsmere grinned. "Interesting thoughts, old man?"

Dominic struggled up out of the depths of his chair. "Damn you, Julian! I was just—"

"Shhhh!" came hissing from all corners of the room.

"Come into the smoking-room," whispered Lord Ellsmere. "I've got some news I think you should hear."

They had been at Eton, then Oxford, together, had shared all the larks and adventures of well heeled young men. And had remained close friends to the present. Which, when they'd found a secluded corner of the smoking-room, allowed Lord Ellsmere to say, "Don't know how deep your interest goes with your sister's protégée, but I just saw her being driven out of town by a rather rum customer. Tow-headed, pasty-faced bounder."

The sudden hardening of the lines of his friend's face told Lord Ellsmere more clearly than words just how deeply Dominic Ridgeley's interest in Georgiana Hartley went.

"When?"

"'Bout twenty minutes. Up the North Road."

Dominic's eyes had narrowed. "Tow-headed?" When Julian Ellsmere nodded, he continued, "Medium height and build? Fair skin?"

"That's the man. Know him?"

But Dominic was muttering curses under his breath and heading for the door. When Julian caught him up in the hall, where the porter was scurrying to find his cane and gloves, Dominic turned to him and said, "My thanks."

Lord Ellsmere waved one languid hand. "Oh, think nothing of it. As I recall, I owe you one." He smiled, then sobered to ask, "You'll go after her?"

"Most assuredly. The silly chit should have known better. I'd go bail that's her cousin she's with. And between Charles Hartley and a viper there's not much difference."

The porter returned, and Dominic pulled on his gloves. As he took his cane from the man, Lord Ellsmere, frowning, added, "One other thing. Might be significant. This tow-headed chap… Saw him leaving Hattringham House t'other night."

The chill in Dominic's eyes was pronounced. "You're sure?"

Julian Ellsmere nodded. "Quite certain." After a moment he asked, "Need any help?"

At that, Dominic smiled in a way that made Julian Ellsmere feel almost sorry for Charles Hartley. "No. I've dealt with Charles before. It'll be a particular pleasure to make it clear to him that Miss Hartley is very definitely out of bounds."

Lord Ellsmere nodded and clapped his friend on the shoulder.

With a fleeting smile, Dominic was gone.

A brisk walk saw him entering Alton House. Immediately the door shut behind him, he issued a string of commands which had his groom and coachman running to the mews and his valet pounding up the stairs in search of his greatcoat.

Dominic waited in the hall, frowning, his cane, still in his hand, tapping impatiently against one booted foot. Julian had said he had seen them. That meant an open carriage. Surely Charles wasn't proposing to drive her all the way to Buckinghamshire in an open carriage? No. When dusk fell, the cold would be intense. Presumably the open carriage was just part of his scheme, whatever that was.

Timms's cough interrupted his thoughts. "I don't know as this is the most opportune moment, m'lord, but this note came some time ago from Lady Winsmere."

Dominic's frown lifted. He took the note and broke it open. The sound of his carriage drawing up in the street coincided with his man's precipitate descent with his coat. An instant later, garbed in his many caped greatcoat and clutching his sister's missive in his hand, Viscount Alton climbed into his carriage.

"Winsmere House. Quickly!"

"OH, DOMINIC! THANK GOD you've come. I've been so worried." Bella's plaintive wail greeted Dominic as he crossed the threshold of her parlour.

"Don't fly into a pucker, Bella. Julian Ellsmere has just told me he saw Georgiana leaving town with a man who sounds like Charles. Has she?"

"Yes!" Bella was wringing her hands in agitation. "She was so set on it, I knew I couldn't stop her. But I don't trust Charles one inch. That's why I sent for you."

Taking note of his sister's unusually pale face, Dominic replied with far greater calmness than he felt. "Quite right." He swallowed his impatience and smiled reassuringly. "Why don't we sit down and you can tell me all about it?"

Haltingly, prodded by gentle questions, the tale of Charles's visit and the subsequent events was retold. By the end of the tale, Dominic was confident he saw the light. He leant forward to pat Bella's hand. "Don't worry. I'll fetch her back."

Bella blinked up at him as he stood. "You'll go straight away?"

"I was setting out when Timms gave me your note. Just as well. At least now I can go directly to the Hare and

Hounds." Dominic's blue eyes critically surveyed his sister. At his insistence she reclined on the *chaise*. Her face was too pale and her agitation was too marked, even given the cause. Shrewdly he drew his own conclusions. He had been going to suggest she come with him, to lend propriety to their return to Green Street. But in her present condition he rather thought any further excitement was to be assiduously avoided. And, if truth be known, he would much rather be alone with Georgiana on the drive back to town. He had every intention of reading her a lecture on the subject of herself—care of. Afterwards, he felt sure he would enjoy her attempts to be conciliatory, not to mention grateful. And it would give him a heaven-sent opportunity to correct her mistaken assumption regarding his conduct at the masked ball. Yes, he was definitely looking forward to the return journey. Propriety, in this instance, could go hang.

He smiled again at his sister. "Don't fret. Arthur will be home shortly. You can tell him all about it. I suspect we won't make it back until late, so you'd best send your regrets to the Pevenseys."

"Lord, yes! I couldn't face a party on top of all this."

Dominic grinned, then bent to bestow a kiss on one pale cheek. "Take care, my dear. You burn the candle with a vengeance."

She grimaced at him but refused to rise to the bait.

Dominic crossed the room, but turned at the door to consider the listless figure on the *chaise*. Had she realised yet herself? One dark brow rose. With a last affectionate smile, he left.

CHAPTER SEVEN

JOYFUL ANTICIPATION OF seeing her mother's face again carried Georgiana through the streets of London, unaware of the man beside her. However, as the phaeton turned northwards and the more populated streets fell behind, a tingling sense of premonition awoke in her mind.

The afternoon remained fine, a brisk breeze whipping at her cloak and bonnet, promising hard frosts for the morning. As the buildings thinned, the air became perceptibly chillier. Charles's conversation, uninspiring though it had been, had disappeared along with the fashionable dwellings. He seemed to be concentrating on driving the carriage at a slow but steady pace.

Georgiana stared ahead, willing the comforting bulk of the Hare and Hounds to loom on the horizon. But, from Green Street, it would take at least an hour to reach the comfort of the posting inn. A frown drew the golden arches of her brows together. Charles had called for her at three, which, now she came to think more clearly, was surely a little late for an expedition of such distance. It would be dark by the time they returned to Winsmere House. Still, there was little she could do about it now, beyond praying that the plodding nag drawing the phaeton would find its second wind. With a discontented grimace, she gave her attention to their surroundings. She refused to give further consideration to the doubt nagging from the deepest recesses of her mind, the little voice which warned that something was amiss.

Ten minutes later, a surreptitious movement beside her had her turning her head in time to see Charles replace his fob watch in his pocket.

He smiled at her. "Not long now."

Georgiana knew the smile was meant to reassure. It missed its mark. Odd how she had forgotten how Charles's smiles so rarely reached his eyes. Her suspicions, unspecified but now fully awakened, took possession of her mind. The horse's plodding hoofs beat a slow accompaniment to her increasingly trepidatious heartbeat as she reviewed the potential threats she might all too soon have to face.

In the end, she was so preoccupied with her imaginary dragons that she missed the sight of the Hare and Hounds. Only when Charles turned the phaeton under the arch of the innyard did she shake off her reverie to look about her.

She had stopped here on her way to London. But that time she had been travelling in the luxury of Lord Alton's coach, with attentive servants to guard her. Now, as Charles handed her down from the open carriage, she glanced about to see the yard full of people. Ostlers hurried fresh horses out of the stables beyond the yard, while others led weary equines freed of the traces to rest. Stableboys rushed hither and yon, under everyone's feet, helping with the harness and carrying baggage back and forth from the inn. Inn servants stood with jugs of steaming ale and mulled wine, ready to refresh the passengers of the coaches pulled up for the change of horses. At the centre of the commotion stood the southbound accommodation coach, a huge, ponderous vehicle, settled like a dull black bullfrog on the cobbles. The passengers were alighting for their evening meal. Georgiana found herself the object of not a few staring eyes. She was about to turn away when one gentleman raised his high-crowned beaver and bowed.

With a start, Georgiana recognised a distant acquaintance of Bella's and Arthur's. She had been introduced to him at one of the balls. With a small smile, she acknowledged the bow, wondering at the hard-lipped, cold-eyed look the man gave her.

Accepting Charles's arm over the uneven surface, more from necessity than inclination, she was about to ascend the two steps to the inn's main door when a sudden commotion on the coach's roof claimed all eyes. Three well dressed youths—roof passengers—were laughingly struggling with each other. At the coachman's loud "Hoi!", they desisted and, shamefacedly realising they were the centre of attention, sought to descend to less exalted positions. Waiting for his companions to climb down the rungs before him, one of the young men looked about the yard and caught sight of Georgiana. Her eyes met his with a jolt of recognition. He was the younger brother of one of the débutantes being presented that Season. She had danced with him at his sister's come-out. His open-mouth stare told Georgiana quite clearly that something was severely wrong.

She had barely time to smile at the young man before Charles tugged her through the inn door. To her surprise, she found that Charles had hired a private parlour for their use. Distracted by the memory of the stares of the two gentlemen in the yard, she paid scant attention to this discovery. As she meekly followed the innkeeper up the wooden staircase, the reason for the stares occurred. Of course! She and Charles shared no more than a fleeting family resemblance. The gentlemen thought she was here, alone, with a man who was no relation. She blushed slightly. There was, of course, nothing wrong with being escorted somewhere by one's cousin. She knew that. It was often the case in Italy, where families were large. She had not thought there was any impropriety attached to her going to an inn with Charles. Surely, if there had been, Bella would have raised some demur? But the disapprobation on the older man's face, and the sheer stunned disbelief in the younger's, stayed with her, banishing all ease.

So, when she heard the click from the parlour door as the latch fell into place behind the burly innkeeper, it was with a heightened sense of suspicion that she surveyed the neat parlour. It was empty. No Pringates. No paintings. Georgiana's heart plummeted. Drawing a steadying breath, she turned to face Charles. "Where are the Pringates?"

Her cousin stood, leaning against the door, watching her with a shrewdly calculating gaze. After a moment, he pushed away from the solid oak panels and strolled towards her. "Doubtless they've been delayed. Let me take your cloak."

Automatically surrendering her cloak, Georgiana forcibly repressed a shudder as Charles's fingers inadvertently brushed her shoulders in removing it. Inadvertently? She risked a quick glance up at his face. What she saw there did nothing for her peace of mind. Quelling the panic rising within, she forced herself to act ingenuously. "Are we going to wait for them?"

Charles straightened from laying her cloak over a chair. Again she was subjected to a careful scrutiny. Georgiana struggled to quiet the hammering of her nerves and face him calmly. Apparently Charles was satisfied with what he saw.

"Having come this far, we might as well wait for a while." His eyes raked her face again. "Perhaps a tea tray would fill in the time?"

Eager to have something to occupy them ostensibly

while she considered the ramifications of her latest impulsive start, Georgiana forced a smile of agreement to her lips.

The innkeeper was summoned and, in short order, a buxom young serving girl bustled in with a tray loaded with teapot, scones and all necessary appurtenances. Charles dismissed her with a nod and a coin, holding the door for her.

Under cover of wielding the teapot, Georgiana watched Charles close the door. She almost sighed audibly when she saw he did not bother to lock it.

With renewed confidence, fragile though she suspected it was, she gave her mind over to plotting her moves. The first imperative was to learn what Charles had in mind. And, she supposed, there was always the possibility that she was inventing horrors where none existed. A slim hope, she felt, with her nerves jangling in insistent warning.

Taking a sip of strong tea to help steady herself, she asked, "There are no paintings, are there?"

Her question coincided with Charles taking a sip from his own cup. He choked but recovered swiftly. His faded blue gaze lifted and fixed on her face, and she had her answer. He smiled, not pleasantly. Georgiana felt her muscles tense.

"How perceptive of you, sweet cousin."

His congratulatory tone purred sarcastically in her ears. For the first time since leaving the Place, Georgiana knew she was face-to-face with the real Charles Hartley. She fought down a wild desire to rush to the door. Charles might not be large, but he was a great deal larger than she was. Besides, she needed to know more. She was sick of mysteries. "Why? Why all this elaborate charade? What do you hope to gain?"

Charles laughed mirthlessly, his eyes never leaving her

face. "What I want. Your hand in marriage." Then his gaze slid slowly over her. "Among other things."

His tone made Georgiana feel physically ill. She forced herself to sip her tea calmly, drawing what strength she could from the strong black brew. Her mind wandered frantically amid the pieces of the puzzle but could not make out the picture.

"Not worked it out yet?"

Charles's taunt broke into her mental meanderings. She looked at him coldly.

He smiled, enjoying her obvious discomfort. He leant back in his chair, balancing it on its back legs. "I'll spell it out for you, if you like."

Georgiana decided that, however distressful, knowing his plans had to be her primary aim. So she allowed a look of patent interest to infuse her features.

Charles's lips twisted in a gloating grin. "My plan is quite simple. We arrived here just as the accommodation coach was unloading. You were seen entering this inn with me by at least two people who know you. That, in itself, will cause only minor comment. However, when we leave here tomorrow morning, while the northbound accommodation coach passengers are breakfasting in the main room downstairs, I feel certain the sight of you leaving at such an early hour with me, without the benefit of maid or baggage, is going to raise quite a few brows."

Georgiana's heart sank as she pictured the scene. He was right, of course. Even she knew what a scandal such a sighting would provoke, regardless of the truth of the matter.

"So, you see, after that you'll have little choice but to accept my proposal." Charles's grin turned decidedly wicked.

Georgiana had had enough. Carefully replacing her cup on the tray, she wiped her hands on the napkin and then, laying the cloth aside, fixed her cousin with a determined stare. "Charles, I have no idea why you are so set on marrying me. You don't even like me."

At that, he laughed. Hand over heart, he bowed from the waist mockingly. "I assure you, sweet Georgie, I'll manage to drum up enough enthusiasm to convince all and sundry of what took place here."

Georgiana shook her head slowly. "It won't work, you know. I won't marry you. There's no reason why I should."

The cynical twist of Charles's lips told her she had not heard all of his plan. "I hesitate to correct you, fair cousin, but, unless you want the Winsmeres mired in scandal, you'll most certainly marry me. It won't have escaped the notice of the gossip-mongers that you're supposedly in their care."

Involuntarily, Georgiana's lip curled. "You really are despicable, you know."

To her surprise, her tone was perfectly controlled. In fact she felt strangely calm. The lack of expression in Charles's cold eyes sent shivers up and down her spine. But now her own, usually latent temper was on the rise. It had been one thing when he had threatened *her;* to threaten her friends was another matter entirely. She folded her hands and met his gaze unflinchingly. "Be that as it may, I repeat, I will not marry you. Unless things have changed rather dramatically in England, I suspect you still need me to speak my vows. That being so, if you persist in your plan to ruin my reputation, then, when I leave here, I will stop at Green Street only long enough to pick up my luggage and servants. I'll return to Ravello." Summoning a disaffected shrug, she lifted her chin and added, "I always meant to go back eventually. And, with me gone, no scandal of any magnitude will touch Bella and Arthur."

For one long moment, Charles stared at her, eyes quite blank. It had never occurred to him, when he had planned this little campaign, that his prey would simply refuse to co-operate. Having seen her riding high in the social whirl, the threat of a catastrophic fall from grace had seemed an unbeatable card. Now, looking into hazel eyes that held far too much calmness, Charles knew he was facing defeat. Typically, he chose to counter with the usual threat of a bully. With a low growl, he rose menacingly, his chair falling back with a clatter on the floor.

Georgiana's eyes widened in dismay. She felt trapped, unable to move, caught and transfixed by the animosity which poured from Charles's eyes. Not until then had she realised just how much he disliked—nay, hated—her. She stopped breathing.

Charles was poised to come around the table, muscles tensed to lay ungentle hands on her, when the unlikely sound of quiet applause broke across Georgiana's strained senses. She turned towards the door.

Deafened by his anger, Charles only turned after seeing her attention distracted.

The sight that met their eyes was, to Georgiana, as welcome as it was unbelievable. The door lay open. Absorbed in their mutual revelations, neither had heard the click of the latch. Leaning against the door-frame, his greatcoat open and negligently thrown over his shoulders to reveal the elegance of his attire, Lord Alton surveyed the room. Having successfully gained the attention of both its occupants, he smiled at Georgiana and, pushing away from the door, strolled towards her.

In a daze, Georgiana stood and held out her hand, bemused by the sudden turn of events. Blue eyes met hers, conveying warming reassurance and something else—something very like irritation. Bewildered, Georgiana blinked.

Dominic took her hand and bowed over it, then placed it on his arm and covered it comfortingly with his own large hand. "Miss Hartley. I am here, as arranged, to convey you back to town."

Georgiana's eyes flew to his and read the silent message there. The warmth of his hand banished her fears. She had complete confidence in him.

With an encouraging smile, Dominic turned and, seeing her cloak, released her to fetch it.

The action broke the spell which had held Charles immobile. His normal pasty complexion had paled at the sight of his childhood nemesis. Now his face flooded with unbecoming colour. "You're out of order, Ridgeley," he ground out through clenched teeth. "My cousin is in my care. And she's not returning to London."

Settling Georgiana's cloak about her shoulders, Dominic raised his brows in fascinated contemplation of the thinly veiled threat. His gaze met Charles's squarely, then wandered insultingly over the younger man's frame. Dominic Ridgeley was a man in his prime, a noted Corinthian, five years older, three inches taller and two stone of sheer muscle heavier than Charles Hartley. And Charles knew it.

To Georgiana's intense relief, he dropped his eyes, blanching, then flushing again. Bella's brother tucked her hand in the crook of his arm and patted it comfortingly.

"Come, my dear. My carriage is waiting."

By some magical machination, Georgiana found herself escorted gently but firmly out of the inn by a route which exposed her to no one other than the innkeeper, bowing obsequiously as they passed. Handed into the same luxuriously appointed coach that she had used on her previous visit to the inn, she sank back against the fine leather with a small sigh of relief tinged with disillusionment. The search for her mother's portrait had nearly ended in nightmare.

The evening was closing in. Georgiana glanced up to see Lord Alton's large frame silhouetted by the light thrown by the flares in the innyard. He paused, one foot on the carriage step, and gazed back at the inn, an expression she could not define on his face. Then, abruptly, he stepped back. "Your pardon, my dear. Unfinished business." He frowned and added, "I won't keep you more than a minute."

He shut the carriage door, and Georgiana heard him call up to the coachman to watch over her. Peering out of the window, she saw him stride purposefully through the main door of the inn.

As the minutes ticked by, the conviction grew that Lord Alton's "unfinished business" lay with Charles. Georgiana fretted, frustrated by her helplessness. She had almost reached the point of sending the coachman in search of his master when Lord Alton appeared on the inn steps. As he strode across the yard, Georgiana scanned his person. He was undeniably intact. His greatcoat swung, impeccable as ever, from his broad shoulders. She expelled a little sigh of pent-up breath and hurriedly moved farther along the seat to make room for her rescuer. Then he was in the carriage and they were moving.

To her consternation, Georgiana found travelling in a closed carriage with Bella's brother was almost as much an ordeal as being in the inn parlour with Charles. But, while with Charles she'd had to subdue her disgust, with Lord Alton it was an entirely different emotion she fought to control. At one level, she revelled in his nearness, in the delicate wafts of sandalwood and leather that subtly teased her senses. Occasionally a deep rut jolted her shoulder against his arm. But the feelings which rose up inside her were too dangerous, too damning. Ruthlessly, she fought to quell them, forcing her breathing to slow and her mind to function.

"Did Bella send you?"

Dominic had been waiting, with what patience he could

muster, for her to recover. He frowned into the gathering gloom and turned towards her. "Both Bella *and* Julian Ellsmere."

"Lord Ellsmere?"

"The same. He saw you leaving London with Charles—a 'tow-headed bounder' was his description."

His clipped tones destroyed any impulse Georgiana had to laugh.

"Then Bella sent around a note and told me where to look for you." Dominic studied his angel's face in the faint glow of light cast back from the carriage lamps. He could see no sign that she understood the danger she had been in, no comprehension of the fear and worry her impulsive start had visited on him. His tone became noticeably drier. "I find it hard to understand why, knowing Charles as you do, you consented to this ill advised junket."

At the clear censure in his voice, Georgiana stiffened. She swallowed the peculiar lump in her throat to say in a small, tight voice, "I'm sorry if I've caused you any inconvenience."

Inwardly Dominic cursed. This interlude was not progressing as planned. He was having the devil of a time holding on to his temper, rubbed raw by the troubled speculation of the hour and more it had taken to reach the inn. The impulse to shake her was strong. Yet, in his present mood, he doubted the wisdom of laying hands on her. And, wise in the ways of young ladies, he knew his angel, far from being adoringly penitent, was close to taking snuff. If he gave in to temptation and read her the lecture burning the tip of his tongue, she might well treat him to a deplorable display of feminine weakness. For once, he wasn't sure of his ability to withstand such a scene. With a "Humph!", he folded his arms across his chest and stared moodily out of the window.

For her part, Georgiana kept her gaze firmly fixed on the passing shadows, concentrating on subduing her quivering lips and blinking away the sudden moisture in her large eyes. It was really too much! First he had taken charge of her, like a guardian, just because she had asked for help. Then he had not had the sense to recognise her at the masked ball and had made her lose her heart with his wickedly sophisticated ways. Now he was treating her like a child again, upbraiding her, blaming *her* instead of Charles!

Trying not to sniff, Georgiana determinedly dragged her mind away from its preoccupation with the gentleman beside her and turned it to consideration of something—anything—else.

Lord Ellsmere's actions, for instance. Why had he gone to Lord Alton, rather than directly to Bella? That Bella should have summoned her brother was no surprise, but why had Lord Ellsmere done so? No answer occurred to her. Giving up on that issue, she wondered how to acceptably ask what he had done when he had re-entered the inn. She felt she had a right to know; it might prove important in any future disputation with Charles. Surreptitiously, she glanced at him.

In the light thrown by the lamps of a passing carriage, she saw a bloody scratch across the knuckles of his right hand.

"Oh! You've hurt yourself!" Without a thought for propriety or the consequences, Georgiana captured his hand in hers, holding it closer to examine the wound in the dim light. "You've been…been milling with Charles!" Settling the large hand firmly in her lap, she whipped out her small handkerchief and wrapped it tightly over the cut, tying a small knot in the lace edging to keep it in place. "There was no need, I assure you."

A deep sigh greeted her protestations. "Oh, there was

every need. Charles needed to be taught a lesson. No gentleman goes about scheming to ruin a lady's reputation."

"What did you do to him?"

His head back against the squabs, Dominic tried to read her expression. "Don't worry, he still lives." When she continued to wait patiently, he grimaced and added, "He was unwise enough to make a number of suggestions I found distinctly ungentlemanly. I took great delight in making him eat his words."

"But you might have been hurt! You *were* hurt." Georgiana looked again at the hand which still lay in her skirts, gently cradled between hers. Suddenly recalling the impropriety of holding a gentleman's hand in her lap, she reluctantly released it, thankful the dim light hid her blushes.

His lips twisting in a smile he knew she could not see, Dominic equally reluctantly withdrew his hand from where it lay, stilling the all but automatic impulse to reverse the situation and capture her hand in his. He had initially been stunned into immobility by her impulsive actions. When his wits returned, he had seen no reason to shorten a moment which had touched him strangely. Now, sensing her unease, he sought for some comment to distract her.

"Anyway, I doubt you'll be troubled by Charles again."

Georgiana heard and nodded, but, suddenly feeling ridiculously weak, sought refuge in silence. Too many emotions swirled in her breast, conflicting with all the accepted precepts, and his nearness only compounded her confusion. She fixed her gaze on the scene beyond the window, the shadows of trees merging into the darkness. Yet her mind remained centred on the man beside her.

Perceptive enough to sense her turmoil, Dominic smiled into the darkness and, smothering a small sigh of frustration, put aside his plans for furthering his suit. She was nervous and on edge. Doubtless, her recent brush with the despicable Charles had contributed its mite to her state. In fact, now he came to think on it, it was wonderful that she hadn't treated him to the vapours. Most young women would undoubtedly be weeping all over him by this juncture, not concerning themselves with his minor hurts. In the dark, his fingers found the lace edging of her handkerchief wrapped tightly about his hand.

The moment was not right, either, for bringing up the subject of the masked ball. He was far too experienced even to contemplate making love to her now, while she was so touchy. There was, after all, tomorrow. And the day after tomorrow. And all the days after that. For, if nothing else had been settled this evening, he had definitely decided that Georgiana Hartley was not going to be allowed to slip out of his life. Whether she realised it or not, she was there to stay.

He paused in his mental ramblings to glance down at the slight figure beside him. She sat absorbed in her thoughts, her hands tightly clasped in her lap. Another half-hour would see them in Green Street. With another smile for the darkness, Dominic settled his head comfortably against the well stuffed squabs and closed his eyes, the better to indulge his fantasies.

Georgiana sat silently, taking herself to task for her forward behaviour. A lecture on the unwisdom of allowing her fanciful dreams to lead her to read more into Lord Alton's actions than was intended followed. He was very fond of Bella. She should remember that he had come to find her in response to Bella's request—brotherly devotion was the emotion which drove him to protect her, nothing else. Her stern admonitions made her flinch inwardly but did little to ease the tightness around her heart.

Gradually, without conscious direction, her tired mind drifted to consideration of its main preoccupation. Of course he had no interest in her. If he had known who she was at the masked ball, he would have mentioned the fact by now. She knew little of the ways of gentleman rakes, but felt sure a coach trip, together alone, must rate as one of those opportunities too good to let slip. Yet the man beside her remained silent. She stole a glance at him from beneath her lashes. His eyes were closed. Emboldened, she allowed her gaze to skim the contours of his face, the wide forehead and squared chin, his firm, well shaped lips… Finding her mind frolicking in fantasies of how those lips would feel against hers, Georgiana forcibly withdrew her gaze and returned it to contemplation of the darkness beyond the window.

Ravello. The image of the villa there, now hers, materialised in her mind's eye. She seized on it. And was suddenly struck by the obvious solution to her troubles. Charles was a bully and totally unscrupulous. He would continue to threaten her peace of mind while she remained in England. And Bella's brother, too, disturbed her rest and reduced her ability to cope with the daily round of fashionable life. Yet she was not particularly enamoured of the social whirl; it would cause her no great pain to eschew the life completely. It was a pleasant diversion, nothing more.

With sudden conviction, she made up her mind. She would see out the Season with Bella, as she had promised Arthur she would. Then she would return to Ravello, a great deal older and a great deal wiser. She stifled a small sigh and forced herself to promise—when winter set in, she would be in Ravello.

The increasing light coming from street-lamps as they entered the capital made it worth while for Dominic to desert his imaginings in favour of the real thing. He had been watching Georgiana for some minutes, wondering what it was that kept her so serious, when a point which had thus far eluded him surfaced as a question. "Georgiana, do you have any idea why Charles wants to marry you?"

As he said the words, he realised they were hardly flattering. Still, he had a high enough opinion of Georgiana Hartley to be sure she was not the sort of flighty young woman who believed all men who wished to marry her were smitten by her beauty. The memory of her numerous suitors, all of whom were most definitely smitten, himself included, brought a wry smile to his lips.

In the flickering, shifting light, Georgiana saw the smile, and her heart turned to lead and dropped to her slippers. To ask a question like that and then smile condescendingly! Well, if anything was needed to convince her Lord Alton had no romantic interest in her it was that. Doggedly, she forced her mind to concentrate on his query. Frowning with the effort, she shook her head and answered truthfully, "I have no idea."

"It was the same while you were at the Place?"

Georgiana nodded. "Exactly the same." She paused, then decided she might as well tell Lord Alton the whole of it. He knew so much already. Choosing her words carefully, she explained Charles's claim of a long-standing-betrothal.

"And you're certain such an arrangement never existed?"

"Quite sure." Georgiana paused, then added in explanation, "My father and I were…very close. He would never have done such a thing and not told me. Not for any reason."

Lord Alton seemed to accept her assurance. He sat silently beside her as the coach rumbled along the cobbles towards Green Street.

Dominic had no doubt that Georgiana's beliefs were true. He only wished he had known of Charles's claim before he had returned to the inn parlour. The tenseness he had felt but not recognised on his drive to the Hare and Hounds had converted to anger once he had got Georgiana safely away—anger that had demanded some outlet. So he had returned to the parlour, to be quite unnecessarily provoked by Charles's animadversions on his cousin. In the end he had administered a thoroughly deserved thrashing. He knew Charles was close to financial ruin—was, in fact, technically bankrupt. Georgiana's small fortune would not come close to meeting his mounting debts. After suggesting Charles would be wise never to approach his lovely cousin again, he had repeated his offer to buy the Place. The sum he named was far more than Charles would ever get from any other, with the Place situated as it was. Charles had only attempted a sneer through swollen and cracked lips.

Dominic contemplated a late-night return to the Hare and Hounds, to pursue further the reason for Charles's apparent fixation with marrying his cousin. Even less than Georgiana did he believe Charles would act for the good of the family. There was something in all this that he was missing, some vital clue which would make all clear. But Charles would almost certainly have left before he could return to the inn.

He turned the anomalies of Charles's behaviour, both with respect to Georgiana and to the sale of the Place, over and over in his mind. Suddenly, the two connected. Dominic straightened in his seat.

"Georgiana, have you been to see your father's English solicitors yet?"

Dragged from the depths of a series of most melancholy thoughts, Georgiana shook her head. "No. I suppose I should, but there doesn't really seem much point."

"But..." Dominic paused, then decided he was going to interfere even though he theoretically had no right. Right be damned. He was going to marry the chit, wasn't he? "Correct me if I'm wrong, but I seem to recall you left Italy before notification of your father's death was acknowledged by your English solicitors. Is that right?"

"You mean," said Georgiana, brow wrinkling in an effort to get the question straight, "before they wrote back after they got the letter from the Italian solicitors?" At Dominic's nod, she agreed. "Yes, that's right."

"And you haven't seen your father's will?"

"No…no. That was left with the English solicitors. But I always knew I would inherit all Papa's money. And the villa at Ravello." She paused, puzzled by his line of questioning, not sure of what possibilities he saw. "But surely if there had been anything more, or anything unexpected, someone would have told me by now?"

"Who are your solicitors here?"

"Whitworth and Whitworth, in Lincoln's Inn."

"Good. I'll take you to see them tomorrow."

Georgiana turned to look at him in amazement. She had not previously had much exposure to the autocratic side of Lord Alton's temperament. She surveyed the satisfied expression on his face with misgiving. "But…why?"

He smiled at her, and she almost forgot her question.

"Because, my dear Georgiana," he said as he captured her hand and raised it to his lips, "Charles, despite all evidence to the contrary, is not a complete gudgeon. His attempts to coerce you into marriage must have some motive behind them. And, as your kinship with him is the only connection between you, I suggest we start looking for the answer with your father's solicitors."

Despite the clear impression that Lord Alton had a stronger motive for insisting she visit her solicitors, Georgiana got no further chance to question him. He had barely ceased speaking when the carriage pulled up outside Green Street. In the ensuing hullabaloo there was no opportunity to do more than thank him prettily for his rescue and meekly accept his instruction to be ready the next morning at eleven.

GEORGIANA RETURNED ARTHUR'S reassuring smile as the Alton town carriage drew up at the entrance to Lincoln's Inn. Both she and her host had been taken up by an irresistible force at eleven that morning, their objective being the office of her father's solicitors. Despite her belief that nothing new would be learned from the Whitworths, Georgiana was enjoying her first view of an area of London she had not previously had cause to visit.

Lord Alton, sitting beside her, had leant forward to speak to the porter. As he leant back, the carriage lurched forward again, over the cobbles and through the large gate of the Inn. The cobbled yard was surrounded by buildings entirely given over to solicitors and clerks. By each doorway leading on to a stairwell hung the bronze plaques of the practitioners within. The carriage drew up before one such door. Lord Alton jumped down and gave her his hand.

Their destination lay on the first floor. A desiccated clerk of indeterminate years, dressed in sombre grey and sporting a tie wig of decades gone by, bade them seat themselves in the small outer office, "While I enquire if Mr Whitworth will see you." He left Georgiana with the definite impression that to be permitted to see the Mr Whitworth was tantamount to being granted an audience with the Regent.

Minutes later he was back, oozing spurious concern. A Mr Whitworth—the elder, as they later learned—followed close on his heels. A portly man of late middle age, he glanced down at the card he held in his hand, given to the clerk by Lord Alton.

Mr Whitworth looked at the two elegant and eminently respectable gentlemen filling his antechamber and became slightly flustered. "My lord…?"

Dominic took pity on him. "I am Lord Alton," he explained smoothly, "and this is Miss Georgiana Hartley, one of your clients. She is presently in the care of my sister,

Lady Winsmere. Lord Winsmere," he added, indicating Arthur for the solicitor's edification, "and I have escorted her here in the hope you can clarify a number of points concerning Miss Hartley's inheritance."

It was doubtful if Mr Whitworth heard the latter half of this speech. His eyes had become transfixed on Georgiana, sitting patiently on a chair between her two protectors. Despite the fact she was now used to being stared at, and knew she looked her best in a soft dove-coloured merino gown with a delicate lace tippet, Georgiana found his gaze unnerving. As Lord Alton finished speaking, and the man continued to stare, she raised her brows haughtily.

Mr Whitworth started. "Miss Georgiana Hartley—Mr James Hartley's daughter?" he asked breathlessly.

Georgiana looked puzzled. "Yes," she confirmed, wondering who else had her name.

"My dear young lady!" exclaimed the solicitor, grasping her hand and bowing elaborately over it. "My dear Miss Georgiana! Well, it's a relief to see you at last! We've been searching for you for months!" Once he had started, it seemed the man hardly paused for breath. "Almost, we had begun to fear foul play. When we couldn't contact you and all our letters were returned unopened and no one seemed to know where you had disappeared to..." Suddenly he paused and seemed to recollect himself. He waved plump hands in sudden agitation. "But what am I thinking of? Please come into my office, Miss Hartley, my lords, and we will sort this matter out at once."

He ushered them into a large office which bore little resemblance to the spartan outer chamber. Here all was air and light, with a rich red Turkey carpet covering mellow polished boards. Through the windows, the branches of the trees in the small lawn in the middle of the yard could be seen, the last yellow leaves tenaciously defying the brisk autumn breeze.

As they entered, a thin, soberly clad gentleman rose from behind one of two large desks. Mr Whitworth, holding the door, proclaimed, "Alfred, Miss Hartley is here!"

The second Whitworth—for, from the similarity of facial features, there was little doubt of who he was—looked startled. He pulled his gold-rimmed pince-nez off his nose, polished the glass, then returned it to its perch the better to view Georgiana. After a moment of rapt contemplation, he sighed. "Thank God!"

Both Whitworths bustled about, arranging chairs for their guests. They set these in front of the large desks which, side by side, faced the room. Once their visitors were seated, they subsided, each behind his own desk.

"Now!" said Whitworth the elder, chins flapping as he settled, hands folded before him. "As you can see, we're delighted to see you, Miss Hartley. We have been trying to contact you since we learned of your father's death, with respect to the matter of your inheritance." He beamed at Georgiana.

"If we might speak frankly...?" enquired Whitworth the younger, his flat tone a contrast to his brother's jovial accents.

Turning to face him, it took a moment before Georgiana understood his query. "Oh, please," she said quickly when light finally dawned, "Lord Alton and Lord Winsmere are my friends. I will be relying on their advice."

"Good, good," said Whitworth the elder, causing Georgiana to swivel again. "Not wise for a young lady so well dowered as you are to be alone in the world."

"Quite," his younger brother concurred drily.

"Now, where to begin?"

"Perhaps at your father's bequests?"

"There weren't many—nothing that interfered with the bulk of the estate."

"A few minor legacies to old servants—the usual sort of thing."

"But the major estate remains intact." Whitworth the elder paused to beam again at Georgiana.

Stifling the impulse to put a hand to her whirling head, Georgiana took the opportunity to quell her impending dizziness. It was like watching a tennis game, the conversational ball passing from brother to brother and back again, before their audience of three. Then his last words registered. "Major estate?"

"Why, yes."

"As the major beneficiary of your father's will, you inherit the majority of his estate."

"Which is to say," Whitworth the elder took up the tale smoothly, "the estate known as the Place in the county of Buckinghamshire..."

"His invested capital," intoned Whitworth the younger. "The house in town..."

"And all his paintings not previously sold."

A pause ensued. Georgiana stared at the elder Mr Whitworth, he who had last spoken. Lord Winsmere, having given up the unequal task of allowing his eyes to follow the conversation, stared out of the window, his lips pursed. Lord Alton, even less enthralled by the vision of the Whitworths, had shifted his gaze long since to the young woman beside him. He showed no surprise at the solicitor's news.

"The Place? But... There must be some mistake!" Georgiana could not believe her ears. "My cousin Charles owns the Place."

"Oh, dear me, no!" said the younger Whitworth. "Mr Charles Hartley is not a client of ours."

"And has no claim whatever on the Place. The estate was not entailed."

"It generally passed through the eldest male..."

"But your grandfather divided his estate equally between his two sons..."

"Your father and his brother, your uncle Ernest."

"Both were given an estate—in your father's case, the Place."

"Unfortunately, Ernest Hartley was a gambler."

"Quite ran through his patrimony, as the saying goes."

"He eventually lost everything and turned to your father for aid."

"Your father was enjoying a great success in London at that time. He had married your mother and was much in demand. Dear me, his fees! Well, quite astronomical, they seemed." Mr Whitworth the elder paused for breath.

This time Georgiana could not restrain her need to put a hand to her brow. The world was whirling.

"If we could condense this history, gentlemen?" Viscount Alton's precise tones jerked both Whitworths out of their rut.

"Er—yes. Well," said Mr Whitworth, with a careful eye on his lordship, "the long and the short of it is, your father and mother wished to spend some time in Italy. So your father installed your uncle as steward of the Place, put his ready capital in the funds, leased the house in London, and left the country. I believe you were a child at the time."

Georgiana nodded absent-mindedly. The Place was hers. It had never been Charles's property, and he had known it.

"When we heard of your father's death," broke in the younger Whitworth, warily eyeing the Viscount, "we wrote immediately to you at the villa in Ravello. The letter was returned by your Italian man of business, stating you had returned to England before learning of your uncle's demise and had planned to stay at the Place."

Whitworth the elder opened his mouth to respond to his cue, but caught the Viscount's eye and fell silent, leaving it to his sibling to continue, "We wrote to you there, but the letters were returned without explanation. In the end we sent one of our most trusted clerks to see you. He reported that the house was shut up and deserted."

The elder Whitworth could restrain himself no longer. "No one seemed to know where you'd gone or even if you'd arrived from the Continent."

Following the tale with difficulty, Georgiana saw what must have occurred. Questions hammered at her brain, but most were not for the solicitors' ears. She fastened on the one aspect that held greatest importance to her. "You mentioned pictures?"

"Oh, yes. Your father left quite a tidy stack of canvases—some unclaimed portraits, and others—in England. He always claimed they were a sound investment." The dead tones of the younger solicitor left no doubt of his opinion on the matter.

"But where are they stored?" asked Georgiana.

"Stored?" The elder Whitworth stared at her wordlessly, then turned to his brother for help. But the younger Whitworth had clearly decided this was one cue he would do well to miss. "Er…" said Mr Whitworth, chasing inspiration, "I rather suspect he must have left them at the Place."

"Are you certain they haven't been sold?" Lord Winsmere bought into the conversation. "From what you say, Ernest Hartley sounds the type to hock his grandmother's spectacles. Excuse me, m'dear," he added in an aside to Georgiana.

But the elder Whitworth waved his hands in a negative gesture. "A reformed character, I assure you. After his—er—brush with the Navy, he was so thankful to be pulled free that he was quite devoted to his brother and his interests."

"Devoted?" echoed Lord Alton incredulously. "Have you seen the Place?"

"Unfortunately, Mr Hartley was unsuited to the task of managing the estate, although he tried his best." The younger Whitworth drew his lordship's fire. "We would seriously doubt he would have sold any of his brother's paintings. He lived quite retired at the Place until his death, you know."

"So," said Georgiana, struggling to take it all in, "the most likely place for my father's pictures—the ones he left in England—is the Place. But they aren't there. I looked."

Both Whitworths shifted uncomfortably but could throw no further light on the matter.

Eventually Mr Whitworth the elder broke the silence. "Are there any instructions you wish to give us, my dear, concerning your property?"

Georgiana blinked, then slowly shook her head. "I'm afraid I'll need a little time to think things through. It's all been rather a surprise."

"Yes, of course. No rush at all," said the elder Mr Whitworth, resuming his genial state. "Mr Charles Hartley will of course be given due notice to quit."

Then, as there seemed nothing further to say, Georgiana rose, bringing the men to their feet.

"One moment, my dear," came Lord Winsmere's voice. "It's as well to know all the facts." He smiled at Georgiana and then turned to ask, "You mentioned capital placed in the funds. What is the current balance?"

The elder Mr Whitworth beamed. The figure he named sent Lord Alton's black brows flying.

An enigmatic smile played on Lord Winsmere's lips

as he turned to a stunned Georgiana. "Well, my dear, I'm afraid you'll have more than your earnest suitors to repel once that piece of news gets around."

ARTHUR'S REACTION WAS echoed by Bella when, over the luncheon table, she was regaled with the entirety of Georgiana's fortune. Arthur told the story; Dominic had declined an invitation to join them, pleading the press of other engagements.

"There's no point in thinking you can hide it, Georgie," Bella said once she had recovered enough to speak. "You're an *heiress*. Even if the Place is all to pieces."

Georgiana was still trying to recover her equilibrium. "But surely, if we don't tell anyone, no one will know."

Bella felt like screaming. What other young lady of quality, with her way to make in the world, when informed she was a considerable heiress, would act so? Inwardly, Bella railed again at the unknown who had stolen her friend's heart. Dominic had not yet found him; that much was clear. After his successful rescue of Georgiana the evening before, he had stayed to partake of a cold supper. She could well imagine what he had done to Charles, even without the tell-tale handkerchief she had seen him quickly remove from his hand and stuff into his pocket before he thought anyone had noticed. She was more than ready to believe his assertion that Charles would not trouble Georgiana again, and would in all probability not remain over long in England. But, after arranging for Arthur to accompany Georgiana and himself to her solicitors' this morning, her brother had merely bestowed a fond pat on her cheek and left...left her to struggle with the herculean task of convincing Georgiana to forget her hopeless love and choose between her lovesick beaux.

Sudden inspiration blossomed in Bella's mind. "Georgie,

my love, we will really have to think very carefully about how you should go on." Bella paused, carefully choosing her words. "Once it becomes known you're an heiress, you'll be swamped. Perhaps it would be better to make your choice now."

Georgiana's gaze rose from her plate to settle on her friend's face. Bella's attempted manipulation was unwelcome, but, seeing the wistful expression in the blue eyes watching her, and knowing that she only meant to help, Georgiana could not suppress a small smile. But, "Really, Bella!" was all she said.

Abashed, Bella retreated, but rapidly came about. "Yes, but seriously, Georgie, what do you plan to do?"

"I'm afraid, my dear," put in Arthur, "that for once Bella is quite right." Bella grimaced at his phrasing. "Once it becomes common knowledge that you have such a fortune, you'll be besieged."

With a sigh, Georgiana pushed her plate away. They had sent the servants from the room to give free rein to their discussion. She rose to fetch the teapot from the side-table. Slipping once more into her chair, she busied herself with pouring cups for both Arthur and Bella before helping herself. Only then did she answer Bella. "I don't know. But please promise me you'll say nothing to anyone about my inheritance?"

Arthur bowed his acquiescence. "Whatever you wish, my dear." His stern eye rested on his wife.

Bella pouted, but, under her husband's prompting, she gave in. "Oh, very well. But it won't help, you know. Such news *always* gets around."

CHAPTER EIGHT

THE ACCURACY OF Bella's prediction was brought home to Georgiana before the week was out. Shrewd assessing glances, condescending and calculating stares—the oppressive, smothering interest of the *ton* made itself felt in a dozen different ways. She could only conclude that the clerks in Mr Whitworth's office, or, perhaps, the Whitworths themselves, were less discreet than she, in her naïveté, had supposed.

Bella, of course, behaved as if all the attention was only her due. Her friend continued to hope she would succumb to the blandishments of one or other of her insistent suitors. In fact, thought Georgiana crossly, the entire charade was enough to put anyone off marriage for life. How could she ever hope to convince herself any gentleman was in earnest, that he truly loved her for herself, rather than for the financial comfort she would bring him, when everyone behaved as if her new-found fortune was of the first importance?

With a disgusted little snort, she turned over on the coverlet of her bed, kicking her legs to free her skirts from under her. She had retreated to her room to rest before dressing for dinner and the Massinghams' rout. For the first time since Georgiana had come to Green Street, Bella had also retired for a late-afternoon nap. While she studied the details of the pink-silk-draped canopy, Georgiana considered her friend. Bella certainly seemed more tired these days, though the bloom on her skin showed none of the subtle signs of fatigue. Still, Georgiana couldn't understand how she kept up. Or why. For her own part, the glamour of the balls and parties was rapidly fading, their thrills too meaninglessly repetitive to hold her interest. Now she had no difficulty in understanding Bella's plea of boredom with the fashionable round.

Her eyes drifted to the wardrobe, wherein resided all her beautiful gowns. Bella was always so thrilled when she wore her latest acquisitions. They were worth every last penny just for that. Georgiana grinned. She could hardly deny Bella such a small pleasure when all her friend's energies were directed towards securing her, Georgiana's, future. Nothing seemly likely to turn Bella from her purpose. Her beloved Georgie must marry into the *ton.*

As an errant ray of sunshine drifted over the gilded cords drawing back the curtains of her bed, Georgiana wondered again at the oddity of having a virtual foster-sister. She was fast learning that receiving care and concern laid a reciprocal responsibility on the recipient. But, despite Bella's yearnings, this was one aspect of her life on which she was determined to hold firm. She would marry for love, or not at all.

Just the thought of love, the very concept, brought a darkly handsome face swimming into her consciousness. Vibrant blue eyes laughed at her through a mask, then turned smoky and dark. Resolutely she banished the unnerving image. Dreams were for children.

In truth, if it had not been for Lord Alton's support, she might well have turned tail and fled back to Italy the first day after their discovery at Lincoln's Inn. The puzzle of Charles and his machinations was now clear. Fiend that he was, devoid of all proper feeling, he had decided to marry her before she found out she owned the Place. That way, Dominic had explained, she would likely never have known the extent of her fortune; as her husband, Charles would have assumed full rights over her property.

Dominic. She must stop thinking of him like that, in such a personal way. If she was to preserve her secret, she must learn to treat him with becoming distance. Unfortunately, this grew daily more difficult.

When he had appeared before her at the Walfords' ball the evening after their momentous visit to the Whitworths', she had offered him welcome far in excess of what might reasonably be excused on the grounds that he was her patroness's brother. She hoped he had put it down to a gush of girlish gratitude, no matter how the very thought irked her. But the warmth in his blue eyes had left her with an uncomfortable feeling of no longer being in control, as if some hand more powerful than hers was directing her affairs.

Dominic—*Lord Alton!*—continued to rescue her from the worst of her importunate court. In fact he was now so often by her side that the rest of her admirers tended to fade into the background, at least in her eyes. Georgiana frowned at the wandering sunbeam which had moved to light the bedpost. Now she came to consider the matter, it was almost as if Lord Alton himself was paying court to her.

Another unladylike snort ruffled the serenity of the afternoon. Ridiculous idea! He was merely being kind, giving her what protection he could from the fortune-hunters, knowing she did not like her prominence one little bit. He was her patroness's brother, that was all.

Nothing more.

THE HUM OF a hundred conversations eddied about Georgiana, enclosing her within the cocoon of the Massinghams' rout party. The bright lights of the chandeliers winked from thousands of facets, none more brilliant than the sparkling eyes of the débutantes as they dipped and swayed through the first cotillion. Laughter tinkled and ran like a silver ribbon through the crowd. It was a glittering occasion; all present were pleased to be seen to be pleased. The ballroom was bedecked with tubs of hothouse blooms, vying with the ladies' dresses in splashes of glorious colour, perfuming the warm air with subtle scents. A small orchestra added its mite to the din, striving valiantly to be heard above the busy chatter.

Newly entered on the scene, Georgiana had taken no more than three steps before being surrounded by her intrepid admirers, all clamouring for the honour of setting their name in her dance card. With a charm none the less successful for being automatic, she set about her regular task of ordering her evening.

"My dear Miss Hartley, if you would allow me the supper waltz I should be greatly honoured."

Georgiana glanced up and found the serious face of Mr Swinson, one of her earnest suitors, who had become even more earnest over the last few days, hovering beside her. All her instincts cautioned her to refuse his request. The supper waltz, with the implied intention of going into supper on the gentleman's arm at the conclusion of the measure, was the most highly prized of the dances at such a gathering. Whenever possible, Georgiana strove to grant that dance to one or other of her refused suitors, so as not to raise any false hopes among others of her court. But what excuse could she give, so early in the evening? A lie? Resolute, she opened her mouth to deny Mr Swinson, hoping he would accept her refusal without excuse, but was forestalled by a deep voice, speaking from behind her left ear.

"I believe the supper waltz is mine, Swinson."

Swaying slightly with the dizziness his nearness always induced, Georgiana struggled to keep her expression within the limits of the acceptable, and knew she failed dismally. Her eyes were alight, her nerves tingling. She turned and gave her hand to Lord Alton. She didn't even notice Mr Swinson huffily withdraw, eyeing the elegant person of the Viscount with marked disfavour.

Lord Alton bowed low over her hand. "Fairest Georgiana."

His words were a seductive murmur, rippling across her senses. Then, knowing it was unwise, but utterly incapable of resisting the compulsion, Georgiana met his eyes, and the warmth she saw there spread through her, leaving dizzy happiness in its wake.

"My lord."

She retained just enough wit to return his greeting, dropping her eyes from his in a flurry of shyness.

With a gentle smile, Viscount Alton tucked the hand he was still holding into the crook of his arm, thereby making life exceedingly difficult for the numerous other gentlemen waiting to pay court to this most desirable of young ladies. Lord Ellsmere, by his friend's side, grinned. Taking pity on Georgiana, he engaged her in light-hearted conversation.

Georgiana's hand burned where it lay on Lord Alton's silk sleeve. Why was he behaving so? Under cover of paying polite attention to Lord Ellsmere as he related the latest *on dit,* she glanced up to find the Viscount's blue eyes regarding her, an expression she dared not place lighting their depths. Another glance around showed her frustrated court dwindling, leaving only those gentlemen she regarded more as friends than suitors. Unlike those whose interest was primarily pecuniary, none of these gentlemen seemed to find Lord Alton's possessive attitude any impediment to conversing with her.

Possessive? Georgiana's thoughts froze. Then, inwardly, she shrugged. If the shoe fitted… And really there was no other way to describe the way he was behaving. This was the third night in a row he had appeared by her side almost immediately she had entered a room. By his mere presence he eased the crush about her, bringing relief which would doubtless be acute if she could feel anything through the sheer exhilaration of having him so near.

With an effort Georgiana forced herself to attend to the conversation, grateful for the distraction of Mr Havelock, who now joined them. By imperceptible degrees, the circle about them grew as more acquaintances stopped to talk. Gradually the sense of being, in some strange way, identifiably his receded, leaving only a subtle feeling of security.

When Lord Aylesham approached to claim the next dance, Lord Alton relinquished her with no more than a warm smile and a whispered reminder of their later appointment.

Released from the mesmerising effect of the Viscount at close quarters, Georgiana determinedly devoted a large part of her mind to a detailed analysis of his actions and motives. None of her partners noticed anything amiss; she was now too thoroughly practised in the arts of dancing, conversing and general entertaining to need to assign more than a small portion of her attention to these endeavours.

Of all the questions revolving in her head, the most insistent was, *Why?* Why was he doing all the things he was? Why was he behaving as he was? Again and again, only one answer came. It was impossible to attribute his actions to any other cause. *He was making her the object of his attentions.* Delicious shivers ran up her spine when she finally allowed her mind to enunciate that fact. Mr Sherry, whose arms she graced at the time, looked at her askance. Georgiana smiled dazzlingly upon him, completely stunning the poor man.

The next instant her sky clouded again. How could she

believe such a magnificent man, with all the advantages of birth, position and fortune, would seriously look in her direction? That he was contemplating anything other than the acceptable was unthinkable. But perhaps he wasn't contemplating anything at all. Maybe she was just an amusing aside, his sister's protégée who needed looking after. Was she simply a naïve foreigner, reading far more into the situation than was intended? Georgiana forgot to suppress her sigh, and was forced to spend the rest of the dance soothing a ruffled Mr Sherry.

While Georgiana struggled with question and answer, alternating between cloud nine and prosaic despondency, the object of her thoughts strolled about the rooms, stopping here and there to chat as the mood seized him. Dominic was in a state of pleasurable anticipation. To his mind, his course was clear. While it was not one he had followed previously, he did not doubt his ability to carry the thing off. The major problem was time—or, rather, the patience required to see the campaign through.

The necessity for taking things slowly was self-evident. This time the object of his desires was not an experienced woman, capable of playing the game with a facility on a par with his. This time he wanted a green girl, an innocent, an angel whose conquest meant more to him than all the others combined. She needed gentle wooing. So the habits of the last ten years were set aside in favour of the strict dictates of propriety. With a wry grin at no one in particular, Dominic wondered how long he could harness the coiled tension that was growing, day by day, beneath the surface of his suave urbanity.

"Dominic! What ho, lad! Up from the princely delights of Brighton?"

Dominic swung to face the speaker, a smile lighting his face. "My lord." He nodded to Lord Moreton, one of his late father's contemporaries. "As you say, sir, the amenities of Brighton palled."

"Palled before the attractions of the young ladies, eh?"

Unperturbed by the close scrutiny of a pair of sharp grey eyes overhung by bushy brows, Dominic smiled in his usual benign way and agreed. "Oh, Prinny's no competition, I assure you."

Lord Moreton guffawed. Slapping Dominic on the back, he resumed his peregrination through the crowd, allowing Dominic to do likewise.

It was, Dominic supposed, inevitable that people would start to speculate. The very fact that he was here, attending all the balls and parties of the Little Season, rather than pursuing a very different course, in very different company, positively invited the attention of the gabblemongers. No one was as yet sufficiently bold to put their speculation into circulation, but doubtless that, too, would come. For his part, he didn't give a damn what the gossips said. He'd weathered far worse. But he would need to be vigilant to ensure no disturbing whispers reached his Georgiana's ears. In truth, he was not sure how she might respond. But, with first-hand knowledge of the spitefulness of some among society's civilised hordes, he was not prepared to take any chances.

For the first time, at the ripe old age of thirty-two, he was seriously wooing a young lady. The pace grated. The slowly compounding returns, when set against the constantly high expense in time and restraint, were hard to bear, particularly for one to whom instant gratification of the smallest whim, however fleeting, had become the norm. And unusual abstinence only aggravated his state.

Still, there was at least one shining beacon on the horizon, holding the promise of safe haven in the end. He was too experienced not to be able to read the signs. Her response to him was gratifying, even at thirty-two. Who would have imagined he would be so susceptible to such flattery? Dominic allowed a slow grin to twist his lips. The pull he sensed between them—that magnetic attraction that drew man to woman and bound them together with silken strands of desire—was so strong that he felt sufficently confident to leave her, essentially unwatched, for half the evening. The other half, of course, would be his. At least this way the gossip-mongers would have to wait a little longer for their *on dit.*

"What on earth are you grinning at?"

Startled, Dominic turned to find Bella at his side. His slow smile surfaced. "Pleasant thoughts, my dear." His eyes scanned her face, noting the pallor she had attempted to hide with rouge. "How goes it with you?"

A small frown worried at Bella's arched brows. "Oh, so-so." she paused, then went on in a rush, "If I wasn't so concerned about Georgie, I declare I would have stayed at home with Arthur. These affairs are becoming a dreadful bore."

The quavering note in her voice alerted Dominic to her state. He drew her hand comfortingly through his arm, stroking it soothingly, a small gesture he had used since she was a child. It had the desired effect. While his sister regained her composure, it occurred to him that time, his present arbiter, was about to place a limit on his courtship. The Season had only two more weeks to run. Then the *ton* would retire to their estates for Christmas and the worst of the winter. He was unsure if Bella had yet recognised her condition. Typically she was not one to coddle herself and could be relied on to fail to consider such possibilities until they became too obvious to ignore. But Arthur was not so sanguine. He would undoubtedly wish to remove from London as soon as the Season ended. Which raised the question of Georgiana's future plans.

On impulse, Dominic turned to his sister. “Incidentally, what are you planning for Christmas?”

Diverted, Bella gave him a clear blue stare. “Christmas?” Then, recovering from her surprise, “I haven’t given it much thought.” She shrugged. “I suppose we’ll go down to Winsmere, as usual.”

“Why not come to Candlewick? You haven’t spent Christmas there since you married. I want to open the house up—just us, but the place needs warming.”

Bella was taken aback by the invitation, but the more she considered it, the more value she could see in the suggestion. While she was very comfortable at Winsmere Lodge, it couldn’t compare with the graciousness of Candlewick. Nothing could. “I’m sure Arthur wouldn’t mind. I’ll speak to him tomorrow.”

Dominic nodded. “What about Georgiana?”

Bella’s brow clouded again. “I’ve already asked, but she seems set on returning to Italy. I’ve tried to talk her out of it, but she’s so stubborn!”

His suspicions confirmed, Dominic, repressing a grin at his sister’s disgruntled tone, said, “Leave it to me. I’ll see what my persuasions can do.”

Big beseeching blue eyes met his. “Oh, Dominic. If you could only persuade her to stay, I just know she’ll make a good match once she gets over this horrible mystery gentleman of hers.” Remembering her brother’s promise, Bella added, “You haven’t found out who he is yet, have you?”

It was Dominic’s turn to frown. Amid the delights of wooing Georgiana, he’d forgotten the existence of her “secret love”. Now, considering the matter carefully, knowing what he did of that young lady, he was hard put to it to credit the notion. If she had ever in truth had a “secret love”, then the man was all but forgotten already. The unwelcome idea that Georgiana’s partiality could vacillate like a darting sunbeam, now here, now there, awoke in his mind. Resolutely he quashed it. Quite simply, he had no intention of allowing her the leeway necessary to vacillate. Seeing the worry etched in Bella's face, he yielded to the impulse to reassure her. "Don't worry your head about your protégée. From all I've seen, she's well on the way to achieving a highly creditable alliance."

The glow in Bella's face brought a smile to Dominic's lips.

"Who? Where...? I haven't noticed any particular gentleman... Oh, Dominic! Don't tease! Who is he?"

But Dominic only shook his head, smiling at her chagrin. "Patience, sister, dear. Don't crowd out the action. Just keep your eyes open and you'll doubtless see it all. But," he said, returning to a sterner tone, "believe me, there's no need for you to worry."

Bella grimaced up at him.

Dominic's brows rose, with that faintly supercilious air that warned Bella he was in earnest. Her rejoinder was destined to remain unuttered as Viscount Molesworth approached to claim her for the cotillion just forming.

Free again, Dominic continued his amble, determined to eschew Georgiana's company until the supper dance provided him with adequate excuse. At the door to the cardroom, he was hailed by his brother-in-law.

"Thought you were at home," Dominic said, strolling up and nodding to Lord Green, standing beside Arthur.

"Finished my last box earlier than I'd thought. You've seen Bella?"

Dominic nodded. "She's dancing with Molesworth."

"In that case, come and join us."

"Just a quiet hand," put in Lord Green with a smile, "but at least more life than you're likely to find out here."

The smile on Dominic's face broadened. "Not tonight. I have other fish to fry."

"Ah." Arthur's pensive eye met his brother-in-law's bright blue gaze. "And what a shock that must be to the system."

Dominic's lips twitched, but he responded calmly. "As you say."

"Still," said Arthur, his eyes now on the figure of his wife twirling down the set with Viscount Molesworth, "it's worth it in the end."

With a nod and a smile, Dominic moved on. The cotillion had ended, and the dancers were taking their places, with a great deal of noisy laughter, for a set of country dances. His eyes were drawn to where Georgiana was standing, partnered by Julian Ellsmere. Dominic stood unobtrusively between a sofa occupied by two turbaned dowagers and a potted palm and watched the dancers, anticipation growing keener by the minute.

Suddenly the irritation of being stared at caused him to lift his eyes and look over the dancers' heads. Directly opposite, Elaine Changley stood watching him.

She smiled as their eyes made contact. Then, completely ignoring the ladies beside her, she glided across the ballroom in his direction.

It was a bold move. Under his breath, Dominic uttered an oath, completely forgetting the proximity of the elderly dowagers. As he watched her progress between the sets, he allowed himself to examine, as if from a distance, her attractions. Other than as a passing diversion, she had failed to activate his interest. He had never encouraged her to believe otherwise. It amazed him that she could confuse the emotion he felt for the lady he would marry with the fleeting passion he had indulged with her.

Elaine Changley was desperate. Just how desperate, she

had not known until she had seen the handsome form of Dominic Ridgeley across the room and realised the smile on his face was caused by the sight of his sister's protégée. Her present play was a gamble. By the time she reached his side, she realised how dangerous a gamble it was.

Dominic greeted her with a formal bow and a cold, "Elaine."

Inwardly, Lady Changley winced, but she kept a bright if brittle smile fixed on her lips and attempted to inject some warmth into her habitually cold gaze. "Dominic, darling," she purred, "how pleasant to find you here. Have you come to alleviate the singular boredom of this party?"

Dominic allowed his gaze, which had returned to the dancers immediately after greeting her, to come slowly about to rest on her face—a handsome face, pale and perfectly featured, but devoid of all softness, all womanly feeling.

The music stopped.

Suddenly nervous, Elaine Changley plied her fan, fluttering it delicately just below her eyes.

Curtly Dominic bowed. "If you'll excuse me, my lady, I am engaged for the next dance."

With that, he left her, aware of the avid interest of the dowagers, and of Elaine Changley's eyes, following him.

Paler than ever, Elaine Changley had no move left on the board. She had perforce to remain where she was, her temper in shreds, and bear the sly feminine whispers of the ladies from across the room and the less subdued cackle of the witches on the sofa beside her. Her apparently impetuous approach to Lord Alton had been designed to draw all eyes. His leaving her after no more than a minute made his uninterest as clear as if the town crier had announced it. And he had gone straight to Miss Hartley's side! Seething and impotent, Lady Changley stood rigid as a post, forced to accept the most comprehensive defeat of her varied career with what very little grace she could muster.

A sudden tingling rippling along her nerves told Georgiana, chatting easily with Lord Ellsmere, that her next partner was close. She turned slightly to find her hand taken in a firm grip and placed, equally firmly, on Viscount Alton's arm. Chancing an upward glance, she found his lordship's blue eyes smiling down at her, that curiously warming expression readily discernible.

"Julian, I believe Arthur is looking for a fourth in the card-room."

Lord Ellsmere laughed at the overt dismissal and, with a smiling bow over Georgiana's free hand, he left them.

There was a slight break between the country dances and the waltz, while the musicians retuned their instruments. Lord Alton seemed quite content to spend the time staring at her. Unnerved, and knowing she would very likely dissolve entirely if she permitted him such licence, Georgiana strove to find a suitably distracting conversational gambit.

"All the *ton* seem to be attending tonight. The rooms are quite full, don't you think?" Breathless and quivering, it was the best she could manage.

"Are they?" Lord Alton replied, brows rising, but his gaze remaining fixed on her face. "I hadn't noticed."

The expression in his blue eyes and the seductive tenor of his voice infused his words with a meaning far in excess of the obvious. Georgiana blushed.

Dominic smiled. "But you remind me of something I had to ask you."

"Oh?" Georgiana struggled to reduce their interaction to the commonplace. If she could only keep talking, and avoid those soft silences that he used so well to steal her mind and her wits and her very soul, she might just survive. "What was that?"

"Why, only that I wondered what your plans for the winter months were." The music restarted, and Dominic drew her gently into his arms and into the swirling drifts of couples on the floor.

Her feet circling dutifully, Georgiana made a desperate effort to focus her mind on his words. "Ah..." She moistened suddenly dry lips with the tip of her tongue, then tried again. "I... That is to say..." She caught his amused look. A sudden little spurt of anger allowed her to regain her composure. Putting up her chin, she stated calmly, "I expect to be returning to Italy."

A woebegone sigh met her declaration. At her look of surprise Dominic said, "Mrs Landy and Duckett will be so disappointed. I'm sure they would love to see the eminently fashionable young lady you have become, if only to congratulate themselves on their far-sightedness."

Georgiana looked her puzzlement.

Effortlessly guiding her about the turns required to negotiate the end of the room, Dominic waited until they were once more precessing up the length of the ballroom before smiling down into her large eyes. "I have invited Bella and Arthur to spend Christmas at Candlewick. It is my earnest hope you will join us."

Wise in the ways of his Georgiana, Dominic watched her thoughts in her eyes. He waited until the desire to accept his invitation had been overcome by her instinctive fears, and a reluctant refusal was about to leave her lips, before allowing a pained expression to infuse his features. "Before you come to any hasty conclusion, I beg you will consider what a refusal would mean to me, my love."

His evident distress, the unacceptable endearment, combined with her own conflicting emotions, which he had skillfully invoked, left Georgiana's head in a whirl.

"What…? Why, what on earth can you mean, my lord?" Her eyes widened. "What did you call me?"

He ignored her last question, and continued in despondent vein, "You must see that it really won't do."

Dizzy, Georgiana made a grab for sanity. She drew a deep breath. "My lord—"

"Dominic."

Georgiana blushed, and was further confounded by his lordship's rising brows and the words, "If I'm to go about calling you 'my love', it's only reasonable for you to use my Christian name."

Georgiana was so flustered that she could think of nothing to say.

"Now where were we?" mused his lordship. "Ah, yes. You were about to accept my invitation to spend Christmas at Candlewick."

Her resolve to flee to the safety of Ravello as soon as she possibly could was melting under the warmth in his sky-blue eyes. "But—"

"No buts," countered Dominic. "Just think of poor Arthur and myself, condemned to a mournful Christmas with Bella all mopey because you've gone off and left her in the dismals again." Glancing down into her sweet face, and seeing that desire was winning his battle, Dominic withheld the news of Bella's condition. He would keep that as an ace up his sleeve, in case of future need. "You couldn't possibly be so cruel."

The music ceased, and for one silent moment they stood, eyes locked. Then, suddenly frightened she would see the strength of his desire in his eyes and be alarmed, Dominic smiled and broke the contact. He raised one long finger to caress a golden curl that hung by her ear. The finger, with a will of its own, moved on to trace the curve of her jaw.

At his touch, Georgiana shivered, pure pleasure tingling along already overstretched nerves.

Dominic's eyes widened slightly. His gaze returned to her eyes, large and luminous under softly arching brows. Instinctively he sought to reassure her. "Besides," he said, his voice no more than a whisper, "there's no reason for you to run away."

Georgiana's tired brain accepted the statement, with all its layered meanings. She understood he knew she had no pressing need to return to Italy, but also, in her heart, heard his vow that she would have no cause to flee him.

"Say you'll come. I promise you Christmas at Candlewick will be everything you could wish." Dominic had not the slightest hesitation in making that vow. He had every intention of seeing it fulfilled.

Entranced, with his darkened eyes demanding only one answer, Georgiana found herself nodding.

A brilliant smile was her reward. Warmed through and through, she allowed him to settle her hand on his arm once more.

The other dancers were leaving the floor, heading for the supper-room. Dominic's appetite had no interest in food, and, from her pensive expression, his Georgiana was not in the mood for lobster patties either. With an imperious gesture he commandeered a footman and sent him on a search for two glasses of champagne.

With the foresight of a man accustomed to success in the field, he had already made arrangements to allow him to appropriate much of the rest of Georgiana's evening without raising any scandalised eyebrows. When the footman returned with their drinks, Dominic handed one to Georgiana and, taking the other himself, steered her away from the crowded supper-room towards the entrance to the ballroom.

With the fizz of champagne tickling her throat, Georgiana held her peace until it became clear he did indeed intend to lead her out of the ballroom. Then she raised her face, her eyes meeting his in mute query.

Dominic smiled slowly, allowing just enough time for her to sense his thoughts and blush delightfully, before saying, "I thought you might like to see the Massingham art collection. It's quite impressive, and includes, I'm told, a number of your father's works."

It was, of course, the perfect ploy. Georgiana was all eagerness to view her father's portraits of the last generation of Massinghams. And no one would remark on their absence on such an errand, particularly not when Dominic had had the forethought to request permission from Lord Massingham to show his sister's protégée around the collection, dispersed about the gallery and the large library downstairs.

Delighted with their excursion, Georgiana relaxed entirely in the enjoyment of fine paintings, many of which she, with her tutored eye, could accurately place and appraise. To her surprise, Dominic proved to have a sound knowledge of the painters whose works were displayed. She eventually forced him to admit to an extended Grand Tour, which had included many of the galleries and great houses of Europe.

He did not press her to speak when they stood before one of her father's portraits, but stood back and perceptively left her to her musings.

After long moments of studying again the brush strokes she knew so well, Georgiana sighed and moved on, coming up again level with Dominic, smiling tremulously at his now serious face with its gently questioning look. She allowed him to take her hand. He raised it and, to her surprise, brushed it gently with his lips before returning it to its accustomed place on his sleeve. Strangely comforted, recognising her need only by its relief, Georgiana felt herself curiously but totally at ease by the side of this man who more normally reduced her to quivering mindlessness.

With no need for words, they descended the staircase and crossed the chequered-tiled entrance hall to the library. The door stood open, glasses and a decanter on a tray bearing witness to the Massinghams' care for their guests, all of whom had apparently succumbed to the lure of the lobster patties. The room was empty. Ushering Georgiana in, Dominic quietly closed the door behind them.

The walls boasted two Tintorettos, a Watteau and one Hartley—a small portrait of one of the sons of the house. It hung between two sets of long windows. Dominic appropriated a three-armed candelabrum from a sidetable and placed it on the sofa table beneath the portrait.

Head on one side, Georgiana studied the small picture. Dominic watched her. The flickering candlelight gleamed on her golden tresses, striking highlights deep in the silken mass, like flames in molten ore. His fingers itched to tangle in those glorious curls, to see her golden eyes widen in surprise, then darken with delight. He could not see the expression in those bewitching eyes, but her lips, warmly tinted and full, were pursed in thought, pouting prettily, all but begging to be kissed. Desperately he sought for some distracting thought. If he continued in this vein, he would never be able to resist the temptation posed by the deserted room.

"It's one of his better works," said Georgiana. She smiled up at her companion, so still and silent beside her. His face was a polite mask, telling her nothing of his thoughts, but his eyes, so intensely blue that they seemed, in the weak light, to be almost black, sent skittering shivers along her sensitised nerves. She found herself wishing she had not donned the latest of Fancon's creations—a sheath of bronze satin which revealed rather more of her charms than she was presently comfortable with. She reminded herself to keep talking. "Papa always said that children were especially hard to do. Their features are so soft—almost unformed—that he claimed it was excessively easy to make them look vacuous."

Dominic, with no interest in anything save the flesh-and-blood woman beside him, asked, "Are there any portraits of you?"

Alerted by the rasping huskiness of his voice, Georgiana moved slightly, ostensibly to gaze out of the uncurtained window, thereby increasing the distance between them. "Of course," she replied, surprised at her even tone. "There are three at the villa in Ravello, and there was supposed to be one, done when I was very young, left in England."

If Georgiana had seen the smile which curved Dominic's lips as she stepped into the window embrasure, she might have recognised the unwisdom of the move. As it was, it was only when, after a moment's silence had further stretched her nerves to tingling awareness, he closed the distance between them, coming to stand behind her, that she realised she was effectively trapped, unable to retreat, her exit blocked by his large body. And he was so close that she dared not turn around.

Dominic's smile was devilish as he moved so that no more than an inch separated them. His hands came up to stroke her upper arms gently, where her ivory skin gleamed bare above her elbow-length gloves. He leant forward so that his lips were close by her ear, and whispered, "In that case, we'll have to make a special effort to locate these mysterious paintings." He grinned at the shiver that ran through her. "Perhaps, now that you own the Place, you should institute a search."

"Mmm-mmm," murmured Georgiana, her mind far from

her father's missing paintings. He was so close! Through the thin satin gown, she could feel the radiant heat of him. His breath wafted the soft curls by her ear, sending all sorts of feelings skittering through her body. The caressing hands, drifting so gently over her skin, had ignited a funny warm glow deep inside her, quite unlike any sensation she had previously experienced. She decided she liked it.

Caught up in her novel discoveries, Georgiana was unaware of her instinctive movement, of leaning back against the hard chest at her back, letting her coiffed head rest against one broad shoulder, exposing the long column of her throat and a creamy expanse of shoulders and breasts to the blue gaze of the man behind her.

Dominic stopped breathing. This wasn't how he had planned it. Suddenly the rules of the game seemed to be shifting, leaving him confused, struggling to control a rampant desire which had somehow slipped its leash. His eyes flicked to hers, and found them half closed, heavy-lidded with the first stirrings of passion. Her lips, luscious and ripe, were slightly parted, her breathing swift and shallow. Full understanding of the effect he was having on her hit him with the force of a sledge-hammer.

A muffled groan escaped him, then, unable to resist, he bent his head and touched his lips to where the pulse beat strongly beneath the soft skin of her throat.

Georgiana stiffened at the intimacy, then, as his lips moved over her skin, warm and gentle, yet teasing, so teasing, promising more of the delicious delight, she relaxed fully against him, accepting and wanting to know more as the fires within her grew.

The click of the door-latch brought Dominic's head up.

"This place is nice and quiet. So much noise up there, can't hear yourself think!" The old Duke of Beuccleugh stumped into the room, accompanied by two equally ancient cronies. They headed across the room towards the deep armchairs by the hearth, but pulled up to stare at the couple engaged in rapt contemplation of the picture on the wall between the long windows.

"Very nice brush strokes, don't you agree?" said Viscount Alton, gesturing towards the painting.

Georgiana choked.

Dominic turned, as if just realising they were no longer alone.

The Duke peered at him, then recognition dawned. "Oh, it's you, Alton."

"Your grace." Dominic bowed.

"Admiring the view?" enquired the Duke, hard grey eyes glinting.

With an expression of bland innocence, Dominic explained, "Miss Hartley's father painted the portrait."

"Ah." His Grace's grey gaze switched to Georgiana, curtsying deeply. "Painter chappie, heh? Vaguely recall him, if m'memory don't serve me false." He nodded benignly at Georgiana, then recalled his purpose in the room. "Dancing's started again upstairs."

Dominic took the hint. "In that case, we should perhaps return." He turned to Georgiana and offered his arm. "Miss Hartley?"

Very correctly, Georgiana placed her hand on his sleeve and allowed him to escort her back to the ballroom. She was deeply shaken. Never would she have believed she would enjoy such a scandalous interlude. Yet she had not only enjoyed it; even now, with her eyes wide open, and no longer under his hypnotic spell, she was conscious of how deeply she resented the interruption that had brought a premature end to proceedings. Her concupiscence shocked her.

Unknown to Georgiana, her response had also shocked Dominic although, in his case, the feeling was purely pleasurable. On the stairs he recalled his as yet unfulfilled intention of making clear to the beautiful creature on his arm that he had, most definitely, known who she was at the masked ball the week before. Determined to be rid of this potential source of misunderstanding, he waited until they had reached the upper landing before stopping to glance down at a still flushed Georgiana. Unable to resist a knowing smile, drawing sparks from her huge hazel eyes, he chose what he thought was a simple but effective means of conveying his information. "I most heartily approve of that dress, my love," he said, his voice a sensuous murmur. "It will doubtless vie for prominence in my memory with that topaz silk creation you wore at the masked ball."

Georgiana blushed furiously, completely missing the implication in her thoroughly unnerved state. With an enormous effort, she gathered sufficient control to incline her head graciously and say, "I think perhaps we should return to the ballroom, my lord."

A deep chuckle answered her. "I'm sure you're right, my love. You've had quite enough adventure—for tonight."

There was a wealth of promise in his suggestive tone, none of which was lost on Georgiana. She willed her jittery nerves to compliance and, with the most serene expression she could muster firmly fixed on her face, allowed him to lead her back into the cacophony of the ballroom.

NOT UNTIL SHE was wrapped in the darkness of the Winsmere carriage on the long drive home from the Massinghams' did Georgiana allow her mind to dwell on the events of the evening. Even in the shielding gloom, she felt herself blush as she recalled those long moments in the library. How could she have been so…so positively *wanton?* Easily, came the damning reply. And now he knew. The thought made her shiver. Drawing her cloak more closely about her, she snuggled into its warmth, feeling the silk lining brush across her bare shoulders. These outrageously fashionable gowns of Fancon's hardly helped. Somehow, scantily clad in satin and silks, she was much more aware of a peculiar need to be held, to be stroked and caressed as she had been that evening. Repressing a little snort of derision, she told herself she could hardly claim it was the dresses which made her feel as she did. They simply made it easier to feel so…abandoned.

Jettisoning that unproductive line of thought, she blushed again as she remembered Dominic's rapid actions when the Duke and his friends had threatened discovery. She had sensed his suppressed laughter and had had to struggle to subdue her own, bubbling up in reply. It was odd, now she came to consider the matter, that she felt no sense of shame, only frustration.

Abruptly refocusing her thoughts once more, she tried to remember what he had said later, before they had gained the ballroom. Her mind promptly supplied the caress in his eyes as they had roamed appreciatively over her face and shoulders before he had complimented her on her gown. What had he said? Something about it being as pretty as her topaz silk.

The carriage jolted over a rut and she slipped sideways on the seat. She resettled herself in her corner, sightlessly watching the house fronts slip past the window.

Then her mind caught hold of the elusive memory, and his words replayed in her head. "It will doubtless vie for prominence in my memory with that topaz silk creation you wore at the masked ball."

Georgiana gasped.

"Georgie? Are you all right?"

Struggling to draw breath, Georgiana managed a reassuring phrase, then, feeling winded, curled up in her corner and gave her full attention to her staggering discovery.

He had known!

Which, as she had long ago worked out, meant... Her mind went completely blank, unable to accept the implication. Yet it was the only explanation possible.

Her heart beating in double time, a host of quivery, fluttery feelings crowding her chest, Georgiana forced her mind to grapple with the unthinkable. He had known, therefore he was... Oh, heavens!

THE NEXT THREE days passed in a haze of happiness. Georgiana hardly dared to believe her deductions, yet, whenever she met Lord Alton, every word, every action, confirmed them. He was paying court to her. Her—little Georgiana Hartley!

Bella seemed quite unaware and, yielding to the promptings of some sixth sense, Georgiana did not explain the source of her sudden elation to her friend. Bella had, certainly, noticed her glow. Uncharacteristically, she had yet to enquire its cause. But Georgiana was too much in alt to worry about such inconsistencies.

She had artfully managed to drop the information that Dominic had invited her to Candlewick for Christmas and she had accepted. Bella had feigned complete surprise, but Georgiana suspected she had known of her brother's intent. The subtle smugness in her smile suggested as much.

It was Lady Chadwick's gala tonight. She would see Dominic there, she was sure. They had yet to meet outside a ballroom, but it had only taken a moment or two to work out his strategy. Young and naïve as she was, even she knew any overt gesture on his part, any attention which could not be credited to a natural assistance to his sister's protégée, would make them the focus of the most intense speculation. She had no wish to figure in the latest *on dit,* and was grateful for his care of her reputation.

So she had to make do with the caress in his eyes every time they met, the gentle promise of his smile, the touch of his fingers on hers. It was nowhere near enough. She contented herself with the thoughts that, when the time was right, he would surely advance their courtship to the stage where the heady delights he had introduced her to in the library of Massingham House would once again be on their agenda.

Bella had retired to rest before the Chadwick gala. Georgiana had come to her room with a similar intention. But her thoughts denied her sleep. Restless, she jumped off the bed and paced the room in small, swirling steps, then broke into a waltz, spinning about as anticipation took hold. Whirling almost out of control, she did not see the door open, and cannoned into Cruickshank as she entered.

"Oh!" Georgiana put a hand to her whirling head. "Oh, Cruckers! What a start you gave me."

"I gave you?" said her dour maid, righting herself and shutting the door firmly. "Now, Miss Georgie, whatever's got into you? Whirling about like a heathen, indeed!"

Georgiana giggled, but made no other reply. She was in love, but she had no intention of letting anyone into the secret. Anyone other than Dominic.

Cruickshank sniffed. "Well, if you're so wide awake, I'll get your bath-water brought up. We may as well spend the time beautifying you."

Georgiana, thinking of the admiration she would see in a pair of bright blue eyes, gladly agreed.

THERE WAS NO supper waltz at the Chadwicks' gala. Dominic had, instead, claimed both the first and the last waltzes of the evening. Twirling down the long ballroom, under the glare of the chandeliers, Georgiana suddenly realised why it was he always chose a waltz. He was holding her far closer than was the norm. And, when she blushed, all he did was laugh softly and whisper, "As I cannot steal you away, my love, to a place where we might in safety pursue our mutual interest, you can hardly deny this lesser joy." The look that went with the words only made her blush more.

At the end of the dance, the last waltz of the evening, she was breathless and very nearly witless. Laughingly declining a most sensually worded invitation to take the air on the terrace—a highly dangerous undertaking, she had not a doubt—she whisked herself off to the withdrawing-room. A glass of cool water and a few moments of peace and quiet were all the restorative she needed. It would never do to let Bella see her return from a dance with her brother in such a state. There was, she felt sure, a limit to her friend's blindness.

When she entered, the withdrawing-room, a large bedchamber on the first floor, was empty of other guests. While she sipped the cool water an attentive maid brought her, Georgiana strolled to the long windows. The cool night air beckoned; Georgiana stepped out on to the small balcony. Behind her, the door of the withdrawing-room opened and shut, but she paid the newcomers no heed.

Not until the words, "Alton's such a cynical devil. D'you think he means marriage this time?" riveted her attention.

Slowly Georgiana turned to face the room. Standing still and silent in the shadows of the billowing draperies, she was concealed from the occupants, two matrons of considerable years and similar girth. They had dropped into two chairs and were busily fanning themselves while they considered the night's entertainment.

"Oh, I should think so," opined one, the fatter, pushing

a wilting ostrich plume from over one eye. "After all, why else would he be dancing attendance as he is?"

"But she's hardly his sort," countered the other, resplendent in blue bombazine. "Just look at Elaine Changley. What I want to know is why an out-and-outer like Alton should suddenly succumb to a sweet young thing whose charms can't possibly compare to those he's become accustomed to."

"But haven't you heard?" The fat matron leaned closer to her companion and lowered her voice in conspiratorial fashion. "It's her land he's after." She sat back in her chair and nodded sagely. "Seems she's inherited a section of land Alton's been chasing for years."

"Oh. Well, that sounds more like it. Couldn't imagine what had come over him." The blue bombazine rustled and shuffled, then stood and stretched. "Come on, Fanny. If we don't get back soon, that boy of yours will catch something you'll wish he hadn't."

Frozen, her senses suspended, Georgiana remained on the balcony while the two ladies fussed over the frills on the gowns before departing for the ballroom.

The Place. Georgiana wished she had never heard of it. And, of course, the words rang all too true. According to Bella, it was an obsession of her brother's. Georgiana's heart turned to ice, a solid chilled lump in her breast. Slowly, hardly aware of what she was doing, she came back into the room, pausing to place the glass she was carrying on a side-table.

Then she looked up and caught sight of herself in the mirror above the dressing-table. Huge haunted eyes stared back at her, stunned and distressed. She couldn't go back to the ballroom looking like that.

Drawing a deep breath, Georgiana shook herself, then straightened her shoulders and blinked several times. Pride was not much comfort, but it was all she had left. Determined to think no more about what she had heard until she had the privacy to indulge her tears, she left the room.

Once back in the crowded ballroom, misery hovered, threatening to engulf Georgiana if she relaxed her superhuman effort to ignore the matrons' words. She had to survive the rest of the gala. But Bella, seeing the stricken look in her friend's eyes, was immediately concerned.

"No, Georgie! We'll leave right now. There's no reason at all we need stay for the rest of this boring party."

With a determined frown, Bella silenced Georgiana's protests, and, within minutes, they were ensconced in the carriage and on their way to Green Street.

Bella yawned. "One thing about leaving just that little bit early—you can always get your carriage straight away." She stretched and settled herself. "Now, what's the matter?"

But Georgiana had had time to get herself in hand. She had anticipated the question and strove to deflect Bella's interest. "Nothing specific. It's just that I seem to have developed a migraine. I find it hard to go on once it comes on."

"Oh, you poor thing!" exclaimed Bella. "You just lie back quietly. As soon as we're home, I'll get Cruickshank to brew a tisane for you. I won't speak to you any further. Now try to rest."

Grateful for Bella's silence, Georgiana sank into her corner of the seat and gave herself up to her chaotic thoughts. After several minutes of totally pointless recollection, she forced herself to view the facts calmly. First of these was the relationship she knew existed between Lord Alton and Lady Changley. There was no doubt it was real—not just from the gossip, but from the evidence of her own eyes, on the terrace that fateful night. The memory of the passionate kiss Lord Alton had bestowed on Lady Changley was imprinted indelibly on her mind. He had never kissed her—let alone with such ardour. She recalled her early conviction that his attitude to her was merely that of helpful friendship, giving what assistance he could to his sister in her efforts to find a husband for her protégée. And his behaviour at the masked ball? Well, she had always thought he had not known who the lady in the topaz silk was. When had he told her he knew? Only a few days ago, long after he had learned of her inheritance. He could easily have found out what she had worn to the ball—from Bella if no one else. And then, too, Bella's ready acceptance of her sudden happiness could be easily explained if her friend knew her brother was paying court to her.

Georgiana stifled a sob. A few hours ago her world had looked rosy indeed. Now all her hopes lay in ashes about her. She had thought he was different, blessed with all the virtues, strong and steady and protective. Now it seemed he was no different from the rest. His love for her was superficial, assumed, of no great depth, called forth only by her possession of the Place. His main interest in life was status and wealth, with all the trappings. Why, he was not much better than Charles. And Bella thought nothing of Dominic's marrying her to gain title to the land. In all probability, he planned to keep Lady Changley as his mistress, even after they were married.

Georgiana tried to whip up her anger, her disdain. She must despise him, now she knew of his plans. But, as the miles rolled by, a cold certainty crept into her heart. She loved him far too much to despise him. Surely love wasn't meant to hurt so much?

Disillusioned on every front, she huddled into her corner and wept.

CHAPTER NINE

A SLEEPLESS NIGHT filled with hours of crying was no remedy for Georgiana's ailment. Bella took one look at her in the morning and insisted she spend the day in bed. Georgiana was in no mood to argue. But she winced at Bella's last words, floating in her wake as, having insisted on tucking her in, she tiptoed out of her bedroom. "For don't forget, we've the Mortons' ball tonight, and that's one event we can't miss."

Georgiana closed her eyes and let misery flow in. But she knew Bella's reasons for attending the ball, the Mortons being old family friends, and knew she could not avoid going. She had revised her opinion of Bella's part in her brother's schemes. No one who was as kind as Bella could possibly be party to such cold-blooded manipulation. And there was Arthur, too. Try as she might, it was impossible to cast Bella's husband in the light of a hard-hearted character who would idly watch while a young girl was cajoled into a loveless marriage. No. Neither Bella nor Arthur knew of Dominic's schemes. Not that that made life all that much easier, for she could hardly ask them for advice on such a matter. Still, she was glad she had at least two friends she could count true.

The evening came all too soon. Under the combined ministrations of Cruickshank and the redoubtable Hills, supervised by Bella herself, the ravages of her imaginary migraine were repaired until only her lacklustre eyes and her pallid complexion remained as witness to her inner turmoil.

Those items were sufficient, however, to immediately draw Dominic's attention to her distress. As was his habit, he gravitated to her side immediately she appeared in the ballroom.

"Georgiana?" Dominic bowed slightly over her hand, his eyes searching her face.

Flustered and weak, Georgiana retrieved her hand immediately, not daring to meet his intent gaze. Her heart was thudding uncomfortably, bruised and aching.

Dominic frowned. "My dear..."

At his tone, desperation flooded Georgiana. She raised her head, but still could not meet his eyes. "I'm afraid, my lord, that my dance card is full."

The silence on her left was complete. She had just entered the ballroom—he must know she was lying.

Dominic felt his face drain of expression. His jaw hardened. The impulse to call her bluff was strong. Then he noticed again her pallor, and the brittle tension in her slim frame, and swallowed his anger.

Stiffly, he bowed. With a cold, "My dear," he forced himself to walk away.

Dominic spent the first two dances watching Georgiana from the side of the room, unsure of his feelings, unsure, for what seemed like the first time in his life, of what to do. What the hell was going on? Then, finding himself the object of more than a few curious glances, he took himself off to the card-room.

He was rapidly inveigled into playing a few hands, but his mind was not on the game, and no one demurred when he left the table and returned to drift idly about the ballroom, keeping an unobtrusive eye on Georgiana. He had been careful enough for their association to have passed for mere acquaintance. If he displayed too overt an interest now, it would be tantamount to a declaration. But the impulse to cross the floor and haul her out on to the terrace and demand an explanation for her extraordinary conduct grew.

If she had betrayed the slightest hint of partiality for any other gentleman, he would have done it, and the consequences be damned. Luckily, she seemed unusually subdued, dancing only with those he knew she deemed her friends, refusing all others.

Slowly, his mind calmed and he started to sort through the possibilities in a more methodical fashion. At the Chadwicks' gala, all had been well, until after their last dance. She had gone off to the withdrawing-room, and he, careful of appearances, had gone to make one in the card-room. When he had returned to the ballroom, he had found the Winsmere party had decamped. That had not surprised him at the time, knowing Bella's condition. But perhaps there had been some other reason for their early departure.

Useless to speculate, when he had no idea what might have occurred. But between that last waltz and this evening, something had happened to destroy the carefully nurtured bond between himself and Georgiana.

Feeling very like hitting someone, but having no idea whom, Dominic scowled and strode out on to the balcony. The cool air brought some relief to his fevered brain. This was ridiculous. He was thirty-two, for heaven's sake! The effect Georgiana's withdrawal was having on him was both novel and highly unnerving. He didn't like it. And he'd be damned if he'd endure it for a minute longer than necessary.

Drawing a deep breath, he frowned direfully at the young couple who, giggling softly, came up out of the secluded garden. Surprised to find him there, arms folded and looking so grim, they fled back to the ballroom. Dominic sighed. If he did not have to be so circumspect, he could have taken Georgiana into the garden and made delicious love to her—

Abruptly he cut off the thought. Right now, it seemed as if she wasn't even speaking to him.

He would have to find out what was upsetting her. From the few comments he had exchanged with his sister, Bella clearly had no idea what had happened—she still had no idea of his interest in Georgiana. He needed to see Georgiana alone. For several moments, he pondered various schemes for attaining this end, finally settling on the one which, although it would not allow the fiction of the avuncular nature of his interest to stand, had the best chance of success.

With his decision made, he left the terrace to lay the necessary groundwork to put his plan into action.

GEORGIANA HAD NO idea how she survived the Mortons' ball. It remained, long afterwards, a dull ache in her memory. She was glad, she kept telling herself, that Lord Alton had accepted her dismissal so readily. It would have been too much to bear if he had insisted she speak with him. Perhaps he had realised she had come to understand his motives and would not be the easy conquest he had expected. Hopefully, he would stay away from her now. Depressed and weary, she slept the sleep of exhaustion, and awoke the next morning, refreshed at least in body, if not in spirit.

Despondent, she trailed into the breakfast-room.

"Georgie! Are you feeling better this morning?"

Bella's solicitude brought Georgiana to her senses. She had no right to wallow in misery and act like a raincloud over her friend. Summoning a wan smile, Georgiana nodded. "Yes. I'm fine."

Bella's face suggested she did not look fine, but, instead

of harping on the subject, Bella started chattering about the events that would fill the next week and bring the Little Season to an end. Georgiana listened with half an ear.

As Bella's catalogue ran its course, Georgiana realised she could not just up and flee to Italy tomorrow, much as she might wish to. She had made a bargain with Arthur, who had stood her friend when she had been in need. She could not shrug off her indebtedness. So she would have to see out the rest of the Season with what interest she could muster, trying not to dampen Bella's enjoyment with her own unhappiness.

She apparently returned sufficiently accurate, if monosyllabic, responses to Bella's opinions, for they rose from the breakfast-table in perfect amity.

"Oh, Georgie! I nearly forgot. Dominic noticed you looked a bit peaked last night, so he's coming to take you for a drive this afternoon."

Bella had preceded Georgiana through the door, so did not see the effect her announcement had on her friend.

"It's really a great honour, you know. I can't even remember the last lady Dominic took up for a drive in the park. He doesn't normally do so—says it's too boring. You must wear your new carriage dress; it'll be just the thing."

Reaching the parlour, Bella turned expectantly.

Georgiana had had enough time to school her features to a weak smile. "I really don't know if—"

"Oh, nonsense!" said Bella, dismissing whatever megrim Georgiana had taken into her head. "Some fresh air is just what you need to blow the cobwebs away."

Sinking on to the window seat and taking up her embroidery frame, Georgiana could not think of any reasonable excuse to decline Lord Alton's invitation. At least, not without explaining a great deal more of the situation to Bella. And that she was definitely not up to doing. Quite clearly, Bella was still in the dark regarding the state of affairs between her brother and her protégée.

Throughout the day, Georgiana formulated and discarded a string of plans to avoid the afternoon drive. In the end, her schemes became so wildly far-fetched that her sense of humour came to her rescue. What on earth did she imagine he'd do to her in the sanctity of the park? Besides, she knew him too well to believe he'd do anything scandalous—at least, not with her. She spent a moment in dim regret over that point, then determinedly stiffened her spine. She would go with him and hope to impress on him that she did not wish to see him again. Perhaps, with one major effort, she could avoid having to live with the dread of dancing with him at every evening entertainment, of being held in his arms, with his blue gaze warming her.

With a despairing sigh, she went upstairs to change.

Cruickshank was waiting with the carriage dress laid out. Having seen the sudden change in her mistress, and having more than a suspicion of the cause, Cruickshank fretted and snorted over every pleat in the elegant brown velvet dress with its snug-fitting jacket. Georgiana, knowing she could hide little from her maid's sharp eyes, was thankful to escape her chamber without a lecture. As she descended the curving staircase, the villager hat she had chosen dangling by its ribbons from one hand, Georgiana imagined such a scene, and what Cruickshank might actually say. The possibilities brought a smile to her face, the first for the day.

A sudden tingling brought her head up. Her eyes met blue—bright blue. Lord Alton was standing in the hall below, Bella by his side, watching her. For an instant she froze. Then, drawing what courage she could from knowing she looked as well as might be, Georgiana descended to the hall and placed her hand in his, curtsying demurely.

He raised her and carried her hand to his lips, and there was no doubt of the warmth in his gaze. Georgiana blushed vividly; her heart fluttered wildly. She had forgotten how devastatingly charming he could be.

She turned to Bella, who remained rooted to the spot, an arrested look on an otherwise blank face. But before Georgiana could make any comment, Dominic said, "We'll be back in about an hour, Bella." And, with a nod for his sister, he firmly escorted Georgiana outside.

Handed into a curricle of the very latest design, Georgiana quickly tied her hat over her curls. The breeze was brisk, stirring the manes of the two black horses stamping and sidling between the shafts. A small tiger held their heads. Dominic climbed up beside her and, with a flick of the reins, they were off, the tiger scrambling for his perch behind.

As he threaded his team through the traffic, Dominic realised that his supposedly straightforward plan to have an hour's quiet conversation with his love had already run off the tracks. For a start, there were no horses which could be described as docile in his stables. Until the present, this had not proved a problem. The pair he had unthinkingly requested be harnessed to the curricle were Welsh thoroughbreds, perfectly capable of stomping on anyone or anything they took exception to. And they had not been out for days and would willingly run a hundred miles if he would just drop his hands and give them their heads. Stifling a sigh, he gave them his undivided attention.

Once the park gates were reached, he set the horses to a trot, letting them stretch their legs at least that much. They tossed their heads impatiently, but eventually responded to the firm hand on the reins and accepted their lot. Only then did he turn to view his second hurdle. What on earth had possessed her to wear that hat? He knew perfectly well that the outfit she wore—the very latest in carriage wear—should have been completed by a tight-fitting cloche, perhaps with a small feather or cockade on the brim. The temptation to tell her as much burned his tongue, but he left the words unsaid. At the moment, he did not think a demonstration of his familiarity with feminine apparel was likely to further his cause.

"Someone is waving to you."

Dominic looked about and returned the salutation, ignoring the invitation to draw up his carriage by Lady Molesworth's barouche.

Georgiana's fingers were clutching her reticule so tightly that she could feel the thin metal brim twisting. She wished he would say something, or that she could think of a safe topic to discuss. Finally, sheer desperation drove her to say, "I believe the weather is turning more cold..." only to hear her voice clash with his.

They both fell silent.

Dominic glanced down at the top of her hat and grimaced. Without being able to see her face, he felt he was groping in the dark. He dropped his voice to a softer tone. "Georgiana, my dear, what's wrong?"

His experience with his sister, on top of his extensive expertise in related spheres, enabled him to get the tone just right, so that Georgiana felt that if he said another word in such a gentle way she would burst into tears in the middle of the park and shame them both. She waved her small hands in distress. "My lord... Please..." She had no idea what to say. Her mind wouldn't function, and her senses, traitorous things, were too much occupied with manifestations of his presence other than his conversation. "There's nothing wrong," she eventually managed in a very small voice.

Swallowing his frustration, Dominic wondered just what he had expected to achieve with a question like that in the middle of the park. He should have guessed that whatever it was that had upset her would prove too distressing to discuss reasonably in such surroundings. The situation wanted improving, and he would get rid of that hat, too.

Without the least effort, he instituted a conversation on recent events, none of which could be construed as in any way disturbing. Gradually, he won a response from Georgiana.

Grateful for his understanding, and believing the worst was behind her, Georgiana set about recovering her composure, and her wits, eventually contributing her half of the conversation. As they bowled along, the horses' hoofs scattering the autumn leaves, the breeze whisked past her cheeks, bringing crisp colour to hide her pallor. Bella had been right: fresh air was just what she needed. By the time they had completed their first circuit, she was chattering animatedly when, to her surprise, the curricle headed for the gates. They had been out for less than half an hour. "Where are we going?"

"Back to Green Street," came the uncompromising reply. "I want to talk to you."

The ride back to Winsmere House was, not surprisingly, accomplished in silence. Georgiana stole one glance up at Dominic's face, but, as usual, his features told her nothing.

The curricle swayed to a halt. Before she could attempt to climb down, he was there, lifting her effortlessly to the pavement. Breathless, she stood for one moment within the circle of his arms and dared to look up into his face. "There's really no need—"

"There's every need." Dominic's face remained shuttered. His hand at her elbow drew her up the steps.

Georgiana, trembling inwardly with an odd mixture of exhilaration and sheer terror, drew a deep breath and swung to face him. "My lord—"

"Ah, Johnson."

Georgiana turned to find the door open and Bella's butler bowing deferentially. The next instant she was in the hall.

"We'll use the drawing-room, I think."

Borne inexorably over the threshold, Georgiana gave up all hope of avoiding the coming interview and crossed the room, her fingers fumbling with the ribbons of her hat.

Dominic shut the door and watched with relief as she cast the offending headgear aside. He moved to a side-table and stripped off his driving gloves, dropping them on the polished surface.

"Now—"

The door opened.

"There you are!" Bella came tripping over the threshold, big eyes bright.

Georgiana looked on her with undisguised relief.

Dominic looked on her with undisguised irritation. "Go away, Bella."

Brought up short, Bella turned to stare at him. "Go away? But whatever—?"

"Bella!" The dire warning in his voice was enough to send Bella about and start her for the door. Then she remembered she was in her own house and no longer needed to heed her brother's orders. She stopped, but before she could turn again a large hand in the small of her back propelled her out of the room.

The drawing-room door shut with a sharp click. Stunned, totally bewildered, Bella turned to stare at its uninformative panels.

Inside, Dominic turned to find Georgiana regarding him with distinct trepidation. Wondering how long his patience was going to last, he crossed the room and took her hands in his, covering her cold fingers with his warm ones. "Don't look at me like that. I'm not going to eat you."

Georgiana smiled weakly.

"But you are going to tell me what's wrong."

Glancing wildly up at him, eyes wide, Georgiana drew breath to reiterate that there was nothing wrong, when she caught his sceptical look and fell silent.

"Precisely." Dominic nodded sternly. "I'm not addle-pated enough to swallow any tale you might concoct, so the truth, if you please."

Standing there, her hands warm in his, the temptation to cast herself on his broad chest and sob out all her woes was dreadfully strong. In desperation, Georgiana sought for some way out, some tale he would accept for her not seeing him again. But another upward glance under her lashes convinced her the task was hopeless.

"It's… It's just that our…our association has become sufficiently marked that people might start talking and…" Her voice trailed away altogether.

She looked up to find an oddly amused expression on Dominic's face.

He smiled. "Actually, our association has, until today, been sufficiently well hidden. However, I dare say they will start talking now."

Distracted, Georgiana frowned. "You mean after our drive in the park?"

Still amused, Dominic nodded. "That. And tonight." At Georgiana's puzzled look, he explained, "It's the Rigdons' ball. And as from now, I'm going to be so very attentive to you that even the blindest of the gossips will know my intentions."

"Your intentions?" Georgiana's voice had risen strangely.

Dominic regarded her with some slight annoyance. "My intentions," he repeated. After a moment he sighed and went on, "I know I haven't proposed, but surely, Georgiana, you are not so scatter-brained you don't know I'm in love with you and intend asking you to marry me?"

Georgiana stared at him. Of course she knew he intended to marry her. But that he loved her? No, she knew that wasn't right. Gently, she tried to ease her hands from his, but he would not allow it.

Dominic frowned. "Georgiana, love, what is the matter?"

Becoming more nervous by the minute, Georgiana shook her head, not daring to look up at him. "I can't marry you, my lord." There, she had said it.

"Whyever not?"

The calm question took her breath away. Inwardly Georgiana groaned. She closed her eyes and wished herself anywhere but where she was. Yet when she opened them again, a pair of large, well formed hands were still clasped firmly around hers. She risked a glance upwards. He was calmly waiting for an answer. Nothing in his face or stance suggested he would let her go without one.

Dominic stood silently and hoped she would hurry up. The effort of keeping his hands on hers, rather than sweeping her into his arms and kissing away whatever ridiculous notions she had taken into her head, was draining his resolution. In the end, he repeated his question. "Why can't you marry me?"

Georgiana drew a deep breath, closed her eyes, and said quite clearly, "Because you're in love with Lady Changley and were planning to marry her."

Sheer surprise kept Dominic immobile and slackened his hold on her fingers.

Instantly Georgiana whisked away and, on a broken sob, rushed from the room.

Even after the door closed behind her, Dominic made no move to follow her. How on earth had she come to that marvellous conclusion? How on earth had she learned of Elaine Changley? Feeling remarkably sane for a man who had just had his first ever proposal thrown in his face, before he had uttered it, Dominic strolled to the sofa and sat down, the better to examine his love's strange ideas.

Within a minute a subtle smile was curving his lips. Another minute saw him chuckling. So that was what all this fuss was about. His ex-mistress. It really was absurd. Undoubtedly Elaine would be thrilled if she ever knew she was the cause of such difficulties. And Julian Ellsmere would laugh himself into stitches if he ever heard. He spent a moment wondering which busybody had told Georgiana of Elaine Changley, then dismissed the subject from his mind. There were any number of loose tongues about town.

Standing, Dominic stretched, then relaxed. He would just have to arrange to explain to his love the subtle difference between what a gentleman felt for the woman he made his mistress and the emotions he felt for the woman he would make his wife. It was, as it happened, a point he was supremely well qualified to expound. His smile broadened. He had told her he would see her at the Rigdons' that night. As he recalled, Rigdon House had a most intriguing conservatory, tucked away in a corner of the mansion, unknown to most guests. The perfect place. As for the opportunity, there would be no difficulty arranging that.

Strolling to the door, relieved of his strange burden of not knowing what had gone wrong, Dominic felt on top of the world. Then, out of the blue, two phrases, heard at widely differing times, coalesced in his mind. He froze. Georgiana's secret love was a man she had met during her earliest days in London who she believed was in love with and about to marry another woman. He had searched her acquaintance to no avail—there was no such man. Now she had just admitted that she thought *he* was in love with and had been about to marry Lady Changley. *Ha!*

Dominic's smile as he left Winsmere House could have warmed the world.

IT WAS WITH a strange mixture of trepidation and relief that Georgiana entered the Rigdon House ballroom. She had initially felt devastated and drained after her interview with Lord Alton, but a peaceful hour in her bedchamber had convinced her that it was all for the best. At least he now knew she would not accept an offer from him and why. She told herself her problems were over. Yet, deep down inside, she was far from sure he would accept her dismissal. And buried even deeper was the uncertainty of whether she really wanted him to.

She had not left her chamber until, arrayed for the evening, she had descended for dinner. Arthur's presence would, she had hoped, inhibit Bella's ability to question her closely about her brother's strange behaviour. As it transpired, Bella had evinced not the slightest degree of curiosity, even in the privacy of the carriage on the way to the ball. Dimly Georgiana wondered if Bella's brother often did such outrageous things.

After being presented to Lord Rigdon, whom she had not previously met, she and Bella drifted into the crowds of guests, chattering avidly while they waited for the dancing to begin.

Joining a circle of young ladies, many of whom she now knew, Georgiana went through the usual process of filling in her dance card, allocating the vital supper waltz to Lord Ellsmere. To her surprise, he also requested another waltz, earlier in the evening. She was puzzled, for he had rarely danced twice with her since she had refused his suit. Still, she numbered him among her most trusted cavaliers and gladly bestowed on him the first waltz of the night.

It was while she was circling the ballroom in Lord Ellsmere's arms that she first became aware of a change in her status. A number of dowagers sat on chairs lining the walls. From the direction of their sharp glances and the whisperings behind their fans, she realised with a jolt that she was the subject under discussion. A few minutes later, as the waltz ended and, on Lord Ellsmere's arm, she joined a small group of young people, she surprised a look of what could only be envy on the face of Lady Sabina Matchwick, one of the Season's *incomparables*.

Slowly, it dawned that, as Dominic had prophesised, people were beginning to talk. Finding Bella by her side, and momentarily alone, Georgiana could not help but ask, "Bella, tell me. Is it really so very unusual for your brother to drive a lady in the park?"

Bella's candid blue gaze found her face. "Yes. I told you. Dominic's never taken any lady driving before."

"Oh."

At her stricken face, Bella burst into a trill of laughter. Impulsively, she hugged Georgiana. "Oh, Georgie! I'm so happy!"

The approach of their partners for the next dance put an end to any confidences. Georgiana dipped through the cotillion and barely knew what she did. As dance followed dance, she realised the nods and smiles denoted not scandalised horror, but a sort of envious approval. Heavens! Just by taking her for a drive, Lord Alton had all but publicly declared himself. How on earth was she to rectify the mistaken impression? Then Georgiana reminded herself that in a few short days her Little Season would be over. And she would go back to Ravello and forget all about Lord Alton and his very blue eyes.

It was almost time for the supper waltz. Lord Ellsmere came to claim her. By some subtle manoeuvre, he separated her from her court and proceeded to stroll down the long room with her on his arm.

"My dear Georgiana, I do hope you won't forever hold it against me, but I've a confession to make."

Startled out of her abstraction, Georgiana stared at him. "Confession?" she echoed weakly. Oh, dear. Surely he was not going to start pressing her to marry him, too?

As if sensing her thoughts, he smiled at her. "No, no. Nothing to overset you. At least," he amended, frowning as if suddenly giving the matter due thought, "I hope it won't upset you."

Georgiana could stand no more. "My lord, I pray you'll unburden yourself of this horrendous secret."

He smiled again. "It's really quite simple. I engaged you for this waltz in proxy, as it were."

Her heart was beating an unnerving tattoo. "Who…?" Georgiana didn't bother finishing her question. She knew who. And as if to confirm her suspicions, she felt a familiar tingling sensation start along her nerves, spreading from the bare skin of her shoulders and neck in a southerly direction. No, Lord Alton had not accepted his dismissal.

"Ah, here he is."

With a smile and an elegant bow to her, Lord Ellsmere surrendered her to the suavely elegant gentleman who had come to stand beside her.

Georgiana felt her hand being raised and the warm pressure of his lips on her fingers.

"Georgiana?"

His husky tone rippled across her senses. Despite all her intentions, she could not prevent herself from looking up. And she was lost. His eyes caught hers and held her gaze effortlessly. Somewhere in her unconscious the subtle perfection of his attire registered, along with an appreciation of face, form and figure, all apparently designed with her own prejudices in view. But her conscious mind was only aware of the total mastery he exerted over her senses, the hypnotic tug which drew her, unresisting, into her arms. Before she knew it, they were waltzing.

With an effort, Georgiana managed to free enough wit to realise he was smiling at her in amused appreciation, quite certain of his conquest. Then, as her senses probed the ballroom about them, the enormity of his strategy hit her. They might have been waltzing amid a host of other couples, but every eye in the ballroom was on them. She blushed vividly.

This evidence of her sudden awareness drew a deep chuckle. "Don't worry. You look radiantly lovely. Just think what a handsome couple we make."

Georgiana tried to summon enough anger to glare at him, but her overwhelmed emotions were not up to it.

Dominic looked down at her, her golden eyes and creamy skin, the glorious riot of her golden curls filling his vision. More than satisfied with her capitulation thus far, he made a mental note to play on her senses more often—a subtle torture, at present, but so very rewarding.

The music drew to a close, Georgiana waited to be released, but, instead of bowing and escorting her back to Bella's side, Dominic simply tucked her hand into his arm and walked out of the ballroom. Entirely unable to resist, and with a sinking feeling that it would be singularly pointless to try, Georgiana found herself wandering the corridors on Lord Alton's arm.

Suspecting that the amble had more purpose than was apparent, Georgiana turned an enquiring gaze upwards, to be met with a smile of quite dazzling effect.

"I thought, my love, that, given your apparent misconception regarding my feelings towards you, we should find a quiet spot where I might endeavour to disabuse your mind of its strange notion."

Georgiana tried, really tried, to come up with some suitable response, but not a coherent phrase came into her head. At the end of the long corridor, Dominic turned right, opening a glass-panelled door and ushering her through.

Vines and species of *ficus* grew out of large tubs artfully arranged to give the impression of a tropical forest. Cyclamens provided bursts of exotic colour amid the greenery. A small fountain played a lonely tune in the middle of a circular tiled courtyard. Of other humans, there was no sign.

With no real idea of what he meant to say, Georgiana was caught between a desire to hear his words and a conviction that it would be unwise to do so. But she was given no choice in the matter as, smoothly compelling, Dominic led her to a rustic ironwork seat. At his nod, she sat, and he sat beside her, retaining possession of her hand and showing no inclination to release it.

Sensing her skittering nerves, Dominic smiled reassuringly and raised her fingers to his lips, placing a leisurely kiss on each rosy fingertip, his eyes all the while holding hers. He watched as her golden eyes widened and her breathing suspended, then started again, more shallowly and less evenly. Entirely satisfied, he grinned wickedly. "Now where were we, when you so abruptly left the room this afternoon? Ah, yes! You believe I'm in love with Lady Changley and was intending to marry her." He directed a look of patent enquiry at Georgiana, clearly seeking confirmation.

Trapped, in every way, Georgiana coloured.

Smiling again, Dominic continued, his voice light but perfectly serious. "I'm not, I'll have you know, in favour of the idea of a gentleman discussing his paramours with anyone, least of all with his intended bride. Young ladies are not supposed to be cognisant of the sorts of affairs women such as Lady Changley indulge in. However, as you have already heard of her, I'll admit we enjoyed a short liaison, which ended some weeks before I met you."

Dominic paused to allow the full implication of his words to sink in. Georgiana's attention was complete; she was hanging on every word, and he doubted not that she would remember what he said, even should she fail to immediately register its import.

Pensively he began to stroke her fingers with his thumb. "Like all rich and single peers, I am high on the list of prey for such as Lady Changley. She, unwisely, believed I was besotted enough to offer marriage. At no stage did I do so. You'll have to take my word for that, although you will notice no public charges for breach of promise have been levelled at me. That's because she knows no one would believe I would be so lost to all propriety as to offer to make her my Viscountess."

To Georgiana his words were every bit as intoxicating as the sensations produced by the insistent pressure of his thumb over the sensitive backs of her fingers. Then his eyes lost their far-away look and his gaze became intent, capturing her own as if to focus her entire being on him. Georgiana felt herself drowning in blue.

Without releasing her from his spell, deliberately, Dominic raised her hand to his lips, but this time turned it to press a warm kiss to her palm. He smiled at the marked shiver the caress produced, but his eyes were nevertheless perfectly serious as he said, "The feelings I have for you, my love, are far removed from the lust a man feels for his mistress, a fleeting emotion which dissipates, usually in months if not weeks. No man marries his mistress. No man falls in love with his mistress."

Georgiana could not have moved if the ceiling fell. She

was mesmerised—by his voice, by his eyes, by him. Drawing a shuddering breath, she waited for what was to come, knowing she could not prevent him from saying the words, knowing that, once said, they would bind her, no matter how hard she struggled, tying her to him, not by his love, but by hers.

Dominic continued to devour her with his eyes, following her reactions. He waited until full awareness returned to her, then said, "What I feel for you is far removed from mere lust. I can hardly deny I know what that is and can readily define it. What I feel for you is not that. I fell in love with you the first moment I saw you, asleep in my armchair by the drawing-room hearth at Candlewick. You belong there." He paused, knowing that his next move was chancy, but, confident he had gauged her responses, and her temperament, accurately, he smoothly continued, "Regardless of what you may say, regardless of how many times you deny it, I know you love me in exactly the same way I love you."

His words, delivered in a low, deliberate, slightly husky tone, sent shivers up and down Georgiana's spine. He was right, of course, at least in defining her love. Oh, what temptation he posed! Still trapped in his gaze, she knew immediately his attention shifted. His eyes were now fixed on a golden ringlet hanging beside her face. One long finger came up to caress the soft curl, then moved on with tantalising slowness to outline the curve of one brow, then the length of her pert nose, and then traced, oh, so lightly, the full bow of her lips. The roaming finger slipped under her chin and tilted her face upwards. Georgiana's eyelids drooped. His lips touched hers in the gentlest of kisses.

When he drew back, she could barely cope with the sense of loss, could barely restrain herself from throwing her arms about his neck and behaving like a wanton. Again, she blushed rosily, not at his actions but at her thoughts.

Entirely satisfied with progress thus far, Dominic sat back and waited patiently until her breathing slowed, watching her through half-closed lids. When she had recovered sufficiently to glance at him once more, he took up his dissertation. "As you've realised, the rest of the *ton* are now *au fait* with my intentions. Our affairs are thus public knowledge, and should, given your age, proceed with all due circumspection."

He smiled, his eyes lighting with a certain devilment that awoke an answering spark in Georgiana. She found herself smiling back in genuine empathy.

"Thus, you will now be wooed in form. I will drive you in the park every afternoon, weather permitting. I will escort you to whichever evening functions it is your desire to attend. The *ton* will be edified by the sight of me at your pretty feet. Therefore, having attained that position, it will be no great difficulty to propose to you at the end of the Season."

Whereat you'll accept me. And thank God there's only a week of the Season to go! Dominic left his last thoughts unsaid, contenting himself with another warm smile. Dropping a last kiss on Georgiana's fingers, he rose.

"Come, my child. We should return you to the ball before the dowagers start having the vapours."

THE INTERLUDE IN the conservatory disturbed Georgiana more than she had believed possible. She had never before been exposed to, let alone been called upon to withstand, anyone as compelling as Bella's brother. The magnetic force he wielded was of a magnitude that rendered mere reason impotent. Settled in her corner of the *chaise* on their way home from Rigdon House, she was conscious that the attractions of Ravello and freedom were dimming in the light of the flame Lord Alton was skillfully igniting.

That he meant to do it, she had not a doubt. Deliberate, calculated, he made no effort to hide his tactics. He wanted the Place. In the darkness of the carriage, Georgiana shivered.

Their discussion had at least relieved her mind of one nagging, guilty worry. He did not and had never loved Lady Changley. Of that, she was certain. She could not decide whether it was the hint of humour that had coloured his voice when he had spoken of his mistress or the coldly unemotional way he had considered her machinations that had convinced her. But convinced she was. Lady Changley might or might not have believed he was in love with her. Whichever way it was, she was only another victim of his lordship's potent charm.

Unfortunately, all that did was prove he had the ability to make women fall deeply in love with him. It hardly proved that he loved her.

The more she considered the matter, the more she doubted the possibility. Why would such a handsome man, so eligible in every way, with all of the last ten years' débutantes to choose from—*incomparables* included—have decided to opt for her? Little Georgiana Hartley, whose head barely topped his shoulder, who knew next to nothing of the fashionable life of England, let alone the political side with which he was so intricately involved. Why had he picked her?

The Place. It was the only answer.

Miserable all over again, Georgiana lay sleepless for a long time after Cruickshank had snuffed her candles. In the dark, she wrestled with demons who all too often had bright blue eyes. He professed love, and she longed to believe him. Yet, when it came down to it, his actions belied his words. Admittedly she had been brought up in Italy, but she couldn't believe national boundaries changed human nature so very much. True love always brought desire in its wake, as was only right and proper. Yet the chaste kiss he had bestowed on her had held no hint of burning passion. And she knew that wasn't how he kissed a woman he desired.

Again and again, her thoughts brought her back to the same depressing conclusion. He was an expert in seduction; she was a novice. Her hand in marriage would secure the Place, so he had calmly set about capturing it. In the world of the *ton,* it would be considered a very fair exchange—her land for the position and wealth he could provide.

As the hours of the night gave way to a grey dawn, Georgiana considered for the first time whether she might be wise to listen to the promptings of her heart, to accept the proposal he had told her was coming, even knowing that her love wasn't shared. She knew he would always treat her well—with respect and affection, if not with the love she craved. She would fill the position of his wife, be able to care for him, bear his children.

A vision of Candlewick swam before her, and she spent some time imagining what might be. But she could not place him in the picture beside her. Instead, he appeared as a nebulous figure, arriving in the dead of night, leaving with the dawn.

With a sob, Georgiana buried her face in her pillow. No. It was impossible. If she couldn't have his love, the rest was meaningless. She would leave for Ravello as soon as the Season ended.

CHAPTER TEN

"Humph!"

The loud snort brought Georgiana awake with a start. Cruickshank stood by the bed.

"You'd better wake up and take a look at these."

With a grim look, Cruickshank drew back the bed curtains. The window drapes had already been opened, letting weak morning sunshine bathe the room. For an instant Georgiana stared uncomprehendingly at her maid, then her attention was drawn to the door. It opened to admit a young girl, one of the parlour maids, all but concealed behind a huge stand of cream roses.

The girl peeked at Georgiana around the delicate blooms, then, with a giggle, crossed to deposit the vase on a table by the window.

To Georgiana's astonishment, her place in the doorway was immediately taken by another maid, similarly burdened. When a third maid entered, with yet more cream roses, Georgiana put her hands to her hot cheeks. Cream roses in October!

Hundreds of cream roses.

By the time the procession of maids had transferred all the blooms delivered to the house by the florist's that morning to her bedroom, Georgiana was speechless. She sat and stared. The sheer outrageous extravagance of the gesture numbed her. About her, the delicate perfume of the flowers took hold, flavouring the air with their subtle enchantment.

She needed no card to tell her who had sent them.

At the Rigdons' ball, he had vowed to woo her formally. His public courtship had started that night, when he had returned her to Bella's side but remained possessively beside her, discouraging all her partners but those he approved of simply by being there. The next day he had swooped down on her morning and taken her driving to Richmond, later producing a picnic hamper for lunch and taking her to the Star and Garter for tea. It was impossible to stand firm against the invitation of his smile. He would accept no denials. Powerless to prevent his whirlwind courtship, she had, unwillingly, reluctantly, been swept along, mesmerised by the blue of his eyes. The following evening she had seen the effects of his strategy. As far as the *ton* was concerned, only the ceremony was required to establish her as the Viscountess Alton.

In the four days that had followed, each filled with unsought joy and a hidden despair, he had succeeded in convincing everyone that theirs would be a marriage made in heaven, until it seemed to Georgiana that only she guessed the truth.

Her moods fluctuated wildly, from ecstatic pleasure when he was with her, to blackest despair when he was not. She was counting the days to the end of the Season, to when Bella and Arthur departed for Candlewick and she could flee to Ravello and safety. She had even tried to sound Arthur out on the possibility of leaving before then. But he had looked at her blankly, seeming not to understand her oblique reference. Incapable of being more explicit, she had been forced to let the matter drop.

Cream roses surrounded her. Her consciousness was filled with him to the exclusion of all else. Georgiana sighed.

Only Cruickshank remained in the room, fussing over

laying out her clothes, sharp eyes stealing covert glances, trying to assess her reaction.

Shaking free of despondency, Georgiana slipped out of bed. Cruickshank held up a blue morning dress for her approval. Through narrowed eyes, Georgiana studied its clean lines. Then, abruptly, she shook her head. "No, Cruckers. The new green velvet, please."

Cruickshank's eyebrows rose comically, but she made no comment beyond the predictable snort.

Stripping off her nightgown, Georgiana washed her face and donned her soft muslin undergarments while Cruickshank brought out the latest of her purchases from Fancon. If her association with Lord Alton had taught her anything, it was to value the added confidence appearing before him in new and fashionably elegant gowns gave her. Besides, in a few days' time, she would no longer have the pleasure of appearing before him at all. Despite the heaviness of her heart, weighed down by unrequited love, she was determined to live these last few days as fully as she could, to store away the bittersweet memories to warm the long winter days, and nights, in Ravello.

THE EAST WIND was chilly. Grey clouds scudded low across the tops of the trees, skeletal fingers emerging to trap them as the summer cloaks were stripped, leaf by leaf, away. Everywhere summer was in decline, giving way to the gusts of autumn, chill harbingers of year's end.

Perched on the box seat of Viscount Alton's curricle, Georgiana was immune from the cold. Refusing to face her bleak future, she revelled in the warmth of the moment. Her wind-whipped cheeks glowed and her eyes, when she managed to wrench them free of his lordship's steady gaze, sparkled with life and love. She had left her inhibitions in Green Street and was happy.

Beside her, Dominic was host to a range of emotions, some of which were both novel and, to one of his experience, distinctly disturbing. That he loved Georgiana Hartley, in the complete fullness of the term, he no longer doubted. But that she could invoke in him the full gamut of desire, to the point where his mind became prey to salacious imaginings, was not something he had expected. She was a young, innocent, inexperienced, green girl. A golden angel. Yet, no matter how many accurate adjectives he heaped about her name, nothing detracted from the sensual spell she cast over him. She was learning quickly. But she had no idea, he felt sure, of the risks she courted. His well honed skills, all but automatic, were in danger of carrying them away.

There were few people in the park. The cold weather had kept most of the fashionable indoors. They completed one circuit, then went about again, content to prolong their time in such unaccustomed seclusion. Few words were exchanged. Their eyes spoke, and that was enough.

When the gates hove a second time into view, Dominic acknowledged the passing hours and headed his team for the street. His gaze flicked to Georgiana's face, catching her wide-eyed hazel stare, and he knew she had enjoyed their time together as much as he had. In that instant, he made his decision.

He had postponed asking her to marry him, wanting his courtship of her to be a recognised fact before any announcement. Quick betrothals between men such as he and sweet delights such as she had a way of being remembered and whispered about. He wanted no breath of a question to touch her.

But there were only two more days of the Season to go. And there was no doubt of their state. And no reason at all to procrastinate.

As the park gates fell behind, Georgiana was conscious of the day closing in, of a dimming of her joy. For the past hour she had been happy. It was so easy to forget, to imagine instead how things might have been. But always reality eventually intruded, reminding her of the real reason for his interest in her.

By the time Green Street was reached and he lifted her down she was thoroughly depressed once more. He escorted her indoors, and she inwardly shrank at the coming meeting with Bella. Her hostess, to whom she owed so much, was *aux anges* at the prospect of having her for a sister-in-law.

She was shaken out of her dismal thoughts by the words, "The drawing-room, I think, Johnson. You needn't inform your mistress that we've returned."

Before her weary mind had time to do more than register that quite improper order, Dominic had deftly ushered her into the drawing-room and shut the door.

Suddenly conscious of the desirability of putting as much space as possible between them, Georgiana quickly crossed the room. Her heartbeat, which had slowed somewhat since they had left the park, picked up its tempo.

From his stance just inside the door, Dominic viewed her impetuous movement, which had about it the air of flight, and frowned. Then, when he saw the agitated flutter of her small hands, clasping and unclasping before her, a slow smile erased the stern look. She was nervous, no more. A strange rapport existed between them. So she sensed his intention and, true to her age and innocence, was disturbed. His features softened. He crossed to stand beside her.

"Georgiana, my love…"

A small gesture silenced him. Georgiana could stand the strain no more. "Dominic, please," she whispered, infusing every particle of persuasion she could into her tones.

After the briefest of pauses, she continued, "My lord,

I am most sensible of the honour you do me, but I cannot marry you."

Dominic suppressed the instinctive retort that he hadn't yet had a chance to ask her and, to his surprise, found himself fascinated, rather than furious. "Why?"

Despite her highly strung state, Georgiana spared a moment to curse silently the incredible evenness in temper that could yield such a mild response. If truth be known, she would infinitely have preferred a more melodramatic reaction. That, she would have known how to deal with. Instead, his deceptively simple question was anything but easy to answer.

In fact, as the minutes stretched, she realised she couldn't answer it at all. In growing panic, she shook her head, dropping her gaze to her nervously clenching fingers.

Dominic sighed. "Georgiana, my love, I should perhaps inform you that I am not one of the school which holds it right and proper that a young lady should refuse her chosen suitor at least three or four times before accepting him, so as not to appear too eager." He waited to see what effect that had, and was not entirely surprised to see her ringlets dance a decided negative.

Allowing silence, so often his ally, to stretch still further, Dominic, close behind her, watched her growing agitation, and chose his moment to murmur, "Sweetheart, I've not got infinite patience."

The gentle tone of his voice cloaked the steel of the words. Georgiana did not miss the implication of either. Her nerves singed by his nearness, she abruptly took a step away, then turned to face him. She had to make him understand the futility of his enterprise.

"My lord, I…must make it plain to you. I will not marry you."

Dominic wasn't really listening. She had not answered

his question, which, in itself, was answer enough. He was not in the mood to listen to missish denials, not when her eyes were so soft and her lips, gently parted, just begged to be kissed.

Seeking to impress on him the inevitability of her refusal, Georgiana allowed her eyes to meet his. And, as had happened so often before, in the warm blue of his gaze, she felt their wills collide and hers melt away. Mesmerised, she could barely breathe as he moved closer, one long finger rising to trace the curve of her cheek, stopping at the corner of her mouth. Unable to move, she watched as his eyes fixed on her lips. Unconsciously, her tongue slipped between them to run its moist pink tip along their suddenly dry contours. He smiled. Then, tantalisingly slowly, his head drew nearer, his lips hungry for hers.

As her eyelids drooped, panic seized Georgiana. In desperation, she put her small hands up before her and met the wall of his chest. She turned her head away. She felt him hesitate. In that instant she seized the tattered remnants of her sanity and, on a choked sob, fled the room.

In utter disbelief, Dominic watched her go. As the door shut behind her he uttered one comprehensive oath and, thrusting his hands deep in his breeches pockets, swung about to glare at the window.

After a moment he glanced around, half expecting the door to open and for her to return. When nothing happened, he muttered irritably and ostensibly gave his attention to a minute inspection of Bella's lace draperies. What the devil did Miss Georgiana Hartley think she was playing at? What the devil did she think *he* was playing at?

When the ticking of the mantelpiece clock made it plain any hope of Georgiana's return was forlorn, Dominic let his head fall back. Scowling at the ceiling, he vented his disapproval in one sharp and pungent phrase, then strode purposefully to the door, his face like granite.

Johnson, unperturbed and imperturbable, met him in the hall.

"Dominic!"

In the act of shrugging on his greatcoat, Dominic swung to meet his brother-in-law's sharp gaze.

Arthur stood in the library doorway. Now he took a step back in clear invitation. "I've some information you might find of interest. If you can spare the time…?"

Even from across the hall Dominic could sense the amusement in the older man's voice. He knew Arthur understood his intentions towards Georgiana. And approved of them. With another shrug, he divested himself once more of his coat and, leaving the heavy garment in Johnson's hands, strolled with as much nonchalance as he could muster past his brother-in-law and into the library.

A delighted chuckle was his reward.

Elegantly disposing his limbs in one of the heavily padded leather chairs, Dominic raised eyes limpid with enquiry to Arthur's face.

Sinking into the chair behind his heavy desk, Arthur met the cool blue glaze with one of unalloyed amusement. "You know, for a man of such vast experience, you're being singularly obtuse in your present campaign."

Dominic's black brows rose haughtily. "Oh?"

"From Georgiana's loss of composure and your own black looks, I assume you've offered for her and been rejected."

From narrowed eyes, Dominic surveyed his brother-in-law. They had always got on well. In truth, there was no one he trusted more. So he dropped his reserve and answered with a languid air, "If you must know, I haven't as yet proposed. I have, however, been refused. Twice."

With an effort that was obvious, Arthur swallowed his laughter. Finally, when he was sure he could command his voice, he said, "Well, that's hardly surprising."

The blue eyes watching him narrowed again. After a pregnant pause Dominic murmured, "Arthur, if you weren't who you are, I rather think I'd take exception to that comment."

Far from being cowed, Arthur only smiled. "I didn't think you'd seen it."

A world-weary expression of dutifully waiting to be informed of what "it" was infused Dominic's countenance.

"Why, the Place, of course."

"The Place?" echoed Dominic, bewildered.

"The Place," repeated Arthur. "You know, it's that little piece of land you've spent half of the last ten years trying to buy."

"But..." Dominic stopped. It came as a shock to realise that desire for the Place, an obsession nursed and fed for years, had simply been forgotten, displaced, rendered unimportant by his desire for Georgiana. In fact he hadn't thought of the Place with a view to gaining possession for weeks. Not since he had met Georgiana. He frowned.

Arthur sat back and watched his friend's face as the pieces fell into place. It wasn't hard to work out the probabilities once the facts had been pointed out. And, despite Dominic's reputation with the ladies, Arthur, remembering the euphoric daydream that had possessed his own sharp wits in the days he had wooed Bella, found nothing odd in the notion that his brother-in-law had completely mislaid his obsession in the whirl of recent weeks.

Eventually Dominic's features relaxed slightly and he glanced up to meet Arthur's grey gaze. "So she thinks I'm marrying her to get my hands on the Place." It was a statement, not a question.

Arthur shrugged. "It's hardly an uncommon event, for men to marry for property. And I doubt she has any idea of the relative value of the Place and your own estates. But I'd go bail Bella's edified her with the tale of your desire for the land." He paused, but Dominic was frowning at the inkstand on the desk. "Has she given you any other reason for her refusal?"

Without looking up, Dominic shook his head slowly. "Not this time. The reason for her first refusal was quite different." He glanced up with a wry grin. "She'd heard the stories of Elaine Changley and had convinced herself I was in love with Elaine."

"And only wanted to marry her for her dowry?"

Dominic looked struck. "She didn't actually say so," he mused, "but I suppose that must have been in her mind. I didn't think further than disabusing her of the idea that I'd ever been truly enamoured of or considered marrying Elaine Changley."

Arthur said nothing.

Then Dominic shook his head. "No, it won't fit. I started paying court to her at the Hattringhams' ball, before any of us knew she owned the Place."

"The masked ball?" said Arthur, tapping one finger against his lips. "I assume she knew you knew who she was, that night."

Dominic shifted in his chair. "No. But I told her I did know later."

"How later?"

Exasperated, Dominic frowned at his brother-in-law. "At the Massinghams' rout."

"*After* our little visit to Lincoln's Inn."

With a long drawn sigh of frustration, Dominic stretched and crossed his arms behind his head. "You're right." He considered the inkstand again. Then he said, as if talking to himself, "So I'll just have to remove that little obstacle from my path."

Perfectly satisfied with the effects of his interference, Arthur leant back in his chair and watched as his brother-in-law planned his next moves. Finally Dominic looked up.

"There are only two more days left to the Season. How long do you plan to remain in Green Street?"

Arthur smiled. "For as long as it takes you to settle this business."

A quick smile lit Dominic's face. "You are coming to Candlewick, aren't you?"

Arthur nodded. "I've already sent instructions for Jonathon and his nurse to travel direct to Candlewick. The weather's closing in and, as you know, I'm not one to take chances. They should be there by now. I'd thought to send Bella down as soon as she's free of her social activities. Mrs Landy can fuss over her more effectively than anyone else. I'll go to the Lodge and check through business there, then come across before Christmas."

To all this, Dominic nodded. "It'll take a day or two to deal with the Place. But once I've cleared that hurdle from my path, I don't expect any further impediment to our affairs." He paused, then added with a slightly grim smile, "I would be obliged if you would inform Miss Hartley that I have some...pressing business to attend to, but will call on her in two days' time to continue our discussion of her future." He considered his words, then shrugged and rose. "With luck, I'll be able to escort both Bella and Georgiana down a few days after that."

"Good," said Arthur. "The news from the country is that there'll be early snows. I'd feel happier once Bella's safely installed at Candlewick." He watched as Dominic crossed to the door, waiting until his fingers were on the handle to say, "By the by, do let me know if you feel the need for any further assistance in this matter."

Dominic smiled sweetly. "My friend, I've often thought it was a good thing for England that you were born an Englishman. God only knows what might have happened if Napoleon and his generals had had you as a quartermaster."

Arthur laughed.

With a neat bow, Dominic left, closing the door softly behind him.

TO GEORGIANA'S DISMAY, relief was not her predominant emotion on waking the next morning to no extravagant gifts, no note requesting her company on a drive, nothing. She sighed. She told herself sternly it was how she wanted things to be. He had at last accepted the fact she would not marry him.

Feeling at one with the gloomy morning, close and grey with drizzle, she dressed without interest and wended her way downstairs, wondering what she could do to fill in the bleak hours.

But she had barely left the breakfast-table to join Bella in the back parlour when Johnson came to summon her.

"A legal gentleman, miss. Name of Whitworth."

Brows rising, Georgiana stood and laid aside her embroidery. "In the drawing-room, Johnson?"

The butler bowed and escorted her to where Mr Whitworth the elder waited patiently, his bright eyes darting curiously about the white and gilt room.

As soon as he had bowed to her, Georgiana waved him to a chair. He looked alarmed when it creaked protestingly under his weight. But Georgiana was too puzzled to waste any time reassuring him. She hadn't sent for him. Why was he here?

Apparently agreeing his presence required immediate

explanation, Mr Whitworth made haste to answer her unvoiced query. "My dear Miss Hartley, forgive my calling on you unheralded, but we have received a very generous offer for the Place. The buyer is most urgent to settle, so I took the liberty of calling in person."

Georgiana's immediate reaction was of immense relief. She would be rid of her albatross of an inheritance. If it hadn't been for the Place, she would not now be subject to the most deadening melancholy. And she would certainly never want to return there, as close as it was to Candlewick. But, hard on the heels of relief, came a swift understanding of what it would mean to Dominic—no! Lord Alton—if she sold the Place to another. A sharp stab of empathy brought an impulsive denial to her lips. But she bit the words back and forced herself to consider more carefully.

Dominic wanted the Place...wanted it so badly that he would even marry to get it. But, although she loved him, he didn't love her. She would not, could not, allow him to sacrifice either himself or her to the misery of a one-sided marriage. But she could give him what he wanted.

Mr Whitworth stirred uneasily, then cleared his throat.

Before he could launch into one of his long-winded discourses, Georgiana held up a small hand, commanding silence.

Only a moment's thought was required to convince her Dominic would not accept the Place as a gift from her. But there was nothing to stop her offering to sell it to him. He had tried to buy it from Charles, after all.

"What were the conditions offered by this buyer? And who is he?"

Mr Whitworth was only too happy to answer Georgiana's first question, naming a sum which meant nothing to her, but which, he assured her ponderously, was, "Very generous. Exceedingly so!"

After a moment, he went on, "But the thing that moved me to come here in this manner, my dear Miss Hartley, is that the buyer wishes an answer by this afternoon."

"This afternoon?" echoed Georgiana. She looked at her solicitor. His excited urgency was apparent in the way he almost bobbed in his chair. "Surely, that's rather unusual?"

Mr Whitworth pursed his lips, and she feared she was about to be told every case of rapid sale he had ever heard of, chapter and verse. But instead his breath came out in a little whoosh. "Well, yes," he admitted. "But whoever has that sort of money to throw down can generally call the tune."

"Who is this buyer?"

"Ah," said Mr Whitworth, eyeing her uneasily. "That's another thing. The man who contacted us is an agent, and he won't reveal the name of his principal."

So she could be selling to anyone. Georgiana made up her mind. "I wish to consult with my friends on this matter. I will undertake to send my answer to you this afternoon."

She rose, in a fever to get on with her latest impulsive start.

As if only too keen for her to put the wheels into motion, Mr Whitworth rose too, and rolled forward to take her hand. "Certainly, Miss Hartley. My brother and I will hold ourselves in readiness to act on your behalf as soon as you have communicated your wishes to us."

With that solemn promise, he bowed low and took his leave.

For some moments Georgiana stood, head bowed, eyes on the patterned rug. Then, resolutely straightening her spine, she crossed the room to the small escritoire. Seating herself before it, she pulled forward a pristine sheet of paper and, after examining the nib carefully, dipped it determinedly into the standish. This wasn't going to be easy, but there really was no alternative.

GEORGIANA'S MISSIVE BROUGHT Dominic to Green Street at noon. As her note had contained little beyond a summons, he used the time while Johnson went in search of her to pace the drawing-room, pondering the possibilities. Avoiding the little tables Bella seemed to have a peculiar penchant for strewing about her rooms, Dominic had arrived for the third time by the fireplace when he heard the door open.

Entering as calmly as she could, Georgiana wished for the tenth time that morning that she did not have to face Dominic—Lord Alton!—over this particular matter. The very thought of the Place rubbed a sore spot in her heart, aggravating its already fragile condition. Thoughts of Lord Alton brought even more pain. But she was determined to go through with it. Unconscious of the worried frown that marred her smooth brow, she pressed her hands together to still their trembling, only to find herself forced, by his outstretched hand, to surrender one into his clasp.

"My lord." Her greeting was little better than a whisper. Pulling herself together with an effort, Georgiana raised her head to look into his eyes, steeling herself for the battle to meet his gaze and remain lucid. To her relief, she found it easier than she had anticipated. He was looking at her with undisguised concern.

"Georgiana, my dear, what's the matter?"

And suddenly it was easy to tell him.

"I've received an offer for the Place. A mystery buyer." She paused, temporarily distracted by the sudden intentness in his gaze, and promptly lost her thread. Luckily her rehearsed phrases came to her rescue. "I remembered how keen you were to buy the property from Charles. I wondered if you still wished to purchase it."

Dominic watched as, gently withdrawing her hand from his, Georgiana subsided into one corner of the sofa, lilac skirts softly sighing, and fixed him with her candid hazel gaze. Outwardly he smiled, warmly, comfortingly. Inwardly he wondered where it was that he had left his usual facility for managing such *affaires de coeur*. He had certainly misplaced it. Ever since Georgiana Hartley had magically appeared in his life, his touch had deserted him. He had told his agent to purchase the Place without revealing his name, purely to spare her any undue embarrassment. Instead, having once again failed to predict her reactions to the events he caused to happen, he had forced her to face the very object he was endeavouring to remove from the relationship.

Capturing her eyes with his, he smiled again. "I'm afraid, my dear, I've a confession to make." He could see from her eyes that she had jumped to the right conclusion, but he confirmed it. "I'm the mystery buyer."

"Oh."

Georgiana's eyes fell. She felt decidedly deflated.

Acutely sensitive where she was concerned, Dominic moved to take her hands in his, and drew her to her feet before him. In his present mood he would not trust himself on the sofa beside her. Standing this close to her, holding her hands so he would not sweep her into his arms, was bad enough, feeling as he did. He looked down on her golden head, bent so he could not see her eyes.

"Georgiana?"

But she would not look up. Her eyes seemed to be fixed on her hands, clasped lightly in his. So, with the patience of one who knew all the moves, Dominic slowly raised her hands, first one, then the other, to his lips. Inevitably, her eyes followed...and were trapped when they met his. He smiled, incapable of entirely hiding his triumph. "Sweetheart, do you know why I want to buy the Place?"

With an effort Georgiana tore her gaze from those fascinating eyes. That blue gaze held untold power over her, giving tantalising glimpses of emotions she did not understand but of which she longed to learn more. But she was returning to Ravello. Forcing a tight smile to her lips, she nodded. "Yes. Bella explained."

"I sincerely doubt Bella could explain." He smiled as she turned to him, hope and uncertainty warring in her big eyes. "Oh, I know Bella told you I've always wanted the Place, to return Candlewick to completeness. That has, in the past, been something of an obsession with me. Recently that obsession has been eclipsed by a far greater desire. It had, in fact, completely slipped my mind. Until..." Dominic paused, then decided to leave Arthur out of his explanation. "Until I realised you might misconstrue my interest in you for an interest in your property."

If the matter hadn't been so intensely important, so vitally crucial to him, he would have been amused by the sheer intensity of her concentration. Her huge hazel eyes glowed with hope, tinged with disbelief. He had expected that and did not let it worry him. He would convince her he loved her if it was the last thing he did in life. Despite his firm intentions, he felt himself drowning in her honey-gold gaze, felt the inevitable effect of her nearness start to test his restraint.

"My love, I want to buy the Place so it can no longer stand as a point of confusion between us." Dominic dropped a kiss on her knuckles and decided he had better get out of the room with all speed. If he didn't, she would be in his arms and he had no idea where it would end. "If you agree, send a message to Whitworth and he'll settle it with my man of business." He paused, looking deep into the darkened centres of her wide eyes. Smiling, he released one of her hands, carrying the other to his lips in a parting salute. "Once the sale is finalised, I'll call on you and we can discuss our... mutual interest further."

His look dared her to deny him, but Georgiana was too dazed to do anything but stare.

With a gentle chuckle, Dominic lifted a finger to her cheek in a fleeting caress, then bowed elegantly and left her.

CHAPTER ELEVEN

THE SHARP CRACK as the wax seal broke beneath Dominic's long fingers echoed hollowly in the library of Alton House. Outside, Grosvenor Square lay somnolent under a blanket of fog. The weather had turned with a vengeance, and all who could were making hurried preparations to quit the capital before the roads became impassable. Hurriedly scanning his agent's letter, Dominic put it aside and spread the folded parchment the packet had contained. In the warmth and comfort of his library, in the glow of expensive wax candles, Dominic stared at the title-deed of the Place, which he had longed to hold for so long. It was his. Candlewick was whole once more.

Conscious of a mild elation on that score, Dominic grinned wryly. Far stronger was the relief that now Georgiana could have no more doubts of his love for her, no more excuses to deny his suit.

His eyes narrowed. The recollection that he had on more than one occasion underestimated her ability to misread his intentions surfaced. For some reason, she seemed unable to believe he truly loved her. Incomprehensible though that was, it would be unwise to ignore that particular foible. First his ex-mistress, then the Place—what would the next obstacle in this particular course be?

Unbidden, laughter bubbled up. He had never had the slightest trouble making offers before, although admittedly for less exalted positions. However, to date, his particular concern had always been to ensure the women involved never imagined him to be in love with them. He had never had to convince a woman of his love before. And here he was, getting his feet in a tangle at every step, no doubt providing Arthur with untold amusement. All in all, wooing an angel was proving the very devil of a task.

With a self-deprecatory smile, he put the title-deed in the top drawer of his desk, locking it with a small key from his watch chain.

There was only one way forward. His mind refused to entertain the thought of any outcome bar success. He did not doubt he would win her in the end. It was his patience he doubted. Still, at least this time he was forewarned. And if, instead, she fell into his arms without raising any more quibbles, he would be doubly grateful.

Imagining how he would express his gratitude to his beloved, he settled his shoulders more comfortably against the leather and fixed his gaze on the ceiling. A smile of anticipation curved his lips.

Ten minutes later his reverie was interrupted by sounds of altercation in his hall. The library door flew open.

Bella entered. Timms followed close behind, trying to retrieve the bonnet she still wore.

"Dominic! Thank God you're here! You'll have to do something. I never imagined she'd do anything so rash!" Succeeding in tugging her bonnet strings free, she paused only to hand her headgear to Timms before impetuously throwing herself at her brother, who had risen and come forward to meet her. Her small hands grasped his arms. "You must go after her!"

"Yes, of course," Dominic replied, gently detaching her before turning her towards the *chaise*. "And I undoubtedly shall, as soon as you have calmed sufficiently to tell me where and why."

His calm, deliberate tones had the desired effect. Bella plumped down on the *chaise* with relief, her bearing losing the frenetic tenseness of a moment before.

"It's just so unexpected. I had no inkling she might do such a thing."

Dominic forced himself to take the seat facing his sister, reminding himself that any attempt to drag stories out of Bella faster than she was prepared to tell them inevitably took longer than allowing her to proceed at her own pace. Relieved to see her colour improving, and assuming from her words that Georgiana was not in any mortal danger, he contented himself with a bland, "What's happened?"

"I didn't know anything about it until I came downstairs half an hour ago. We were at the Ranleighs' last night—such a crowd! The rooms were so stuffy, I was quite worn out, so I slept late." Bella opened her reticule, hunting through its contents. "I found this on the breakfast-table."

Dominic took the single sheet of delicately tinted paper and smoothed it out. As he scanned its contents, his jaw hardened. Undoubtedly, it was past time someone took Georgiana Hartley in hand. The note blithely informed Bella that its writer had decided to ask the tenants of her father's London property whether they had any idea where his missing pictures might be. As she had ascertained that the house was located in Jermyn Street, she did not imagine she would be away long.

"She told me that when she wrote to Mr Whitworth to instruct him to sell the Place she remembered to ask about the London house. Johnson says she received a letter this morning."

"Jermyn Street!" Dominic stood and paced the room, incapable of remaining still. The words, Doesn't she know better? rang in his brain, but he didn't utter them—he knew the answer. There were times when Georgiana Hartley was too much the impulsive innocent for her own good. Over the past ten or more years, Jermyn Street had become the popular address for the well-heeled bachelors of the *ton,* which number included a disproportionate percentage of the most dangerous rakes and roués in England. His gaze returned to Bella's anxious face. "Do you have any idea of the number?"

Bella blushed. Under cover of fossicking in her reticule once more, she explained, "In the circumstances, I thought I should see if I could find the letter from the Whitworths. It was on her dresser." She looked up to hand the plain white envelope to her brother.

Dominic received it with undisguised relief and a fleeting smile for Bella's notions of propriety. "Good girl." Then he was reading the fine legal script. "Seventeen. Who lives at 17 Jermyn Street?"

Bella shook her head, her gaze on her brother's face. He was clearly going through his acquaintance. Then she saw his expression drain.

"Good God!"

Bella paled. "Who is it?"

"Harry Edgcombe."

"Oh, dear." Bella's wide blue gaze had not left her brother's face. Recognising from uncomfortable experience the emotions flaring in his eyes, she suddenly wondered whether she would have done better by Georgiana to have tried to find Arthur, instead of flying to Dominic.

Abruptly Dominic headed for the door. "Wait here until I get back."

Seriously alarmed now, Bella half rose. "Don't you think I should come, too?"

Dominic paused, hand on the door-handle. "It would be best if this was done with as little fuss as possible. I'll bring her back here."

And with that grim promise he was gone, leaving Bella with nothing to do but sink back on the *chaise,* wondering if Georgiana was strong enough to weather both Harry Edgcombe's advances *and* Dominic's temper.

DOMINIC DIDN'T BOTHER with his carriage. As the hackney he'd hired pulled up outside 17 Jermyn Street, he reflected that the anonymity of the hack was an added advantage, distinctly preferable to his carriage with his liveried coachman. Instructing the driver to wait for him, he ascended the three steps to the polished oak door and beat a resounding tattoo. Heaven help Harry if he'd gone too far.

The door was opened by a very correct gentleman's gentleman. Recognising the Viscount, he smiled politely. "I'm afraid his lordship is currently engaged, m'lord."

"I know that. I'm here to disengage him."

And with that the astonished retainer was set firmly aside. Dominic closed the door behind him. His gaze swept the hallway and found Cruickshank, seated in a stiff-backed chair in the shadows. Surprised, she came to her feet.

"Where's your mistress?"

Trained to respond to the voice of authority, Cruickshank immediately bobbed a curtsy. "In the drawing-room, m'lord." With a nod, she indicated the door opposite her chair.

Stripping off his gloves and handing them, together with his cane, to Lord Edgcombe's bemused valet, Dominic said, "I suggest you return to Winsmere House. I will be taking your mistress to meet Lady Winsmere. I would imagine they'll return home in a few hours. Should Lord Winsmere enquire, you may inform him they're in my charge."

Bright blue eyes met faded blue. Cruickshank hesitated, then bobbed again in acquiescence. "Very good, m'lord."

With Lord Edgcombe's valet distracted by Cruickshank's departure, Dominic strolled forward and, after a fractional hesitation, opened the drawing-room door.

The sight which met his eyes would have made him laugh if he hadn't been so angry. Georgiana was seated in a chair by the hearth and had clearly been listening with her customary intentness to one of Harry's tales. He was leaning against the mantelpiece, negligently attired in a green smoking jacket, his pose calculated to impress the viewer with his particular brand of assured arrogance. Despite himself, Dominic's lips twitched. The door shut behind him with a sharp click. Both fair heads turned his way.

While most of his attention was centred on Georgiana, Dominic did not miss the relief which showed fleetingly in Harry's eyes. Relieved in turn of its most urgent worry, his mind went on to register the expression in Georgiana's hazel gaze. Total innocence. Then, as he watched, she blushed deliciously and, flustered, looked away.

Inwardly, Dominic smiled. He did not make the mistake of imagining her sudden consciousness was due to delayed guilt on being discovered in such a compromising situation. Oh, no—*he* was the cause of Georgiana's blushes, not Harry. Which fact compensated at least in part for his agony of the past ten minutes.

An interested spectator to Georgiana's reaction, Harry pushed away from the mantelpiece, a smile of real mirth lighting his face. "Ah, Dominic. I wondered how long you'd be."

Acknowledging this greeting, and the information it contained, by shaking Harry's offered hand, Dominic turned to find Georgiana rising to her feet.

"I had no idea… I wasn't expecting…"

"Me to arrive so soon?" suggested Dominic. He advanced upon his love, capturing one delicate hand and raising it to his lips. "I finished my business rather earlier than I had hoped. I take it you've finished yours?"

Georgiana was completely bemused. The last person she had thought to meet this afternoon was Lord Alton. And none of his words, nor Lord Edgcombe's, seemed to make any sense. Entirely at sea, she simply stared into his lordship's blue eyes, traitorously hoping he would take charge.

"No sign of these paintings, I'm afraid," put in Lord Edgcombe, shaking his head. He added in explanation to Dominic, "Moscombe has been with me since I moved here, and he insists the place was completely empty. Even the attics."

Dominic nodded, and tucked Georgiana's hand into its accustomed place in the crook of his arm. "It was a long shot. Still," he added, blue eyes intent on Harry, "no harm done."

Harry's eyes widened in mock alarm. "None in the least, I assure you." Then a gleam of wicked amusement lit his grey eyes. "Mind you, it did occur to me that Miss Hartley might like to view my art collection."

Dominic's black brows rose. "Your etchings, perhaps?"

Harry grinned. "Just so."

"Etchings?" queried Georgiana.

"Never mind!" said Dominic in the voice of a man goaded. He gazed down into wide hazel eyes and wished they were in his drawing-room rather than Harry's. "Come," he added in gentler tones. "I'll return you to Bella."

Walking beside him to the door, Georgiana struggled to free enough of her mind from its preoccupation with Lord Alton to make sense of what was going on. Emerging into the hall, she looked about for Cruickshank.

"I've sent your maid on." Dominic was beside her, holding her coat.

"Oh," said Georgiana, suddenly aware of a disturbing

glint in his lordship's blue eyes. Did that mean she would be travelling in a closed carriage alone with him?

Settling Georgiana's coat over her shoulders, Dominic cast a sharp glance at their host, standing genially beside them. "Harry...?"

Lord Edgcombe's grey eyes met his over Georgiana's head. A slight frown and a shake of the head was all the immediate response Harry made as Georgiana turned to thank him for his trouble. He charmingly disclaimed all effort, bowing with easy grace over her hand. As he straightened, his eyes intercepted Dominic's blue gaze.

"Not a word, I assure you." The grey eyes glinted, amusement in their depths. "You have my heartfelt thanks. Can you doubt it? Any word from me would cook my own goose, after all."

Reassured but puzzled, Dominic raised his brows in question.

Harry grinned and waved an airy hand. "M'sisters are a mite pressed at the moment, it seems. Can you imagine their joy if they learned of—er—what so recently transpired? Why, it would spell the end to my distinguished career." He fixed Dominic with a winning smile. "No, no, m'lad. Rather you than me."

Walking towards the door ahead of the two men, Georgiana, no longer subject to Viscount Alton's mesmerising gaze, tried to follow the gist of their conversation, to no avail. When she turned in the doorway to bid Lord Edgcombe goodbye, it was to see both men cordially shaking hands. Piqued, feeling that something was going on literally over her head, Georgiana tilted her chin a fraction higher and coolly responded to Lord Edgcombe's farewell.

Turning to the street, she majestically descended the steps, but had barely gained the pavement before Lord Alton's long fingers grasped her elbow. A spurt of anger urged her to shake off his hand, but the memory of that odd glint she had seen in his eye undermined her confidence. Before she had time to do more than register the fact that it was into a hackney rather than one of his own carriages he was helping her, she was inside. He followed her, taking the seat beside her. Immediately the driver whistled up his horse and they moved off.

Georgiana strove to quiet her nerves, aquiver with an unnameable emotion. She kept her eyes on the streetscape while she tried to make sense of events. Why had he come to fetch her? Bella? Impulsively, she turned.

"Is Bella all right?"

His face was a mask. At her question, one black brow rose. "As far as I am aware." After a moment he added, "She's waiting at Alton House."

Alerted by the chilled crispness of his tone, Georgiana eyed him warily. "Did she send you for me?"

Suddenly noticing the tension in his long frame, Georgiana tensed too. But his calmly enunciated, "Yes. She sent me," gave her no clue to the cause of what she suspected was his displeasure.

Irritated by his odd behaviour, Georgiana frowned and asked, "Why?"

"Because, having learned that you had taken yourself off to visit a house in Jermyn Street, which, to one who knows London, means almost certainly to call on a bachelor alone, she needed someone to rescue you."

"But I didn't need rescuing," declared Georgiana, turning to face him more fully. "There was nothing the least wrong."

At his strangled laugh she flushed and went on, "I admit it was a relief to find it was Lord Edgcombe who lives there, but that just made it easier. And I made sure I took Cruickshank with me so I wasn't alone."

"When I entered the house, Cruickshank was in the hall

and you were most definitely alone with Harry." With an effort, Dominic kept his voice even.

Flushing at the censure in his tone, Georgiana swung her gaze to the street. "Yes, but there wasn't… I was in no danger of…" Georgiana broke off. Now she thought it over, she was no longer so sure she hadn't been in danger. There had been a rather disquieting gleam in Lord Edgcombe's grey eyes when she had first arrived. However, the more they had talked, the more she had become convinced he was merely slightly nervous over something. Maybe she had misread the signs. Still, he had done nothing to deserve Lord Alton's suspicions. "Lord Edgcombe was most truly the gentleman."

"I would imagine Harry would always act the gentleman he undoubtedly is," Dominic retorted, asperity colouring his words. "But that doesn't mean he isn't a rake and a gamester, and therefore totally unsuitable as private company for a young lady. Such as yourself."

There was no mistaking the anger in the clipped words. Amazed, her own temper flying, Georgiana turned an incredulous face to him. "But you're a rake and a gamester, too. Why is it safe for me to be alone with you but not with him?"

At her question Dominic closed his eyes in exasperation and thought determinedly about his old nurse, about climbing trees at Candlewick—anything to shut out the urge to sweep her on to his lap and kiss her witless. Safe? She was pushing her luck.

Anger growing at his refusal to answer, Georgiana continued, her long irritation with the oddities of English mores finding sudden outlet. "Why did you send Cruckers away? Surely it's not acceptable for me to be riding in a carriage alone with you?"

Forcibly keeping his eyes shut, Dominic answered, "The

only reason it's acceptable for you to be alone with me is because we're soon to be married." He waited for her "Oh" of understanding. When no sound came, he slowly opened his eyes.

Georgiana was staring at him in total confusion.

Quickly Dominic closed his eyes. She was definitely not safe.

For long minutes Georgiana could do nothing but stare. But the fact that he had his eyes closed made it easier for her to think. He should have received the deed of the Place that morning. Dominic had said he would visit her once the sale was finalised, *to discuss their mutual interest.* She had no idea what he had meant by that. Now that he owned the Place, she could see no reason why he would still want to marry her.

In real perturbation, Georgiana stared at the handsome face, wishing she could read his motives in the even features. Then, like a beacon on a hill, she saw the light. He had gone too far, too publicly, to draw back now. And that old scandal, the one that had started his rakish career, hung like Damocles' sword, forcing him to offer for her or face the censure of the *ton.*

Which meant she would have to deny him again, one last time. And make it convincing.

She knew he did not love her, not as she understood love. He had shown no fiery passion, uttered no impassioned speeches nor indulged in any melodramatic gestures—all components of love as she knew it. The only time he had kissed her, it had been like a magic caress, so light that she could have dreamt it. But she was in love with him. And, because there seemed to be developing a strange conduit of communication between them, one that did not need words, or even gestures, a sensing that relied on something other than the physical, because of this, she would have to end it now. Or he would know.

And that would be even harder to bear.

Despite his wanting to marry her for her property, something she was honest enough to acknowledge was commonplace in his world, she had always felt safe with him. He had never intentionally done anything to cause her grief. If he ever learned she loved him—not gently, as a well bred young lady should, but to distraction—she doubted he would accept a denial of his suit. He would not cause her pain.

Could he be made to understand that loving him as she did, being married to him, knowing he did not love her in the same way, would cause her even greater pain that if she was never to see him again?

His eyes remained shut. Georgiana could not resist the temptation to study his face, memorising each detail, storing the vision in her heart to last her for a lifetime. She saw his eyelids flicker, then slowly rise. Ill prepared to meet his blue gaze, she straightened and turned slightly away, furiously blinking back the tears which suddenly threatened, pressing her hands tightly together to still their trembling.

Dominic took one look at his love, all but quivering with suppressed emotion, and his anger abruptly vanished.

"Georgiana?"

When she made no answer beyond a small wave of her hand, Dominic drew back, giving her the time she needed to compose herself, ruthlessly stilling the instinctive urge to wrap her in his arms and comfort her. He didn't dare touch her. Frustrated beyond measure, he felt an insane desire to laugh, to catch her to him and kiss her worries, whatever they were, away. Her silence screamed the fact that she was still labouring under some delusion sufficient to make her balk at the very mention of marriage. Her forlorn countenance showed he had his work very much ahead of him.

His eyes on her guinea-gold curls, Dominic sighed. He wanted her, and he was tired of the roundabout the prescribed methods of courtship had put them on.

He waited until her breathing became less laboured, until the pulse at the base of her throat beat less tumultuously. Then he tried again. "Georgiana, my dear, what is it?"

Georgiana put up one small hand in a gesture he found both imperious and, in her present state, endearing.

"Please, my lord. You must let me speak." Her voice was low, urgent and breathless.

"Of course, my dear." Dominic managed a politely attentive tone. He made no move to take her hand, but continued to sit beside her, the flounce of her skirt brushing his boots, his head inclined to watch her face. She did not look up at him, but fixed her gaze on her clasped hands, tensed in her lap.

Georgiana drew a shuddering breath at his easy acquiescence. If only he would remain so calm, she might manage to accomplish her task. But he was near, so near. Speak—she had to speak or her resolution would crumble. "My lord, you must believe that I most earnestly value your friendship, and the…the proper feeling that lies behind your wish to marry me." She paused, reaching deep to dredge the remainder of her strength, before continuing, "I am aware—have always been aware—that my ownership of the Place was fundamental to your interest in me. Now that you own the Place, there is no reason for any further talk of marriage between us." Resolutely she swallowed the sob that rose in her throat and hurried on. "I realise that, if I were of the *ton* and chose to continue living in London, our association these past weeks might give rise to awkward conjecture. However, as I intend returning to Ravello shortly, I beg you will not let such considerations sway you."

Beside her, Dominic allowed his brows to rise. A smile, soft and gentle, curved his lips.

Georgiana drew a deep breath. "My lord, I hope you will see that, in the circumstances, there is no reason for you to offer for me. Indeed," she said, struggling to subdue her treacherous tears, "I beg you will not renew your offer."

"Of course not."

The calm words brought Georgiana up short. One moment she was about to dissolve in tears, the next she had turned and her eyes met his. "I beg your pardon?" she asked weakly.

Smiling sympathetically, Dominic said, "My dear, if my offering for you will cause you distress, then of course I'll not do it. I would never knowingly distress you."

The look which accompanied his words warmed Georgiana through and through, despite the total depression which now hung like a cold black pall over her. He was convinced. He was going to make it easy for her. Tremulously, she smiled.

Seeing this evidence that she had pulled back from the brink, Dominic smiled back and possessed himself of one small hand.

Georgiana was so relieved that she only just stopped herself from leaning against him, so close as he was. Her head was spinning. Was it possible to feel so cherished and yet know one was unloved? She wasn't sure. In fact she was no longer sure of any number of things. But thankfully he had taken charge. She was sure he wouldn't press her for further words.

Words, especially from his beloved, were very far from Dominic's mind. He had no intention of giving her the opportunity to refuse him again. It occurred to him that there were other routes to his desired goal. The time had come to consider alternatives—his patience was wearing wafer-thin. On impulse, he raised the hand he held and touched it to his lips, then, yielding to a need he was endeavouring to subdue, turned it and pressed a kiss to her palm. He heard the sharp intake of her breath, and glanced up to smile reassuringly at her.

"My dear, you're overset. I give you my word I'll press you to do nothing unless it is your wish, urge you to nothing beyond what is in your heart to do. Remember that."

Georgiana blushed. As a parting speech, it held a note of promise entirely out of place with its supposed intent.

Dominic watched her confusion grow, turning her eyes a deeper shade, like toffee. Repressing the all but overwhelming urge to kiss her, he reluctantly released her hand, adding in a conversational tone, "It's very likely I'll be out of town for the next few days, but I'll see you before you leave town." It would take a day or two to organise his trap, but he had no intention of letting her escape.

The hack turned into a square and pulled up before an imposing mansion. Within minutes Georgiana was ushered inside to find Bella anxiously waiting.

"DUCKETT? WHAT THE devil are you doing here?"

Slouched in the armchair before the fireplace, Dominic frowned as his head butler, whom he had supposed still at Candlewick, entered the room. Unperturbed by his greeting, Duckett held a long taper to the fire and proceeded to circumnavigate the room, lighting candles as he went.

"Timms is ill, m'lord. You'd given orders to shut up this house, so the lad very properly sent for me."

Dominic snorted. Lad? Timms was all of thirty-five if he was a day. But he was one of Duckett's protégés and, provided he obeyed Duckett's guidelines to the letter, would always be assured of the head butler's protection.

Turning the fragile glass balloon he held so that the candlelight caught and reflected from the golden liquid within, Dominic found himself staring at the glowing colour, the same colour as her eyes. With an effort, he withdrew his gaze and found his head butler engaged in the demeaning task of making up the fire.

"Duckett, I have a problem."

"My lord?"

"A problem with a lady, you understand."

"I understand perfectly, my lord."

"I sincerely doubt it," replied Dominic. He eyed his henchman appraisingly. It wasn't the first time he had unburdened himself to Duckett, and doubtless wouldn't be the last. Duckett had started service as a stableboy with his grandfather. He had rapidly progressed through the ranks, reaching his present position shortly after Dominic had attained his majority. They'd been firm friends forever, it seemed, despite a good twenty years' difference in age.

"I'd value your opinion, Duckett."

"Very good, m'lord." With the fire blazing, Duckett rose and unobtrusively busied himself, straightening books and stacking magazines.

"The situation," said Dominic, "can only be described as delicate. The lady in question is both young and innocent. The crux of the problem is that she has great difficulty in believing herself to be loved."

Dominic waited for some response, but none came. He turned and saw Duckett flicking the dust from a book before replacing it on the shelf.

"Are you listening, Duckett?"

"Naturally, m'lord."

Dominic let his head fall back against the chair. "Very good." Taking a moment to gather his thoughts, he went on, "This being so, the said lady invents the most tortuous reasons to account for my wanting to marry her, and for refusing my suit. The first was that I was in love with a courtesan and intended marrying her. Having convinced her this was untrue, I then found she believed that I wished to marry her in order to gain title to the Place, which she owns. Owned, I should say, because today I bought it from her. The title-deed now resides in my strong-box and has lost all relevance to the proceedings. The last twist in the tale is that she now perceives that I feel I must marry her because, due to the public nature of my pursuit of her, not to do so would leave her open to the usual opprobrium." Dominic paused to take a swig of the fiery liquid in his glass. "You now have the facts, Duckett. I am presently searching for ways and means of removing her to a suitably isolated locale, sufficiently private to allow me to convince her that I do in fact love her while at the same time rendering her opinion on the subject irrelevant."

A slight frown marred Duckett's majestic countenance. "I take it the young lady returns your affections, my lord?"

"The young lady is head over heels in love with me, if you must know."

"Ah," said Duckett, nodding sagely. "Just so."

Dominic eyed his impeccable retainer through narrowed eyes. Duckett's gaze was fixed in the far distance. Then, quite suddenly, a smile quirked at the corners of his mouth.

"What are you thinking of, Duckett?"

The soft question brought Duckett to himself with a start. Then he smiled at his master. "It just occurred to me, m'lord, that now that you own the Place you'd want Jennings and me to put our people through it—to tidy it up, as it were."

Puzzled, Dominic nodded. "Yes, but—"

Duckett held up a restraining hand. "That being so, m'lord, I dare say there'll be personal belongings—things to do with the Hartleys—that we'd need to know what to do with. And, I should warn you, old Ben says the snows are no more than a few days away."

Dominic's eyes, vacant, remained trained on his butler's face as the grandfather clock in the corner ticked on. Then, to Duckett's relief, the blue gaze focused. Dominic smiled wickedly. "Duckett, prince of butlers, you're a rascal. I'd be shocked, if I weren't so grateful. No wonder I pay you so well." Struggling upright, Dominic drained his glass and handed it to the waiting Duckett. "We'll set out at first light."

"Very good, m'lord," replied Duckett.

CHAPTER TWELVE

BEING TRULY ALONE again was worse than Georgiana had expected. Bella's brother had come to fill a void in her heart she hadn't even known existed. Until he was gone.

Idly plying her needle over the slippers she intended leaving as a parting gift to Arthur, Georgiana stifled a despondent sigh. The day outside was dull and grey, but no more dismal than the state of her heart. Bella, reclining on the *chaise* in the middle of the room, flicking through the latest *Ladies' Journal,* seemed almost as subdued as she. But, in her friend's case, there was a peacefulness in her quiet which Georgiana, in her tortured state, could only envy.

The Season had come to an end two days before. During the last ball, at Lady Matcham's, there had been much talk of country visits and plans for the annual festivities. Georgiana had listened and tried to summon an enthusiasm she could not feel. To her, the future looked cold and bleak. She waited for Arthur's decision on when they would leave Green Street, Bella and he bound for Candlewick, she for the Continent. He had asked her if she would stay until his business in London was completed, to keep Bella company. Naturally, she could not possibly refuse such a request. Particularly now that Lord Alton had left London.

He had sent a short note to Bella, simply informing her he had business in the country and would welcome her to Candlewick whenever she chose to quit town.

There had been no word to Bella's protégée.

Casting another glance at Bella, Georgiana couldn't help feeling guilty that she had not been able to satisfy her friend's ambition, and, worse, would not be returning to London to continue their friendship. Arthur would have to find some other distraction for his wife next Season. Georgiana knew she would never return. She would never be able to face Lord Alton's bride. He would eventually marry—an inescapable fate for one such as he. Already she felt a potent jealousy for the beautiful woman who would be his wife. Feeling despair weigh heavily on her shoulders, she forced away her unhappy thoughts and bent over her embroidery.

The door opened.

"A note for you, miss."

Frowning, Georgiana reached for the white rectangle on Johnson's salver, images of Charles and Lord Ellsmere in her mind. But one glance at the strong script emblazoned across the white parchment dispelled those weaker images, replacing them with a handsome, dark-featured face with warm blue eyes.

With the unnerving sensation of having her heart in her throat, Georgiana nodded a dismissal to Johnson and broke open the seal.

"What is it?" asked Bella, struggling to sit up.

Slowly Georgiana scanned the single sheet. Then, absentmindedly, she said, "Your brother wants me to go down to the Place. His people want to know what to do with the furniture and so on."

Bella, now sitting, nodded. "Yes, of course. You must tell them whether you want anything set aside."

"But I don't think there could possibly be anything I would want—" Georgiana began.

"You can't tell that," said Bella seriously. "Who knows?

They might even stumble across those paintings of your father's."

Bella put her head on one side, the better to view her friend. To her mind, something was not entirely right between Georgiana and Dominic. Why on earth Georgie should fall into such a lethargy just because Dominic repaired to the country for a few days she could not imagine. As she saw it, it was only to be expected that her brother would want to see his affairs at Candlewick organised before he took his intended bride down for a prolonged stay. Despite the fact Dominic had apparently not as yet proposed, Bella was quite sure he would and that Georgiana's plans for removal to Italy would never be realised. She knew her brother well enough to be certain he would view any interference with his schemes in a dim light. But, in this case, her confidence in the eventual outcome was supreme. Consequently, she was waiting with perfect equanimity for the time to come for them to leave for Candlewick.

"When are you to go?" Bella asked.

"He says he'll come and fetch me tomorrow," answered Georgiana, still struggling with conflicting emotions. The note was little more than a polite summons, its wording leaving no room for manoeuvre and even less for escape. Lord Alton would give himself the pleasure of fetching Miss Hartley at ten the next morning. He would undertake to return her to town that evening.

"Perhaps I should come down with you," Bella suggested. "There's nothing to keep me here, and I would like to see Jonathon."

Georgiana readily agreed. In her present state, spending two hours and more in a closed carriage alone with Lord Alton was an undertaking too unnerving even to contemplate.

But when the subject was broached with Arthur that evening he surprised them both by vetoing his wife's part in it.

"I'm afraid, my dear, that I would prefer you to remain in London for the next day or two. As Dominic plans to bring Georgiana back the same day, I really don't think you should leave Green Street just yet."

Put like that, it was impossible to argue the point.

Georgiana retired for the night, trying in vain to quell the entirely inappropriate leaping of her heart whenever she thought of the morrow. All was at an end between Lord Alton and herself. Why, then, did anticipation run in tantalising shivers down every nerve?

PRECISELY AT TEN the next morning, Lord Alton's travelling chaise pulled up outside Winsmere House. Strolling unannounced into his sister's back parlour, Dominic could not repress a smile at the picture that met his eyes. On the window-seat, his beloved sat, perfectly ready, fingers nervously twisting in the ribbons of her bonnet. Her gaze was fixed on the garden, a dull prospect beyond the glass.

His sister lay on the *chaise,* staring at the ceiling, a slight frown puckering her brows. It was she who first saw him.

"Oh!"

With that exclamation Bella sat up, putting up a hand to straighten the wisp of lace she had started experimenting with atop her dark curls. Dominic held out a hand to assist her to right herself, bending to drop an affectionate kiss on her cheek. Then he stood back and eyed her headgear.

Bella held her breath.

After a moment, Dominic's brows rose. "Has Arthur seen that yet?"

"No," said Bella.

"In that case, I suggest you burn it before he does."

"Oh!" Spots of colour flew in Bella's cheeks, eliciting

a chuckle from her unrepentant brother. "If you've a mind to be disagreeable, I'll leave you," she replied haughtily.

But Dominic only smiled. "Don't trouble yourself. It's I who am about to leave you. If Miss Hartley is ready?"

Finding herself the object of his calm blue gaze, Georgiana nodded and rose. Within a matter of minutes her cloak had been gently placed about her shoulders and she was settled in the luxury of his carriage, a warm brick at her feet, a soft rug wrapped protectively about her knees.

Taking his seat beside her, and giving the order to start, Dominic turned and smiled. "The journey should not be too tedious, I hope."

At his smile, all Georgiana's fears dissolved. She smiled back.

They preserved a comfortable silence as the coach wended its way through the crowded streets. Once the outskirts of town were reached, and the power of the four horses began to make itself felt, Dominic turned to Georgiana. "Have you heard of Prinny's latest start?"

She hadn't, of course. Without effort, he entertained her with stories of the *ton* and other suitable anecdotes, until she had relaxed enough to ask some questions of her own. These, not surprisingly, were focused on the Place. Perfectly content with the topic, Dominic described the actual land attached to the Place, and how it related to his own far-flung acres.

"So, you see, the Place all but cuts my holdings in two, at least in that area. It has meant that my people constantly have to route all their movements around the Place, often tripling distances. Aside from being purely a nuisance, it has in recent years become an eyesore—a blot on the landscape. It's been irritating to me, as much as to my farmers, to see good land go to ruin."

Georgiana nodded, the memory of the Place as she had last seen it vivid in her mind.

Dominic paused to glance once more out of the window. The one subject he was most assiduously avoiding was the weather. He had ensured that Georgiana was seated on the left on the carriage, so her gaze, should it wander, dwelt only on the relatively clear skies to the west. On his side the eastern horizon was obscured by slate-grey clouds of the peculiar quality which, to one country-bred, denoted but one outcome. Snow. By nightfall.

The temperature was starting to fall precipitate, even though it wanted half an hour to noon. He did not think Georgiana would notice, wrapped up as she was. Still, it wouldn't do to become too complacent on that score. With a wicked grin, he turned to her once more, his brain making a rapid inventory of the latest *on dits,* selecting those suitable for his purpose.

By his order, the coach took them direct to the Place. It was well after noon when he alighted and handed Georgiana down. His steward, Jennings, and Duckett were there to meet them.

"I'll leave you with Duckett, my dear," Dominic said. "I'll be with Jennings if you need me."

Recognising Duckett, Georgiana was relieved to have his comforting presence beside her as she walked the old rooms of the Place. There was no piece of furniture she remembered with any particular affection. When appealed to, Duckett suggested the vicar's wife, who managed the local charity, and promised to convey the furniture to her.

"There's just one more matter, miss," said Duckett, pausing at the top of the stairs.

Dominic, having finished his instructions to Jennings, approving the steward's suggestion that the Place be made over as a single unit into a farm, came to stand at the foot of the stairs. Spying Georgiana and Duckett in the shadows at their head, he ran lightly up to join them.

"I was just telling Miss Hartley, m'lord, that when our people went through the attics they found one of them sealed up. An old cupboard had been moved across the door. Took three men to shift it. Then it was a struggle to force the door—looked to have been left locked for years. The room inside seems to have been used for painting—bits of rag and dabs of paint all over. There were lots of old paintings stacked by the walls. We didn't know what to do with them, so we left it until you came. Would you care to take a look, miss?"

Her father's paintings? His studio at the Place? Georgiana simply stared at Duckett.

Correctly gauging his love's reaction, Dominic took her hand and drew it through his arm. "Lead the way, Duckett."

Escorted in Duckett's wake, Georgiana drew a deep breath. "Oh, Dominic! If only…"

He glanced down, smiling, inordinately pleased to hear his name on her lips. "Patience. A moment and we'll see."

He helped her up the narrow stairs to the low-ceilinged attics. A white patch on one wall of the first room showed where the old cupboard had been. Now the concealed door stood ajar.

Duckett pushed it open and stood aside to allow Georgiana to enter. Dominic released her and, when she hesitated, gave her an encouraging nudge.

Dazed, she stepped over the threshold, lifting her skirts free of the dusty floor. There was little doubt this had been her father's eyrie. Long windows all but filled the outer wall. Now half covered with creeper, clear, they would have allowed light to flood the large room. An easel stood in the middle of the floor, empty; a paint-stained rag hung on a nail at one corner. Georgiana gazed about. The odd smell of old paints was still detectable, wafting like a ghost about the room.

For one instant, reminded so vividly of the life that had been, she felt the past threaten to engulf her. She struggled to keep back the tears. Then she heard a soft movement behind her and Dominic was there, his hands closing gently on her upper arms, comforting by his touch, by his solid warmth so close behind her. Like an anchor, he held her in the present, defying the past to claim her.

Georgiana drew a deep breath. Calm once more, she put up a hand to touch one of his. Her gaze fell on the canvases, stacked against the side-wall. She moved to touch them and he released her immediately, following her across the floor.

Without words, they set about the task of examining her father's last legacy.

Most of the portraits were of adolescent youths. After a pensive moment, staring at one of a gentle-eyed young man with reddish tints in his hair, Dominic grinned. "Ah! Now I understand."

Patiently Georgiana waited to be educated.

Dominic's smile warned her. "Your father was clearly an astute man. He wanted to leave you something which was sure to retain its value, regardless of the vacillations of fashion. So he left you these." Still Georgiana waited. Displaying the canvas in his hand, Dominic said, "This one's William Grenville as a young man." When Georgiana still looked blank he explained, "Grenville was one of our recent Prime Ministers. His family will pay a small fortune for this. And," he continued, replacing the portrait and picking up another, "unless I miss my guess, this one is Spencer Perceval, another Prime Minister. That one," he said, pointing to another study of an earnest young man, "could be Castlereagh, though I'm not certain." He bent again to flick through the portraits.

There were sixteen in the series, and Dominic could put a name to nine and guess at the others. But the three portraits at the bottom of the pile, once they were uncovered, claimed his and Georgiana's complete attention.

The first was of a young woman, with a sweet face crowned by masses of brown hair. Her eyes, startlingly clear hazel, shone out of the canvas, bright and clear. It was the portrait of Georgiana's mother.

Leaving Georgiana to gaze on her mother's face, Dominic pulled the next from the pile. A young baby rolled playfully on the grass beside the same woman. A gentle smile, full of love, curved the woman's fine lips.

Wordlessly offering this picture to Georgiana, Dominic reached for the last. This showed a young girl, of six or so summers, long golden hair hanging in plaits down her back, honey-gold eyes alight with mischief. A dusting of freckles was scattered across the bridge of her pert nose. Dominic smiled. Turning to Georgiana, he put one finger under her chin and turned her face towards him. After a careful examination, which ignored her brimming eyes, he stated, "You've lost your freckles."

Georgiana smiled tremulously, recognising his attempt to lighten her mood and grateful for it.

Dominic smiled back and released her, gently flicking her cheek with his finger. He glanced about them. "Now that this room has been opened again, I rather think these pictures should be removed from here."

Georgiana looked blank.

"Shall I get Duckett to pack them up and take them to Candlewick? You can decide what to do with them later."

Still dazed by their discoveries, Georgiana nodded her agreement. Duckett began to move about her, carefully stacking the paintings into smaller piles to be carried downstairs by his minions.

"And now," Dominic said, coming once more to stand beside her, "you must be famished. I'll take you to Candlewick, and Mrs Landy can feed us."

Quite forgetting the long trip back to London, Georgiana, happiness filling her heart, and enjoying the novelty of having someone to share it with, allowed herself to be escorted downstairs and into the carriage.

Mrs Landy had a meal waiting. She scolded Dominic for keeping Georgiana so long in the cold, causing Georgiana's brow to rise. But Dominic only laughed.

When they had eaten, he left her in Mrs Landy's care while he went out to talk with his bailiff.

It wasn't until, over tea and scones in the housekeeper's rooms, she noticed the day drawing in that Georgiana started to become uneasy. As the hour dragged by and Dominic did not return, her sense of premonition grew.

The light had faded to a premature dusk when he finally appeared. He came into the drawing-room, where she had retreated, stamping his feet to restore the circulation. He crossed to the fire and bent to warm his hands. Straightening, he smiled at her reassuringly, but his words dispelled the effect. "I'm afraid, my dear, that we won't be able to return to town tonight. The weather's turned nasty and the roads are freezing. There's snow on the way, and I doubt we'd make the Great North Road before we were stuck in a drift."

At the sight of his satisfied smile, Georgiana's eyes grew round. He'd planned this, she was sure. But why, for heaven's sake?

But her host gave her no opportunity to ponder that vital question. He challenged her to a game of chess, to which she had admitted fair knowledge, and, by the time Georgiana had conceded her king, Mrs Landy was at the door, smiling and waiting to take her to her room to freshen up before dinner. The clouds of worried questions that flitted through Georgiana's mind seemed ridiculous when faced with the solid respectability of that worthy dame.

A sense of unreality hung over her during dinner, eaten in the large dining-room. The huge table, which Mrs Landy had informed her could seat fifty, had thankfully had all its leaves taken out, rendering it a suitable size for household dining. She was seated on Dominic's right, and so attentive was her host that she had no time to question the propriety of the proceedings. The food was delicious, and the wine Dominic allowed Duckett to supply her with was cool and sweet. A discussion of the portraits her father had left her occupied much of their time, until, with the removal of the last course, Dominic pushed back his chair and rose, waving Duckett aside and coming to assist her to her feet. "Come. We'll be more comfortable in the drawing-room."

The presence of Duckett behind her chair had soothed her troublesome conscience, pricking with half-understood suspicion. Now, as the drawing-room door closed and she realised he was no longer in the room with them, her jitters woke afresh. Her nervousness spiralling upwards, she crossed the room towards the *chaise* angled before the big fireplace, conscious that he followed close behind.

"Georgiana."

The single word, uttered in the most compelling of tones, stopped her before the marble hearth. Recognising the futility of attempting evasion, Georgiana turned slowly to meet him. He was closer than she had realised. She found herself enfolded in his arms, like delicate porcelain. Looking up, she felt her eyelids automatically drop as his head lowered to hers and he kissed her, so gently that the caress captivated her senses. This time, the kiss did not end, but went on to steal her breath, and her wits. Her nervousness disappeared, chased away by the warm glow of desire which spread insidiously through her veins. In response to some inner prompting, she slipped her arms free of his hold and twined them about his neck. His lips firmed against hers, until she parted her lips in welcome and, by imperceptible degrees, the kiss deepened.

Suddenly her mind, all alive to every incoming sensation, registered the restraint in his body, the tightness in the muscles holding her so gently, the iron control which stopped him from crushing her to him. She moved closer, letting her body press, soft but firm, against his.

Dominic stiffened with the effort to hold his passions in check. He raised his head to look down into her face. In surprise, he viewed hazel eyes smoky with desire, lips parted slightly in flagrant temptation. The siren he had glimpsed in the Massinghams' library stood within the circle of his arms, her body pliant against his. And it was all he could do to draw breath and, his voice husky, demand, "Marry me, Georgiana."

His words slowly penetrated the fog of desire which swirled through Georgiana's mind. They made no sense. Nothing made any sense any more. He had the Place. This wasn't supposed to be happening. Georgiana ignored his talk and, instead, tightened her hold on him, forcing his lips back to hers.

With a groan, Dominic recognised her state. But he was powerless to resist her blatant demands. His lips closed on hers and he tried very hard to think of other things—anything other than the slim form snuggling so invitingly against him. His plan of gentle wooing had not taken into account the possibility of such responses on her part. In the dim hope that her mind would return presently if he kept their lovemaking in a frustratingly light vein, he rained gentle kisses on her lips and face, ignoring her attempts to ensnare him in a deeper caress.

Gradually her flaring passion abated somewhat—enough, at least, for him to try again.

"Georgiana?"

"Mmm." She moved seductively against him, and he caught his breath.

"Marry me, love. Say yes. Now."

"Y… What?" Abruptly Georgiana's eyes focused. Slowly her mind followed. Then, still dazed, she shook her head.

To her amazement, she found herself looking up into eyes darkened with desire but lit by underlying sparks of anger.

"I do hope, my love, that you are not going to tell me you won't marry me."

The clipped accents sobered her. The warmth of his arms still surrounded her, making it difficult to think. Her hands on his shoulders, Georgiana tried to ease from his embrace, only to find the arms holding her so gently were, in fact, made of steel. "I can't think," she murmured protestingly.

"Don't think," came his voice, so close that his breath caressed her cheek. "Just say yes."

Again she shook her head, not daring to meet his eyes. Unequal to this battle, she leant her forehead against his shoulder. She felt his arms come up to draw her closer against him, his solid warmth comforting rather than threatening. Ridiculous, she thought, to feel so wholly at peace in the arms of a man who did not love her.

"Why?"

The question drifted softly, a murmur in her mind.

"Because you don't love me." She answered aloud without realising it.

"What?"

Abruptly he held her from him, staring at her in stunned disbelief. His eyes searched her face, then his lips twitched.

Closing his eyes in exasperation, Dominic drew her head back until it was once again pillowed on his shoulder.

Georgiana snuggled against him, still dazed from his kisses, still wanting more, but not, at this juncture, daring to tempt him further. His insistence on marriage baffled her. Her own responses confused her even more. How wanton she became, with him.

Dominic waited until he had regained some measure of control over his reeling senses before asking, in a perfectly amiable tone, "Do you think, my love, you could explain to me why you think I don't love you?"

The effort required to return their interaction to an acceptable footing was entirely beyond Georgiana. She contemplated attempting to retreat without explaining herself, but doubted she had the strength to win free of his arms, let alone his presence. So when his lips found her ear and nuzzled gently, inviting her confidence, she sighed and said, "You don't really love me, you only say you do. I saw you kiss Lady Changley once. You never kiss me like that."

Put into words, it did not sound particularly rational, but it was the best she could do, with him so close.

Silence greeted her revelation. After a moment she glanced up to find him regarding her, an odd expression in his eyes.

"Do you mean to say that *that* is why you've held me off for so long? Because I *didn't* kiss you the way I did Lady Changley?"

His voice sounded strangled. Georgiana looked up at him in concern. When she neglected to answer, he shook her slightly. She nodded.

A groan rewarded her honesty. "Georgiana!"

Then she was swept into his arms and ruthlessly kissed, passionately kissed, until her legs collapsed under her and she had to cling to him for support. And still the kiss went on, demanding, commanding and utterly devastating. When at long last she was allowed to emerge, she was shaken to the very depths of her being.

"Oh!"

It was all she could say. She looked up at him, love, joy and wonder dancing in the golden flames of her eyes.

With a wordless groan, Dominic crushed her to him once more, burying his face in her silken curls.

"But why?" asked a dazzled Georgiana. "Dominic, why didn't you kiss me like that before?"

To her amazement, she felt his shoulders shake.

Dominic could contain his laughter no longer. And, although his love struggled in his embrace, he held her tightly until he felt rather less crazed and more capable of answering her sanely. Only then did he ease his hold enough to allow her to look up into his face.

Reassured at seeing her own love reflected in his blue eyes—eyes which held warmth and gentle affection as well as the passion she had not recognised before—Georgiana smiled and waited patiently.

Drawing a deep breath, Dominic sought for words to explain how her innocence had tripped him up yet again. "I was most careful, I'll have you know, not to expose you to my desire, because my sweetest love, it is generally held that innocent young ladies are not—er—sufficiently robust to withstand such raw passions."

The incredulous widening of his love's innocent stare nearly had him in stitches again.

"Aren't I supposed to like…? No, that can't be true."

Dominic was nuzzling her ear again. "I assure you it is," he murmured. "If I'd kissed any of the gentle debs as I've just kissed you, seven out of ten would faint dead away and the other three would have had the vapours."

Georgiana giggled.

Then she felt the arms around her shift slightly and one strong hand found her chin, tilting it up so that he could gaze into her eyes, his own burning again with the dark lights she now understood. A sensuous shiver ran through her.

A slow and infinitely wicked smile curved Dominic's lips. When he spoke, his voice was husky and deep. "Enough of the rest of this crazy world. Come, let me see if I can convince you of just how irrevocably I love you."

His lips closed over hers, and Georgiana, swept away on a tide of passion, gave herself up wholeheartedly to that enterprise.

"Ahem!"

The discreet cough from the doorway brought Dominic's head up. "What the devil?" Frowning direfully, he turned his head and located the intruder. "Duckett?"

At the door, Duckett stood correctly to attention, his gaze fixed on the far wall. "I'm sorry to interrupt, m'lord, but I thought you'd want to know that Lady Winsmere has just arrived."

"Bella?" Dominic's incredulous question hung quivering in the air, but Duckett had already gone, leaving the door ajar.

Brows flying in disbelief, Dominic looked down at the woman still held securely in his arms. "I suppose we'd better go and see what your chaperon has to say."

Georgiana smiled. "I wonder why she's come."

"Precisely my question. We'd better ask her." Keeping Georgiana within the circle of his arm, Dominic strolled to the door.

In the doorway, they paused to take in the scene. Only one of the large double doors was open, with one of the footmen standing in its protection with a branch of candles, trying to cast some light on to the steps outside. Blasts of cold air hurled into the hall, bringing swirls of snowflakes to flutter and melt on the tiles. On the porch a carpet of snow, already some inches thick, bore witness to the intensity of the storm outside. As Georgiana and Dominic watched, two footmen emerged from the darkness, bearing Bella between them. Duckett followed immediately behind, the shoulders of his dark coat already dusted with snow.

As soon as everyone was inside, the footmen slammed the door shut against the elemental fury ravaging the night.

Immediately her feet hit the floor, Bella glanced about. Her eyes found Georgiana and Dominic, side by side in the drawing-room doorway. "There you are! Really, Georgie, you're going to have to be more careful!" She bustled up and embraced Georgiana before turning a censorious look on her brother. "And you, of all people, should have known better!"

Intrigued, Dominic allowed one brow to quirk upward. Holding the door wide, he bowed slightly, ushering both Bella and Georgiana into the drawing-room. He closed the door firmly.

"Now, Bella, cut line. What on earth made you leave Green Street in this hoydenish fashion?"

In response to her brother's crisp question, Bella simply stared.

"*Hoydenish?* Dominic Ridgeley! To call me hoydenish when you've all but compromised Georgiana by unthinkingly bringing her here when you might have guessed the snows were coming on. Why, if I hadn't set out as soon as the first snowflake fell, she'd have had to spend the night here with you unchaperoned. I would have thought with all your experience you would have seen the danger as well as I."

"Precisely."

The exasperated tone brought Bella's eyes to his face.

Her confidence faltered. "You knew..." Bewildered, she glanced from Dominic's face to Georgiana's, then back again. "I don't understand."

Dominic sighed. "Before your arrival interrupted us, Georgiana and I were examining a number of the reasons for our impending marriage. As my affianced wife, she most definitely does not need the services of a chaperon when with me."

"Oh." Bella looked at Georgiana, but her protégée was watching Dominic, a strange little smile on her lips.

Dominic, meanwhile, had crossed to the bell-pull. "Yes. *Oh!* And, what's more, you'll have brought your husband out in these foul conditions—"

"But Arthur doesn't know," Bella interrupted to assure him.

"Most assuredly Arthur didn't know when you left Green Street. However, he will certainly have found out long since and be close behind you. Talking about people who should know better, dear sister, in your condition you have no business to go gallivanting around the country in snowstorms."

Bella gasped. "My condition? Whatever do you—?"

"My lord?"

Dominic turned to the door. "Ah, Mrs Landy."

But before he could give any orders, there came again the sound of the great front doors opening. Voices, all masculine, were heard in the hall.

Bella put a hand to her lips.

Dominic glanced at her but said nothing, his attention returning to the door.

Arthur walked in. One glance was sufficient for everyone to see he was displeased. He nodded a wordless greeting to his brother-in-law, then fixed his wife with a stern eye. "Bella, what's the meaning of this?"

Small hands fluttering, Bella went quickly to his side. "Arthur, you're frozen." When her husband's gaze did not waver, she hurriedly explained, "But really, you must see. If I hadn't come, Georgiana would have been alone here with Dominic."

"My dear, your brother is perfectly capable of managing his own affairs. You're my affair, and I cannot condone your careering across the countryside in this fashion. Not in your condition."

For the second time that evening, Bella was struck dumb.

Before she could recover her wits, Dominic smoothly intervened. "I suggest you let Mrs Landy take you upstairs, Bella. You should get to bed immediately."

"Quite so," agreed Arthur, turning to nod to Mrs Landy, still standing by the door. "My lady is expecting and needs to rest."

Abruptly Bella found her voice. "Whatever do you mean? I'm not—"

"Yes, you are!" said two male voices in emphatic unison.

Bella blinked. Then, as the truth dawned, she smiled beatifically. "Oh," she said.

"Arthur," pleaded Dominic, in a tone of desperation, "take her away. Please?"

Arthur smiled.

Mrs Landy took her cue and bustled forward. "Now if you'll just come along, Miss Bella, we'll get you nicely settled…"

Within a minute, an unresisting Bella had been borne away.

"I'm sure Duckett can organise some dinner for you," said Dominic to Arthur.

Arthur nodded. "If you don't mind, I'll take a tray upstairs with Bella. But first I think I'll go and find some of that excellent brandy you keep in your library." The shrewd grey gaze came to rest on Georgiana's face. "I'm glad to see you've come to your senses, Georgiana. You belong here, my dear." With a smile and a nod to each of them, he left.

"Now where were we?" asked Dominic, as he came to stand once more in front of Georgiana and drew her back into his arms.

Georgiana stared up into his face, her eyes alight with love and laughter. "Did you really plan to compromise me?"

From under heavy lids, Dominic's blue eyes watched her. He smiled, slowly, knowing what it did to her. "Mm-hm," he assented, nodding solemnly. "After all, you did beg me not to offer for you. If I couldn't get you to agree any other way, then I was quite prepared to compromise you shamelessly."

Returning the smile, his golden angel turned into a golden siren and wound her arms about his neck. "Shamelessly?"

It was the last word Georgiana uttered for quite some time. A log crashing into the stillness of the room finally broke the spell that held them. Dominic raised his head and glanced around to make sure the log had not rolled from the hearth. Turning back, he surprised an impish smile on his love's face. One dark brow rose in question.

Georgiana saw it. She hesitated, then, her smile broadening, she explained, "I was remembering the first time I saw the Fragonard." She inclined her head in the direction of the masterpiece above the fireplace. "I wondered then what sort of man would hang such a painting in such a place."

A rakish smile lit his face. "The same sort of man who has two other Fragonards."

Her golden eyes begged the invitation.

"Would you like to see the other two?"

"Mm-hm," Georgiana murmured, one tiny fingertip tracing the line of his jaw. "Where are they?"

"Upstairs," Dominic said, in between dropping tantalising little kisses along her lips. "In the master bedroom."

"Ah," said Georgiana, far more interested in his kisses than in any painting. After a moment she moved closer and asked, "Does that matter?"

With mock-seriousness, Dominic considered the point. One brow rose sternly. "It occurs to me, my love, that, as you have yet to formally accept my offer, such an excursion would be highly improper."

Georgiana smiled, letting her fingertip wander to trace the line of his lips. She glanced up at him through her lashes. "And if I were to accept your offer?"

The blue eyes gleamed. "That, of course, would cast an entirely different light on the matter."

Their gazes locked. For one moment, all was still. Then a slow smile twisted Dominic's lips.

"Georgiana, my love, will you marry me?"

Her face alight, Georgiana squealed as his arms tightened about her. "Yes!" she said, laughing. Then, as his head bent to hers, "Oh, yes."

Much later, curled on his lap, warm and secure and pleasantly intoxicated, Georgiana recalled the paintings. She looked into his face. His eyes were closed, but as she watched they opened. One brow rose in query.

Suddenly shy, she dropped her gaze to where her fingers played in the folds of his cravat. "Will you take me to see the Fragonards?"

As a deep chuckle rumbled through his chest, she blushed vividly. But when she glanced again into his face, his expression was perfectly serious.

"Maybe you should see them. Just so you know what kind of man you're marrying."

His lips twisted into a smile that held a gentle promise. The glow in his eyes thrilled her to the core. Feeling suddenly light-headed, her heart thundering, Georgiana managed to nod her agreement.

A few minutes later they left the drawing-room with some semblance of normality and started up the stairs, Georgiana going ahead. On the landing they met Duckett, on his way down. As he drew abreast of his butler, Dominic paused to murmur, *sotto voce,* "Just remember, Duckett, this is all your fault."

Duckett's rigidly correct demeanour did not alter. He inclined his head. "Very good, m'lord."

Duckett continued down the stairs, pausing at their foot to listen to the soft murmur of lovers' voices, cut off by the closing of a door overhead.

Then he smiled. "Very good, m'lord."

* * * * *

Also available from Michelle Willingham and Harlequin Historical and Harlequin Historical Undone! ebooks

Warriors of Ireland
(linked to *The MacEgan Brothers*)

Warrior of Ice

Forbidden Vikings

To Sin with a Viking
To Tempt a Viking

The MacKinloch Clan

Claimed by the Highland Warrior
Seduced by Her Highland Warrior
Tempted by the Highland Warrior
Craving the Highlander's Touch

And coming soon

Warrior of Fire

THE ACCIDENTAL PRINCESS

Michelle Willingham

To Elizabeth, my own special princess.

Acknowledgments

I'd like to thank the library staff of the Mariner's Museum in Newport News, Virginia, for their invaluable help in researching the interior of a steamship. In particular, thanks to library researcher Bill Edwards-Bodmer, who guided me in choosing the best steamship to use as a model for my own ship. I had a great time poring over old photographs, and I was very inspired by the luxurious interiors of these historic vessels.

CHAPTER ONE

London, 1855

SHE COULD FEEL his eyes watching her from across the room. Like an invisible protector, warning away anyone who would bother her. Lady Hannah Chesterfield smiled at one of the ballroom guests, but she hadn't heard a word the woman had said. Instead, she was all too aware of Lieutenant Thorpe's gaze and the forbidden nature of his thoughts.

Though she'd only met him a few weeks ago, she hadn't forgotten his intensity. Nor the way he'd stared at her like a delectable sweet he wanted but couldn't have.

He'd brushed his lips upon the back of her hand when her brother had introduced them. The unexpected kiss had made her skin flush, awakening the strange desire to move closer to him. He looked as though he wanted to kiss every inch of her, and the thought made her body tremble. His interest had been undeniable.

It was nearing midnight, the hour of secret liaisons. More than a few ladies had disappeared into the garden with a companion, only to return with twigs in their hair and swollen lips.

Hannah wondered what it would be like to indulge in such wickedness, feeling a man's mouth against her lips, his hands touching her the way a lover would. There was something about the Lieutenant that was dangerous. Unpredictable. He didn't belong here among London's elite, and yet he fascinated her.

She risked a glance and saw him leaning against the back wall, a glass of lemonade in one hand. His black tail-coat was too snug across his broad shoulders, as though he couldn't afford one that fit. His matching waistcoat accentuated his lean form, while the white cravat he wore had a careless tilt to it. His dark hair was too long, and he was clean-shaven, unlike the current fashion.

His mouth gave a slight lift, as though daring her to come and speak to him. She couldn't possibly do such a thing.

Why was he here tonight? It wasn't as if Lieutenant Thorpe could seek a wife from among the ladies. He might be an officer, but he did not possess a title. Furthermore, if it weren't for his unlikely friendship with her brother Stephen, the Lieutenant wouldn't have been allowed inside Rothburne House.

'Hannah!' A hand waved in front of her face, and she forced herself to pay heed to her mother, who had crossed the room to speak with her.

'You're woolgathering again, my dear. Stand up straight and smile. The Baron of Belgrave is coming to claim his dance with you.' With a slight titter, Christine Chesterfield added, 'Oh, I do hope the two of you get on. He would make such a dashing husband for you. He's so handsome and well-mannered.'

An unsettled feeling rose up in her stomach. 'Mother, I don't want to wed the baron.'

'Why? Whatever is wrong with Lord Belgrave?' Christine demanded.

'I don't know. Something. It feels wrong.'

'Oh, for heaven's sake.' Her mother rolled her eyes. 'Hannah, you're imagining things. There is absolutely nothing wrong with the baron, and I have little doubt that he would make an excellent husband.'

A sour feeling caught up in her stomach, but Hannah didn't protest. She'd learned, long ago, that her mother and father had carved-in-stone ideas about the man she would marry. The gentleman had to be well-bred, wealthy and titled. A saint who had never transgressed against anyone, who treated women with the utmost respect.

And likely rescued kittens in his spare time, she thought sourly. Men of that nature didn't exist. She knew it for a fact, being cursed with two older brothers.

Though she wanted to get married more than anything, Hannah was beginning to wonder if she'd ever find the right man. Having her own home and a husband was her dream, for she could finally have the freedom she wanted.

She craved the moment when she could make her own choices without having to ask permission or worry about whether or not she was behaving like a proper lady. Although she was twenty years old, she might as well have been a girl of five, for all that she'd been sheltered from the world.

'Now, Hannah,' her mother chided. 'The baron has been nothing but the soul of kindness this entire week. He's brought you flowers every day.'

It was true that Lord Belgrave had made his courtship intentions clear. But despite his outward courtesy, Hannah couldn't shake the feeling that something was wrong. He was almost *too* perfect.

'I'm not feeling up to a dance just now,' she said, though she knew the excuse would never hold.

'You are perfectly well,' her mother insisted. 'And you cannot turn down an invitation to dance. It would be rude.'

Hannah clamped her lips together, suppressing the urge to argue. Her mother would never bend when it came to appropriate behaviour. With any luck, the dance would be over in three minutes.

'Smile, for the love of heaven,' her mother repeated. 'You look as though you're about to faint.'

Without waiting for her reply, Lady Rothburne flounced away, just as the Baron of Belgrave arrived to claim his dance.

Hannah forced a smile upon her face and prayed that the remaining hours would pass quickly. And as the baron swept her into the next dance, she caught a glimpse of the Lieutenant watching them, an unreadable darkness upon his face.

MICHAEL THORPE HAD a sixth sense for trouble. He often perceived it before it struck, which had served him well on the battlefield.

It was happening again. Intuition pricked at his conscience, when he saw Lady Hannah about to dance with the Baron of Belgrave. Whether she knew it or not, the suitors were circling her like sharks. There wasn't a man among them who didn't want to claim her.

Including himself.

She was an untouched angel. Innocent of the world, and yet he recognised the weariness in her green eyes. Her caramel-brown hair had been artfully arranged with sprigs of jasmine, while her gown was purest white. It irritated him that her parents treated her as a marital offering to be served out to debauched males.

Like the dog that he was, he wanted to snarl at her suitors, warning them to stay the hell away. But what good would come of it, except to embarrass her among her family and friends?

No. Better to remain in the shadows and keep watch over her. He'd seen so much death and war in the past few months, he felt the need to protect something fragile and good. Soon enough, he'd have to go back to the Crimean Peninsula. He'd have to face the demons and ghosts he'd left behind, and, more than likely, a bullet would end his life.

For now, he would savour this last taste of freedom before the Army ordered him back to the battleground. He glared at Belgrave, watching the pair of them on the dance floor. For a brief moment he imagined himself holding a woman like Hannah in his arms.

His good friend, the Earl of Whitmore, approached with an intent glare upon his face. A moment later, Whitmore's younger brother, Lord Quentin Chesterfield, joined them.

'I hope, for your sake, Thorpe, that you weren't eyeing my sister.' The Earl spoke the words in a calm, deliberate fashion. 'Otherwise, I'll have to kill you.'

Lord Quentin leaned in, a mischievous smile on his face. 'I'll help.'

Michael ignored their threats, though he didn't doubt that they meant them. 'Your sister shouldn't be dancing with Belgrave. I don't trust him.'

'He might be a baron, but he looks a bit too polished, doesn't he?' Lord Quentin agreed. 'Like he's trying too hard to impress the women.'

'You could try a bit harder with your own attire.' Whitmore grimaced at his younger brother's dark purple jacket and yellow waistcoat.

'I like colourful clothing.' Lord Quentin shrugged and turned his attention back to the dancing couple. 'I suppose we shouldn't worry. Our father isn't going to allow Hannah to wed a man like Belgrave, even if he does propose.'

Glancing at the ceiling as if calculating a vast number, Lord Quentin thought to himself. 'Now how many proposals does that make for her this Season…seventeen? Or was it twenty-seven?'

'Five,' Whitmore replied. 'Thankfully, from no one appropriate. But I'll agree with you that Belgrave wouldn't be my first choice.' Crossing his arms, the Earl added, 'I'll be glad when she finds a husband. One less matter to worry about.'

From the tension in Whitmore's face, Michael suspected that impending fatherhood was his greater fear. 'How is the Countess?' he asked.

'One more month of confinement, and then, pray God, we'll have this child. Emily begged me to take her to Falkirk for the birth. We're leaving at dawn. Still, I'm not certain I want her to travel in her condition. Our last baby arrived weeks earlier than we'd expected.'

'Emily *is* approaching the size of a small carriage,' Lord Quentin interjected.

Whitmore sent his brother a blistering look, and Michael offered, 'I'll hold him down while you break his nose.'

A smile cracked over the Earl's face. 'Excellent idea, Thorpe.'

Changing the subject, Michael studied Lady Hannah once more. 'Do you think the Marquess will choose a husband for her this Season?'

'It's doubtful,' Whitmore replied. 'Hannah might as well have a note upon her forehead, telling the unmarried gentleman: "Don't Even Bother Asking."'

'Or, "The Marquess Will Kill You If You Ogle His Daughter",' Quentin added.

The brothers continued to joke about their sister, but Michael ignored their banter. Beneath it all, he understood their fierce desire to protect her. In that, they held common ground.

But regardless of what he might desire, he knew the truth. A Marquess's daughter could never be with a soldier.

No matter how badly he might want her.

'LADY HANNAH, YOU are truly the loveliest woman in this room.' Robert Mortmain, the Baron of Belgrave, led her in the steps of the polka, his smile broad.

'Thank you,' she murmured without looking at him.

She couldn't deny that Lord Belgrave was indeed charming and handsome, with dark brown hair and blue eyes. Born into wealth, nearly every unmarried woman had cast her snare for him—all except herself. There was something about him, a haughtiness that made Hannah uncomfortable.

Don't worry about it, she told herself. *Papa isn't going to force you to marry him, so there's no need to be rude.* The problem of Lord Belgrave would solve itself.

Hannah's skin crawled when the baron touched the small of her back, even with gloved hands. As they moved across the floor, she tensed. The smug air upon his face was of a man boasting to his friends. He didn't want to be with her; he wanted to show her off. A subtle ache began to swell through her temples.

Just a few minutes more, and the dance will be over, Hannah consoled herself. Then she could escape to the comfort of her room. It was nearly midnight, and though she was expected to remain until after two o'clock, she might be able to convince her father that she didn't feel well.

Lord Belgrave scowled when they danced past the refreshment table. 'I didn't realise *he* would be here tonight.'

He was speaking of Lieutenant Thorpe, who was now openly staring at them. Displeasure lined the Lieutenant's face and he gripped the lemonade glass as though he intended to hurl it towards the Baron.

'Why did your father invite him, I wonder?' Lord Belgrave asked.

'Lieutenant Thorpe saved my brother Stephen's life a few years ago,' she admitted. 'They are friends.'

Though how Stephen had even encountered such a man,

she'd never understand. Despite his military rank, Thorpe was a commoner—not the second son of a viscount or earl, as was customary for officers in the Army. And were it not for her brother's insistence, she knew the Lieutenant would never have been invited.

There was nothing humble or uncertain about the way he was watching them. Anger ridged his features, and though the Lieutenant kept himself in control, he looked like he wanted to drag her away from Belgrave.

'He's trying to better himself, isn't he?' Belgrave remarked. 'A man of his poor breeding only poisons his surroundings.'

From his intensity and defensive stance, the Lieutenant appeared as though he were still standing on a battlefield. Likely he'd be more comfortable holding a gun instead of a glass of lemonade.

'I don't want you near a man like him.' The baron scowled.

Lord Belgrave's possessive tone didn't sit well with her, but Hannah said nothing. It wasn't as if she intended to go anywhere near the Lieutenant. Even so, what right did Belgrave have to dictate her actions?

None whatsoever. The dance was nearly finished, and she was grateful for that. Her headache was growing worse, and she longed for an escape to her room. When the music ended, she thanked Lord Belgrave, but he held her hands a moment longer.

'Lady Hannah, I would be honoured if you'd consent to becoming my wife.'

She couldn't believe he'd asked it of her. Here? In the middle of a ballroom? Hannah's smile grew strained, but she simply answered, 'You'll have to speak with my father.'

No. No. A thousand times, no.

The baron's fingers tightened when she tried to pull

away. 'But what of your wishes? If you did not require the Marquess's permission, what would you say?'

I would say absolutely not.

Hannah kept her face completely neutral. She didn't like the look in his eyes. There was a desperate glint in them, and she wondered if Belgrave's fortunes were as secure as he'd claimed. Forcing a laugh she didn't feel, Hannah managed, 'You flatter me, my lord. Any woman would be glad to call you her husband.'

Just not me. But then, a word to her father would take care of that. Although the Marquess presented an autocratic façade to his peers, he was softer towards her, probably because she'd never embarrassed him in public, or even hinted at rebellion. Obedient and demure, she'd made him proud.

Or at least, that's what she hoped.

Hannah managed to pry her hand free. Even so, she could feel the baron's eyes boring into the back of her gown. She walked towards her father and brothers, who were standing near the entrance to the terrace. From the serious expressions on their faces, she didn't want to interrupt the conversation. She took a glass of lemonade and waited outside the ballroom, in the darkened shadows near the terrace. It wasn't good to be standing alone, but she hoped she was near enough to her brothers that no one would bother her.

Everyone else was still inside, dancing and mingling with one another. Her head was aching even more, a dreadful pressure that seemed to spread.

Oh, please, not tonight, Hannah prayed. She'd suffered headaches such as these before, and they were wretched, attacking her until she was bedridden for a full day or longer.

'You don't look well,' came a male voice from behind her.

Without turning around, she knew it was Lieutenant Thorpe. His voice lacked the cultured tones of the upper class, making his identity obvious. Hannah contemplated ignoring him and approaching her father, but then that would be rude. And whether or not she wanted to speak to him, good manners were ingrained within her.

'I am fine, Lieutenant Thorpe. Thank you for asking.'

Despite her unspoken dismissal, he didn't move away. She could feel him watching her, and, beneath his attention, her body began to respond. It felt too hot, even outside on the terrace. The silk of her dress felt confining. She fanned herself, not knowing why his very presence seemed to unnerve her so.

She didn't turn around, for it wasn't proper for her to be speaking with him alone. Even if he was completely hidden behind her, she didn't want to take a chance of someone seeing them. 'Was there something you wanted?'

He gave a low laugh, a husky sound that was far too intimate. 'Nothing you can give, sweet.'

Her face flushed scarlet, not knowing what he'd meant by that. She took a hesitant step closer to her father, sensing the Lieutenant's presence like a warm breeze upon her nape. Her gown rested off her shoulders, baring her skin before him. The strand of diamonds she wore grew heavy, and she forgot about her aching head. Instead, she was intensely conscious of the man standing behind her.

'You look tired.'

It was so true. She was tired of attending balls and dinner parties. Tired of being paraded around like a porcelain doll, waiting for the right marriage offer.

'I'm all right,' she insisted. 'You needn't worry about me.' She wanted him to leave her alone. He shouldn't be standing behind her, not where anyone could come upon them. She was about to step away when a gloved hand touched her back. The heat of his palm warmed her skin, and she jerked away out of instinct.

'Don't touch me,' she pleaded.

'Is that what you want?'

Her shoulders rose and fell, her breathing unsteady. Of course that's what she wanted. A man like Michael Thorpe was nothing but trouble.

But before she could say another word, his hand moved to her shoulders. Caressing the skin, gently easing the tension in her nape.

Step away from him. Scream, her brain insisted. But it was as though her mouth were stuffed with cotton. Her limbs were frozen in place, unable to move.

Her breasts prickled beneath the ivory silk, becoming aroused. He'd removed a single glove, and the vibrant intimacy of his bare palm on her flesh made her tremble.

'Don't do this,' she pleaded. Her voice was a slight whisper, barely audible. 'You—you shouldn't.'

Well-mannered ladies did *not* stand still while they were accosted by a soldier. She could only imagine what her mother would say. But she had never been touched by a man like this, and the sensation was a secret thrill.

The Lieutenant's fingers slipped beneath the chain of her necklace, teasing her neck before winding into the strands of her coiffeur. 'You're right.'

His fingers were melting her resistance, making her feel alive. She was beginning to understand how a woman might cast off propriety, surrendering to a stranger's seduction.

'My apologies. You were too much temptation to resist.'

Her fingers clenched at her sides. 'Sir, keep your hands to yourself. Or you'll answer to my brother.'

'I'll try.'

Then she felt the lightest brush of his mouth upon her nape, a kiss he shouldn't have stolen. Wicked heat poured through her, and she gasped at the sensation.

Hannah whirled around, prepared to chastise him. But

he'd already gone. She stared out at the gardens, but there was not a trace that he'd been there. Only the gooseflesh on her arms and the storm of churning fire inside her skin.

'Why are you out here alone, Hannah?' The Marquess of Rothburne approached, having finished his conversation with her brothers. Her father frowned at her, as though she'd transgressed by avoiding a chaperone.

She prayed he didn't see her flushed cheeks or suspect the improper thoughts racing through her head. 'I would like permission to retire,' she said calmly. 'It's been a long evening. My head hurts, and I need to lie down.'

'Do you want me to send your maid with laudanum?' he asked, becoming concerned.

Hannah shook her head. 'No, I don't think it's going to be one of those headaches. But if you please, Papa, I'm very tired.'

Her father offered his arm. 'Walk with me for a few minutes, if you will.'

Hannah was hesitant, but she suspected her father had something else to discuss with her. He led her outside the terrace and down the gravel walkway toward her mother's rose garden. The canes held hints of new growth, though it would be early summer before the first blooms came. She raised her eyes to look out at the glittering stars, wishing she had brought a shawl.

Her skin was still sensitive from the Lieutenant's touch, her mind in turmoil. He'd awakened a restless side to her, and she didn't like it. Even while she walked, the shifting of her legs sent an uneasy ache within her body.

What had he done to her? And did that make her a wanton, for enjoying his fleeting touch?

Her father led her through the gardens toward the stables, their feet crunching upon the gravel as they walked. Hannah found herself comparing the two men. James Chesterfield was every inch a Marquess, displaying a haughty exterior that intimidated almost everyone except herself. Never did he stray from the rules of propriety. In contrast, Lieutenant Thorpe had a devil-may-care attitude, a man who did exactly as he pleased.

She shivered at the memory.

When her father's silence stretched on, Hannah guessed at the reason. 'You turned another proposal down, didn't you?'

James paused. 'Not yet. But the Baron of Belgrave asked for permission to call upon me tomorrow.'

It wasn't a surprise, but she felt it best to make her feelings known. 'I don't want to marry him, Papa.'

'He possesses a large estate, and comes from an excellent family,' her father argued. 'He seems to have a genuine interest in you.' He escorted her back to the house.

'Something about him bothers me.' Hannah paused, trying to find the right words. 'I can't quite explain it.'

'That isn't a good enough reason to reject his suit,' the Marquess protested.

She knew that, but was counting on her father to take her side. To change the subject, she asked, 'What sort of man are you hoping I'll wed? I do want to get married.'

The Marquess cleared his throat. 'I'll know him when I see him. Someone who will take care of you and make you happy.' He took her hand and gave it a gentle squeeze, though he didn't smile. Streaks of grey marred his bearded face, his hair silvery in the moonlight.

He led her back to the house, where they passed the ballroom filled with people. Music crescendoed amidst the laughter of guests, but it only made her headache worsen. Finally, her father escorted her to her room, bidding her good night.

At the door he added gruffly, 'Lady Whitmore brought

over some ginger biscuits earlier this afternoon, when she visited. I had a servant place some in your room. Don't tell your mother.' Shaking his head in exasperation, he added, 'You would think that a woman in her condition would know better than to work like a scullery maid. It's ridiculous that she wants to bake treats, like a common servant.'

While most women rested in their final month of pregnancy, her sister-in-law Emily had gone into a flurry of baking during the past several weeks. Stephen humoured his wife, allowing her to do as she wished during her confinement.

Acting upon her father's unspoken hint, Hannah slipped inside her room for a moment and returned with two of the ginger biscuits. She handed them to her father, who devoured them.

'If I see Emily, I'll tell her how much you liked them,' she said.

He grimaced. 'She shouldn't be in the kitchens. Her ankles are swelling, so she said. If you see her, order her to put her feet up.'

'I will,' Hannah promised. Though he would never admit it, the Marquess thoroughly enjoyed his arguments with Stephen's wife.

After her father left, Hannah rang for her maid. She sat down at her dressing table, wondering if she would need the laudanum after all. Her headache hadn't abated and seemed to be worsening.

She massaged her temples in an attempt to block out the pain. It frustrated her, being unable to control this aspect of her life.

Then again, so much of her life was out of her hands. She should be accustomed to it by now. Her mother made every decision concerning her wardrobe and which balls and dinner parties she attended. Christine controlled what she ate, which calls she made…even when she was allowed to retire for the night.

Hannah ran her hands over a silver hairbrush, praying for the day when she could make those decisions for herself. Though she supposed it was her mother's way of showing she cared about her welfare, as time went on, her home felt more and more like a prison.

Her gaze fell upon the list of reminders her mother had left behind. She'd received one every day since the age of nine, since, quite often, she didn't see her mother until the evening.

1. Wear the white silk gown and the Rothburne diamonds.
2. Wait for your father and brothers to introduce suitors to you.
3. Do not refuse any invitation to dance.
4. Never argue with any gentleman. A true lady is agreeable.

Hannah could almost imagine instruction number five: Never allow strange gentlemen to touch you. Her eyes closed, her head pounding with pain.

Folding the list away, she rested her forehead upon her palm. A slow ache built up in her stomach when she saw a morning dress the colour of butter laid out for tomorrow. She had never cared for the gown, and would have been quite happy to see it burned. It made her feel as though she were six years old.

But she would never dream of arguing with Christine Chesterfield. Her mother alternated the colours of her dresses, selecting gowns of white, rose and yellow. When Hannah had tried to suggest another colour once, Christine had put her foot down. It wouldn't surprise her if her mother measured each and every one of her necklines, to be sure that she wasn't revealing too much skin.

Just once, Hannah wished to have a scarlet dress. Or amethyst. A wild burst of colour to liven up her wardrobe. But she supposed real ladies weren't supposed to wear colours like that.

Hannah raised the hem of her gown, and at the glimpse of her petticoats, she thought of the man who would one day become her husband. Would he treat her with tenderness, bringing friendship and possibly love into their marriage?

Or was there…something more? Her mother had not breathed a word about the intimacy between a man and a woman. Only that she would learn of it, the night before her wedding. Any mention of the marriage bed made her mother blush and stammer.

The unexpected memory of Lieutenant's Thorpe's kiss made Hannah shiver. He never should have caressed her, especially with an ungloved hand, but then that was the sort of man he was. A man who made his own rules and broke them when he liked. The Lieutenant hadn't offered tired compliments or begged her father for permission to call upon her. Instead, he'd touched her in the shadows, and she'd come alive.

Nothing you can give, sweet.

What had he meant by those words? Her hands moved to her shoulders, over the sensitised skin. Her mother would have a fit of the vapours if she knew the Lieutenant had stolen a kiss. His mouth had touched her here, on the nape. Almost like a lover's kiss. A cold realisation dawned upon her when her fingers touched bare skin.

Her diamond necklace was gone. *No. Oh, no.* Panic shot through her, for the diamonds were worth nearly a thousand pounds.

Hannah threw open the door to her room and fled down

the stairs. Keeping towards the wall, she tried to avoid notice.

She hid behind the doorway, searching the floor of the ballroom, but saw nothing. Nothing by the refreshment table, either.

Thoughts of the Lieutenant's hands around her throat made her wonder. Had he unfastened the clasp? She didn't want to believe that he'd taken the diamonds, but the last time she remembered wearing the necklace was in his presence.

With fear in her throat, she sought him out. The Lieutenant wasn't among the ballroom guests, but instead stood alone on the edge of the terrace. Before him, the boxwood hedges rose tall, like silent sentries.

His arms were crossed in the ill-fitting formal wear, causing the seams of the coat to stretch against his shoulders.

'I beg your pardon,' she murmured, stepping towards him, 'but may I speak with you a moment, Lieutenant?'

His gaze flicked across hers, but he shrugged. 'Aren't you afraid of your father? I believe it isn't proper for a lady to be in the company of a soldier.'

She ignored his mocking tone. She knew well enough that what she was doing was highly improper. 'I must ask you if you've seen my necklace. I've lost it, you see, and—'

'You think I took it.'

His posture had changed, and she wished she hadn't spoken. Just like her father, he was a man of pride. Soldiers valued their honour above all else, and she'd just insulted his.

Hannah chose her words carefully. 'The clasp may have slipped when you—when you touched my neck. I thought it dropped where I was standing.'

That sounded reasonable enough, didn't it? Surely he wouldn't take offence—

'I stole nothing from you.' A hard edge accompanied his remark. 'And there's nothing of yours that I want.'

His harsh words stabbed her pride. He wasn't merely speaking of the necklace any more. Hannah forced herself to nod, though her cheeks were burning. 'I didn't mean to imply anything.'

'Yes, you did. I'm the only man here who would need diamonds. A man without a fortune.'

'You aren't the only one,' she argued. 'But that's neither here nor there. You don't have the necklace, and that's that.'

She gathered her skirts and strode towards the rose garden without bidding him goodbye. Rude, yes, but she had no desire to speak to him any longer. It was possible that his wayward fingers had loosened the clasp, and the necklace had fallen on to the ground when she'd walked outside.

The idea of the Lieutenant being a thief didn't sit well with her. He was her brother's friend, and she wanted to believe that there was honour in him.

Her headache had intensified to an unbearable level, as though someone were bashing rocks against her temples. The sooner she found the necklace, the sooner she could rest.

Hurrying towards the rose canes, Hannah dashed back to where she'd spoken with her father last. She retraced her footsteps, searching everywhere. But there was nothing. She turned the corner, only to stumble into the Baron of Belgrave.

'Oh! I'm sorry. I didn't expect to see you here,' she apologised. The moonlight spilled a faint light over his face, and his gloved fingers withdrew something glittering from his pocket.

'Were you looking for these?'

Belgrave held out the diamonds in his palm, and Hannah breathed a sigh of relief. 'Yes, thank you.'

She reached for them, but he pulled his hand back. 'I saw them lying on the ground after your father escorted you back to the house.' He returned the necklace to his pocket and held out his arm for her to accompany him. 'I thought you might come back for them.'

Hannah didn't take his elbow, for she had no desire to walk alone with the baron. Her instincts prickled, for she had once again crossed the line of what was proper. If anyone saw them unchaperoned, the gossip tales would spread faster than a house fire.

But he had her necklace, and she needed it back. Reluctantly, she placed her hand upon his arm. Perhaps if she gave him a moment, he would return the jewels.

The baron led her away from the house, and with each step, her headache worsened. When they neared the stables, Hannah had endured enough. 'Lord Belgrave, give me my diamond necklace, if you please.'

And go away. Where were her father and brothers when she needed them most?

Belgrave's hawkish face appeared fierce in the moonlight. Diamonds or not, she'd made a terrible mistake in approaching him. She took a step backwards, wondering if she dared flee.

The baron retrieved the necklace from his pocket and held the diamonds in his hand, stroking the gems. 'I overheard you speaking to your father about me.'

Hannah's heartbeat quickened, and she cast a glance around the garden, searching for another escape. 'Wh-what did you overhear?'

'You lied to me.' Cold anger edged his voice. 'You led me to believe you wanted my courtship.'

'I didn't want to hurt your feelings,' she explained. His anger made her uncomfortable, and she was ready to get away from him. The necklace be hanged. Her safety was far more important than a strand of diamonds. With an apologetic look, she added, 'I'll send a servant to collect my necklace from you.'

'What's the matter? Are you afraid of me?' he murmured.

Hannah ignored the question and picked up her skirts, striding towards the house. Before she could reach the terrace, a firm hand clamped over her upper arm.

'I haven't finished our conversation.'

'We weren't having one,' she corrected. 'And I'll ask you to remove your hand from my arm.'

'You think you're better than me, don't you? Because your father is a Marquess and I a mere baron.' He bent closer, and her stomach wrenched, the pressure in her head rising higher.

Dear heaven, she felt like fainting. The headache was like a dagger grinding into her skull.

She opened her mouth to call for help, but Lord Belgrave cut off her scream. She struggled against his grip, but he pinched her nose. With the lack of air, the headache roared into a fury. Dizzy and sick, she stopped fighting, and he dragged her across the gravel. Nausea gripped her, and the agony in her head was so intense, it nearly brought her to her knees. It couldn't have come at a worse time.

The baron lowered his voice. 'You said that any woman would be fortunate to wed me.' He drew so close, Hannah could see the vengeance in his eyes. 'It looks like you're about to become very fortunate indeed.'

CHAPTER TWO

MICHAEL RETURNED TO the ballroom, his posture stiff with anger. Lady Hannah had all but accused him of stealing her diamonds. He might be poor, but he wasn't a thief. Yet she wouldn't believe that, would she? Her blush had revealed how she viewed him: as a lowborn man, a soldier who wouldn't hesitate to take advantage of a lady.

True, he had a weakness for beautiful women. But never if they were unwilling. And that was the curious part, wasn't it? He'd dared to touch Lady Hannah...and she hadn't protested. The aristocrat with impeccable manners hadn't slapped him with her fan, nor called out for help. She'd leaned into his touch, as though she were thirsty for it.

God, she'd smelled good. Like seductive jasmine, haunting and sweet. He hadn't been able to resist her. He'd wanted to run his mouth over her neck, sliding the ivory gown over those bare shoulders until he revealed more of her delicate skin, but then her brother would murder him where he stood.

Normally, Michael had no interest in husband-seeking innocents, but Lady Hannah captivated him. He didn't for a moment believe she would cast him a second glance. Not only because of her suspicions about the necklace, but also because of his status. As a lieutenant, he wasn't worthy of a woman like her.

He had no title, unlike the other officers who had bought their commissions. He'd been granted his own commission within the British Army as a gift from the Earl of Whitmore, after he'd saved the Earl's life five years ago. And last October he'd learned what it meant to give a command, knowing that men would die because of it.

He'd tried to save whatever men he could, after his Captain had died at Balaclava. But he'd failed to protect the vast majority of his company. Of the six hundred, less than two hundred had returned. He'd been one of them.

Even now, he could still hear the bullets ripping through flesh, the moans that preceded death. He couldn't erase the nightmares, no matter how hard he'd tried. A lump tightened in the back of his throat, and he went to get another drink. As he passed the entrance to the terrace, he wondered if he should check on Lady Hannah.

Though she wanted to find her diamonds, she was far too lovely to be venturing out alone. She needed someone to protect her from unsavoury men.

Before he could follow her, a gentleman stepped into his line of sight, clearing his throat. He was accompanied by Hannah's brother Stephen Chesterfield, the Earl of Whitmore.

'Forgive me, Thorpe, but there is someone whom I'd like you to meet.'

The older man wore a black cloth tailcoat, expertly tailored to his form. His salt-and-pepper beard and mustache were neatly groomed, while the rest of his head was bald. Gold glinted upon the handle of his cane, and every inch of the gentleman spoke of money. Idly, Michael wondered if the man wanted a personal guard.

'This is a friend of my father's,' Stephen said. 'Graf Heinrich von Reischor, the Lohenberg ambassador to England.'

Lohenberg. Uneasiness slipped over him like a gust of cold air. The mention of the country provoked a distant memory he couldn't quite grasp. His mouth tightened, and he forced himself to concentrate on the gentleman standing in front of him.

Whitmore finished the introduction, and Michael wondered if he was expected to bow before an ambassador. He settled upon a polite nod.

Graf von Reischor leaned upon his cane. 'Thank you, Lord Whitmore. I am most grateful for the introduction. If you will excuse us?' The Earl nodded to both of them and departed.

Now what was this all about? Michael wondered. The Lohenberg Graf fixed his gaze upon him in an open stare, as though he were intrigued by what he saw. Then the man lowered his voice and spoke an unfamiliar language, one that sounded like a blend of German and Danish.

Michael wondered if he was supposed to understand the words, but he could do nothing but shake his head in ignorance.

Graf von Reischor's interest never wavered. 'Forgive me, Lieutenant Thorpe. I thought you might be from Lohenberg, given your appearance.'

'My appearance?'

'Yes.' The man's gaze was unrelenting, though there was a trace of surprise beneath it. 'You look a great deal like someone I know. Enough that you could be his son.'

'My father was a fishmonger. He lived in London all his life.'

The Graf didn't appear convinced. 'And your parents… they were both English?'

'Yes.' It didn't sit well with him that the Graf von Reischor was implying anything about his parentage. He had been their only son, and though it had been four years since they'd died of cholera, he hadn't forgotten Mary Thorpe dying in his arms. She'd been a saint, his mother. It shamed him that he'd never been able to provide more for them, though he'd done his best.

Graf von Reischor didn't appear convinced. 'It may be a coincidence. But I don't know what to believe. You have no idea how strong the resemblance is.'

It was difficult to keep his anger in check. 'Paul Thorpe was my father. No other man. You have no right to suggest otherwise.'

'We should discuss this more in private,' the Graf said. 'Call upon me tomorrow at my private apartment at Number Fourteen, St James's Street.'

'I have no intention of calling upon you,' Michael retorted. 'I know who I am and where I come from.' He started to leave, but a gold-handled cane blocked his path.

'I'm not certain you understand, Lieutenant Thorpe,' the Graf said quietly. 'The man you resemble is our king.'

MICHAEL PUSHED HIS way past the Graf, refusing to even acknowledge the man's words. He had no desire to be the brunt of a nobleman's joke. A Prince? Hardly. Von Reischor was trying to make sport of him; he wasn't foolish enough to fall prey to such nonsense.

As he made his way through the room of people, his anger heated up. Who did the Graf think he was, implying that a common soldier could be royalty? It was ridiculous to even consider.

A coldness bled through his veins, for the encounter had opened up the dreams that sometimes haunted him. Dreams of a long journey, voices shouting at him and a woman's tears.

He gripped his fists. It wasn't real. None of it was. And he refused to believe false visions of a life that wasn't his.

To take his mind off the ludicrous proposition, he decided to find Lady Hannah. She'd been gone a long time, and he hadn't seen her return to the terrace.

He retraced her path toward the roses. She'd been wearing a white gown, so it shouldn't be difficult to find her amidst the greenery. But after an extensive search of the shrubbery and rose beds, there was no sign of her.

She'd been here. He'd swear it on his life. Michael thought back to the direction she'd gone, and he knelt down near the walkway. It was an easy matter to slip back into his military training.

Light footprints had left an imprint upon the gravel. Michael tracked her path around the side of the house, when abruptly the footprints were joined by a heavier set. Then something…no, someone, had been dragged off.

His instincts slammed a warning into him—especially when he spied Lady Hannah's diamond necklace lying in the grass.

Michael raced toward the stables, cursing that he hadn't followed Lady Hannah immediately. There was no sign of her anywhere.

Michael clutched the diamonds, and near the end of the walkway, he spied a single landau and driver. Surely the driver would have seen anyone coming from the stables.

'Lady Hannah Chesterfield,' he demanded. 'Where did she go?'

The man shrugged, his hands buried in his pockets. 'Ain't seen nothing.'

He was lying. Michael grabbed the driver by his coat and hauled him off the carriage. A handful of sovereigns spilled onto the ground, and the driver scuttled to pick them up.

A haze of red fury spread over him as he pressed the man up against the iron frame of the carriage. 'Who took her?'

When the driver stubbornly kept silent, Michael tightened his grip on the man's throat. 'I'm not one of those titled gentlemen you're used to,' he warned. 'I'm a soldier. They pay me to kill enemies of the Crown. And right now, I see you as one of my enemies.' Holding fast, he waited long enough until the man started to choke.

Michael loosened his fingers, and the driver sputtered and coughed. 'The—the B-Baron of Belgrave. Said they was runnin' off t'be together. Paid me not to talk.'

'What does his carriage look like?'

The driver described an elaborate black brougham with the baron's crest. Michael stepped aboard the carriage. 'I'll be needing this.'

'But—but you can't steal his lordship's landau! I'll lose me post!'

Michael took the reins and nodded to the man. 'And what do you think will happen when you explain to the Marquess of Rothburne that you allowed his daughter to be abducted for a few sovereigns? You had best alert him immediately, or you'll face much worse than dismissal.' Snapping the reins, Michael drew the landau around the circle and toward the London streets.

There were a thousand different places Belgrave might have taken her. As he struggled to make his way through the London traffic, Michael went through the possibilities. Was the baron trying to compromise her or wed her?

If the intent was to compromise her, then likely he would take Lady Hannah back to his town house where they would be caught together. Michael's fist curled into the diamond necklace. No innocent young lady deserved this. By God, he wanted to kill the baron for what he'd done.

Luck was on his side, for when he reached a side street past Grosvenor Square, he spotted the baron's brougham, which had pulled to a stop by the side of the road. *Thank God.*

Michael raced forward, urging the horses towards the

vehicle. He barely waited for the landau to stop before he ran to Belgrave's carriage and jerked the door open.

Lady Hannah was lying on the floor of the carriage, moaning with her eyes closed. Lord Belgrave appeared slightly panicked, his face pale.

Michael wasted no time and dragged the baron out, pushing him up against the black brougham. 'I should kill you right now.'

Belgrave blanched, and Michael punched him hard, taking satisfaction when he broke the baron's nose.

Blood streamed from the wound, and Belgrave snarled, trying to fight back. 'I'll see you hanged for assaulting me.'

Michael leaned in close, his grip closing over Belgrave's throat. 'I haven't yet decided if I'm going to let you live. I'm sure Lady Hannah's brother wouldn't mind at all if I rid London of an insect such as yourself.'

He clipped the baron across the jaw, following it up with another punch to the man's ear. The blow sent Belgrave reeling before he lost consciousness and slid to the ground. Michael glared at Belgrave's driver, who hadn't lifted a finger to help defend his master.

'My lord, I had no choice,' the driver apologised. 'The baron insisted—'

Michael cut him off. 'Take Belgrave back to Rothburne House in this landau. Tell the Marquess what happened, and I'll bring Lady Hannah home.'

The driver didn't argue, but took possession of the landau immediately, loading Belgrave's slumped form inside. Michael waited until he'd gone, then climbed inside the brougham to Lady Hannah.

'Are you all right? Did he harm you?'

Lady Hannah clutched her head, tears streaming down her face. 'No. But my head hurts. The pain—it's awful.'

Her eyes were closed, and she was holding herself so tightly, as if trying to block out the torment.

'Just try to hold on, and I'll bring you home to your father's house.' Gently, Michael placed her back into the carriage seat and closed the door. Taking control of the reins, he turned them back towards Rothburne House. The other driver had already departed with the Baron of Belgrave.

It had been tempting to leave Belgrave in the streets for thieves or cut-throats to find. A man like the baron didn't deserve mercy.

Michael increased the pace, turning towards Hyde Park, when he heard Hannah call out, 'Lieutenant Thorpe! Please, I need you to stop.'

Damn it. If she were ill, he needed to get her home. Get her a doctor. Stopping the carriage would only blemish her reputation even more.

He slowed the pace of the carriage and asked, 'Can you hold on a little longer?'

'I can't. I'm sorry,' she pleaded. 'I'm going to be sick.'

Michael expelled another curse and pulled the brougham toward a more isolated part of the park. With any luck, no one would see them or ask what they were doing.

He opened the carriage door and found Hannah curled up into a ball, her face deathly pale. 'What can I do to help you?'

'Just…let me stay here for a bit. You don't have any laudanum, do you?'

He shook his head. 'I'm sorry. Do you want me to go and fetch some?' But even as he offered, he knew it was a foolish thing to say. He couldn't leave her here alone, not in this condition.

'No.' She kept her eyes closed, resting her face against the side of the carriage. 'Just give me a few moments.'

'Let me help you lie down,' he suggested.

'It hurts worse if I lean back.' Her breathing was shaky, and Michael sat across from her. A gas lamp cast an amber glow across the carriage, and she winced. 'The light hurts.'

He'd never felt so helpless, so unable to help her through this nightmare. She was fighting to breathe, her face grey with exertion.

And suddenly, his worry about her family and her reputation seemed ridiculous in light of her illness. This was about helping her to endure pain, and that was something he understood. He'd watched men suffering from bullet wounds, crying out in torment. On the battlefield, he'd done what he could to ease them. It was all he could do for her now.

Michael closed the carriage door, making it as dark as possible. He removed his jacket and covered up the window to keep out the light.

'I can't…can't breathe.' Her shoulders were hunched, her eyes turning glassy.

He didn't ask permission, but unbuttoned the back of her gown in order to loosen her stays. Hannah didn't protest, and she seemed to breathe easier once it was done. He held her upright in his arms, keeping silent.

AN HOUR PASSED, and in time, he felt her body begin to relax. She slept in his arms, but Michael couldn't release his own tension. Her father would be looking for them. He needed to get her out of here, take her home. But he was afraid of causing her more pain.

Her hair had fallen loose from its pins, and the dark honey locks rested against his cheek, smelling sweetly of jasmine. He'd heard that some women suffered from headaches as excruciating as this one, but he'd never witnessed it before. Nonetheless, her unexpected illness had probably saved her from Belgrave's unwanted attentions. It was a blessing in that sense.

The night air was cold, but Hannah's body heat kept him warm. His neck and shoulders were stiff, but that didn't bother him. She was no longer in pain, and he was grateful for it.

It had been a gruelling experience, one he didn't care to repeat. He was unbearably alert, attuned to Hannah in a way he'd never expected. Against his chest, he could feel the rise and fall of her breathing.

There would be hellish consequences. And yet he wouldn't have changed what he'd done. He'd rescued her from that bastard Belgrave and protected her innocence. She could go into her future marriage as an untouched bride, the way she should. That is, if he could get her home without anyone realising where she'd spent the last hour or two.

He had his doubts.

Michael watched her sleeping, the strands of hair twining around her throat and spilling over the curve of her breasts. Her beauty stole his breath away.

Innocence and purity. Everything he didn't deserve.

From his pocket, he withdrew the strand of diamonds and fastened them around her throat. Bare skin peeped from the open back of her dress where he'd loosened her corset. He wanted to kiss her, to run his mouth over that silken skin. Like forbidden fruit, she tempted him to taste.

Only a few hours ago, he'd touched her back, indulging himself in a bit of wickedness. She'd allowed him liberties he never should have taken.

Not for you, his brain warned.

An honourable man would leave her alone to sleep, taking the reins and driving her home again. He wouldn't run his palms over her arms, watching her skin tighten with gooseflesh. A good man would ignore the seductive glimpses of female skin and set his baser urges under control.

But he wasn't good. He wasn't honourable. Right now,

he'd been given a few stolen moments with this woman. And he intended to take them.

Michael lowered his mouth to her shoulder blade, tracing the fragile skin up to her nape. Hannah shivered, lifting her face towards his as she awakened from sleep. He took possession of her softened mouth, not asking for permission.

HANNAH AWOKE WITH her body temperature rising, as though she were suffering from a fever. The Lieutenant was kissing her, and she was sitting in his lap.

She couldn't move from the shock of feelings coursing through her. No man had ever kissed her before, and she trembled beneath the onslaught. It was as though he were starving for her, his mouth hot and hungry.

His tongue slid inside her mouth, caressing her intimately. Hannah had never imagined such a thing, and desire poured through her, making her skin hotter.

Push him away. Beg for him to stop.

But her mind was disconnected from her body, once again. She felt herself arching towards him, needing to be closer. His hands slipped beneath the open back of her gown, and dimly she remembered the Lieutenant unlacing her, to help her breathe easier.

The touch of his bare hands on her skin made her cry out, 'No! Stop, please.'

The remnants of her headache pressed into her, and tears spilled out. Not because of his unexpected kiss, but because of her guilt. He'd evoked shameful feelings inside of her, arousing her. And though she wanted to lay the blame at his feet, she knew in her heart that she couldn't. She'd allowed him to kiss her, to touch her in ways that no good girl would allow.

'I'm not going to apologise for that.' His voice was low

and deep, a man who had seized what he'd wanted. 'You kissed me back.'

'I didn't want to.'

Liar. An aching throbbed within her womb. She felt damp, restless. The touch of his hard body against her pliant flesh was almost too much to bear.

'Yes, you did.' The the Lieutenant broke away, his breathing harsh. He moved to the opposite side of the carriage, resting his wrists on his knees. His head hung down, dark hair shadowing his face. He looked as though he'd been in a fist fight. 'I need to drive you home.'

'Please.' She tried to hold the back of her gown together, but the edges wouldn't hold. Exposed to him, she wanted to die of embarrassment.

'I'll help you get dressed,' he said. 'You'll never manage by yourself.'

'I don't want you to touch me,' she snapped. 'Take me back.'

'What do you think your father will say when he sees you like this?'

'You should be more worried about yourself,' she countered. 'He'll want to kill you.'

The the Lieutenant sent her a patronising smile. 'For saving your virtue?'

'You're the one who tried to attack me just now.'

'Sweet, I'm not a man who has to attack anyone.' He pulled his coat from the carriage door, and Hannah winced at the flash of light from one of the street lamps.

She said nothing, her thoughts drifting back and forth, trying to decide whether he was a rogue or a man of honour. Yes, he'd kissed her when he shouldn't have. But he'd also taken care of her.

Though he should have brought her home immediately, he'd listened when she'd begged him to stop the carriage.

The excruciating, jarring sensation from the horses had made each mile an unending torture.

Another man wouldn't have done the same. He'd have ignored her needs, riding as fast as he dared, back to Rothburne House. But not the Lieutenant.

So many questions gathered up, needing to be asked. Hannah traced her swollen lips, wondering what had driven him to do such a thing.

'You don't need to be afraid of me,' he said quietly. 'I'm not going to kiss you again.' His cravat was loosened from his collar, while he donned the ill-fitting jacket.

'I should hope not.'

He raised his gaze to hers, and she caught a glimpse of green eyes with flecks of brown. His cheeks held a light stubble, and for a moment, she wondered why the texture hadn't scratched her skin.

'You really are an innocent, aren't you?' He glanced over her ivory silk gown, and the remark didn't sound like a compliment.

'I suppose. You speak of it as though it's a bad thing.'

He glanced outside the carriage window, as if searching for someone. 'It's what most men want.'

'But not you.'

A dark laugh escaped him. 'I'm not a good man at all.'

She didn't entirely believe that. 'Please take me home,' she reminded him. 'My family will be worried.'

'Turn around,' he ordered.

She knew what he needed to do, but she hesitated to let him touch her corset. It didn't matter that he'd already done so; she'd been half out of her mind with pain. 'No, it isn't proper.'

The Lieutenant didn't listen to her argument, but forced her to turn around. His hands fumbled with the stays, pulling them tight before tying them. 'Proper or not, I won't let your father think I ravaged you in a carriage.'

He was right. Her father would be angry enough at both of them, without him drawing the wrong conclusions.

'How long have we been gone, do you think?' Her stomach didn't feel right, and her head still ached.

'Longer than an hour. Two or three, perhaps. It isn't dawn yet.' His large hands struggled with the tiny buttons, and she couldn't help but be even more aware of him. He muttered, 'I'm better at taking these off than buttoning them up.'

Hannah didn't doubt that at all. When he'd finished, she rested her head against the side of the carriage, waiting for him to go back to the driver's seat.

'Are you feeling better?' he asked.

'I'll manage.' Thank heaven, it had been one of the shorter headaches, swift and furious. The after-effects would dwell with her for a while, but the worst was over.

'What are you going to tell my father?' she asked.

Michael opened the door to the carriage, leaving it slightly open. 'The truth. Neither of us has done anything wrong.'

I have, Hannah thought. The kiss might not mean a thing to him, but it had shaken her. The sensation of his mouth upon hers had been the most sinful thing she'd ever experienced. She'd fallen under his spell, wanting to know his touch in a way she shouldn't.

Michael opened the carriage door the rest of the way, about to disembark, when they heard the sounds of men shouting and the rumble of another carriage approaching. Her father's voice broke through the stillness, and within moments, he was standing in front of the door.

'Are you all right?' the Marquess demanded of Hannah.

Hannah gripped her hands together, cold fear icing through her. For she suspected the truth was not going to be enough to pacify her father.

CHAPTER THREE

'GET AWAY FROM my daughter,' the Marquess of Rothburne ordered.

Hannah tried to rise from her seat, but the Lieutenant motioned her back. With a horrifying clarity, she realised what her father must think. With a pleading look she insisted, 'Papa, this isn't what it looks like. Lieutenant Thorpe rescued me from Lord Belgrave.'

Though she tried to find the right explanation, her father looked more interested in murder than the truth.

Hannah continued talking, though she knew how unlikely it must sound. 'Lieutenant Thorpe tried to bring me home but… I had one of my headaches. I didn't have any laudanum, and the pain was unbearable. He obeyed me when I ordered him to stop the carriage.'

Her father gave no indication that he'd even heard her speaking, but gave a nod to one of his footmen. The large servant reached to seize hold of the Lieutenant, but Michael's hand shot out and stopped him. With a twist to the man's wrist, the footman had no choice but to release him.

'Enough.' The Lieutenant climbed down from the carriage and regarded the Marquess. 'Instead of having this conversation here in the park, I suggest we return to Rothburne House. Take Lady Hannah home with you, and see to her health. I will follow in this carriage.'

'I should have the police drag you off to Newgate right now,' the Marquess countered.

'He didn't dishonour me, Papa.' Hannah moved forward, but when she exited the carriage, the world tipped. A rushing sound filled her ears, and Michael caught her elbow, steadying her. 'I swear it. He protected me while I was ill.'

'Because of him, you may be ruined.' Her father stared at her as though she'd just run off with a chimney sweep. 'You just spent the night with a common soldier.'

But she hadn't. Not really. Heated tears sprung up in her eyes, for she didn't know how to respond to her father's accusations. Never could she have imagined he'd be this unreasonable.

A defence leapt to her lips, but Lieutenant Thorpe shook his head. 'As I said before, this is not the place to talk. Take Lady Hannah home.'

Hannah had never heard anyone issue an order to her father before, but the Lieutenant didn't appear intimidated by the Marquess.

'No one knows about this,' she whispered. 'My reputation is still safe.'

'Is it?' Her father's face was iron-cast. 'The Baron of Belgrave knows all about what happened to you. Nonetheless, he has graciously offered to wed you.'

She'd rather die than wed Belgrave. 'Papa, it isn't as bad as all that. Lieutenant Thorpe did nothing wrong.'

'Belgrave informed me that Thorpe assaulted him and took you away in a stolen carriage.'

'That lying blackguard,' Hannah blurted out, then clamped her hand over her mouth. Insults wouldn't help her cause.

Horrified, she met her father's infuriated expression, hoping he wouldn't believe the lies. Surely he would trust her, after all the years she'd been an obedient daughter. One mistake wouldn't eradicate everything, would it?

Thoughts of the Lieutenant's forbidden kiss flayed her conscience. She could have fought him off, but instead, she'd kissed him back. It had been curiosity and shock, mingled together with the first stirrings of desire. She'd wanted to know what a real kiss would be like. But not at this terrible cost.

'Harrison, take my daughter home,' the Marquess commanded to his footman. 'I will accompany Lieutenant Thorpe in this carriage.'

The Lieutenant gave an abrupt nod, and Hannah tried to fathom the man's thoughts. His hazel eyes were shielded, his face expressionless.

She prayed that they could undo the mistake that had been made. Surely they could keep matters quiet. She'd been a victim and didn't deserve to be punished like this. If anyone deserved to be drawn and quartered, it was Lord Belgrave.

As the footman closed the carriage door, Hannah twisted her hands together. Thank goodness the Lieutenant possessed no title. Were he an earl or a viscount, no doubt her father would demand that he marry her.

As a common officer in the British Army, that would never happen. She should feel relieved, but her nerves wound tighter. Her father was so angry right now, he might do something rash.

And she didn't know what that might be.

'YOU SHOULD KNOW that the only thing that prevents me from killing you where you stand is the fact that I don't want your blood staining my carpet.' The Marquess of Rothburne pointed to a wingback chair in his study. 'Sit.'

'I am not your dog,' Michael responded. He was well aware that he was only tossing oil upon the fire of James Chesterfield's rage, but he refused to behave as if he'd seduced Lady Hannah.

Kissed her, yes. But that wasn't a crime.

Michael rested his forearms upon the back of the chair and met the Marquess's gaze squarely. 'I don't regret rescuing Lady Hannah from the Baron of Belgrave. You know as well as I that the man isn't worthy of her.'

'And neither are you.'

'You're right.' There was no reason to take offence at the truth. He possessed enough to live comfortably on his army salary, but it wasn't enough to support a Marquess's daughter. He didn't want a wife, or any family who would rely upon him.

'Because of you, her reputation is destroyed.'

'No.' Michael drew closer to the desk, resting his hands upon the carved wood. 'Because of Belgrave. Were it not for him, she'd never have been taken from Rothburne House.'

'You should have brought her home immediately!' The Marquess's face was purple with wrath.

He knew it. But she'd been in such pain, he hadn't wanted to make it worse. At the time, he'd thought it would only be for a short while—not hours. Perhaps he should have driven her home, despite the agony she would have endured. Still, it did no good to dwell upon events he couldn't change.

'She's had headaches like that one before, hasn't she?' Michael said softly. 'She told me she keeps laudanum in her reticule.'

'That is beside the point.'

'Is it? I presume you've seen how much she suffers? That any form of light or sound gives her pain beyond all understanding? I've seen men take a bullet through their shoulder and suffer less than what I saw her endure.'

He didn't add that there were moments when he'd wondered if she was going to die. She'd been so pale, in such agony.

'Even if what you say is true, it doesn't change the fact that you stayed with her alone for hours.' James reached out for a letter opener, running his finger along the edge. 'She is my only daughter. My youngest child.'

'This wasn't her fault.' Yet, Michael didn't see a clear solution. It wasn't fair for Hannah to endure the sly gossip of the society matrons, nor to be shunned if word got out.

'No, it's yours.' The Marquess folded his arms, adding, 'Don't think that I would allow a man like you to wed her. You won't touch a penny of her inheritance.'

Michael stepped back, his anger barely controlled. Keeping his voice steady, he said, 'I don't want anything from either of you. She was in trouble, and I went to help her. Nothing more.'

The Marquess set his pen down. 'I want you to leave England. I don't want her to ever set eyes upon you again.' Picking up his pen, he began writing. 'I am going to ask your commanding officer to see to it. I'll contribute enough funds to the Army to make sure you stay far away from London.'

Michael didn't doubt that the Marquess's money would accomplish anything the man wanted. 'And what will happen to Lady Hannah?'

The Marquess set down his pen. 'Belgrave has offered to wed her.'

'No. Not him.' Michael clenched his fist. 'You would offer her up to a man like that?'

'There is nothing wrong with Belgrave. He's going to keep Hannah's reputation safe.'

'You mean he's going to reveal the scandal to everyone if she doesn't wed him,' Michael guessed.

The Marquess didn't deny it. 'I won't let my daughter be hurt. Not if I can prevent it from happening.'

HANNAH HAD SEEN her mother cry before, but never like this. Usually Christine Chesterfield used her tears to dramatic effect, whenever her husband wouldn't let her opinion sway him.

This time, Christine simply covered her mouth with her hand while the tears ran down her cheeks. Hannah sat across from her, while two cups of tea went cold. The grandfather clock in the parlour chimed eight o'clock. Eight hours was all it had taken to change her life completely.

'I promise you, Mother, I am fine,' Hannah murmured. 'Neither of them compromised me.' She refused to cry, for the shock was still with her. 'I don't know what else to say, when you won't accept the truth.'

'This isn't about truth.' Christine dabbed her eyes with a handkerchief. 'It's about appearances.'

'It will be all right,' Hannah insisted. 'My friends will believe me, if they hear rumours. They know I would never do anything of that nature.' She stood up, pacing across the carpet. 'I don't see why we cannot simply tell everyone what happened.'

Christine blew her nose. 'You are far too naïve, my dear. We can't risk any of this scandal leaking to anyone.'

'I am not ruined.'

'You are. Your only hope of salvaging what's left of your honour is to marry Lord Belgrave and to do so quickly.'

'I will not marry that horrid man. He's the reason all of this happened!' Hannah arranged her skirts, tucking her feet beneath them. 'He kidnapped me from my own home, Mother! Why won't you believe me?'

Her mother only shook her head sadly. 'I believe you, Hannah. But the greater problem is that you spent hours alone in a carriage with a soldier. Lord Belgrave is right: nothing will cover up that scandal, if it gets out.'

But no one knew about it, except...

'He's threatening you,' Hannah predicted, suddenly realising the truth. 'Belgrave plans to tell everyone about the scandal unless I wed him. Is that it?'

Her mother's face turned scarlet. 'We won't let that happen.'

Hannah couldn't believe what she was hearing. Her parents were allowing themselves to be manipulated for her sake.

Christine avoided looking at her. 'You have nothing to fear from the baron, Hannah. I believe him when he says he has nothing but remorse for his actions. He wants to start again, and I think you should give him a second chance.'

'I'd rather kiss a toad.'

'He is coming to pay a call on you tomorrow. And you *will* see him and listen to what he has to say.'

Without meeting Hannah's incredulous gaze, Christine retrieved a sheet of paper from a writing desk and chose a pen. Hannah clenched her fingers together, for she knew her mother was composing another list.

'Mother, no,' she pleaded. 'There has to be another way. Perhaps I could go to Falkirk with Stephen and Emily.' Her brother would offer her the sanctuary of his home without question.

'They have already left, early this morning,' her mother said. 'And your brother has enough to worry about with Emily due to give birth in a few weeks. He doesn't know what happened last night, and we are not going to tell him until it's all sorted out.'

Her mother handed her the list, and walked her to the door. 'Now. Go to your room and rest until eleven o'clock. When you rise, wear your rose silk gown with the high neck and pagoda sleeves. We will discuss your future over luncheon. The baron will come to call upon you tomorrow to discuss the arrangements.'

'I don't want to see that man again, much less marry him,' Hannah insisted.

'You no longer have a choice. You'd best get used to the idea, for your father is making the arrangements now. You'll be married within a week.'

AFTER HER MOTHER's door closed, Hannah stormed down the stairs, her shawl falling loose from her shoulders. There was no hope of finding sleep, not now.

With a brief glance at the list, she saw her mother's orders.

1. Rest until eleven o'clock.
2. Wear the rose silk gown.
3. Drink a cup of tea with cream, no sugar, to calm your nerves.

Hannah read the list three times, her hands shaking. Her entire life, she'd done everything her parents had asked. She had studied her lessons, listened to her governesses and done everything she could to please her family.

It made her stomach twist to see them turn against her this way. Her parents no longer cared about her future happiness—only their reputations.

Though she was supposed to return to her room, she kept moving towards the gardens. Tears of rage burned down her cheeks. All her years of being good meant nothing if she had to wed a man like Belgrave.

The list no longer held the familiarity of a mother's love, helping her to remember the tasks at hand. Instead, it was a chain, tightening around her neck.

Hannah crumpled up the paper and threw it into the shrubbery. Rules, rules and more rules. Once, she'd thought that, by obeying the rules, her reward would come.

Did her mother truly expect her to wed the man who

had caused her such misery? She'd sooner drown herself in the Thames than marry Belgrave.

She stumbled through the garden, the remnants of her headache rising up again. Why? Why did this have to happen to her? Only yesterday, she'd had so many choices before her. Now, she had nothing at all.

Hannah wrapped her arms around her waist, as if holding the pieces of herself together. With each step forward, she released the sobs, letting herself have a good cry. She wandered down the gravel pathway, to the place where she had lost her necklace last night.

Unexpectedly, her hand rose to her throat. The diamonds were there. The Lieutenant must have returned the necklace to her early this morning. She didn't remember him wrapping the strand around her neck, for most of the night had been a blur of pain.

After she'd been abducted, the baron had grown flustered at her illness, demanding that she cease her tears. He'd cursed at her, but she'd been unable to stop weeping.

Then the Lieutenant had rescued her. He'd covered up all light, keeping her warm. Not speaking a sound. Holding her in the darkness.

Hannah pulled her shawl around her shoulders. She didn't know what to think of him. One minute, he'd been her saving grace, and the next, he'd stolen a kiss.

Shielding her eyes against the morning sun, she saw him standing near the stables while a groom readied his horse. Almost against her will, Hannah's feet moved forward, drawing her closer to the Lieutenant. She didn't have the faintest idea what to say, or why she was even planning to speak to him.

The Lieutenant's hazel eyes were tired, his cheeks covered in dark stubble. The white cravat hung open at his throat, and he held his hat in his hands.

Hannah dipped her head in greeting, and out of deference, the groom stepped away to let them talk. She kept her voice low, so the servant wouldn't overhear their conversation. 'I'm glad my father didn't murder you.'

Michael shrugged and put on one of his riding gloves. 'I'm a difficult man to kill.'

Hannah found her attention caught by his long fingers, and she remembered his bare hand caressing her nape. No one had ever made her feel that way before, her skin sparking with unfamiliar sensations.

She closed her eyes, clearing her thoughts. Then she reached for what she truly needed to say. 'I never thanked you for rescuing me. It means a great deal to me. Even despite all of this.'

The Lieutenant gave a slight nod, as though he didn't know how to respond. He didn't acknowledge the words of gratitude, but instead glanced over at the house. 'Lord Rothburne said you're going to marry Belgrave.'

Hannah tensed. 'My father is ready to marry me off to the next titled gentleman who walks through the gate.' She stared him in the eyes. 'I won't do it. He'll have to drag me to the altar.'

'I thought you were the obedient sort.'

'Not about this.' She could hardly believe the words coming out of her mouth. It wasn't like her, not at all, but then she felt like someone had taken a club to her life, smashing it into a thousand glass pieces.

Obedience had brought her nothing. And right now she wanted to voice her frustrations to someone who understood.

'Why is this happening?' she whispered. 'What did I do that was so wrong?'

'Nothing,' the Lieutenant said. His hand started to reach for hers, but he drew back, as if remembering that it wasn't proper. 'Your only fault is being the daughter of a Marquess.'

'I wish I weren't.' Hannah lowered her head. 'I wish I were nothing but an ordinary woman. I would have more freedom.'

No lists, no rules to follow. She could make her own decisions and be mistress of her life.

'You wouldn't want that at all.' The Lieutenant gestured toward her father's house. 'You were born to live in a world such as this.'

'It's a prison.'

'A gilded prison.'

'A prison, nonetheless.' She raised her eyes to his. 'And now I'll be sentenced to marriage with Lord Belgrave. Unless I can find a way out.'

He didn't respond, but she saw the way his mouth tightened, the sudden darkness in his eyes. 'You will.'

'And what about you?' She realised she'd never asked what had happened to him. Surely the Lieutenant had faced his own lion's den, courtesy of the Marquess. 'What happened between you and my father?'

He hesitated before answering, 'My commanding officer will see to it that I stay on the Crimean Peninsula.'

'What exactly…does that mean?' A shiver of foreboding passed through her.

'I'll be sent to fight. Possibly on the front lines.' He shrugged, as if it were to be expected. But she understood what he wouldn't say. Men who fought on the front lines had essentially been issued a death sentence without a court-martial. Certainly it was no place for an officer.

She stared at him, her skin growing cold. Though he might be an unmannered rogue who had taken unfair advantage of her, he didn't deserve to die.

This is your fault. Her conscience drove the truth home

like an arrow striking its target. If it weren't for her, he'd be returning to his former duties.

'You were wounded before,' she said slowly. 'With the Light Brigade.'

He gave a nod. 'I would have been returning to duty anyway. I've made a full recovery.' He spoke as if it didn't matter, that this was of no concern.

She looked into his eyes, her heart suddenly trembling. 'It's not right for you to be sent away again.'

'I've no ties to London, sweet. I always expected to return. It doesn't matter.' He started towards his horse, but Hannah stopped him.

He was going to lose everything because of her. Because he'd rescued her and taken care of her that night.

'It matters.' She touched the sleeve of his coat, feeling obligated to do something for him. There had to be some way she could intervene with her father's unnecessary punishment.

'Stop looking at me like that,' he murmured, his eyes centering directly on hers.

'What do you mean?'

'Like you're trying to rescue me.'

'I'm not.' She lifted her face to his, studying those deep hazel eyes. He was a soldier, trained to strike down his enemies. Right now, he looked tired, but no less dangerous.

'Trust me, sweet. I'm not a man worth saving.' He took her hand in his and, despite the gloves, she felt the heat of his skin. 'You'd do well to stay away from me.'

The evocative memory of his stolen kiss conjured gooseflesh on her arms. The Lieutenant never took his eyes from her, and Hannah held herself motionless.

It went against everything she'd been taught, to hold an unmarried man's hand while standing in the garden where anyone could see. He was so close, the barest breath hung between them.

Something wanton and unbidden unfurled from within her, making her understand that Michael Thorpe was no ordinary man. He fascinated her. Tempted her.

And the daughter of a Marquess could never, never be with a man like him. He was right.

At last, she took her hand from his, ignoring the pang of disappointment. It was better for her to stay away from him. He was entirely the wrong sort of man.

Yet he was the only man who had noticed her absence at the ball. He hadn't stopped to notify her father and brothers, but had come after her straight away. An unexpected hero.

The Lieutenant's ill-fitting coat had a tear in the elbow. Shabby and worn, he didn't fit into the polished world in which she lived. But beneath his rebellious air was a man who had fought to save her.

Would he do so again, if she asked it of him?

'Lieutenant Thorpe, I have a favour to ask.'

He eyed her with wariness. 'What is it?'

It felt so awkward to ask this of him. She dug her nails into her palms, gathering up her courage. 'If I am forced into marriage with Lord Belgrave, would you…put a stop to the wedding?'

A lazy smile perked at his mouth. 'You're asking me to kidnap you from your own wedding?'

'If it comes to that—yes.' She squared her shoulders, pretending as though she hadn't voiced an inappropriate request. 'I shall try to avoid it, of course. You would be my last resort.'

He expelled a harsh laugh and went over to his horse, bringing the animal between them. Grasping the reins in one hand, he tilted his head to study her. 'You're serious.'

'Nothing could be more serious.' It was an arrangement,

a practical way of preventing the worst tragedy of her life. And though it might cause an even greater scandal, she would do anything to escape marriage to Belgrave.

'I have to report to duty,' the Lieutenant warned. 'It's likely I would be gone within the week.'

She gave a brisk nod, well aware of that. 'Believe me, my parents want to see me married as soon as possible. It's likely a wedding will be arranged in a few days. I simply refuse to wed Belgrave. Any other man will do.'

'Even me?' He sent her a sidelong smile, as though he, too, couldn't believe what she was asking.

'Well, no.' She pinched her lips together, realising that she'd led him to believe something she'd never intended. 'I couldn't possibly—'

'Don't worry, sweet.' His voice grew low, tempting her once again. 'I'll stop your wedding, if it's in my power.'

She breathed once again, her shoulders falling in relief. 'I would be most grateful.' Knowing that he would be there in the background, to steal her away from an unwanted wedding, gave her the sense that somehow everything would be all right. She held out her gloved palm, intending to shake his hand on the bargain.

The Lieutenant took her gloved hand in his. Instead of a firm handshake, he raised her palm to his face. 'If I steal the bride away,' he murmured, pressing his lips to her hand, 'what will I get in return?'

CHAPTER FOUR

'WHAT DO YOU WANT?'

Michael's response was a slow smile, letting her imagine all the things he might do to a stolen bride, if they were alone.

Hannah's expression appeared shocked. 'I would never do such a thing. This is an arrangement, nothing more.'

Her face had gone pale, and Michael pulled back, putting physical distance between them. 'Don't you recognise teasing when you hear it, sweet?'

She looked bewildered, but shook her head. 'Don't make fun of me, please. This is about Belgrave. I simply can't marry him.'

'Then don't.'

'It's not that simple. Already my mother has decided it would be the best future for me.' Hannah rubbed at her temples absently. 'I don't know what I can do to convince her otherwise.'

'It's very simple. Tell her no.'

She was already shaking her head, making excuses to herself. 'I can't. She won't listen to a thing I say.'

'You've never disobeyed them, have you?'

'No.' She seemed lost, so vulnerable that he half-wished there was someone who could take care of her. Not him. There was no hope of that. She was far better off away from a man like himself.

'No one can force you to marry. Not even your father.'

He adjusted her shawl so it fully covered her shoulders. 'Hold your ground and endure what you must.'

Visions flooded his mind, of the battle at Balaclava where his men had obeyed that same command. They'd tried valiantly to stand firm before the enemy. A hailstorm of enemy bullets had rained down upon them, men dying by the hundreds.

Was he asking her to do the same? To stand up to her father, knowing that the Marquess would strike her down? Perhaps it was the wrong course of action.

'I don't think I can,' Hannah confessed. She tugged at a finger of her glove, worrying the fabric. 'Papa can make my life a misery. And I'll be ruined if I don't marry.'

Though she was undoubtedly right, he could not allow himself to think about her future. They were worlds apart from one another. She would have to live with whatever choices she made.

'Time to make your own fortune. If you're already ruined, you've nothing left to lose. Do as you please.'

Hannah stared at him, as though she hadn't the faintest idea of how a ruined woman should behave. 'I don't know. I've always…done what I should.'

She took a step towards the house, away from him. He suddenly understood that she'd asked him to rescue her, not because of her parents, but because the need to obey was so deeply ingrained in her. If he kidnapped her from the wedding, she could lay the blame at his feet, not hers.

She's not your concern, his brain reminded him. *Let her make her own choices. Tell her no.*

But he didn't. Though he shouldn't interfere, neither would he let her marry a man like Belgrave. He let out a breath, and said, 'Send word to me if anything changes. Your brothers know where I can be found.'

'Will you be all right?' she asked in a small voice. 'What if my father—?'

'He can do nothing to me,' Michael interrupted. Within a week or two, there would be hundreds of miles between them. He'd be back with the Army, fighting the enemy and obeying orders until he met his own end. Men like him weren't good for much else.

The troubled expression on her face hadn't dimmed. Instead, a bright flush warmed her cheeks. 'Thank you for agreeing to help me.' Hannah reached up to her neck and unfastened the diamond necklace. 'I want you to have this.'

'Keep it.' He closed her fingers back over the glittering stones. An innocent like her could never conceive of the consequences, if he were to accept. Her father would accuse him of stealing, no matter that it had been a gift.

'If you're planning to keep watch over me, then you'll need a reason to return.' She placed it back in his palm.

He hadn't considered it in that light. 'You're right.' The necklace did give him a legitimate reason to return, and so he hid the jewellery within his pocket.

'Return in a day or two,' she ordered. 'And I'll see to it that you're rewarded for your assistance, whether or not it's needed.'

He wouldn't accept any compensation from her, though his funds were running out. 'It's not necessary.'

'It is.'

In her green eyes, Michael saw the loss of innocence, the devastating blow to her future. Yet beneath the pain, there was determination.

She crossed her arms, as if gathering her courage. 'I won't let my father destroy my future.' Her expression shifted into a stubborn set. 'And I won't let him destroy yours, either.'

THE OLDER WOMAN wandered through the streets, her crimson bonnet vivid in the sea of dark brown and black. Michael pushed his way past the fishmongers and vendors, minding his step through Fleet Street.

Mrs Turner was lost again. He quickened his step, moving amid sailors, drovers and butchers. At last, he reached her side.

'Good morning,' he greeted her, tipping his hat.

No recognition dawned in her silver-grey eyes, but she offered a faint nod and continued on her path.

Damn. It wasn't going to be one of her better days. Mrs Turner had been his neighbour and friend for as long as he could remember, but recently she'd begun to suffer spells of forgetfulness from time to time.

He hadn't known about her condition until he'd returned to London last November. At first, the widow had brought him food and drink, looking after him while he recovered from the gunshot wounds. He'd broken the devastating news of her son Henry's death at Balaclava.

And as the weeks passed, she began to withdraw, her mind clouding over. There were times when she only remembered things from the past.

Today she didn't recognise him at all.

Michael tried to think of a way to break through to her lost memory. 'You're Mrs Turner, aren't you?' he commented, keeping up with her pace. 'Of Number Eight, Newton Street?'

She stopped walking, fear rising on her face. 'I don't know you.'

'No, no, you probably don't remember me,' he said quickly. 'But I'm a friend of Henry's.'

The mention of her son's name made her eyes narrow. 'I've never seen you before.'

'Henry sent me to fetch you home,' he said gently. 'Will you let me walk with you? I'm certain he's left a pot of whisky and tea for you. Perhaps some marmalade and bread.'

The mention of her favourite foods made her lower lip tremble. Wrinkles edged her eyes, and tears spilled over them. 'I'm lost, aren't I?'

He took her hand in his, leading her in the proper direction. 'No, Mrs Turner.'

As he guided her through the busy streets, her frail hand gripped his with a surprising strength. They drew closer to her home at Peabody Square, and her face began to relax. Whether or not she recognised her surroundings, she seemed more at ease.

Michael helped her inside, and saw that she was out of coal. 'I'll just be a moment getting a fire started for you.' Handing her a crocheted blanket, he settled her upon a rocking chair to wait.

AFTER PURCHASING A bucket of coal for her, he returned to her dwelling and soon had a fire burning.

Mrs Turner huddled close to it, still wearing her bright red bonnet. He'd given it to her this Christmas, both from her love of the outrageous colour, and because it made it easier to locate her within a crowd of people.

'Why, Michael,' she said suddenly, her mouth curving in a warm smile. 'I didn't realise you'd come to visit. Make a pot of tea for us, won't you?'

He exhaled, glad to see that she was starting to remember him. When he brought out the kettle, he saw that she had hardly any water remaining. There was enough to make a pot of tea, though, and he put the kettle on to boil.

'You're looking devilishly handsome, I must say.' She beamed. 'Where did you get those clothes?'

He didn't tell her that she'd loaned them to him last

night, from her son's clothing. Bringing up the memory of Henry's death would only make her cry again.

'A good friend let me borrow them,' was all he said. When her tea was ready, he brought her the cup, lacing it heavily with whisky.

She drank heartily, smacking her lips. 'Ah, now you're a fine lad, Michael. Tell me about the ball last night. Did you meet any young ladies to marry?'

'I might have.' The vision of Lady Hannah's lovely face came to mind. 'But they tossed me out on my ear.'

She gave a loud laugh. 'Oh, they did no such thing, you wretch.' She drained the mug, and he refilled it with more tea. 'I'm certain you made all the women swoon. Now, tell me what they were wearing.' She wrapped the blanket around herself, moving the rocking chair closer to the fire.

While he answered her questions about the Marquess and his vague memory of the women's gowns, he tried to locate food for her. Scouring her cupboards, he found only a stale loaf of bread. Beside it, he saw a candle, a glove and all of the spoons.

He searched everywhere for marmalade, finally locating it among her undergarments in a drawer. He was afraid to look any further, for fear of what else he might find. Ever since she'd begun having the spells, he'd found all manner of disorganisation in her home.

He cut her a thick slice of bread and slathered it with marmalade. God only knew when she'd eaten last.

Mrs Turner bit into it, sighing happily. 'Now, then. Who else did you meet at the ball, Michael?' She lifted her tea up and took another hearty swallow.

'A foreign gentleman was there,' he added. 'Someone from Lohenberg.'

The cup slid from Mrs Turner's hand, shattering on the floor. Tea spilled everywhere, and her face had gone white.

Michael grabbed a rag and soaked up the spill, cleaning up the broken pieces. 'It's all right. I'll take care of it.'

But when he looked into Mrs Turner's grey eyes, he saw consummate fear. 'Who—who was he?'

'Graf von Reischor,' he said. 'The ambassador, I believe. It was nothing.'

He said not a word about the man's impossible claim, that he looked like their king. But Mrs Turner gripped his hand, her face bone white. 'No. Oh, no.'

'What is the matter?' He stared into her silver eyes, wondering why the mention of Lohenberg would frighten her so. Neither of them had ever left England before.

A few minutes later, Mrs Turner's face turned distant. She whispered to herself about her son Henry, as though he were a young child toddling toward her.

It was useless to ask her anything now. The madness had descended once more.

HANNAH WASN'T ENTIRELY certain what a ruined woman should wear, but she felt confident that it wouldn't be a gown the colour of cream. This morning, Christine Chesterfield had inspected every inch of her attire, fussing over her as if she were about to meet the Queen.

'Now remember,' her mother warned, 'be on your very best behaviour. Pretend that nothing happened the other night.'

Nothing did happen, she wanted to retort, but she feigned subservience. 'Yes, Mother.'

Christine reached out and adjusted a hairpin, ensuring that not a single strand was out of place. 'Did you read my list?'

'Of course.' Hannah offered the slip of paper, and her mother found a pen, hastily scratching notes.

'I've made changes for tonight. At dinner, you are to

wear the white silk gown with the rose embroidery and your pearls. Estelle will fix your hair, and you should be there by eight o'clock.'

Her mother handed her the new list. 'I have advised Manning not to serve you any blanc mange or pudding. And no wine. You have been indulging far more than you should, my dear. Estelle tells me that your figure is a half-inch larger than it should be.'

Her throat clenched, but Hannah said nothing. She stared down at the list, the words blurring upon the page. Never before had she questioned her mother's orders. If she couldn't have sweets, then that was because Christine wanted her to have an excellent figure. It was love, not control. Wasn't it?

But she felt herself straining against the invisible bonds, wanting to escape. Her mother was worried about the size of her waistline, when her entire future had been turned upside down? It seemed ridiculous, in light of the scandal.

With each passing moment, Hannah's discomfort worsened. 'Mother, honestly, I don't feel up to receiving visitors. I'd rather wait a few days.' She hadn't slept well last night, and her mind was preoccupied with the uncertain future.

'You will do as you're told, Hannah. The sooner you are married, the sooner you can put this nightmare behind you.' Her mother stood and guided her to the parlour. 'Now wait here until Lord Belgrave arrives. He told your father he would come to call at two o'clock.'

Hannah realised she might as well have been speaking to a stone wall. In her mind, she envisioned her parents chaining her ankle to the church pew, her mouth stuffed with a handkerchief while they wedded her off to Belgrave.

At least she had an hour left, before the true torment began. She contemplated escaping the house, but what good would it do to run away? Nothing, except make her parents angrier than they already were.

No, if she had to face Lord Belgrave again, she would tell him exactly what she thought of him. Perhaps he would call off his plans.

Her father, the Marquess, stood beside the fireplace, his pocket watch in his hands. Disappointment and sadness cloaked his features as he put the watch in his waistcoat. He paced towards the sofa and sat down, his wrists resting upon his knees.

Hannah went and sat down beside her father. She reached out and took his hand. Anger would never win a battle against her father. But he had a soft spot for obedience.

'I know that you are trying to protect me,' she said gently. 'And as your only daughter, I know that you want someone to take care of me.'

His grey eyes were stormy with unspoken fury, but he was listening.

'I beg of you, Papa, don't ask me to marry Lord Belgrave,' she pleaded. 'I don't care if he reveals the scandal to everyone.'

'I do.' Her father's grip tightened around her knuckles. 'I won't allow our family name to be degraded, simply because you lost your judgement one night.'

Hannah pulled her hand away. 'I will marry no one.' Rising to her feet, she added, 'Most especially not the Baron of Belgrave.'

'It won't be Michael Thorpe. God help me, you will *not* wed a soldier.'

The thought had never entered her mind, but at the reminder of the Lieutenant, a caress of heat erupted over her body. Sensual and rebellious, a man like Michael Thorpe would never treat her with the polite distance so typical of marriage. No, she suspected he was the sort of man who would possess her, stealing her breath away in forbidden pleasure.

Hannah shook her head. 'Of course not.'

Plunging forward, she revealed an alternate plan. 'Send me somewhere far away from London until the talk dies down. We have cousins elsewhere in Europe, don't we?'

'Germany,' he admitted. His countenance turned grim, but she though she detected a softening in his demeanour. *Please, God, let him listen to me,* she prayed.

At that moment, the footman Phillips gave a quiet knock. 'Forgive me, my lord, but the Baron of Belgrave has come to call upon Lady Hannah.'

The Marquess hesitated a moment before speaking. Hannah gripped her fingers together so hard, her knuckles turned white. She shook her head, pleading with her father.

'Give him another chance, Hannah,' the Marquess said quietly. 'Despite his reproachable actions, the man does come from an excellent family. He can provide you with anything you'd ever need.'

She couldn't believe the words had come from her father's mouth. She'd known that he cared about appearances, that upholding model behaviour was important to him. But she'd never thought it was more important than her own well-being.

'Papa, please,' she whispered again. 'Don't ask this of me.'

Her father's face tensed, but his tone was unyielding when he spoke. 'Tell the baron my daughter will await him in the drawing room.'

CHAPTER FIVE

MICHAEL STOOD AT attention when Colonel Hammond entered the room. He'd been summoned to the War Office this morning, but it wasn't the commander-in-chief who'd prepared his new orders. Instead, he'd been shown into a smaller sitting room. 'Colonel, you asked to see me?'

'Yes. I'm afraid there's been a change in your assignment,' the Colonel admitted. The senior officer's red jacket gleamed with brass buttons, the gold epaulettes resting upon his shoulders. Michael felt ill at ease in his own slate-blue uniform, which still bore the bloodstains he hadn't been able to wash clean.

The Colonel gestured towards a wooden chair, and Michael took a seat. 'You won't be returning to the front, after all.'

'I've made a full recovery,' Michael felt compelled to point out. 'I'm ready to fight again.'

Colonel Hammond looked uncomfortable. 'That will have to wait, I'm afraid. Though I should like to see you return to battle as well—we can always use men of your fortitude—I'm afraid the Army has other plans for you.'

An uncomfortable suspicion settled in his gut. Had the Marquess used his powers of influence so soon? He'd known that he would probably be sent away from England, but he'd expected to return to duty.

'What are my orders?'

The Colonel sat across from him, a large mahogany

desk as a barrier between them. 'You will accompany the ambassador from Lohenberg, the Graf von Reischor, to his homeland. He has proposed to send supplies to the Crimean Peninsula, offering aid from their country to our troops. You will assist the Commissariat by choosing what is most needed for the men.'

Michael's hand clenched into a fist. He didn't believe for a moment that the Graf was acting out of concern for the British troops. This was nothing but a stranger meddling in his military career, all because he'd ignored the summons. Why should he care whether or not he resembled the King of some tiny, forgotten country?

He'd given years of service to the Army, obeying orders and doing his best to keep his men alive. And with a single stroke of the pen, the Lohenberg Graf had turned his military career from a soldier into an errand boy.

'You honour me, Colonel,' he lied, 'but I'm nothing but a lieutenant. Why not one of my commanding officers?'

'The ambassador requested you. I suggested another officer as a liaison, but he insisted that it must be you, or he would reconsider the offer.' There was a questioning note in the Colonel's voice, but Michael gave no response. He couldn't tell his commander why the Graf wanted him to travel to Lohenberg, when he didn't know the man's intent.

'I'd rather be back with my men,' he said quietly. 'I owe it to them, after what happened at Balaclava.' He'd tried to save whatever lives he could until he'd fallen, shot and bleeding on the field.

'I understand Nolan spoke well of you and your bravery before the battle.' The Colonel's voice was also quiet, as though remembering those soldiers who had not returned.

He turned his attention to pouring a cup of tea. 'While we would welcome you back on the Peninsula, Lieutenant Thorpe, this alliance is far too important. I'm afraid your orders are clear. The Graf has requested you, and it is our hope that you can convince the Lohenberg Army to join in our cause.'

Bitter silence permeated the room, and Michael rose from his seat. Damned if he was going to allow the Graf to ruin everything he'd worked for. He would go and try to convince the man to choose another officer. Then, perhaps he could rejoin what was left of the 17th Lancers.

Michael bowed and offered a polite farewell to Colonel Hammond, who shook his hand afterwards and wished him well.

'I will give your regards to the men, upon my return to Balaclava, Lieutenant. You will report to Graf von Reischor at eight o'clock tomorrow morning.'

His heart filled with anger; numb to all else, Michael gripped the Colonel's hand and murmured another farewell.

It was becoming quite clear that Graf von Reischor believed himself to be a puppet master, jerking his strings toward a path that was not his.

As he left the War Office, Michael shoved his hands inside his pockets, only to find the tangled strand of diamonds Hannah had given him.

He slid his hands over the hard stones, feeling the chain warm beneath his fingertips. Although Hannah believed the diamonds would grant him an excuse to return to Rothburne House, that wasn't a wise idea. The Marquess would murder him if he so much as set foot upon a blade of Rothburne grass.

It's not your battle to fight.

He knew he shouldn't be involved. Their lives were too distant from one another, and despite the night they'd spent in the carriage, she was better off if he left her alone. Most likely Hannah would be all right, with her father and brothers to protect her.

The way they had on the night Belgrave took her? his conscience reminded him. His trouble instincts were rising up again.

He expelled a foul curse and continued walking through the streets. An hour. He could spend that much time ensuring for himself that she hadn't been dragged off by Belgrave.

Hackney cab drivers called out, offering to drive him, but he ignored them. It wasn't such a long walk, and he didn't have the money for it anyway.

The thin soles of his shoes were worn down, and as he continued on the walk to Rothburne House, he felt the cobbled stones more than he'd have liked. He hadn't broken his fast this morning, and the thought of food made his stomach hurt. It didn't help matters to see a vendor selling meat pies and iced raisin buns.

After half an hour, he finally reached Rothburne House. He recognised Lord Belgrave's carriage waiting outside. A grim resolution took root inside him, to get rid of Belgrave.

He couldn't approach the front entrance, however. Rothburne's footmen would throw him out. His military uniform also made it impossible to reconnoitre without being easily noticed.

Quickly, Michael stripped off his jacket and shako, hiding the plumed military cap and outer coat beneath a trimmed boxwood hedge. Beside it, he placed his officer's sword. He removed Hannah's necklace from the jacket and placed it in his pocket.

Traversing the perimeter of the house, he spied an open window on the first floor. Time to discover exactly what Belgrave was up to.

LORD BELGRAVE'S HARDENED face transformed into a smile when he saw her. 'Lady Hannah, you look lovely, as always. Well worth the wait.' The baron bowed in greeting, and Hannah felt an unladylike sense of satisfaction at the bruises darkening his cheek and the bandage across his nose. No doubt the wounds were from his brawl with Lieutenant Thorpe.

Only years of training made her dip into a curtsy. She'd changed her gown three times in an effort to delay the inevitable. Only when her mother had arrived to escort her in person did she finally enter the drawing room.

Lady Rothburne sent the baron a blinding smile, gripping Hannah's wrist so hard that the skin turned white. 'Lord Belgrave, it was kind of you to pay a call under these...circumstances.'

'It was my pleasure, Lady Rothburne.'

Another jerk of the wrist, and Hannah understood her mother's silent rebuke. All right. If she had to endure this charade, so be it.

'Lord Belgrave.' She didn't care how icy her tone was; the sooner she could get rid of him, the better.

'Lady Hannah, I believe you know why I have come.' He patted the seat beside him in an obvious invitation.

'And I believe you know what my answer is.' Hannah remained standing, her arms crossed. 'Your visit was a waste of time, I am afraid.'

'Hannah—' Lady Rothburne implored. 'Do be kind enough to at least listen to Lord Belgrave.'

Though she wanted to fight back, to lash out at her mother, Hannah found herself sinking into a chair. Out of habit, she fell silent, as if a shroud had fallen over her. Choking off any hint of defiance, she listened to Belgrave speak.

'I offer my apologies for what happened the other evening,' the baron began. 'But, Lady Hannah, I believe it would be in your best interest to consider my offer.' He went on to describe his different estates, both in London and Yorkshire. And of course, how much of an honour it would be to join their families together.

Hannah didn't listen to a word of it. Did Belgrave honestly believe that she would consider him, after the abduction? And were her parents so swept up in his money and family name that they would ignore what he'd done?

'We are pleased that you would still consider our daughter,' Lady Rothburne said. 'I am sure Hannah understands the necessity of protecting her reputation.' Brightening her smile, the Marchioness offered, 'I have ordered a picnic basket from Cook, and you both may wish to discuss wedding plans outside in the garden. It is a lovely day, and it would allow you to become better acquainted.'

'I would welcome the opportunity,' Belgrave answered.

'But, Mother, I—'

'Would next Tuesday morning suit, for the wedding?' the Marchioness interrupted.

'I am certain I can procure a special licence in time,' Belgrave reassured her mother. 'The archbishop will understand the need for haste.'

Say it. Tell them you'll never marry a man like him.

Hannah gripped the edge of her chair, and finally broke in. 'No.'

Her word came out too softly, and neither her mother, nor Lord Belgrave, seemed to notice.

'A quiet wedding would be best,' Belgrave suggested. 'Don't you think?'

'No,' Hannah tried again, this time louder and filled with all of her frustration. 'I don't think so.'

Lord Belgrave rose from his seat and came to stand beside her chair. His large fingers reached out to rest upon her shoulder. The weight of his palm was a firm reminder, not an act of comfort.

And suddenly, her mother's discussions of how a husband would have full dominion over her body made Hannah jerk away. She couldn't lie on her back and let a man like Belgrave do what he wished. Good wives were supposed to submit to their husbands, but, God help her, she could never let him touch her.

She didn't know where the words came from, only that she couldn't bear it any longer. 'There will not be a wedding.' Her voice shook with nerves, sounding more uncertain than she'd intended. 'I won't agree to it. And if you will excuse me, I intend to retire to my room.'

Her mother scurried forward to try to stop her, but Belgrave lifted his hand. 'Forgive me, Lady Rothburne, but perhaps if I had a moment in private with Lady Hannah, I could reassure her that I have only the best of intentions.'

The Marchioness hesitated, and Hannah prayed that her mother wouldn't dare allow such a thing.

'Wait in Lord Rothburne's study,' her mother advised the baron. 'I will speak with my daughter first.' She gestured for Hannah to sit down, and Lord Belgrave followed a servant into her father's study.

The grim expression on her mother's face was not at all encouraging. Christine sat across from her, and her face held nothing but disappointment.

'Hannah, you must know how much your father and I want what's best for you,' Christine began. With a tremulous smile, her mother wiped at her eyes with a handkerchief. 'We want you to have a wonderful marriage with every comfort you could possibly want.'

'Not with him,' Hannah insisted. 'Mother, I won't do it.'

'Is he really as awful as all that?' her mother asked softly. 'He's handsome and wealthy. You got off to a terrible start, I'll grant you that much. But couldn't you possibly give him a chance? This isn't only about your future. The scandal will darken your father's good name.'

'There must be another way.'

The Marchioness rose and drew close, putting her arms around her. 'Talk to him, Hannah. That's all I ask. If, after this, you still don't wish to wed him—' Her mother broke off, tears glistening in her eyes.

I don't, Hannah wanted to say. But she kept silent, knowing that to pacify her mother was the easiest way to get rid of Belgrave. 'Very well. I'll talk to him.'

Christine embraced her again, wiping her eyes. 'Thank you, my dear. It won't be so bad. You'll see.' Her mother took her by the hand and escorted her into the study. 'I'll be right here in the hall,' she offered. With an encouraging squeeze of the hand, she stepped back into the hallway, leaving the door wide open.

It was dark inside her father's study, with the curtains pulled shut. Hannah waited for Lord Belgrave to speak. Instead, he approached the door and closed it. Seconds later, he turned the key in the lock.

She stood immobile, stunned at his actions. What was he doing? Did he plan to assault her in her own home? Hannah's paralysing fear suddenly transformed into rage.

'Be thankful that I will forgive this defiance,' Belgrave murmured. 'You seem to be under the delusion that you have a choice in whom you wed. No other man will marry a woman who was defiled by a soldier.'

'Lieutenant Thorpe did nothing wrong. And I'd rather be a spinster than wed you.'

She wouldn't simply stand here and become Belgrave's victim. Good manners weren't going to protect her virtue, only actions.

Hannah eyed the contents of the study, dismissing the books or the large globe in one corner. Where was a medieval sword when she needed one? Or, better yet, a chastity belt.

He sent her a thin smile. 'Once you and I are married, no one will worry about the hours you spent with the Lieutenant.'

'It was your fault,' she shot back. 'All of this. And I know you've threatened to spread gossip about me.'

'Only the truth,' he said, with a shrug. 'But if you marry me, I'll forget all about it.'

'Do you honestly believe I would forgive you for threatening my family's name?'

'How else am I to wed the daughter of a Marquess?' he asked, his hand moving to her cheek. 'The ends justify the means. Perhaps tomorrow you and your mother might begin shopping for your trousseau.'

That was it. Just being in the same room with Belgrave made her feel like insects were crawling over her skin. When his mouth lowered to kiss her nape, Hannah reached for the gleaming brass candlestick. Swinging hard, she struck Belgrave across the skull, while another attacker hit him with a dictionary.

The baron crumpled to the floor.

'THAT WAS WELL DONE,' Lieutenant Thorpe complimented her, emerging from the shadows. He wore only part of his slate-blue military uniform, while his jacket, shako and sabre were missing.

Dear God, where had he come from? Not that she wasn't grateful, but he'd scared the life out of her.

Hannah choked back her shock and stared down at the fallen body of Belgrave. Her heart was still pounding with horror at what she'd done. 'Did we kill him?'

That was all she needed now. To be hanged for murder.

'I doubt it.'

She slumped into a leather chair, resting her forehead on her palm. Relief poured through her. 'What are you doing here? I thought you'd wait a few days at least.'

Michael pulled a chair across from her and sat. 'A soldier's instincts. You asked me to prevent a marriage between you and Belgrave. I saw his carriage when I passed by the house.'

It was a mild way to state that he'd been spying on her. And yet, she was grateful. Knowing that he'd kept his promise to watch over her made her feel safe. 'How did you get in here without anyone seeing you?'

The Lieutenant pointed towards the window. 'It's not difficult. I thought I'd sneak in, see that you were all right and leave.'

Her breath caught for just a moment. He'd planned to rescue her with a dictionary. A choked laugh bubbled in her throat, but Hannah tamped it down as she studied Belgrave's unconscious form. 'I should probably get some smelling salts.'

'Leave him. He looks good on the floor, after what he did to you the other night.'

She agreed with the Lieutenant, but didn't say so. 'No, it's really not a polite thing to do. I shouldn't have struck him with the candlestick. My mother would faint if she learned of it.'

He turned serious, resting his forearms on his knees as he regarded her. 'If you hadn't done so, he would have forced his attentions on you.' The Lieutenant's words were brutally blunt. 'And your parents could not have stopped him.'

Hannah's hands started to shake. It was cold in the study, and she gripped her arms to try to warm them.

A squeaking noise caught her attention—the Lieutenant was occupied with pushing the curtains aside and raising the window. 'Come on. We'll leave him here while you make your escape.'

'Not out there.' Anyone might see her, and it was impossible in her skirts. 'I'll just go back through the study door.'

'Do you plan to rummage through his pockets for the key?' he enquired. 'Or will you shout for one of the servants to break down the door?'

Hannah winced at the thought of touching Belgrave. 'There's no other way, Lieutenant Thorpe. Even if I wanted to go out the window, my skirts wouldn't fit.'

'You could remove some of your petticoats.'

'Never.' The thought made her ill. He might catch a glimpse of her ankle. Or worse, part of her stocking-clad leg. 'It's a terrible, ridiculous idea.'

He sat on the window sill, one leg in, one leg out. 'I never said it was a good idea. It's simply one of your options.' He shrugged. 'Either way, I am leaving through this window.' He disappeared from the sill, and Hannah stared at the study door.

Outside, she heard the voices of servants and her mother. She was about to approach the locked door, when Belgrave suddenly stirred.

His eyes snapped open, and he groaned, rubbing his head. When he staggered to his knees, Hannah didn't wait any longer. There wasn't time to get the key.

She raced towards the window and saw that it was about a six-foot drop. Not as bad as she'd expected. Below, the Lieutenant was waiting.

'Did you change your mind?'

'Don't let me fall,' Hannah ordered. She had a fleeting image of flying into the shrubbery, with her skirts over her head. The vision made her stomach lurch. Ladies did not jump from the window into an unmarried man's arms.

But her alternative was to face Belgrave again.

Why in the name of heaven did this have to happen to her? Hannah bemoaned the indignity of it all as she sat upon the window sill. Her tiered skirts fluffed around the window, the petticoats amassing in a large pile before her.

'I'll catch you,' came his voice. Glancing down, she saw the Lieutenant standing with his arms outstretched. His face was confident, his arms strong. He looked as though he would never let anything happen to her. 'Trust me.'

With a backwards glance, she saw Belgrave stumbling towards her. Squeezing her eyes shut, Hannah let herself tip backwards. Though she longed to release a scream as she fell, only a muffled 'oomph' left her lips as she landed in his embrace.

Sure enough, every petticoat remained in place. The Lieutenant lowered her down, and as they stood outside the servants' entrance, she marvelled that she'd done such a thing.

'To the garden,' she ordered. 'Quickly, before anyone sees us.'

He didn't argue, but led her towards the tall hedge, ducking around the corner. A crooked grin creased his mouth. 'I suppose that's the first time you've ever thrown yourself out a window.'

She flushed. 'I had no choice. Belgrave woke up.'

His smile faded into a tight line. 'You're safe from him now. You can go back through the front door and tell your mother what happened. I doubt if they'll force you to marry him now.'

'I should think not.' Hannah brushed at her gown, to give herself a way of avoiding his gaze. He was looking at her as though he wanted to kiss her again, and her nerves tightened. The boxwood hedge dug into her neck as she pressed herself against it. 'Thank you, Lieutenant.'

He acknowledged her thanks with a nod, but didn't leave

immediately. She noticed the way his attention shifted towards the kitchen. His features grew tight, and she understood suddenly that he was hungry.

Though she wanted to send the Lieutenant to the kitchen for a hot meal as a reward, she didn't dare, for fear her father would discover his presence.

'Go to the gardener's shed, and wait for me. I'll be right back.'

The Lieutenant shook his head. 'Lady Hannah, I have to leave.'

'You're hungry,' she said quietly. When he was about to protest, she held up her hand. 'I can see it. I'll get a basket of food for you from the kitchen. You'll have a meal as repayment for rescuing me.'

He took another step away from her. 'It's not a good idea for you to be seen with me again.'

'It sounds as though you're afraid of my father.'

He grimaced at her implication, and Hannah moved in for the kill. 'Don't worry, Lieutenant.'

She stepped towards the kitchen, her mood improving. 'If Papa dares to try to kill you, I promise to defend your honour, just as you did mine. I'm quite good with a candlestick.'

CHAPTER SIX

WHEN HANNAH OPENED the back door to the kitchen, she saw the servants busy chopping vegetables at the long table on the far side of the room. Their backs were to her, and they were busy talking amongst themselves. Near the wall beside her, she saw a tea tray with the picnic basket her mother had ordered earlier. Perfect.

Holding fast to her skirts, Hannah slipped inside and snatched the basket. She didn't wait to find out if anyone had seen her, but hastened back outside, ducking behind the arborvitae hedge. Within a few minutes more, she reached the gardener's shed.

The Lieutenant sat on the floor of the shed, but he'd spread out a few burlap sacks for her to sit upon. She handed him the basket. 'It's not much, but it's the only reward I could think of on such short notice. Thank you for rescuing me.'

He didn't take the basket immediately. 'No reward was necessary. I wasn't about to let Belgrave raise a hand against you.'

The words were spoken with a casual air, as though it were nothing. But even as he rested with one knee up, she saw his wrist hanging down, she saw a caged alertness. This was a man who would defend someone to the death. A ruthless soldier, one who showed no mercy to his enemies.

'A dictionary,' she remarked. 'Not a weapon I'd have

expected. It seems you are a man of more words than I'd thought.'

A hint of a smile twitched at his lips, and she avoided further discussion by opening the basket. She found a china plate and began loading it with slices of ham, bread and creamed spinach.

Concentrating on the food made it easier to forget that she was alone in a gardener's shed with a man who was far too handsome. Her nape prickled with awareness of him, and she tried to ignore his scrutiny.

Her hand reached up to straighten a strand of hair, and she felt completely improper without a bonnet or gloves.

'Aren't you going to eat?' he asked, after he'd made a sandwich out of the bread and ham. He ate slowly, but from the flash of relief on his face, Hannah knew she'd made the right decision to offer food.

'I'm not hungry.' She'd lost her appetite after the ordeal with Belgrave. Her emotions were bottled up so tightly with the knowledge that her family's reputation was about to be destroyed.

The awful pressure was building in her chest, and she clenched her skirts, staring down at them. A tear dripped down on her palm, and she struggled to keep herself together.

'Lady Hannah,' came the Lieutenant's deep voice. 'What is it?'

'Shh.' She raised a hand, unable to look at him. 'I just need a moment to…fall apart before I collect myself. It's been a most difficult morning.'

'Go ahead and cry,' he said. 'You deserve it, after the way he threatened you.'

Hannah couldn't stop the sobs from breaking forth, her shoulders huddled forward as she released the anger and disappointment.

'He's going to ruin me, after this,' she cried. 'All because I refused to marry him.'

Strong arms enveloped her in an embrace, but there was no judgement, only comfort. He said nothing, but she sensed his anger toward Belgrave.

'What am I supposed to do now?' Hannah whispered, feeling ashamed that her tears were dampening his shirt.

He held her against his chest, gently patting her back. 'I think you should leave London.'

'I agree.' A change in her surroundings was the only thing that would allow the gossip to die down.

She dried her tears, extricating herself from his arms. Though she'd expected to feel abashed at being in his embrace, strangely, she didn't.

Afterwards, she sat down upon one of the sacks, keeping a respectful, proper distance. Across from him, she felt small, almost fragile. He remained alert, as though he expected to leave at any moment.

'I am grateful for your help today. Tell me, did anyone else see you?'

'I don't think so.' His eyes held a glint of mischief. 'It's a good thing your father opened the window earlier.'

Smoothing her skirts, she straightened her posture. 'I do appreciate your help.'

'I suspect, after you struck Belgrave with the candlestick, Lord Rothburne will be less likely to force you into marriage.'

Hannah nodded, hoping that was true. 'When do you have to leave for the Crimean Peninsula?'

The Lieutenant tensed, and he busied himself with finishing the ham sandwich. After a moment, he replied, 'My orders were changed. I've been asked to go to Lohenberg instead.'

Lohenberg? Hannah frowned, wondering what the Army

would possibly want with the tiny country, nestled between Germany and Denmark. In school, she'd learned Lohenisch, among her studies of European languages, but it was hardly an important principality.

Hannah stared at him, unable to comprehend what he'd just informed her. 'Do you mean you're not going to fight any more?' Before he could answer, she plunged on. 'This is my fault, isn't it? My father—'

'—had nothing to do with it,' he finished. 'Another man is involved.'

'Who?'

'The Graf von Reischor.' He shook his head, stabbing at a bite of creamed spinach. 'It's a long story.'

'He was at Papa's ball the other night, wasn't he?' Hannah mused. Her father was good friends with the Lohenberg ambassador, but she'd hardly spoken with the man beyond an introduction, over a year ago. 'What would the Graf want with you?'

She bit her tongue as soon as she spoke, for it sounded as though she'd denigrated the Lieutenant's rank. 'I mean, why would he interfere with your orders?'

'I presume he will tell me that tomorrow morning.' His stiff posture made it clear he had no desire to discuss it further.

He was about to leave, but Hannah stopped him with a hand. 'Wait. You haven't finished everything.'

She removed a covered container and offered it to him, along with a spoon. 'It's Cook's newest dessert. She copied it after the Sacher Torte, which my parents tasted in Vienna. You'll want to try it.'

She'd never been allowed to partake of the rich dessert, but there was no reason why the Lieutenant should not enjoy the rare delicacy. Setting the container into his hands, she made him accept it.

Hannah lifted the lid, and against her will, her mouth watered. Rich chocolate covered the cake, while the inner layers were filled with apricot jam. What would it be like to taste such decadence?

The Lieutenant dipped his fork into the cake, and Hannah stared at the forbidden dessert.

Was it as good as it appeared to be? The soft icing looked so tempting, she forced herself to look away.

'You look as though you're ready to snatch my cake away,' he observed. 'Did you want some?'

'No, that's all right.' Lies. All lies. She breathed in the scent, wishing for just the tiniest taste. 'I'm not allowed to have sweets very often,' she admitted. 'Mother has my waist measured every day.'

The Lieutenant set his fork down, studying her as though she were a foreign creature. 'What do you do when you attend the dinner parties and balls? Surely you would offend the hostess if you refused to eat the dessert.'

She gave a reluctant smile. 'There are ways to play with your food, so it appears that you've eaten it. Don't tell me you never tried it, when you were a boy.'

'I ate everything my parents gave me. I was glad if it wasn't rancid.'

Hannah rested her hands in her lap. She'd never worried about where her food came from. It was always there, in endless variety. Only the best cuisine would meet her mother's impossible standards.

It was sobering to remember that most people worried about whether or not they had enough to eat. She should be grateful for her circumstances, despite the lack of freedom.

'Close your eyes,' the Lieutenant said suddenly.

'Why?'

'Do it.'

She obeyed, wondering what he intended. A moment

later, she felt the light brush of metal tines against her lips. His thumb urged her mouth to open, and the fork slid inside.

The sweetness hit her tongue first, then the bittersweet chocolate icing of the cake. Hannah breathed in as she held the unbelievable flavours against the roof of her mouth. She almost didn't want to swallow, it tasted so good.

When at last she did, she opened her eyes. The Lieutenant was staring at her, his gaze filled with heat. 'Don't ever look at a man like that,' he murmured. 'Else you'll find yourself in his bed.' There was wickedness in his tone, as if he wanted to be that man.

She returned the fork to him, suddenly conscious of the intimacy of sharing it. Michael set the plate aside, rising to his feet. 'I'm going to go now. Thank you for the food.'

'You're welcome.' She held the taste of the torte against the roof of her mouth, savouring the last remnants. And despite the terrible temptation, she would *not* lick the plate after he'd gone away.

'Wait here for a few moments, then go and sit in the garden,' he suggested. 'They'll find Belgrave and come looking for you.'

'Heaven help me when I'm found.'

He took her shoulders, looking her straight in the eye. 'You were brave enough to defeat Belgrave once before. You'll manage it again.'

She wished she felt the same confidence. Even so, it wasn't as if she had any choice. Lifting her gaze to his, she saw the faith in his eyes. And suddenly, she grew aware that he hadn't pulled his hands back.

His palms dominated her narrow shoulders, while hazel eyes bore into hers. He seemed to struggle with an invisible decision, but his hands remained where they were. She was caught by the memory of his fingers caressing her skin, and the unexpected brush of his mouth on her nape. The stolen kiss in the carriage…all of it made Hannah's sensibilities drift away.

If it had been the Lieutenant whom her parents wanted her to marry, she might have had a very different response. There was something forbidden about him. Something tempting.

'I'm not brave at all,' she whispered. 'I'm nothing but a foolish girl.' She lifted her hands to his shoulders, knowing that she was provoking him. Knowing that he wasn't safe at all, nor was he a gentleman.

The effect of her hands upon him was instantaneous. His hands stilled, and he leaned in, his cheek resting against hers. 'Tell me to stop.'

But she didn't. She had broken so many rules today, shaming her family and behaving like the worst sort of daughter.

'Push me away, Hannah. Take a damned spade and strike me over the head.' His gaze was heated, his eyes burning with a warning she couldn't possibly heed.

She couldn't have moved if she'd wanted to. Something about this man drew her in, tantalising her with the promise of physical pleasure.

'Don't stop. I need this…for a moment.' She didn't even understand what she was asking for.

'So innocent.' His mouth moved over her skin, caressing her with his warm breath. Like before, her body came alive, needing him to touch. To taste.

No matter how many books she'd read or how many languages she spoke, in physical matters she was completely ignorant. A secret part of her thirsted for the knowledge.

Michael pulled her against the shed, though he didn't hold her tight. 'This is your last chance to run away. I'm not above taking what's offered.'

'Show me what it's supposed to be like,' she murmured.

The words were all the encouragement he needed. He trapped her against the wood, covering her breathless mouth with his own. Instinct took over, and Hannah kissed him back, ignoring every warning that flew into her mind. She didn't care. Soon enough, she'd never see him again.

And, by heaven, if she was going to be ruined after today, she might as well have a memory to show for it.

His tongue slid inside her mouth, evoking a shocking sensation. Her breasts ached against the fabric of her gown, her nipples rising. Michael slipped his hands around her waist, his wide palms resting upon her ribs. His kiss grew more fierce, his mouth conquering hers. She opened to him, and raw desire pummelled her senses, making it impossible to stop, even if she'd wanted him to.

And God help her, she didn't. He pulled her close and she felt the hard length of his body nestled against her. Something unexpected blossomed inside, and she shifted her thighs, not understanding what was happening.

His mouth moved over her throat in a forbidden caress. 'You shouldn't have started this. I was going to let you go untouched.'

'I know.' She shuddered as his tongue flicked over her pulse. The secret longings made it impossible to think clearly, and she couldn't bring herself to pull away. 'But there's no harm in a kiss, is there?' When he didn't answer, she prompted, 'Lieutenant?'

'Michael,' he corrected. 'And you're wrong, if you think that's all I want from you.' His hands moved over her bodice, resting just beneath her breasts. Hannah grew feverish, her skin blazing with wanton needs.

'I don't know what you want.' *Or what I want,* she thought.

With his thumbs, he stroked her nipples, tantalising her.

His breathing had grown harsh, and she cradled his head, kissing him deeply.

'Are you trying to punish yourself?' he asked, his lips resting upon her skin. 'By kissing a man like me?'

'You're not a punishment,' she whispered. 'It's just that—I wanted to know what it was like. To be desired.' She lowered her head. 'Not for my fortune, not for my hand in marriage. But for me.'

He took her lips again, this time softly. A lover's kiss, one that made her tremble. Michael broke away, resting his face against hers. 'I should never have come here. You're a complication I don't need right now.'

Her throat was burning, but she managed an apology. 'I'm sorry.'

He cupped her cheek then pulled away. 'Be well, Lady Hannah.' The door clattered shut behind him.

Hannah stayed inside the shed, the privacy cooling her unexpected desire. Regardless of what he said about himself, Michael was no ordinary soldier. He didn't let any man intimidate or threaten him. Instead, he carried himself with self-assurance, a man accustomed to guarding others.

And yet, there was no one protecting him. Her spirits dimmed at the thought of the Lieutenant enduring hardships he'd never admit. Like hunger.

Her mother had always cautioned her to think of the poor, to put others before her own needs. The Lieutenant needed someone to look after him.

But it could never be her.

CHAPTER SEVEN

THE FOLLOWING MORNING, Michael stood in front of Number Fourteen, St James's Street, the Graf von Reischor's residence. All night, he'd thought of Lady Hannah.

He'd never intended to kiss her again. It had been a monumental mistake, and one he wouldn't repeat. She'd been distraught after the events of the afternoon, and he'd taken unfair advantage. Again.

But when she'd clung to him, kissing him back, he hadn't been able to stop the rush of desire. Like a train, crashing through him with unstoppable force, he'd touched her the way he'd wanted to. Like the bastard he was.

She was well rid of him. Though he intended to keep his promise of ensuring that she didn't have to wed Belgrave, the sooner he was free of Lady Hannah, the better.

He had his own mess to unravel. The Lohenberg ambassador had left him no other choice but to see this through. Michael intended to get his answers today, no matter how long it took.

A sense of uneasiness rippled inside. Last night, he'd had the nightmare again. In his dream, he'd seen pieces of images, one after the other. Falling from a high distance, wounding his leg. A hand gripping his, dragging him down the street. Frigid waves, striking against a ship's hull. He'd woken up shaking, his body cold with fear. But whenever he tried to recall the details, the dreams faded into nothingness.

Though he wanted to pretend that this was nothing but a distorted trick, that these were nothing but idle visions, he wasn't convinced. As he stood before the door, he quelled the anxiety in his stomach, steeling himself for whatever confrontation lay ahead.

Michael removed his shako when the footman led him into the drawing room, tucking the hat beneath one arm. The ambassador's residence held a deceptive opulence. At first glance, the room appeared no different than the others he'd been inside. But the mahogany side table was polished to a sheen, the wood almost warm in its deep color. Inlaid wood formed a geometric pattern of shapes, like a fine mosaic.

The silver tea service was polished and gleaming, and the tray probably cost more than his yearly salary. Two porcelain cups painted with blue flowers rested upon the tray. The butler offered to pour him a cup, but Michael refused.

He waited for a full half-hour in the drawing room, ignoring the refreshments. His frustration mounted with each passing minute, until finally, he rose from his seat.

'I see you've had enough of waiting,' a cultured voice spoke. The Graf von Reischor entered the drawing room, leaning upon his gold-handled cane. The man's bald head gleamed, his salt-and-pepper beard framing a gnarled face. 'Have you finally decided to confront your past?'

'No. Only the present.' Michael strode forward, standing directly in front of the Graf. At the sight of the ambassador's smug expression, his anger sparked. 'You had no right to interfere with my orders.'

A faint smile tipped at the Graf's mouth. 'You enjoyed being shot, did you?'

'I need to return to my men and finish the campaign. I owe it to them.'

The Graf's expression grew solemn. 'Yes, I suppose you

must feel an obligation. I apologise for that, but it couldn't be helped.' He gestured for Michael to sit, and withdrew a cloth-wrapped parcel.

'I made some enquiries, after you refused my initial invitation to come and discuss this mysterious resemblance. I learned from your commanding officer that you had an anonymous benefactor who ordered you brought back from Malta.'

Michael's gaze narrowed, not understanding what the Graf meant. 'I was sent back because of my gunshot wounds.'

'Did you never wonder why your return to service was delayed for so long? Or why none of the others were brought back to London?'

He hadn't, not really. But then, he'd been in and out of consciousness, fighting for his life. He doubted if he'd have been aware of anything, not after nearly losing his leg. 'I thought other soldiers had returned with me.'

'None but you.' The Graf held out the cloth-wrapped package. 'I find that rather curious, don't you? It must have cost a great deal, both to locate your whereabouts and to bring you back to London. Someone obviously wanted to keep you alive. But who?'

Michael took the cloth package and unwrapped an oval miniature. He didn't know what he expected to see in the painting, but it wasn't an aged version of himself. The resemblance was so strong, he couldn't find any words to respond.

'You see?' The Graf held out his palm, and Michael returned the miniature to him.

Right now, he felt as if the ground had cracked open beneath him, sending him into a darkened chasm of uncertainty. Though he'd successfully ignored the frequent nightmares, now he could no longer be sure.

'It could be a coincidence.' But even as he spoke the words, he knew it wasn't.

The ambassador levelled a piercing stare at him. 'That, Lieutenant Thorpe, is what we must find out.' He poured two cups of tea, but Michael refused the hot drink. The ambassador added milk and sugar to his own cup.

'There is a legend in Lohenberg. One that has persisted for nearly twenty-three years, of a Changeling Prince.'

'Changeling?'

'Only a fairy tale, perhaps. You know how rumours spread.'

Michael waited for the Graf to continue. The ambassador rubbed his beard, lost in thought. 'Some believe the true Prince was stolen away, switched with another child on All Hallows Eve.'

'Wouldn't the King or Queen have noticed, if the boy was different?'

'The King saw the child for himself and proclaimed that Karl was indeed his son. He silenced the rumours.' The Graf sipped his tea.

'Do you think the King was telling the truth?'

'I don't know. But I want to be sure that the right man is crowned.' The Graf finished his tea and set down the cup. 'Forgive me for interfering with your orders, but I saw no other choice.'

Michael preferred to face enemy bullets, rather than unlock a past that might or might not belong to him. He knew, deep down, that he was the very last sort of man capable of leading a country.

'If I am wrong,' the Graf offered, 'you may return to the Army with no further interference from me. I will repay you handsomely for your co-operation, and I will see to it that Lohenberg provides several ships full of supplies and clothing for your fighting men.'

'In the meantime,' Reischor continued, 'you'll want to pack. I've arranged for your passage upon a steam packet, and we sail for Lohenberg at the end of the week.'

A FULL DAY passed before Hannah's parents addressed the subject of Lord Belgrave. She heard not a word of gossip from the servants, only that the baron had returned home with a headache.

An understatement, that.

After dinner, her parents awaited her in the parlour. The silence was so grim, Hannah wondered if they could see the guilt she was feeling right now. Did they know she had kissed the Lieutenant in the shed yesterday? Had any of the servants seen her after she'd gone out the window?

Already, she'd chastised herself for her act of rebellion with the Lieutenant. The kiss had gone too far, but he'd warned her, hadn't he? She could blame no one but herself.

Just thinking of it made her body go warm, her shame multiplying. All she needed was a scarlet letter to brand upon her gown to make her sins complete.

'Lord Belgrave has withdrawn his offer of marriage,' her father began. His tone was flat, his face careworn. 'I imagine you are not surprised.'

'No,' she managed. Few men would appreciate being bashed upon the head. Twice.

'Your mother has something she wishes to say to you.' The Marquess sat back in his chair, nodding to Lady Rothburne.

Her mother paled, her gloved hands twisting a handkerchief. 'Your father...was unaware that I allowed Lord Belgrave to speak with you privately.'

From the dark look on her father's face, she realized with shock that he was on her side. A frail flame of hope burned within her.

'I never dreamed Lord Belgrave would lock himself inside with you.' Her mother's face appeared sickly, and suddenly, she began to weep. 'Hannah, I am so sorry. I was naïve to think he would behave like a gentleman. You were right about him.'

'Then you're not…angry that I struck Lord Belgrave with the candlestick? Or—' she thought wildly for an explanation '—or the dictionary?' She directed her query towards her father, who cleared his throat, looking uncomfortable.

'There were other ways to handle the matter, but, no, I do not blame you. Hannah, I must ask you this—how on earth did you get out of the study? It took us nearly half an hour to find the other key. I was so worried, I nearly ordered Phillips to break down the door.'

'Belgrave was starting to wake up, so I went out the window.' There. Best to tell as much of the truth as she could.

'You could have broken your ankle,' her mother protested. 'I can't believe you risked such a fall.'

Hannah shrugged. 'Better an ankle than my virtue.'

Her mother's expression was incredulous. 'Why didn't you cry out to us for help?'

'What good would it have done?' she shot back. 'You didn't believe me when I told you what sort of man he was.'

Her mother blanched, staring down at her handkerchief. The Marquess regarded Hannah with a solemn face. 'We needn't discuss Belgrave any further. That matter is closed.'

And thank heaven. Hannah let out a sigh of relief. But there was no satisfaction on her parents' faces, only worry. It led her to wonder what they intended to do next.

Her father stood, answering the unspoken question. 'I have decided to send you away for a time. No doubt Belgrave will spread whatever rumours he can. Your mother and I will weather his accusations and do what we can to discredit the stories. In the meantime, I will arrange for your passage to Bremerhaven, Germany. You'll stay with our cousins Dietrich and Ingeborg von Kreimeln.'

Hannah had never heard of the cousins, and uneasiness threaded through her mind. Being sent away was what she'd hoped for, but she hadn't expected it to be half a continent away.

'When must I leave?'

'In three days' time.'

Three days? Though her father continued to explain his plans for her temporary exile, she hardly comprehended a word of it.

He cleared his throat, adding, 'I sent your cousins a letter yesterday, explaining what has happened. I've promised to provide a stipend for your care. No doubt they will be glad to take you in.'

'For how long?'

When her father didn't answer at first, Hannah suspected that he wasn't certain either. An unexpected loneliness spread inside her stomach at the thought of spending years away from her family. London had been her home all her life, and she couldn't imagine being away for an extended time.

'Until talk has ceased,' her father acceded. 'Or until you find another gentleman to wed. Perhaps someone from Germany or Denmark, who doesn't know of the scandal.'

He wanted her to hide the truth, then. The dishonesty didn't sit well with her, and Hannah decided that if she did meet a possible husband, she would tell him exactly what had happened.

'I've ordered the servants to pack your trunks in the morning,' the Marquess added. 'Quentin will escort you to the ship, and after that, the Graf von Reischor has promised to take you the remainder of the journey.'

The ambassador? She recalled Lieutenant Thorpe's confession that he was accompanying the Graf to Lohenberg. Most certainly her father knew nothing of this.

And neither did Lieutenant Thorpe. Hannah suppressed a shiver, wondering if she dared to travel with them. Even with an army of servants to chaperone her, she was afraid of falling prey to her own weakness. The Lieutenant had awakened something inside her, and she feared that the more time she spent with him, the easier it would be to let go of her strict rules of proper conduct.

The Marquess crossed the room and opened the door. 'We will speak more about your journey in the morning.'

It was a dismissal, and Hannah bid her parents good night. Once she left the parlour, she returned to her room, where she found another list of reminders from her mother.

1. Wear the rose silk gown tomorrow morning with the cream gloves.
2. Supervise the packing for Germany.
3. Send farewell notes to your friends.

The last reminder was one she hadn't thought about. She didn't know when she would see her friends again. It hurt to think of them getting married and going on with their lives, without her there to see it. She would miss Bernadette, her dearest friend from boarding school. And Nicole.

She couldn't possibly explain everything in a note. No, tomorrow she would pay a few calls and bid them farewell in person.

Her maid Estelle began unlacing Hannah's dress, helping her into a nightgown. 'Lady Hannah, I am so dreadfully sorry about what happened yesterday afternoon. I can't think of the ordeal you must have endured.'

'Yes, well, it's over now. I won't have to see Belgrave again.' She didn't want to dwell upon the past, not any more.

Hannah dismissed her maid and sat down upon her bed, drawing her legs beneath the covers and reaching for a book. Though she tried to read a bit of Goethe, practising her German, she couldn't concentrate on the words. Her mind kept returning to the Lieutenant. They would spend two nights upon the ship, and several days more by coach, until she reached her cousins' home in Germany.

It would be all too easy to ignore the years of proper comportment, letting herself explore the strange yearnings she felt. But, in spite of the forthcoming scandal, she was still untouched. There was no reason to let go of that.

Fluffing her pillow, Hannah rolled over. Beneath it, her fingers brushed against something cold and hard. She lifted up the glittering strand of diamonds, and her heartbeat quickened. The Lieutenant had been here, in her room. He'd touched her bed, and no one had seen him. Not even her.

An invisible phantom, keeping her safe, just as he'd promised.

Hannah returned the diamonds to her jewellery chest, wondering how and when he had managed to enter her room. He'd given the necklace back, successfully avoiding her. Once, she'd offered him the jewels as an excuse to return. Now, that reason was gone.

A slight disappointment filled up the crevices of her heart. But then, what had she been expecting? He was a soldier and she a lady. There was no possible future for them, except an illicit affair.

She'd never consider such a thing. Michael Thorpe was not the man for her. It didn't matter what he'd made her feel when he'd kissed her. Like a decadent chocolate torte, he'd provided nothing but forbidden temptation.

And no matter how badly he provoked her, she would

not allow herself to fall beneath his spell. They would be acquaintances, nothing more. On the ship, she simply had to avoid him at all costs.

THAT NIGHT, SHE had dreamed of the Lieutenant. Of his mouth, arousing such feelings within her. Hannah awoke in the early morning darkness, her skin alive with unspoken needs. Her cotton nightgown was gathered up around her thighs, and she tried to still the rapid beating of her heart.

A beam of moonlight rested upon her coverlet, the silvery light reminding her of the hours she'd spent in the Lieutenant's arms, only a few nights ago. She rested her hands upon her waist, calming her breathing.

Her hand crept up to her throat, her elbow grazing against her breasts. Instantly, the nipples hardened, provoking the memory of his kiss. She let her hand fall to the curve of her breast, touching herself. The nipples were hard nubs, and the sensation was painfully delicious.

Michael had touched her there, making her body desire so much more. A swell of arousal filled her up inside, and she drew her legs together, her breath quickening. She squeezed the tips of her breasts, and the aching sensation made her damp between her thighs. Never had she felt this way before. She twisted the sheets against her core, craving something she didn't understand.

God help her, she wanted to know more. Michael had given her a taste of sin, leaving her unsatisfied and curious.

But it was wrong. She knew that, and in time, she would learn to forget about him. There was no alternative.

CHAPTER EIGHT

MICHAEL STOOD ON board the ship *Orpheus*, staring out at the brown waters. The ships he'd sailed on earlier had been far smaller, perhaps 150 feet in length. In contrast, this one was nearly 600 feet long.

A large central funnel released a light steam, while six more masts rose high above them. The sails were tied up, and the wooden decking shone new. The rigging ropes were as thick as his wrist, the ratlines stretching up to the top mast.

As he looked aft, he saw the wheelhouse enclosed within glass windows. The *Orpheus* had made its first voyage only a month ago, and the ship was in prime condition.

It felt strange, being a first-class passenger.

Michael tugged at the tight sleeves of his new double-breasted black cloth frockcoat. Though it was a fine cut, he felt conspicuous in the expensive clothing. The shawl collar and cravat abraded his neck, and he felt stiff. His attire had cost more than three years' salary, and he longed for the familiarity of his own worn clothing.

He hadn't wanted to transform his appearance, but the Graf had insisted. 'If you are, in fact, related to the royal family, then you must dress as such. No one will accept your rank unless you appear as the King's son.'

'I may not be his son.'

But he'd succumbed to the changes because his only other attire was his military uniform. The Graf insisted that he travel under the guise of a nobleman, reminding him that his co-operation would help improve the living conditions of the soldiers.

Hundreds of men on the Crimean Peninsula had starved to death, due to lack of rations. It made him sick to think about the shipments of vegetables and meat left to rot because there was no one to transport the supplies to the soldiers' camp.

There would be changes when he returned to the front; he would see to it.

Michael gripped the cuffs of his coat, the guilt erasing any enjoyment he might have had from this journey. He didn't deserve fine clothing or luxurious accommodations upon a steamship bound for Bremerhaven.

His gaze drifted downward to the gleaming buttons on the coat. *Bide your time,* he warned himself. Already the Graf had given him two new suits of clothing that he could sell. He'd loaned hundreds of pounds in spending money, meant for a new wardrobe, once they arrived in Lohenberg. Michael didn't intend to touch a penny, if at all possible.

Behind him, he heard the conversational noises of more passengers boarding the ship. He'd made arrangements for Mrs Turner to be brought with the servants, not trusting anyone to look after her welfare. She'd be lost within a week and forget to eat.

The Graf had protested, but Michael's insistence had won over. No doubt Mrs Turner was pestering the servants about her trunk, making sure no one bumped it or put a scratch upon the wood.

He heard the tones of her voice, anxious and excited, while she inspected the ship. With a quick glance, he saw that today would be one of her more lucid moments. She stared up at the tall masts and funnels, shielding her eyes from the sun while a broad smile creased her cheeks.

God help him, he hadn't told her their true destination. He'd let her believe that it was a trip to Germany, and had ordered the other servants not to reveal their true destination. There was no reason to upset her.

Other passengers boarded the ship, pretending as if they didn't see the elderly woman. He could guess their ranks, without knowing a single name. Dukes and viscounts, ladies and lords. Those who believed themselves too good to mingle with the public.

Michael kept an eye upon Mrs Turner, watching to ensure that no one bothered her. A few of the men cast quizzical looks towards him, as though trying to decide whether or not they were acquainted.

He pretended as though he didn't see, for he didn't belong among them. He'd learned that on the night he'd dared to accept Whitmore's ball invitation.

There was no use in attempting a conversation with London's elite. What could he say, after all? *Have you shot any men recently?* No, he couldn't mingle with them. Far better to stay away.

But then, he heard the soft tones of another woman's voice. He knew her voice, knew the timbre and the familiar way it rose and fell.

Lady Hannah Chesterfield. What in the name of God was she doing upon this ship? Had she followed him?

Michael spun around, intending to confront her. When her gaze met his, she blushed and nodded in greeting.

Clearly, she'd known they would be traveling upon the same ship. Why hadn't she mentioned it the last time he'd seen her?

She wore a grey cashmere pelisse trimmed with a fringe, and beneath the outer garment, he caught a glimpse of a dark blue gown. Her grey bonnet was adorned with lace, ribbons and cream roses. Impeccably attired, she held herself like a queen.

From the vast quantity of trunks and luggage brought on to the ship by her servants, it appeared she was travelling for an extended period. He saw her brother Quentin bringing up the last of the servants, and he spoke softly to his sister, offering an embrace. It was a farewell.

What was going on? Michael didn't believe for a moment that her presence upon the ship was a mere coincidence, even if the *Orpheus* was one of the most luxurious passenger steamers.

His question was answered a moment later, when the Graf brought Lady Hannah towards him. 'Lieutenant Thorpe, there will be an addition to our travelling party,' he said. 'The Marquess of Rothburne asked me to escort his daughter, Lady Hannah Chesterfield, to their cousins' estate in Germany, after he learned I was returning home.'

There was no doubt in his mind that the Lohenberg Graf had arranged this little detail for a reason—most probably as a means of manipulating him. Michael wouldn't allow any harm to come to Lady Hannah, and the Graf knew it.

'Lady Hannah,' Michael greeted her. He let nothing betray his emotions, for he didn't want her caught in the middle of his disagreement with Reischor.

Like him, Hannah kept her reaction cool and veiled. 'Lieutenant Thorpe.' It was as if an icy wall had gone up between them. If Michael hadn't been there himself, he'd have doubted that their kiss had ever taken place. The prim and proper Lady Hannah was back, with no glimpse of the woman who had struck down her last suitor with a candlestick.

Graf von Reischor cleared his throat to interrupt them. 'Lieutenant Thorpe has agreed to accompany me to Lohenberg, conducting business on behalf of the British Army.'

'I am glad to hear that you have been tasked with something so important.' Although she had already known of his orders, he suspected Lady Hannah was itching to ask more questions. Nonetheless, he didn't want her to know anything about the Graf's theory with regard to his heritage.

'When did your father make the decision about this journey?' he enquired, directing the conversation back to her.

'A few days ago.' Hannah twisted at one of her gloves, and the conversation fell flat between them.

Exile was a better word for it. The Princess locked away in a tower, away from those who might scorn her.

'Forgive me,' Graf von Reischor excused himself. 'I must speak with the Captain about our cabin arrangements. I shall return shortly.' He gestured for one of Hannah's maids to remain nearby, as a chaperone.

As soon as he was out of earshot, Michael lowered his voice. 'Why would your father choose Reischor for an escort? Has he lost his wits?'

Hannah seemed taken aback, but a moment later, she raised her chin. 'Papa wants me to wed a foreign count or duke, and Graf von Reischor has many acquaintances.'

That didn't surprise him at all. Lady Hannah was the sort of woman who belonged among high society, her blue blood too good for anything less. If the London suitors wouldn't have her, certainly her father's money would pave the way for a foreign wedding.

'So long as he has the proper title and enough money, not much else matters, does it?' The words came out before he could stop them. He felt like a bastard for voicing them.

But proper to a fault, Hannah didn't let any hurt feelings show. 'I am not allowed to marry a man who does not possess the means to take care of a family.'

'Your father wouldn't let you wed a merchant, sweet. Not even if he possessed a million pounds.' Men like the Marquess were only interested in bettering the family name. 'The higher the title, the more likely you'll gain his permission.'

'There are titled gentlemen who are good men,' she pointed out. 'Not all of them are like Belgrave. Many would value a virtuous woman who wants to provide a comfortable home for him.'

'Like you?'

She turned crimson, and he wished he'd kept his mouth shut. None of this had been her fault. He ought to reassure her that nothing had changed, that she was still the same woman as before. But that was a lie. She would never be the same, not with a scandal shadowing her.

Then, too, he hadn't behaved with honourable intentions, either. He'd taken full advantage of Hannah's innocence, claiming stolen embraces and touching her in a way that was forbidden.

Right now, she was perfectly composed, every button fastened, every hair in its proper place. She looked nothing like the woman who had clung to him in the shed, kissing him as though time were running out.

The high-collared pelisse hid her neck, and he asked, 'Did you receive your necklace back?'

'I did. You could have returned it yourself.' There was a hint of scolding in her tone.

'I thought it best not to see you again.' His voice came out rougher than he'd intended.

The wind buffeted Hannah's bonnet, and she kept her gaze fastened upon a seagull circling the boat. Her green eyes were almost grey this morning, mirroring the darkness of the water.

'You're right, of course.' She drew the edges of her pelisse tighter against her body. 'We've caused enough scandal. It's better for us to stay away from one another.'

She said it so firmly, he wondered whom she was trying to convince. Her face held a lonely cast to it, her eyes glimmering with unshed tears. She watched the shoreline, as though she didn't know when she would see England again. And from the way Hannah was glancing over her shoulder, he suspected she didn't want to keep his company any longer.

Sailors began releasing the ropes from the dock. The steam engines rumbled as they began to take the vessel away from its landing and down the river.

Michael wanted to offer her words of comfort, but he suspected it would only make her feel worse about her exile. He rested his wrists on the side of the boat, staring out at the water. Waiting for her to leave.

But long moments passed, and she stood a short distance away, resting her own gloved hands upon the wood. He ventured a glance at her, and she kept her eyes averted. Her lips were pressed together, her cheeks pale from the cool sea air. He remembered just what her mouth tasted like, as sweet as a succulent berry.

'Why are you watching me?' she whispered. Her hands came together, and she rubbed her palms.

He didn't tear his gaze away. Instead, he looked his fill, memorising her green eyes and flushed cheeks, down to the prim-and-proper body he wanted to touch.

'Don't you want to retire to your cabin?' he prompted.

It was a veiled dare, to see if she truly wanted to be rid of him. He waited for her to march off, sweeping her skirts clear of a man like him.

Her face reddened, but she held her ground. 'I don't want to just yet.' Taking a deep breath, she confronted him. 'I think we are both capable of being civil to one another. We've agreed that there will be nothing improper at all about our behaviour.'

They had? He raised an eyebrow, but she seemed completely unaware of it.

'As travelling companions, we have no other choice, if we wish to avoid future gossip.' She squared her shoulders. 'If we attempt to avoid one another, that may cause further talk. Instead, I suggest that we behave with politeness and decorum.'

It was with great difficulty that he held back his own opinions. Instead, he studied the other passengers on board the ship.

'Well?' she prompted. 'Is that acceptable to you?'

His gaze fixed upon Mrs Turner at that moment. It occurred to him that he could not watch over the widow at night. He needed someone to protect her, in case she suffered from one of her spells.

Facing Lady Hannah, he said, 'You want to pretend as though we're strangers. As though I never kissed you.'

A slight shiver passed over her, but she nodded.

'Then I want a favour in return.' Before she could protest, he continued, 'There is...an elderly woman I've known for many years. Abigail Turner is her name, and she has joined our travelling party.'

Though he could have found another place for Mrs Turner, he didn't trust anyone else to handle the widow's welfare. Others wouldn't understand her condition, nor would they sympathise. He didn't want Mrs Turner sent to an asylum if she suffered from one of her spells.

Hannah didn't answer, and he wasn't certain she'd heard him until at last she said, 'Go on.'

He stepped in front of her line of sight, forcing her to look upon him. 'Mrs Turner is starting to grow forgetful. Sometimes she doesn't remember her name or where she lives.

'She needs someone to look after her,' he continued, in

all seriousness. Staring directly at Hannah, he added, 'She tends to find trouble when she isn't looking for it.'

Hannah shielded her eyes as she stared behind him at the tall funnel. 'What is it you want from me?'

He raised his voice above the din of the engines. 'Would you allow Mrs Turner to join your maids? I cannot watch over her at night, and there are no other female servants travelling with us.'

'She may join us.' Then Hannah studied him, searching his expression. 'Why is she so important to you?'

He had never been asked the question, and he didn't really want to explain it. Abigail Turner had lived near his family all his life. She was the woman who had slipped him sweets when his mother wasn't looking, allowing Henry and him to build fortresses in the bedroom out of sheets and old pillows. As long as he could remember, she'd been like an aunt or a godmother, watching out for him.

'She saved my life,' he admitted. 'After I was shot at Balaclava, I was sent back to London. Mrs Turner nursed me back to health.' He pointed out the widow to Hannah as the woman strolled around the deck.

'How badly were you hurt?'

He sobered. 'I'm alive. Which is more than I can say for most of my men.' He thought of Henry Turner, whose body he'd lain beneath. There wasn't a day that went by when he didn't wish he'd been the one to die instead of Abigail's son.

'I should be glad to look after her for you,' Hannah offered, holding out her hand for him to shake.

He stared down at her gloved hand, and she snatched it back, caught off guard by what she'd done. But he reached forward, taking her palm in his. The sudden touch seared his consciousness.

He took a step forward, and in turn, she stepped back,

her shoulder brushing against one of the ratlines. Interesting.

He hadn't truly intended to start this game of cat and mouse, but her reaction was intriguing. She appeared flustered, as though she didn't know what to do about his sudden attention.

But her eyes held no fear. No, there was anticipation in them.

Michael reached up and took hold of two of the ropes. Though he didn't touch her at all, it was the hint of an embrace. Hannah coloured, but held her ground as though it were the most natural place to be, with her back against the ratlines. She glanced around, to see if anyone saw them, but they were further back on the ship, with no one nearby.

'Why would your father force you to travel with strangers?' he asked.

'The Graf isn't a stranger. He's Papa's friend. They've known each other for years.'

Michael took a step closer, lowering his voice. 'How well do *you* know him?'

'Not well.' Stiffening at his comment, she added, 'But Papa would never place me in harm's way.' She glanced at his arms pointedly, but he refused to move them. He wanted to see what she would do. Would she push him aside? Or surrender, waiting for him to let her go?

Right now, he wanted to take her below the deck, away from everyone else. To kiss her until she could no longer stand. To feel her naked skin beneath his.

'And there's you,' she said softly. 'You would protect me, if I needed it.'

'Don't try to put me on a pedestal, Hannah.' The more time he spent near her, the more he desired her. Michael let his hand brush against hers, and she started at the contact. She truly had no idea of the sort of danger she was in.

Twice, he'd kissed her. And though he possessed a slight bit of honour, even that was beginning to unravel.

'You're trying to intimidate me,' she accused. 'And I know none of this is real. You wouldn't dare hurt me.'

Michael leaned closer so that his breath was against her cheek. 'Sweet, you don't know me at all, do you?'

'You—you don't know me, either.' She squared her shoulders, lifting her chin until her mouth lay only inches from his.

'I know enough about ladies such as you.'

'And what is that supposed to mean?'

'You live your life bound by a strict set of rules. I'm the sort of man who breaks those rules.'

'Do you truly believe I enjoy living that way?' she asked. 'I'm not allowed to choose my own clothing or decide what to eat.' Her eyes held frustration, and she stared down at the wooden decking, her face pale.

'I can't go back to the life I had,' she murmured. 'It's gone forever. This time, I want to make my own choices.' She pushed his hands aside and broke free of him.

'I want to eat whatever I want and wear a gown of my own choosing.' She calmed herself, taking a deep breath. 'I want my freedom.'

He saw the desperate need within her, and knew he could do nothing to destroy that hope. 'You have two days before we reach Germany. Perhaps less.'

Staring hard at him, she whispered, 'Then I'll have to make the most of my voyage.'

God help him, he hoped she would.

CHAPTER NINE

HANNAH SPENT A good part of the afternoon exploring the ladies' saloon and the promenade deck with her maid Estelle. She'd met several of the other ladies travelling in first class, and most seemed friendly enough. One had urged her to explore the ship further, and Hannah was delighted at what she'd found. She'd expected this passage to be gruelling, but instead the ship was designed for luxury at every turn.

She spied *portières* of crimson velvet at each of the doorways, while the maroon carpet was thick and comfortable. Within the saloon, the sofas were made of Utrecht velvet, while the walnut buffets were covered with green marble tops. Grand chandeliers hung throughout the saloons, giving them the appearance of ballrooms.

In one corner, a string quartet was rehearsing their set of music. Standing with his back to her was Lieutenant Thorpe. He looked ill at ease, pacing slightly as he appeared to stroll through the saloon.

Hannah almost turned on her heel and walked away. He hadn't seen her, so there was no need to greet him. She could leave right now, and he'd never know differently.

But then, that was the coward's way, wasn't it? He'd cornered her this morning, intimidating her without actually laying a finger upon her. She pressed a hand to her heart, trying to calm the rhythm. Just thinking of it made her even more aware of him.

He was intensely handsome, in an uncivilised manner.

Although his new clothing fit him perfectly, it didn't change the man he was. Unpredictable. And…not at all safe. He'd been right about that.

Without warning, he turned around and saw her. His gaze held none of the polite greeting that most men would have offered. No, he looked as though he wanted to cross the room and take her away with him.

Her senses grew weak just thinking about it.

Gesturing for Estelle to remain a short distance behind her, Hannah braved a polite smile. Best to say hello and leave as quickly as possible. But as soon as she reached his side, he turned away.

The ship's funnel casings were enclosed with mirrors, and a rich pattern of gold and white covered the wall surfaces. 'Are you studying the wallpaper?' Hannah asked. 'It's lovely enough but a bit boring, I'd imagine.'

'Listening to the music,' he corrected. 'And trying to remain unnoticed.'

That much was doubtful. A man like the Lieutenant could never escape attention. His height and handsome demeanour made that impossible, not to mention he walked like a man in command.

'You're not a very good wallflower,' she said.

He shot her a sidelong glance. 'I was doing quite well before you arrived. No one approached me or spoke to me.'

'They were afraid you'd wrestle them to the ground or throw them into the mirror.' She took a discreet step away from him.

'It's possible,' he admitted. His mouth turned up at the corners, and Hannah relaxed, glad that she'd made peace with him. 'What do you want, Lady Hannah?'

'Nothing, really. I thought it would be rude to leave without saying hello.'

'You've said it. Duty accomplished.'

She refused to be put off by his abrupt air. 'You don't feel comfortable here, do you? Amidst all this.' She gestured toward the opulent decorations.

'I'd rather be on a battlefield. Shooting enemies.' A wicked look of amusement lit up his eyes. He glanced over at a group of matrons talking in a corner.

'Target practice?' she suggested.

'You're tempting me.' His gaze flickered toward two gentlemen, whom she just now noticed were staring at them. 'I don't think you should be standing here, speaking to me alone.'

'My maid is here.' Hannah glanced over at Estelle. 'And we're already acquainted. For all those guests know, you could be my brother.'

He sent her a lazy smile that made her skin turn to gooseflesh. 'I'm most definitely not your brother, sweet.'

She stared down at the floor, uncertain of how to respond. 'Well. What happened between us is all in the past. Right now, we are travelling companions, nothing more.'

'Really?' The dangerous glint in his eyes sent a blush through her cheeks.

'Of course.' She took another step back, pretending everything was fine.

At that moment, the two gentlemen strolled forward. They looked as though they were about to ask for an introduction, but Michael sent them a dark glare. Hastily, they tipped their hats and continued on their way.

'Now what was that about?' Hannah demanded. 'You looked as though you were about to tear them apart with your bare hands.'

'I was acting like any brother would.' Michael's gaze fixed on the doorway as though he expected the two gentlemen to return. 'Keeping you safe, just as you asked.'

If he'd had a firearm at that moment, Hannah had no

doubt it would be aimed at the gentlemen. His behaviour bordered on barbaric, with a hint of jealousy.

'If a gentleman asks me to dance this evening after supper, I have no choice but to accept,' Hannah pointed out. 'You can hardly prevent it from happening.'

'Can't I?'

She ignored the remark, continuing, 'I suspect you don't dance at all, do you?'

'Do I look like the sort who enjoys dancing?' he gritted out.

'No, you look like the sort who enjoys glowering at others.' She tilted her head to study him. 'I would wager that you don't know how to dance.'

He took a glance around the saloon. Except for her maid Estelle, there was no one else in sight. Even the matrons had already strolled away.

The musicians were still practising a set; without warning, Michael took her in his arms. He didn't ask but began dancing with her. His hand pressed against the curve of her waist, guiding her masterfully through the steps.

She couldn't have been more surprised. When had a soldier learned how to dance like this?

He took her through the steps of a waltz, spinning her around without a single misstep.

'In school,' he replied, answering her unspoken question. 'Every last one of us learned to dance. I hated every minute.'

'But you're good,' she whispered. 'Better than I thought you'd be.'

He whirled her around, bringing her against one of the mirrors. The cool glass pressed into her back, and he stopped short.

'I'm good at many things, sweet.' His voice held the undertones of a forbidden liaison. Caught in his embrace, he kept his hands at her waist, looking into her eyes. She saw the rise and fall of his breathing, the desire that he held back.

'And what is something you're not good at?' she asked softly.

'Letting go of something I want badly.'

Without a single word of farewell, he left the saloon. Hannah leaned back, resting her head against the mirrored panel. *Neither am I.*

HANNAH LIFTED OUT a sage-green dress with a high collar and fitted long sleeves. She was grateful for the new travelling clothes in other colours besides rose and yellow. Though the gown covered every inch of her body, at least the colour complimented her light brown hair.

'Lady Hannah, this is not the gown your mother selected for this evening's dinner,' her maid Estelle protested.

'No, it isn't.' And she didn't care. The midnight-blue gown Christine Chesterfield preferred reminded Hannah of mourning garb. 'I prefer this one,' she added, handing it to Estelle so she could dress her.

As soon as she arrived in Germany, she would visit a dressmaker to order new gowns that were more flattering. Perhaps she would even cut her hair shorter. Hannah smiled at the thought, fingering the long strands.

While Estelle finished styling her hair, she thought back to what Lieutenant Thorpe had said—*I'm not safe at all.*

It was a warning to stay away. To guard her virtue at all costs. And she should, no doubt. Yet there was a part of her that wanted to know more about the man behind the soldier. He intrigued her, awakening the rebellious side of herself. What would it be like to live her life, not caring what others thought?

Or was it merely a façade, a means of keeping people

away from him? He isolated himself from others, and it troubled her.

A knock sounded at the door, and Estelle went to open it. Hannah caught a glimpse of Mrs Turner, the elderly woman whom Michael had asked her to watch over.

The woman appeared nervous, twisting a red bonnet in her hands. 'Lieutenant Thorpe sent me here to assist you, Lady Hannah. I am Abigail Turner.'

'Come in.' Hannah gestured toward a chair. 'Would you care to sit down?'

'No, thank you, my lady.' The woman stood near the door, as though trying to fade into the papered walls. The small cabin held three berths, one for each of them. Against the far wall were two chairs and an end table. On the wall adjacent to the berths, stood a large chest of drawers.

Estelle began helping Hannah into the sage-green gown, and a moment later, signalled to Mrs Turner. 'You, there. Fetch Lady Hannah's silk fan from inside that trunk.' Without waiting for a response, the maid began fastening a pearl necklace around Hannah's throat.

'Emeralds would look better,' Mrs Turner suggested.

Estelle sent the widow a tight smile. 'I do not believe you are responsible for Lady Hannah's wardrobe. Her mother has taken great pains to organise each of her gowns with the appropriate matching fan, jewels, stockings and gloves, and has made lists of what outfit should be worn upon which occasion. Your help is not needed.' With a flourish, Estelle produced a small handful of papers.

'Estelle, Mrs Turner is here at my request,' Hannah corrected.

Mrs Turner did not react to the maid's arrogant tone, but instead, a light appeared in her eyes as though she were squaring off for battle.

Estelle pressed the lists into Hannah's hand, and she

glanced at them before setting them down on the table. Orders of what to wear, what not to eat, how to greet the other first-class passengers…the reminders went on and on.

Her mother was *still* trying to give orders, even while they were miles apart.

Enough. Balling up the lists into a crumpled heap of paper, Hannah tossed them in the wastebasket. Her maid gave a cry of dismay, but left the lists alone.

'Did you pack the emeralds, Estelle?' she enquired.

'Yes, my lady, but your mother's orders were—'

'I beg your pardon.' Mrs Turner cleared her throat and turned a sharp eye upon Estelle. 'Are you arguing with your mistress?'

'Do you dare to criticise me?' The maid puffed up with anger. 'Lady Rothburne is one of the greatest ladies in all of London. I take pride in following her explicit orders.'

Mrs Turner frowned and began looking around the cabin. She lifted a cushion, spying beneath it. 'Well, I don't see Lady Rothburne here, do you?'

Hannah had difficulty concealing her smile.

'If your lady wishes to wear emeralds instead of pearls, what does it matter?'

'Emeralds are not proper for a young lady.' The maid glared at Mrs Turner. 'And you should learn your place, if you expect to remain in Lady Rothburne's employ. I shall write to her about you, see if I don't.'

Hannah didn't like her maid's attitude. She'd considered getting rid of the woman even before now, but she'd had enough of this rudeness. 'Estelle, if you wish to stay, you will obey my orders.'

Mrs Turner drew close. 'May I help you with that clasp, Lady Hannah?'

Hannah turned, and Mrs Turner unfastened the pearls,

replacing them with an emerald pendant Estelle grudgingly gave her.

'Go and find some refreshments for Lady Hannah,' the matron suggested to Estelle. 'A glass of lemonade, perhaps, or a bit of cake.'

'Chocolate cake,' Hannah breathed, like a prayer.

'Chocolate, then.'

'But Lady Rothburne has strictly forbidden—'

Mrs Turner shut the cabin door in the maid's face. Dusting off her hands as though they were well rid of her, the widow offered a broad smile. 'I've been wanting to thank you for granting me a place to sleep.'

'It's no trouble.' Hannah struggled with her stockings, and Mrs Turner helped her to adjust them.

The widow added, 'If you don't mind my saying so, I think you should get a lady's maid who is a bit more loyal to you than to your mother.'

'You may be right.'

Mrs Turner fussed over her, helped her finish dressing, and exclaimed over the gown. When Hannah was ready, the older woman smiled. 'He really does like you, you know. My Michael. He spoke of meeting you at the ball that night. You made quite an impression upon him.'

Why a stranger's words would make her stomach flutter, Hannah didn't know. She picked up her fan, feeling like an awkward fifteen-year-old girl once again. She resisted the urge to ask what he'd said about her. It didn't matter.

And if she told herself that a hundred times, she might actually start to believe it.

A knock sounded at the door, and Hannah saw the Graf von Reischor waiting to escort her to dinner. He murmured a compliment in his native language. Before Hannah could respond with her thanks, Mrs Turner followed behind them, adding, 'Yes, she does look lovely, doesn't she?'

The Graf turned, staring at the widow. 'Do you speak Lohenisch, Mrs Turner?'

'No, of course not.' A curious smile rested upon her lips. 'Why ever would you think that?'

THE DINING ROOM was exquisite and could hold nearly four hundred first-class passengers. Long tables set with white linen tablecloths gleamed with silver and bone-china plates. Above, an ornate brass chandelier provided lighting while potted tropical plants added a splash of greenery to the tables.

Several guests were already seated, and the gentlemen rose at the sight of her, Michael among them. He wore black evening clothes and a white cravat. His dark hair was sleek and combed back. Even with his grooming, there was an air of impatience about him, as though he were uneasy about being here. He looked like he'd rather be dining in steerage than among the elite.

Hannah nodded politely to the other women after the Graf von Reischor introduced her. One of the ship's butlers poured her a glass of water and another of wine.

She'd never been allowed to taste spirits before, and she wondered what it would taste like. Would it lure her into a life of sin and greed, the way her mother insisted?

But when she saw that no one else had touched theirs, Hannah restrained herself.

The Graf began introducing her to their dinner companions. 'The Marquess of Rothburne is a close friend of mine,' the Graf explained. 'He asked me to escort Lady Hannah to her cousins' home in Germany. She received so many offers of marriage, her father thought it best that she take some time away from London to make up her mind.'

Hannah nearly choked on her soup. It wasn't at all what she'd expected him to say. After a few more introductions to those seated around her, one of the gentlemen offered her a warm smile, then nodded to the Graf. 'I hope she has not made a decision as of yet, Graf von Reischor.'

'She hasn't,' came a clipped voice. The Lieutenant sent the would-be suitor a warning look, and Hannah's fingers curled over the stem of her wine glass. What gave him the right to be so rude? He was behaving as though he had some sort of claim over her. The glare in his eyes held a shadow she didn't recognise. Not exactly jealousy, but something that made her skin prickle against the fabric of her gown.

The first course was served shortly thereafter, a bowl of turtle soup. Hannah noticed the Lieutenant subtly observing her and the other gentlemen before lifting his own spoon. Surely he must have attended formal dinners before? But then, her father's ball was the first time she'd ever seen him among her social peers.

Michael sat across from her, and she felt his gaze, like a forbidden caress. There was also a sense of reluctance, as though she were a temptation he didn't want.

Hannah reached for her glass of white wine, taking a first sip. It held a slight tang, a sweetness that didn't taste sinful at all. When she glanced over at Michael, he lifted his own glass, and she found herself watching his mouth, remembering his kiss.

The memory pooled through her skin, past her breasts and between her legs. He was staring at her as though he didn't care who was watching. In a ship such as this, there were a hundred different places to hold a secret liaison. And no one would know.

Across the table, he didn't take his eyes from her. She recalled the warmth of his lips, wondering if she would taste the sweetness of wine upon his mouth.

'Lady Hannah?' the Graf prompted her. She hadn't heard

a word of his questioning. She took another sip, and managed a smile.

'I'm sorry. What was it you were saying?'

'I was introducing the Lieutenant to our dinner companions,' he replied. 'This is Lieutenant Michael Thorpe, an officer in the British Army,' the Graf said to the others.

A spoon clattered from a woman's hand into the soup tureen. Hannah turned in curiosity and saw a dark-haired woman with a large ruby necklace and matching rings upon her fingers. She covered her blunder by pretending as though someone else had dropped the utensil.

'You said you are travelling to Lohenberg?' a stout English gentleman enquired. 'My wife is from that country.' He offered a nod toward the woman who had dropped the spoon, then raised a quizzing glass to one eye. 'You look familiar to me, somehow. Have we met before?'

'He looks like the King of Lohenberg,' his wife answered. Though she kept a smile fixed upon her face, her answer held a cold tone.

Lieutenant Thorpe's knuckles clenched upon the spoon. He looked as though he'd rather take a bullet through his forehead than endure this dinner. But he didn't rebut the woman's claim.

What was that about? Hannah tried to catch Michael's attention, but he kept his gaze averted, almost as if he were hiding something.

'Why, you're right, m'dear.' The stout man beamed and speared a bite of asparagus. To his companions, he added, 'I was privileged to have met His Majesty, King Sweyn, when he was visiting Bavaria last summer. Splendid mountains there, I must say.'

The Graf introduced them. 'Lady Hannah and Lieutenant Thorpe, may I present the Viscount Brentford?'

Lord Brentford greeted her heartily and presented his wife Ernestine and his daughter, Miss Ophelia Nelson.

'I am glad to make your acquaintance, Lady Brentford,' Hannah said. Offering a smile of friendship to the younger woman, she continued, 'And yours, Miss Nelson.'

'Delighted, of course,' the matron said, though she didn't look at Hannah when she spoke. Her wide smile emphasised a double chin, and she added, 'Ophelia has just been presented to the Queen and will enjoy her first Season after we return to London.'

Michael didn't respond, and Hannah kicked him under the table to get him to look at the young woman. He sent her a nod of acknowledgement, but a moment later, Hannah felt his shoe nudge against her stockinged calf.

Mortified, she reached for her water glass and took a deep swallow. Only to find out that it was wine she'd drunk instead. She clamped her mouth shut to keep from coughing, and the spirits burned the back of her throat.

Though the Lieutenant didn't look at her, his foot moved against hers once again. Though it was nothing more than a casual touch, the caress distracted her from the dinner conversation. Like a silent admonition, he touched her the way a secret lover might.

Hannah kept her knees clamped together, pushing her ankles as far beneath the chair as she could. He seemed to sense the effect he had on her, and his lips curved upwards.

The Viscount nodded towards his daughter, sending the Lieutenant a knowing look. 'Ophelia is quite talented and has the voice of an angel.' Hannah supposed the Viscount was waiting for someone to suggest that Miss Nelson offer entertainment later that evening.

When neither the Graf nor the Lieutenant responded, Lord Brentford continued, 'Perhaps she might sing for the King of Lohenberg, if the opportunity presented itself on our journey. If someone were to…suggest it.' The Viscount gave a pointed look toward the ambassador.

Miss Nelson turned to the Graf and offered a shy smile.

'I have no doubt that Ophelia will have her opportunity one day,' Lady Brentford interjected. She patted the young girl's hand and discreetly slid the wine glass away from Miss Nelson's place setting. 'It is my country, after all.'

Without an invitation, the Viscountess launched into a dissertation describing the principality. 'And of course, the winters are simply enchanting.'

'No, it's quite cold in the winter,' the Lieutenant interrupted. His eyes were distant, as though he'd spoken without thought.

The Viscountess stopped short, waiting for him to elaborate. When he didn't, she continued, pretending that he hadn't spoken at all.

Hannah caught the Graf's discerning gaze, and he shook his head discreetly. More and more, she was curious about their journey. She suspected the military orders did not reveal the entire story.

'Forgive me, Graf von Reischor,' Viscount Brentford interrupted, 'but I've heard rumours, and I wonder if you could verify them. Is it true that Fürst Karl is going to be crowned king within the next few weeks?'

The Graf set down his fork and regarded Lord Brentford.

'King Sweyn has been ill, but we do not know for certain whether or not a new king will be crowned.'

'How exciting,' Miss Nelson breathed. 'I suppose there must be many men in line for the throne, even for so small a country.'

'There is only one Crown Prince,' the Graf admitted. His gaze turned to Michael, and Hannah felt an icy chill shiver through her. 'And one true heir.'

CHAPTER TEN

MICHAEL ENDURED THE remaining hour of dinner, hating every moment of it. He watched the other guests to determine which forks to use, how much of the food to eat, and whether or not he was supposed to drink the contents of a bowl or wash his hands in it.

What bothered him most was the sheer waste. The ladies picked delicately at their plates, tasting a bite of fish or a spoonful of soup before the course was taken away. It was as if eating were out of fashion.

The men adjourned with brandy and cigars, the ladies retreating to their own saloon after the dinner was concluded. Michael took his moment to escape, though the Graf had ordered him to return for the parlour games.

He had no intention of letting the Lohenberg ambassador dictate what he would or would not do. He wasn't a trained animal to be led about on a leash.

With each moment, his resentment rose. The eyes of everyone at dinner had bored into him, and when Lady Brentford had mentioned his resemblance to the King, no doubt they thought he was a bastard son. Michael hated being the centre of attention, much less the subject of gossiping tongues.

Outside, the sky was black, the white sails taut with wind while the paddle wheel churned through the water. The promenade deck was partially shielded from the winds, but the rocking of the ship sent several guests falling over.

Raucous laughter accompanied one poor woman's misfortune as her skirts went flying.

Michael gripped one of the ropes leading to the foresail. Though the sea had turned rough, his mind was in greater turmoil. He didn't want to believe that his childhood had been a lie, that his parents were not whom they seemed to be. Surely the strange, fleeting memories that caught him from time to time were nothing but dreams. They had to be.

He caught a glimpse of Mrs Turner strolling around the deck, and he took a step towards her. It wasn't good for her to be alone. But before he could reach her side, Lady Hannah appeared, followed by her maid. She wore no outer wrap, only her sage-green gown. In the frigid air, she rubbed her arms for warmth.

'Lieutenant Thorpe,' she asked quietly, 'I want to know what's going on.'

'About what?'

'Your resemblance to the King of Lohenberg. I saw the way the Graf was watching you.'

'It's nothing. Merely a coincidence.'

She stepped in front of him, preventing him from going any further. 'He thinks it's true, doesn't he? The Graf believes you're connected to the royal house of Lohenberg.'

'It doesn't matter what he thinks. I've never set foot in the country.' He strode past her, but Hannah dogged his footsteps.

'You said it was cold there, in the winter.'

He had no idea what she was talking about. 'As I said, I've never been to the country before.'

'Are you lying to me? Or to yourself?' She touched his arm lightly.

'I'm a soldier, nothing more.'

'Are you certain?'

No, he wasn't certain of anything. Nothing except the

way she made him feel. Michael inhaled the light citrus scent she wore. Lemon and jasmine mingled together, seductive and sweet.

'Go back to your cabin, Hannah,' he ordered. It was all he could do not to kiss her again. This time, if he touched her, he wouldn't hesitate to try to seduce her.

'The evening isn't over yet,' she said. 'The entertainment will begin shortly. And whether or not you're too afraid to join us, I intend to participate.'

'Hoping to find a husband, are you?'

She shot him a dark look. 'Whether I am or not doesn't matter to you at all, does it?'

'It matters.' His palm cupped her cheek, his gloved hand sliding against her skin. Ripples of desire erupted all over her skin. She wanted him to kiss her. He tempted her in all the wrong ways. Or perhaps, all the right ways.

It took all of her willpower to break free of him. 'Run away, if you're too afraid,' she taunted. 'Or join us. The choice is yours.'

HANNAH HAD PLAYED a few parlour games during boarding school. Blind Man's Buff and charades were quite popular. But as these games involved men and women, she supposed they must be rather different.

A group of twenty gentlemen and women met in the Grand Saloon. The ship's waiters had arranged several chairs in a circle, and a small table stood at the front. Hannah spied a pocket watch and a slipper upon the table, while other guests were rummaging through their belongings. They would be playing Forfeit, she realised.

Each player would surrender a personal item to be auctioned. In order to get it back, he or she had to perform a forfeit, such as singing or dancing. Viscount Brentford had claimed the role of auctioneer, and from his amused expression, it seemed he was looking forward to the position of power.

A moment later, the waiters brought a large screen to shield the contents of the table, allowing guests to walk behind it, one at a time, to deposit their forfeited item. Reaching into her reticule, Hannah chose an embroidered handkerchief, keeping it hidden in her hand. After she passed behind the screen, she added it to the pile of gloves, shoes, jewellery and cravats.

She took her seat among the other ladies, hoping to see the Lieutenant. A glass of sherry was passed to her, and she sipped at the drink. It was smooth and sweet, and she felt herself beginning to relax. It wasn't nearly as wicked as her mother made it sound. She set it down on a table beside her, feeling her skin flush.

Two of the gentlemen moved the screen away, revealing a large pile of personal belongings.

'My friends, I know many of you are familiar with the game of Forfeit,' the Viscount began. 'However, tonight, I am suggesting that we use this game to raise money for an appropriate charity rather than strictly for amusement.'

He exchanged a glance with his wife and daughter. 'Ladies may bid to win a forfeit from the gentlemen, and gentlemen may bid on the ladies' items. The winning bidder shall send the promised amount to the poor and orphaned children of London. The owner of the item shall perform a forfeit of the bidder's choice.'

It was a scandalous game, one that could involve public humiliation or even a kiss. From the way the sherry, wine and brandy continued to be passed around, Hannah suspected things might indeed get out of hand.

'The winner of the auction will return the item to its owner, after the forfeit is paid.' Viscount Brentford reached behind the screen and picked up a black cravat. He cast a wicked look toward the ladies. 'Shall we start the bidding?'

Poor Henry Vanderkind, the owner of the cravat, was forced to crawl about on all fours while singing 'Woodman Spare That Tree'. Lady Howard, a widow nearing the age of sixty, howled with laughter and promised to send fifty pounds to the orphan fund.

As revenge, Henry Vanderkind bid thirty pounds on Lady Howard's quizzing glass and made her bleat like a goat in order to get it back again.

As each item was auctioned off, Hannah found herself wiping her own tears of laughter. She'd lost count of how much sherry she'd drunk, for a waiter kept all of the glasses full.

The room seemed to tilt, the voices buzzing in a haze. She pushed the glass aside, hoping that another headache would not come upon her. Someone passed a plate of cheeses, and she took a slice, thankful for the food to settle her stomach.

At that moment, she caught a glimpse of the Lieutenant. He didn't look at all entertained by the revelry.

But when he caught Hannah looking at him, his hazel eyes narrowed with interest. He rested his hands upon the back of a carved dining-room chair, and for a moment, she felt like the only woman in the room. The rest of the crowd seemed to melt away, and her body grew warmer as she met his gaze.

It was improper, certainly, but she couldn't stop herself from staring back. Her dress felt too tight, her heartbeat quickening. Though she finally looked away, she was aware of him taking a glass of wine. His mouth pressed against the crystal in a sip, and she again imagined his lips upon hers.

The Lieutenant crossed the room to stand at the other side, effectively distancing them. Hannah noticed that only two items remained on the table: her own handkerchief and a man's pocket watch.

The Viscount gave a silent nod to his daughter and lifted the watch. From the tension emanating from the Lieutenant, she supposed it must be his.

'The last gentleman's item is this pocket watch. It's quite heavy, I must say—no doubt made of the finest gold. Shall we start the bidding at five pounds?'

A flurry of female hands rose into the air, and Hannah saw Michael's discomfort rising. He held his posture stiff, his eyes staring off into the distance. He had loosened his cravat, while his black cloth jacket was unbuttoned to reveal a bright blue waistcoat. The pocket watch he'd worn was missing.

The bidding rose higher, the women laughing at the thought of the forfeit they would ask.

'With a handsome one like that, I'd ask for a kiss,' one woman remarked.

Another giggled. 'I'd kiss him without the auction, if he asked me to.'

Hannah didn't join in, but neither did she want Michael to pay a forfeit that would embarrass him. From the way he eyed the doorway, it wouldn't surprise her if he left the room. He didn't seem to care whether or not the watch was returned to him. It probably belonged to the Graf von Reischor.

When Miss Nelson held the highest bid of eighty pounds, the Viscountess shook her head sharply, whispering in her daughter's ear. Hannah didn't like the look of it. They were plotting against Michael, she was sure. It angered her, for she didn't want him to be the target of anyone's humour.

'One hundred pounds,' she heard herself saying. If nothing else, she might prevent the Lieutenant from being made into a fool.

A ripple of gasps resounded through the crowd of ladies. One woman sent her a dark look, as though she wanted to stab Hannah with a hat pin.

'One hundred and ten pounds,' Miss Nelson countered.

'Two hundred pounds.' Hannah didn't know whether the sherry had loosened her tongue or where this daring feeling had come from. All she knew was that she didn't want to lose the bidding war.

You can't have him, she wanted to say to Miss Nelson. But it seemed her bid of two hundred pounds had silenced the young woman. Viscount Brentford asked for any final bids, but none was forthcoming. Hannah rose from her seat, grasping the arms of the chair for support. With a determination she didn't quite feel, she moved towards the watch.

'What forfeit will you ask from Lieutenant Thorpe?' the Viscount asked.

Hannah looked into Michael's face. His hazel eyes held a rigid expression, his hands clenched at his sides. He didn't know why she'd bid upon him, and the tension in his stance suggested he had no intention of doing her will.

'No forfeit at all,' she whispered.

His eyes stared at her in disbelief for a long moment. When she brought the pocket watch to him, there was a barely perceptible acknowledgement.

'Now, now, Lady Hannah. That isn't playing by the rules,' another matron protested. 'He must pay his forfeit to get back his pocket watch. Perhaps you should have him sing. Or give a demonstration of his fighting skills.' The woman's gaze shifted to Michael's muscled form beneath the tightly fitted jacket.

'I'll reserve the right to ask for my forfeit later,' she said. The ladies squealed in delight, and Hannah instantly regretted the scandalous remark. A moment later, their attention was turned to the last item—her handkerchief.

Viscount Brentford lifted up the handkerchief, sending her a mischievous smile. 'Gentlemen, should we start the bidding for this lovely embroidered handkerchief?'

Michael stood from his seat. 'A thousand pounds,' he said softly.

There was a flurry of discussion over the exorbitant amount.

'For what, Lieutenant?' Viscount Brentford asked.

'For Lady Hannah's handkerchief.' His eyes never left hers when he added, 'That is my bid.'

The room grew uncomfortably quiet, and Hannah wanted to sink beneath the table. Dear God. Did he realise what he'd done? Now, the entire room would believe they were having an affair. She was mortified to think of it.

There were no other bids. Michael took the handkerchief and pocketed it, leaving the guests behind as he exited the dining room. He asked for no forfeit, and Hannah knew she was expected to follow him.

The Graf silently shook his head in disapproval. Hannah didn't know what to do. The game was not yet at an end, not to mention, Michael did not possess a thousand pounds.

Her embarrassment rose even higher as she overheard two ladies speculating about their relationship and whether or not Michael would offer for her. She knew, full well, that it would never happen.

Miss Nelson insinuated herself beside Hannah. 'Aren't you going to return Lieutenant Thorpe's pocket watch?'

It took Hannah a moment to realise she was still holding the watch. 'Oh. Eventually, I suppose.'

'Why did he bid a thousand pounds for your handkerchief?' Miss Nelson asked. 'Are you betrothed to one another?'

Hannah shook her head. 'I'm not certain why. I suppose it gave him an excuse to leave the game.'

Her explanation didn't appear to satisfy the young woman. 'Would you like me to return the watch to him?'

Hannah's fingers curled over the gold. It was a way out, a means for her not to see the Lieutenant again. She looked over and saw the hopeful light in her eyes. Miss Nelson honestly believed that Lieutenant Thorpe was a marriageable man, an officer from a noble family.

'No, thank you.' Hannah stood from her chair. 'I'll take care of this.'

The other ladies had begun a new game of Look About, searching for a hidden item. After several minutes, Miss Nelson joined them, seemingly disappointed that Hannah had not accepted her offer.

Graf von Reischor caught her arm as Hannah reached the door to the staircase, warning beneath his breath, 'Don't, Lady Hannah. It would do your reputation no good.'

'Whatever was left of my reputation, Lieutenant Thorpe just destroyed with that bid. He's going to answer for it.' She tightened her lips and strode forward.

There were less than twenty-four hours where she would be permitted to make her own decisions. Escort or not, the Graf would not control her actions tonight.

'I'm going to return the watch,' she said.

The Graf opened the door for her, gesturing for her maid to accompany them. Lowering his voice, he asserted, 'Regardless of what there might have been between you once, do not compromise yourself. He cannot wed you.'

Marry Lieutenant Thorpe? A man who had said she was nothing but a complication he didn't want? Frustration poured through her, and Hannah clenched her fan tightly. 'You see things which are not there.'

'I see more clearly than you, it seems. And neither your mother, nor your father, would allow you to speak to a man alone.'

She took a calming breath. ‘I will not be alone. And you insult me by implying that I am trying to seek out an affair.’

‘An affair is all you could ever hope to have with him.’

‘Why? Because you think he’s related to the royal family of Lohenberg?’

The guess was an impulsive prediction, but the Graf’s face paled. ‘Keep such theories to yourself, Lady Hannah.’

She closed her mouth to keep from gaping. ‘You’re not serious.’

‘I have eyes, Lady Hannah. Any Lohenberg native who encounters Lieutenant Thorpe would see it. He looks like König Sweyn, enough to be his son.’

‘You have no proof of his birthright.’

‘No. But I intend to find out the truth.’ He rested his hand upon the stair banister. ‘You should be aware that any contact with him bears a risk.’

She took the remaining steps and rested her hand upon the door leading to the promenade deck. ‘I am returning a watch, nothing more. I see no reason to be afraid.’

As she left, she heard the Graf speaking softly. ‘He has enemies you can’t even comprehend.’

MICHAEL TUCKED THE handkerchief into his coat pocket, contemplating whether or not he dared ascend to the upper deck. The sea waves were still rough, the ship swaying in spite of the roaring steam engines and paddle wheel.

He wanted fresh air and the coolness of the night. As he entered the upper deck of the *Orpheus*, the rocking motion of the ship became more pronounced. Wind billowed through the sails, and he heard the groaning of ropes straining against their knots.

The game of Forfeit had taken a turn he hadn’t intended. He’d been angry at becoming an object for ladies to bid on. Lord Brentford had practically offered his daughter’s hand in marriage, when he'd only just met the girl. No doubt if she'd won the bid, Miss Nelson would have asked him for a kiss. He wouldn't have given it. He despised people staring at him with expectations he couldn't possibly fulfil.

But Lady Hannah had intervened, casting a bid to guard his privacy. She'd faced down the women, protecting him from having to make an idiot out of himself.

There wasn't a man at the dinner table who hadn't wanted her to pay their choice of a forfeit. The thought of any man touching her was enough to make him snap a silver fork in half.

She's not yours. Never will be.

He knew that. And he'd done his best to keep his hands off her. She was a woman of Quality, a diamond who needed a polished setting in order to shine.

But he wasn't a damned saint. He desired her, knowing exactly the way he wanted to worship her body. He wanted to taste her skin, to run his mouth over her flesh until she cried out with pleasure.

What did it matter whether or not a gentleman bid upon Lady Hannah's handkerchief? She deserved the opportunity to make a good marriage. Certainly, the gentlemen on board the ship had no idea of the scandal.

For so long, she'd been trapped in her father's cocoon. Now was her chance to rip away the rigid rules and gain her freedom. He was a selfish bastard, wanting her to surrender to him.

Michael rested his hand upon the wooden railing, staring out at the dark waters. What was it about her that drew him in, like a seedling to the sun? She wasn't anything like the women he'd known while he was in the Army. Kindhearted, well-bred and beautiful, she belonged with an English lord who would sleep in a separate bedroom and let her plan the household menus and entertainment.

She didn't belong with a man like him. A man with baser urges, who would much rather unravel those sensibilities than uphold them.

When he'd made the ridiculous bid of a thousand pounds, it hadn't been a true charitable contribution. It had been a warning to the other men to stay away from Lady Hannah, or they would regret it. Like a beast marking his territory, he'd laid claim to her.

But now what was he supposed to do?

Footsteps sounded behind him. He didn't turn around, expecting Hannah to move beside him.

Instead, a rope slid around his neck. Stars glimmered in his consciousness, his lungs burning for air. Michael fought against the tight noose, throwing himself to the decking and knocking his assailant's feet beneath him.

Tearing the rope away, he reached for the man, intending to find out what in God's name was going on.

CHAPTER ELEVEN

A STRONG WAVE shook the ship, and Michael skidded backwards. His head struck one of the masts, and he grimaced at the impact. Salt water sprayed the deck, while in the distance, he heard the crew shouting orders to one another.

When he scrambled to the place where he'd been attacked, there was nothing. Not a trace of the man, as though his assailant had been a phantom. Only the raw abrasions on his throat gave any evidence that he'd very nearly been strangled.

'Lieutenant Thorpe?' Lady Hannah called out to him. She hadn't seen what had happened, from the questioning tone of her voice.

Michael didn't turn, his attention fully upon the shadows. He didn't want to endanger Hannah if his attacker returned.

'Is everything all right?' she enquired, drawing closer to stand beside him. 'You seem distracted.'

'I'm fine.' His voice came out hoarser than he'd intended, and he coughed to disguise it. He withdrew her handkerchief from his waistcoat pocket and offered it back. She took it, handing him his watch. Her fingers lingered upon his palm.

Behind him, he heard a slight shuffling. He didn't know whether it was another passenger or the assailant, but he didn't intend to remain standing about.

'We need to get off the upper deck. Now.' Without waiting to find out who the intruder was, he grasped Hannah's hand and pulled her through a door. The stairs led to the private state rooms, and Michael continued through the maze of first-class rooms until he located hers. Thankfully, she didn't argue with him, but let him escort her back.

'Where is your maid?' he demanded. 'Why are you alone?'

'I dismissed her to our room a few moments ago. I didn't think—'

'It's not safe for you to be alone on this ship. Not ever.' Though he didn't mean to snap at her, he didn't want her risking her well-being on his behalf.

Before he could open the door to her room, Hannah reached up to his neck. 'Dear God, what happened to you? You're bleeding and the skin is raw.'

'Don't concern yourself over it.'

He was about to leave when she held up her hand. 'Wait over there while I send away my maid and Mrs Turner. And if you disappear, so help me, I will seek you out. We are not finished talking.'

He didn't doubt that. She was stubborn, far more than was good for her. But once she had entered her room, he ducked behind the corner to wait.

Several minutes later, the cabin door opened, and he saw her maid Estelle leading the way down the hall, followed by Mrs Turner. Michael waited until the women reached the far end, and then approached Hannah's door.

She stood waiting for him, her expression hesitant. He knew, as she did, that it was entirely improper for him to even be near her cabin, much less inside it.

'You didn't need to send them away.'

'You wouldn't tell me the truth if they were here. And it's best if no one knows about our conversation.' Hannah steeled her posture, nodding. 'Come in and let me tend that for you.' Without waiting for a reply, she turned and went to her dressing table.

She poured water into a basin, dipping her handkerchief into the liquid. When she risked a glance at his neck, she gave a perceptible wince. Though her intentions were good, he doubted if she'd ever tended a wound before in her life. To avoid embarrassing her, he took the damp cloth from her and swabbed at his throat, surprised that there was more blood than he'd thought.

'Tell me what happened,' she demanded, keeping her gaze firmly fixed upon his eyes and not the abrasions. 'I want the truth.'

'Someone tried to strangle me, just before you came.'

'Were they trying to rob you?'

'Trying to kill me, more like,' he admitted.

She froze, her hands falling away. Her complexion paled, and she clenched her fingertips. 'Do you really believe that?'

'It's not the first time someone has tried to do so,' he admitted. 'Usually it was someone on the opposite side of the battlefield.' Reaching out for one of her hands, he asked, 'Are you afraid he'll come after you as well?'

Her hand was cool within his, and she swallowed, as if trying to find her courage. 'Would you protect me if he did?'

His lips curved slightly. 'What do you think?'

She didn't answer, but tried to pull her hand back. He retrieved the damp handkerchief and touched the raw skin at his throat again.

Hannah stopped him, her hand bumping against his. 'Wait. You're missing it.'

Without asking permission, she loosened his collar, untying his cravat to reveal his skin.

Though the water was probably cold, he hardly felt the

temperature. Instead, he was intensely aware of Hannah standing between his legs, her hands upon his skin. He was growing aroused, just being near her. The green gown she wore accentuated the swell of her breasts, the curve of her waist. But it was her innocence that was even more alluring. She didn't seem to understand what her simple touch was doing to him.

Awkwardly, she dabbed at his flesh, her lower lip caught between her teeth as though trying to overcome her distaste for blood. He held himself motionless, willing himself not to respond.

'Why would anyone want to kill you?' she asked. A slight shiver crossed over her before she studied his skin, searching for any other wounds.

He didn't answer, offering a shrug.

'Someone believes it's true,' she murmured. 'That you have royal blood.'

Michael didn't acknowledge her guess, though he agreed with her prediction. There was no other reason for anyone to kill him.

'Fairy tales aren't true, Hannah. A common soldier doesn't simply become a Prince.'

He could smell the faint scent of jasmine, and when she'd finished washing his throat, she kept her hands upon his shoulders. 'Unless he already was a Prince. And didn't know it.'

Catching her wrists, Michael drew her hands away. 'Don't do this, Hannah.'

Confusion clouded her gaze. Then abruptly, she seemed to grasp his meaning. Her face coloured, first with embarrassment, then anger.

'Were you trying to make a fool of me?' she demanded. 'Bidding a thousand pounds for a handkerchief?'

He kept his mouth shut, with no intention of explaining himself.

'You made them believe that we were lovers. That I'd given myself to you.'

'Is that what you're doing?' He stood up so suddenly that her hands fell away.

He needed her to realise that she was tempting the devil, whether or not she intended to do so. Possibly frighten her a little, so she wouldn't risk coming too close.

'You had no right to blemish my reputation before all of those people,' she whispered. 'I left London to start over again. And now they are talking about us.' She stepped backwards, her hands clenched.

He stared hard at her, willing her to see the truth. 'You don't want your freedom as much as you think you do. You like the rules you pretend to despise.'

She held still, like a wild animal about to flee. 'You don't understand.'

'I understand perfectly.' He closed the distance, resting his hands on the wall behind her. 'You want it both ways, don't you? You want them to believe you're a lady, when you secretly desire something else.'

'No. That's not it.' She shielded herself with her arms, hugging them to her chest.

He let his hands slide down to her small waist, feeling the tightness of her corset beneath the gown. 'Why did you bid on the pocket watch?'

She looked guilty. 'Because I didn't want the women treating you that way. Like a piece of meat fought over by dogs.'

'I don't care about what other people think of me.'

'Perhaps you should.' Her breath hitched when his hands slid up her spine once more. 'You're not at all the man you pretend to be.'

'I'm the kind of man you shouldn't be alone with.' Lowering his mouth to her chin, he let his mouth nip the edge of her flesh. He tasted the light sweetness of sherry upon her mouth and waited for her to strike out at him. The kiss made her tremble, but again, she didn't order him to leave.

Instead, her eyes filled with indecision, almost as if she were considering letting him ruin her.

'You'd better find that candlestick,' he warned. 'Or I won't be responsible for what happens. I'm going to take that forfeit now.'

'You would never harm me,' she whispered. To emphasise her prediction, she rested her palms upon his heart. The slight touch made the muscle contract faster within his chest.

He wasn't quite so confident. Just being near her, touching her in this way, was making it difficult to concentrate.

Her scent was shredding his restraint, and he realized she was waiting for him to act. Her mouth was softened, slightly open in anticipation. But he didn't take her offering. Not yet.

He pressed his mouth to her throat, kissing a path down to her exposed collarbone. She shuddered in his arms, not offering a single protest.

The taste of her skin, the way her palms moved up to cup his neck…he wasn't certain he would be able to stop if she let things go much further.

Michael removed his gloves, letting them fall to the floor. His hands moved to the back of her gown, unbuttoning the first few buttons. 'This isn't part of the forfeit any more.' He grazed her shoulder with his teeth, kissing the soft place and evoking a sigh from her throat. 'Order me to leave.'

One word, and he would go. She could lie in her nightdress tonight and imagine the things he wanted to do to her. But she would remain untouched.

'I'm going to take my forfeit, too,' she whispered. 'You're going to make me forget all the rules.'

Deliberately, she caressed his head, bringing her hands back down to his shoulders. Her touch made his body tighten with a greater frustration.

He unfastened another three buttons, baring more silken skin, before tilting her face to look at him. Her body had been touched by no other man, he was certain. Only him.

He didn't know why she was letting him take such liberties, but he suspected she wasn't thinking clearly. 'Do you want another kiss as your forfeit from me?'

She inhaled sharply when his bare palm touched her back. 'Yes.'

He smiled against her mouth and guided her to sit down. He knelt down at her feet, reaching for her ankles.

'Wh-what are you doing?' She held down her skirts, her face pale.

'I'm going to kiss you, all right.' Michael slid his hands up her calves, his palms caressing the silken stockings. 'But you never said where.'

'No. That's not what I meant. I wasn't intending for you to—to ruin me.'

'I'm not going to ruin you, sweet. I'm going to pleasure you. Unless you're too afraid?'

She had gone so pale, her fingers dug into the arms of the chair. And though it was painful to stop this wicked game, he started to draw back. His desire for her was strained to the breaking point, so it was probably for the best.

She shocked him by bringing his mouth to hers. Against his lips, she whispered, 'I'm more terrified than I've ever been in my life. But I don't want you to stop.'

God forgive him for what he was about to do. Michael took her mouth hard, kissing her roughly. He pulled her body tightly to his, letting her legs fall open around his waist. Her shoulders rose and fell as she struggled to catch her breath. To ease her, he unlaced more of her corset.

'But what if someone comes—?'

He kissed another bit of revealed skin, swirling his tongue over it. 'The risk makes it more arousing.'

She shivered in his arms, and he could almost hear the second thoughts racing through her mind. 'I shouldn't let you do this. I know it's wrong.'

'But it feels good to you.'

She lowered her head, as if in surrender. 'Yes. And I'm beginning to wonder what I have left to lose.'

'You would lose far too much.' He took her hands, lifting them to her bodice. Her palms cupped her own breasts, and he held them in place, forcing her to touch herself the way he wanted to.

Though her nipples were beneath the heavy corset, he knew her mind was imagining the sensation.

'You're tempting me down a path I should never tread.'

'I'm a sinner. I live for temptation.'

Hannah leaned back against him, letting him guide her hands. It was hard to breathe, the room swimming in heady sensations.

She never should have let Michael enter her room. Her mother's warnings haunted her, but she couldn't bring herself to step away. Not yet.

This forbidden pleasure coursed through her, for she'd never been touched like this before. She didn't even know such feelings existed. Her body was hot, the skin fiery and unbearably sensitive. Between her legs, she felt empty, swollen and aching. And yet she knew that, regardless of what he said, Michael would stop at any time she asked.

He might be a man who neglected the rules of propriety when it suited him, but beneath it all he possessed an unfailing honour.

With her last vestiges of control, she pushed him back, away from the chair. She stood, needing to know whether she was making the right choice to be with him tonight.

As she'd expected, he held back from her, his face expressionless. The black cloth jacket fitted his broad shoulders perfectly, the evening clothes making him even more handsome. In the lamplight, his hazel eyes were nearly black, heated with desire.

Someone had tried to kill him tonight, yet he gave no indication of being afraid. She supposed soldiers were accustomed to the risk of death. But if someone had just tried to murder her, she would be a sobbing mess.

His strong will and courage intrigued her. Tempted her in ways she didn't understand.

'Michael?' she whispered. She'd never used his first name before, always distancing him with his rank.

'What?'

Touch me again. Kiss me. She didn't say it, the words caught up in a trap of her own morals. And yet, she didn't want him to leave, as he surely would.

She didn't know what was coming over her. Perhaps it was the wine. Perhaps her desire to make her own decisions. All she knew was that she didn't want to be alone.

'What if… I asked you for more than a kiss?'

Michael held so very still, she wondered if she'd made a grave mistake. Her cheeks burned with embarrassment as the silence stretched longer.

'I'm not the right man for you, Hannah. I can't ever marry you.'

His honesty was meant to quell her desire. But she'd always known there could be no future for them. And he didn't love her, either.

'I know that,' she heard herself saying. 'It's not what I want from you.' She held her posture erect, as though it would keep her sensibilities from crumbling. What would it matter if she let him kiss her, let him show her the mysteries of a forbidden liaison? Her reputation was already in shambles.

She stood an arm's length from him, but an invitation rested in the space between them. Michael took a step closer, until she could feel the warmth of his breath upon her forehead. The physical closeness of him turned her thoughts erratic.

Her body tingled, imagining his body atop hers. Never in her life had she known such an experience. The weight of her gown upon her breasts, the heavy skirts covering her legs… It made her uncomfortable, as if too many layers separated them.

He caught her palm and grazed it with a slight kiss. 'You're not yourself.'

'You're right.' She pulled his hand to her cheek, not caring that it was wrong. The need to rebel was rising higher with each moment. 'I have exactly fifteen hours to not be myself. Before we leave this ship.'

His hand drifted to her back, and she felt his bare palm upon her skin. He loosened a few more buttons, sliding his hand beneath the back of her gown.

This was her last chance to say no. Did she want to ruin herself with a soldier? With a man who had no future and could not take care of her? With a man who made her heart beat like the wings of a hummingbird?

Yes.

Hannah reached out and rested her hands upon his evening jacket, tracing the breadth of his shoulders. Before she could talk herself out of it, she lifted her mouth to his in a defiant kiss. He tasted of champagne and a hint of almonds.

That was the last thought in her mind before he took command. He pressed her against the wall, his hot kiss possessing her with no chance of escape. She was aware of his hands unbuttoning the rest of her gown. In turn, she removed his jacket, untying the cravat.

'I loathe women's fashion,' Michael gritted out. Despite her layers of skirts, he managed to reach beneath them to untie a few of the petticoats, and divest her of the heavy crinoline. Without the weight to support her gown, the fabric hung down. She felt small, completely at his mercy. He undressed her, each piece falling away until she was standing in her undergarments.

The reality of her decision hit her like a bucket of freezing water. Why was she casting aside all of her inhibitions, everything she'd been taught, for a man who had already admitted he could give her no future?

He is nothing, her mind insisted.

He is everything, her body contradicted. Only hours ago, someone had tried to kill him. The thought of losing this man, when she'd only just begun to know him, crept into the spaces of her heart, making her ache. And tonight, he belonged to her.

The war between her body's needs and her mind's agonising control was growing even hotter.

His tongue slipped inside her mouth, and her breasts grew taut as though he'd kissed the nipples. Between her thighs, she grew moist, and Hannah shifted her legs together. No one had ever prepared her for this, and she was too afraid to ask him what was happening.

Michael extinguished the lamp, flooding the cabin in darkness. 'Come here,' he urged, taking her hand. He guided her towards him, and when she realised he was seated in the chair, he pulled her onto his lap.

Her womanhood was intimately pressed against the hard length of his arousal, with only her drawers and his trousers as a barrier. She clung to him, her fingers pressed against his hair.

In the darkness, her skin became even more sensitised. She didn't know what he would do next, and it both excited and terrified her.

Michael slid his hands into her hair once again, and the pins scattered across the wooden floor. His fingers spread through the silken locks while he kissed her.

Her hands rested upon his chest, and he sensed her desire to touch. He loosened his shirt, moving her hands beneath the cambric. His pectoral muscles were rigid, his pulse rapid. Bare skin warmed her fingertips, and her bravado was beginning to disappear.

'Are you certain you want this?' he murmured, kissing her deeply.

When he broke free, she couldn't answer, not knowing what she should say. Things had already progressed too far, hadn't they? Her silence weighed down upon his question.

She wanted him. But was the cost too great?

When his hand moved between her legs, she shivered. His fingers moved to the thin drawers, and she flushed, knowing that he could feel the wetness dampening the cloth. She didn't understand why, and it embarrassed her.

'I know you're afraid of me.' His voice was deep, the rich timbre making her quiver.

'A little,' she confessed. 'I don't know what to do.'

His hand moved against her woman's flesh, arousing her. 'Surrender to me, Hannah. And let me touch you the way I've dreamed.'

She didn't know what he meant by that until his thumb rubbed a small nub above her entrance. A harsh cry caught in the back of her throat, and she forced herself not to moan. With a soft rhythm, he nudged it, sending a shock of warmth spiralling into her womb.

Though she wanted to pull away, she couldn't bring herself to move.

'You're beautiful, Hannah.' He leaned her back, nuzzling her throat as he increased the rhythm. 'If I could, I'd be inside you right now.'

Was that what happened between a man and a woman? She could feel the hard length of his manhood against her inner thigh. The thought of him entering her body conjured a response that made her even wetter. He teased the moisture, using the fabric to abrade her sensitive node.

Hannah fought against the rising wave of pleasure that threatened to drown her. He dipped his finger slightly, caressing the opening of her womanhood.

'I don't understand,' she admitted, her face burning with discomfort. 'How could you be inside me?'

She'd never been taught anything about lovemaking, and she half-wondered if this touching was what husbands and wives did. Somehow, she suspected not. It felt like forbidden temptation, to experience such desire.

He brought her hand to his trousers, letting her feel the firm length straining beneath the cloth. She was startled at the thickness of him, the hard ridge of male flesh.

'This part of me would slide deep inside you,' he said gruffly. His hand moved beneath her drawers to her feminine centre. He dipped his hand against her sensitive flesh, inserting a single finger to demonstrate. 'When you're wet, it makes it easier for both of us.'

He captured her mouth again, using his fingers to stroke her. Before she could beg him to understand the unfamiliar longings, something unexpected began to break through. Her breathing quickened, her back arching out of instinct.

His hand rubbed faster without warning, crumbling away her inhibitions until a hot, piercing sensation pushed her closer to the edge. Then abruptly, he slowed the pace, deepening the pressure.

'Let go for me, Hannah.'

She was fighting against the maddening heat building up. Her inner thighs were silken, craving more.

Without warning, pleasure rammed into her, making her writhe against his hand. Never had she felt anything like this before. He rode his palm against her centre, until she was trembling with aftershocks.

Michael removed his palm, his own breath shaken. His mouth pressed light kisses over her temple, while she clung to him. Nothing could have prepared her for such unexpected ecstasy.

'Would it…have been like that if you'd…made love to me?' she panted.

'Better,' he swore. There was pain in his voice, as though he were fighting off his own frustration. A moment later, he lifted her to her feet, turning the lamp back on. The light speared her eyes, breaking through the spell.

She stood in her underclothes, feeling the shock of reality striking through her. She might as well have been naked before him. He didn't look at her, but reached for his fallen jacket.

Oh, dear God above, what had she done? Why had she fallen into temptation this way? And what could she possibly say to him now?

When Michael turned to face her, all emotions were masked, as if they had done nothing but conversed. The back of her throat ached, while her cheeks burned with humiliation. To distract herself, she reached for her own fallen clothing.

'I'll help you dress, before I leave,' Michael said at last.

Hannah would have refused, if she could have managed it herself. She tied the layers of petticoats, unable to face him. Irrational tears stung her eyes, but she kept them at bay. Michael held up her dress and lifted it over her head and arms, helping her to rebutton it.

Despite the deep languor that permeated every inch of her skin, she felt like a piece of crystal teetering on the edge, ready to shatter.

'Are you all right?'

No. No, she wasn't all right. But she forced herself to nod. 'Of course. Why wouldn't I be?' Her voice came out too bright, and his hands caressed her shoulders.

His hazel eyes stared at her, gazing at her with such an intensity, she wondered what he wanted to say but couldn't. Instead, he held himself motionless.

'Be careful when you go back to your room,' she offered.

Michael inclined his head. 'Lock your door until Mrs Turner and your maid return.' There was a forced coolness to his voice, and the invisible mien of a soldier seemed to slide over his face.

Humiliation at succumbing to the liaison, without any future promises from him, made her throat go dry. But she'd known it. There would never be any sort of vow from Michael Thorpe.

'Don't trouble yourself about me.'

He took another step backwards, and a faint tinging noise resounded. Michael reached down to the floor to pick up the object. In his hand, he held a fork.

'How strange,' Hannah remarked. 'I didn't bring any silver into the room.'

Both of them stared at the interior of the state room, suddenly seeing pieces neither of them had noticed before. Pieces of silverware, hair pins, a strand of pearls… seemingly random items now were arranged in a pattern. A rectangle had been constructed around the room, framing the contents.

'How curious. What is it, do you think?' Hannah asked.

But Michael ignored the question, already opening the door. 'Where did you tell Mrs Turner to go?'

Hannah shrugged. 'I only told them to return in an hour. I assumed she stayed with my maid Estelle.'

He cursed, stepping into the hallway. 'I have to find her.'

Not we, she noticed. *I.*

Was he so eager to cast her aside now? Her disgruntled feelings pricked her like the numerous forks lying about the room.

But she didn't understand why a strange arrangement of utensils would cause him to worry so. 'What is it that you're not telling me?'

He pointed towards the perimeter of silver. 'She's having another of her spells. I need to find Mrs Turner before she harms herself.'

It would be easy enough to send him away, to wish him luck in finding her. But she felt responsible for the woman's disappearance. Were it not for her, Mrs Turner would still be inside her room, probably sleeping.

Hannah reached for her pelisse and pulled on a bonnet. 'I'm coming with you.'

CHAPTER TWELVE

OUTSIDE ON THE upper deck, the ship rose and fell with the waves. The darkness was broken only by a handful of scattered oil lamps. Several deck hands adjusted the sails while the dull noise of the steam engine droned on.

Michael kept Hannah's hand firmly in his, wondering why he'd agreed to this. There was no reason to bring her with him, where her presence would be noticeably out of place. It was irrational and dangerous.

But he didn't want to leave her alone. Not after he'd been attacked tonight. And especially not after what had just happened between them.

It had taken an act of the greatest restraint not to seduce her. He didn't doubt for a moment that he could have. Her body responded to him with a passion he'd never expected. More than anything, he'd wanted to strip off her remaining undergarments, joining their bodies together.

The sensual image of her legs wrapped around his waist while he buried himself deep within was like a fire igniting his lust. She was a lady, not a woman to be trifled with. Softhearted, stubborn and highly intelligent, everything about her captivated him.

And yet he couldn't bring himself to dishonour her. If he took her innocence, she would pay the price. And he couldn't destroy her chance to make a strong marriage, no matter how much he might want her.

The thought of another man being intimate with Hannah made him clench his fists. At dinner tonight he'd seen the way the gentlemen watched her. He had no right to feel possessive towards her. Not then, and not now.

He gripped her hand, studying the area for any sign of Mrs Turner. When they passed by one of the sailors, he drew Hannah closer, both to protect her from the rocking of the ship and to send an unmistakable warning to the other sailors.

The bo'sun stepped forward and intercepted them. 'Pardon me, m'lord, but passengers aren't allowed on deck at this hour. Best be returnin' to your cabin. Captain's orders.'

Michael wasn't surprised to hear it, but he didn't give a damn what the Captain's orders were. Whenever Mrs Turner had one of her spells, there was no telling what she'd do. He didn't want her to fall into the sea and drown, if her madness tempted her to do something rash. Abigail Turner was the only family he had left, and he would keep her safe at all costs.

He faced the bo'sun and drew upon his officer's hauteur. Had they been in the Army, he would outrank this man. 'One of Lady Hannah's servants has disappeared.' He nodded to the bo'sun, adding, 'We believe she may be lost.'

The bo'sun shrugged. 'Haven't seen her. She might've gone to meet someone.' His disrespectful leer suggested that he suspected Hannah and Michael had done exactly that.

Michael sent the man a blistering look. He was well aware of the implications of bringing Hannah with him, but he wasn't about to let anyone insult her. The sailor straightened, his smirk disappearing at once.

'She is a woman of about sixty-three years, with curling grey hair and light brown eyes,' Michael added. 'About this plump.' He held out his arms to show her girth, though Mrs Turner had lost a good deal of weight since he'd first known her. Too often she forgot to eat.

The bo'sun shook his head. 'Sorry, m'lord. I'm in charge of the rigging and the deck crew. But I'll send one of the hands to look for you, if y'like.'

'Do that.' And in the meantime, he and Hannah would continue searching. He gave a brusque nod before taking Hannah's hand. He intended to survey every inch of the upper deck, to ensure that they hadn't missed her.

Turning away, he pretended to escort Hannah to the stairs of the promenade deck, but at the last moment he guided her around the side of the boat, towards the forecastle.

Together, they traversed the upper deck, slipping into the shadows when any of the deck hands or officers came close. In the dim amber light of the oil lamps, it was nearly impossible to see.

Luck was with them; a few minutes later he spied a red bonnet rolling across the deck.

'She's here.' He kept Hannah's hand firmly gripped in his. 'Tell me if you see her.'

IT TOOK NEARLY a quarter of an hour before they both heard the singing at the same time. The quavering voice of Mrs Turner came from above them. Michael lifted his gaze and saw her holding onto the rigging, her body swaying as the ship rocked on the waves.

'Oh, dear heaven,' Hannah breathed when she spied her. 'What's she doing up there? She'll fall and break her neck.'

'Not if I can get to her first.' Michael removed his jacket and grasped the heavy rope, climbing up the ratline toward Mrs Turner. Calling out to her, he said, 'Mrs Turner, let me help you down.' It was so dark, he doubted if she could see his face. If she didn't recognise him, it would be a problem.

'Henry?' she cried out, asking for her son. 'Is that you?'

He thought about lying, if that would bring her to safety. But if she glimpsed his face, she might panic and fall.

Instead he admitted, 'No. It's Michael Thorpe.'

At first, she didn't reply, which gave him hope. Her skirts and petticoats billowed in the night air, while she held fast to the ropes.

'Will you let me help you down?'

'I don't know anyone named Michael. Now stay away from me while I wait on my Henry.' She began singing again, her voice high-pitched. 'Mad. She's gone mad, for her boy has gone away.' Her voice grew tighter, mingling with tears. 'My fault. It's my fault that it happened.' Sobbing harder, she moaned, 'I didn't want him to die, you see.'

'Shh—' Michael reached up take her by the waist, but she slapped his hands.

'You're not my Henry. I don't know you. Get away from me!' The wind whipped at the ratlines, and Mrs Turner's hand slipped. She shrieked as the line spun, making her swing downwards. Michael caught her hand and put it back to the rope, though she screamed at him.

Damn it. The precarious balancing point on the ratlines stretching up to the mast made it too dangerous to seize her against her will. Either of them could lose their grip and fall. Mrs Turner was nearly twenty feet up in the air, and though she was primarily over the decking, there was still the possibility that she might slip and fall overboard.

He glanced down and caught a glimpse of Hannah climbing up to them. 'Let me try, Michael. I'll coax her down.' When she drew closer, he saw that she'd tied her skirts to each of her ankles.

There was no hesitation in his refusal. 'No.' He wouldn't risk Hannah's safety, no matter that she was already close to them. 'Climb down.'

But she ignored his orders, reaching up higher. The combined weight of the three of them made the line stretch tight.

'You're frightening her,' Hannah insisted. 'I'm a woman. She'll let me help.'

When he was about to argue again, she touched his elbow. 'Stay below us, in case either of us falls.' Mrs Turner had begun singing again, her frail voice turning hoarse.

'Michael, please,' Hannah begged. 'If you try to force her down, she'll fight you. And you'll both be hurt.'

He knew she was right. Though he didn't want to endanger Hannah, he would give her one chance. With great reluctance, he lowered himself below them, to ensure that neither of them fell. He heard Hannah speaking to Mrs Turner softly.

'I've asked him to leave us alone,' she murmured to the older woman. 'He's gone now and won't harm you.'

'They tried to take him away,' she wept. 'My boy.'

Hannah spoke so quietly to Mrs Turner, Michael couldn't make out what she was saying. He held tightly to the ratlines, watching both of them. Endless minutes passed, and his grip tightened while he watched.

Then Mrs Turner slowly began to descend, with Hannah beside her. Michael kept his hands poised on the lines, prepared to break their fall, if either slipped.

Several of the deck hands had gathered around, and Michael ordered them away. The bo'sun tried to apologise, but Michael cut him off, shielding the women from his gaze. 'I will escort them back to their state rooms,' he said firmly.

Relief filled him up inside that both women were safe on deck. Lady Hannah held Mrs Turner's hand and was speaking quietly to her.

What Hannah had just done was completely unheard of. Women didn't climb twenty feet in the air to rescue a stranger. It was scandalous, dangerous and right now he wanted to shake her. But he also wanted to hold her tightly, thankful that she hadn't been hurt.

She shouldn't have taken such a bold risk. His anger and fear built up to the point where he gritted his teeth to keep from lashing out at her.

Though his rational mind pointed out that both of them were all right, it might have been a very different outcome. He couldn't let Hannah take such chances again.

THE AIR WAS frigid, and Hannah's teeth were threatening to chatter from the cold. Mrs Turner's hands were icy, and Michael led them all back to Hannah's state room, where she found Estelle waiting.

The maid's eyes widened at the sight of Hannah and her windblown, dishevelled appearance.

'Lady Hannah, whatever happened to you?' Estelle looked appalled, but Hannah had no desire to explain herself. Nor did she want a word of this spoken to her mother.

Ignoring the question, she said, 'I ordered you to look after Mrs Turner, but you neglected your duty, it seems.'

Excuses stammered from Estelle's lips, but Hannah had endured her fill of them. 'Enough. Go and help Mrs Turner prepare for bed.'

The maid cast a glance at Michael, and he stared back at Estelle, until she returned her attentions to Mrs Turner.

Hannah was about to help them, when the Lieutenant refused to surrender her wrist, leading her into the dimly lit hallway. He forced her to follow him around the corner to a spot hidden from view.

Keeping his voice in a whisper, he leaned down to her ear. 'Whatever possessed you to do something so dangerous?'

Her teeth started chattering, his words breaking apart the false confidence that was holding her together. She knew it had been perilous, but standing below on the decking hadn't been useful, either.

'I don't know. I just thought…you needed help,' she whispered, thankful when he rubbed her hands to warm them.

'I didn't need you breaking your neck.' He pulled her body close to his, letting his body heat warm her freezing skin. The actions were in opposition to his words. 'You could have been killed.'

'So could you.' She pulled back, trying to calm the chattering of her teeth. 'You asked me to help look after Mrs Turner. And you were frightening her. It seemed like the only way to get her down.'

He said nothing but stroked her hair. His wide hands moved over her scalp, down her back. 'Don't ever do something like that again.' Right now, he was holding her like he didn't want to let go. He fitted his body to hers as though he wanted to shield her from all harm.

Against her better judgement, Hannah embraced him back. In their fleeting solitude, his mouth brushed against her temple. She closed her eyes, wishing to God there weren't so many obstacles between them.

He'd made no promises to her, nor could he. She knew that. All they had was a few stolen moments together. Tomorrow evening, they would arrive in Bremerhaven. And the day after that, she would be left behind at her cousins' house.

He framed her face with his hands. 'Thank you for what you did.'

She braved a smile, startled by his unexpected offering. 'You're welcome. I hope Mrs Turner feels better in the morning.'

'Get some sleep,' he ordered.

'I doubt it.' Her insides were still churning, after everything that had happened, and most especially after the way he'd touched her.

'Michael,' she murmured. 'About what happened between us earlier—'

'It won't happen again,' he swore. He jerked his hands back, as though he couldn't get away from her fast enough. The deep embarrassment returned, for she'd given so much of herself to him. Like a wanton woman, she had laid herself bare before him, seeking the mindless pleasure he'd offered.

'Good,' she echoed. 'That's good, then.' Without another word, she turned back to her room so he would not see the tears.

LADY HANNAH WAS absent from breakfast that morning. Her maid said she'd taken a tray in her state room, and Michael supposed she needed the extra sleep after the night they'd endured.

Earlier, he'd gone back to the upper deck where they had rescued Mrs Turner. Seeing the narrow ratlines in the morning sunlight made his breath catch. If either of them had fallen overboard, they might have become trapped beneath the large paddle wheel.

He never should have let Hannah climb up. It would have been so easy for her to be harmed or killed. The failure would have fallen upon his shoulders, just as he'd failed his fellow soldiers at Balaclava.

He returned to the promenade deck, but saw no sign of Mrs Turner or Lady Hannah. He wasn't about to knock on her state-room door, for he'd already broken enough rules of propriety. It was better for him to keep his distance and hope that he met her by chance.

After exploring the many rooms of the ship, he found them in the Grand Saloon. Hannah wore a long-sleeved, flounced rose gown adorned with lace. The trim was sewn across her bodice down to a narrow vee at the waist. A matching bonnet with ribbons and more lace cradled her face. Were it not for the dull exhaustion in her eyes, no one would notice anything out of order. Her gaze went to his neck, but he'd hidden the abraded skin with a high cravat.

Beside her sat Mrs Turner, wearing her black mourning gown. The elderly woman beamed, calling out, 'Michael! You will join us, won't you?' In her hands, she held out a deck of cards. 'I am teaching Lady Hannah to play piquet.'

He wasn't certain that was such a good idea. 'I thought ladies weren't supposed to play cards.'

Mrs Turner pulled out a chair. 'Oh, we're not going to be ladies today, are we?'

It was then that he saw the enormous slice of chocolate cake on the plate beside Hannah. She took a bite of the dessert, as if defying the etiquette for proper breakfast food. Watching her devour the cake reminded him of the expression on her face last night when he'd showed her the pleasures of her secret flesh.

He hastily took a seat to hide his reaction to the memory.

Mrs Turner dealt out the cards to each of them. 'I know you've played before.'

He let his gaze rest upon Hannah's face while she ate her cake. 'Yes.'

'Then you'll be able to teach Lady Hannah all that she needs to know.'

He made no response, watching as Hannah's tongue slipped out to lick her fingertip. There were many things he wanted to teach Lady Hannah, and not a single one of them having to do with cards.

Hannah picked up the hand dealt, a sheepish smile upon her face. 'I'm not very good with cards. I was never allowed to play.'

He picked up his own cards, barely glancing at them. 'Why not?'

'My mother believed that any cards were a form of gambling. She didn't want me to risk eternal hellfire.'

'There are far worse ways to sin,' he pointed out.

Hannah's face turned scarlet, as though she were thinking of the time she'd spent in his arms. She forced her attention back to the cards.

'Which of us will be the dealer?' Michael asked Mrs Turner.

'Why don't you take on that role? Let Lady Hannah draw first.'

Michael deferred to the widow's wishes and dealt the cards. He picked up his hand, studying the two jacks and the queen of spades amid the other numbered cards. 'Were you wanting to wager on the game?'

Mrs Turner beamed. 'Well, of course we should have a wager. That's what makes playing cards so entertaining. And wicked.'

'There's nothing wrong with a bit of wickedness...once in a while.' Michael shifted his cards, laying them facedown on the table while he waited for Hannah.

When she glanced up, her gaze settled upon his mouth. He spied the traces of chocolate upon her lips. Right now he wanted to lick it off, devouring her mouth and pulling her close.

'What should we wager with?' Hannah asked, a faint blush of colour upon her cheeks. 'Money we don't have?'

He knew she was referring to the fictional thousand pounds he'd offered in return for her handkerchief last night. 'Not for money.'

'What, then?'

A flash of inspiration struck him, and Michael signalled

to one of the ships' waiters. After a brief discussion, the waiter nodded, disappearing behind closed doors.

'Wait and see.'

When the waiter returned, he held a tray of miniature pastries, caramels and confections.

'We'll play for sweets,' Michael said.

'Lieutenant Thorpe, you are a man of genius,' Hannah breathed. Her face beamed with anticipation and a new determination to win.

He rested his wrist upon the table, watching her as she focused on her cards. Mrs Turner explained the rules, urging Hannah to choose five cards to exchange from her hand.

'The seven is the lowest card and ace is the highest,' the widow explained. 'You should try to exchange the most cards, in order to hold the advantage. Then you will count the number of points in your hand.'

Hannah's mouth was pursed, as though she were contemplating the best combination to discard. After she picked up her new cards, Mrs Turner explained more of the rules while Michael exchanged his own cards.

'The winner of each trick will receive her choice of confections from the tray,' the widow said, reaching for one of the chocolates. 'I had best sample these to ensure that they are of good quality.'

'Shouldn't we each sample a bit?' Hannah offered, eyeing the sweets.

'Not unless you win.' Michael arranged his cards. 'That would be cheating.' After she'd arranged her hand, he asked, 'What is your opening bid?'

Before she answered, Hannah took another glance at her cards. 'What penalty will the loser pay, for losing a trick?'

'There's no penalty for losing. The winner gets the sweets, and that's fair enough.'

'No, Lady Hannah is right,' Mrs. Turner said. 'The loser should pay a forfeit.'

'I will not bleat like a goat. Or sing.' He didn't care what the women wanted; some things were beneath his dignity.

Hannah offered him a stunning smile. 'I think it should be answering questions. The loser has to tell the winner the truth, no matter what is asked.'

'Even better,' Mrs Turner said. 'We will take turns playing against one another.' From the bright colour in the woman's cheeks, it appeared that she had not suffered unduly the night before. Michael wondered if she had any memory of what she'd done. Probably not.

Hannah won the first trick. Her lips curved upwards with victory as she chose one of the caramels. Her eyes closed as she chewed the confection. 'I could eat a hundred of these,' she breathed.

And didn't he want to be the one to give them to her? The exquisite expression on her face was like a woman in the throes of sexual fulfillment.

Michael focused his attention back on his cards, ignoring the rigid arousal he was forced to hide beneath the table.

'Time for your forfeit,' Hannah demanded. She reached for a glass of lemonade that the waiter had brought earlier, thinking to herself. After a moment, she asked, 'How did you and my brother Stephen become friends?'

Her question surprised him. He'd expected her to inquire about Reischor or about the journey to Lohenberg.

'I met Whitmore at school, years ago.'

Her face turned curious. 'I didn't know you'd gone to Eton.'

Michael dealt the next set of cards, shrugging. 'I did receive an education. My mother insisted on it, though it was an unnecessary hardship.'

Mrs Turner's face turned serious. 'It was important to

Mary. She wanted our Michael to have a better life than they could give.' With a smile, she added, 'He was the best student there.'

'Really.' Lady Hannah's mouth softened in thought as she arranged another card.

Michael sensed the unspoken questions. Common men rarely attended schools that educated the upper classes. The truth was, he didn't know why he'd been allowed to attend. The headmaster had never made mention of it, though Michael was certain his fellow students had suspected his humble beginnings.

Knowing that each day he spent at school was another coin taken away from his parents, he felt he had no choice but to excel at his studies. And though he'd learned Latin and French, he'd found little use for it. A gentleman's education didn't amount to much without a title.

In the end, he'd followed the path of several friends, joining the British Army. Whitmore had been his closest friend and had considered a military career as well, before he'd become the heir.

Mrs Turner played against him in the next round, and Michael spied Graf von Reischor approaching. Though he nearly lost his concentration, he managed to win the trick.

When Hannah offered him the tray, he chose a chocolate-dipped cream.

'Take it,' he bade Hannah.

'But it was your win. The sweet belongs to you.'

'My win. My choice.' He held it out, and Hannah smiled before she slipped the confection inside her mouth. The pleasure on her face made the decision worthwhile.

'And what question would you have me answer?' Mrs Turner prompted. She eyed the confection tray with a forlorn look.

He thought a moment. 'Tell me the earliest memory you have of my mother.'

The Graf greeted them, pulling up a chair. 'I hope you don't mind if I join in your conversation.'

'Not at all.' Mrs Turner beamed.

Michael tensed, unsure if he wanted the Graf to hear stories about his mother.

'Mary Thorpe was my closest friend, you know.' Mrs Turner's expression turned distant as she remembered. 'She and Paul worked hard and always remembered those less fortunate than themselves.' She rubbed her chin, smiling wistfully. 'They loved you very much. After so many years of being childless, you were their gift.'

In the fraction of a moment, her voice faded to a whisper. 'You were only three years old.'

He saw the Graf's face narrow. 'Three years?'

The widow frowned at the Graf. 'Until you have won a trick, you are not allowed to ask questions.' She sent the Graf a stern look. 'I believe it's your turn to deal, Lady Hannah.'

Michael chose another sweet off the tray and passed it to the widow, as a silent means of thanks. The elderly woman popped it into her mouth.

'Later tonight, we will arrive at the home of Lady Hannah's cousins,' the Graf informed them. 'They live inland, a few hours beyond Bremerhaven, near the Lohenberg border.'

Michael saw Mrs Turner's hands begin to shake. 'Lohenberg?' she whispered. 'You never said we were going to Lohenberg. You said Germany.'

He hadn't, because he'd suspected she would react in this way. 'We are passing through Germany,' he admitted. 'But the trip to Lohenberg will only be for a few weeks. There's nothing to worry about.'

'No.' She stood up, raising her voice. 'No. You can't go back.'

Go back?

Mrs Turner had turned deathly white, wringing her hands. Turning on the Graf, she demanded, 'You can't force him to go.' Muttering to herself, she pushed the cards away, overturning the tray of confections.

Michael caught her before she could run off. Hysteria was etched in her face. 'Why?' he asked softly. 'Why can't I go?'

'Because they'll kill you if you do.'

CHAPTER THIRTEEN

Later that evening

THE COACH JOSTLED across the rough roads, while outside, clouds obscured the landscape. The ship had docked at Bremerhaven, and now they were journeying towards her cousins' home near the border.

Hannah had sent Estelle to travel with the Graf and his servants in another coach while she travelled with Michael and Mrs Turner. She didn't want to agitate the older woman after her outburst earlier. It had taken most of the day and a dose of laudanum to calm her down. Now, the slight noise of Mrs Turner snoring was the only sound to disturb the interior of the coach.

In the meantime, Hannah's head was starting to ache, but she pushed away the pain. Only a few more hours, and she could sleep in a real bed. She imagined soft pillows and warm covers.

Michael looked as though he were on the way to his execution. There was a grim cast to his face while he stared out the window.

'Are you all right?' Hannah asked. 'Is there something I can get for you?' There was a basket of food and drink at her feet, which neither of them had touched. Mrs Turner hadn't yet awakened to take her share of the meal.

'I don't need anything,' he said. But his hands were curled into fists at his sides, his gaze staring out the window.

'You're hoping that this turns out to be nothing,' she predicted. 'That you have no ties to Lohenberg.'

He nodded, his face dark with tension. Though he might deny it, she wasn't so certain his past was that simple. Someone had tried to strangle him after dinner. Not only that, but the widow knew something about Michael's past. Something ominous.

Whenever Hannah had tried to ask Michael about his own journey to Lohenberg, he'd redirected her questions. He, too, was holding secrets.

'What if you are royalty?' she asked. 'Would it be so bad?'

He shook his head. 'There's no evidence of that. Any resemblance to the King is a coincidence.'

'What about Mrs Turner?'

'Mrs Turner has slowly been losing her wits over the past year. Nothing she says can be trusted.'

'She was singing about a lost child last night. What if she was talking about you?'

'She was singing about her son, Henry.' Michael stared outside the window. 'It was her child who was lost. And it was my fault he's dead.' The heaviness in his voice suggested he felt responsible for the widow's madness.

'How did he die?'

Michael rested his hand on his knee, tapping at his hat. 'It was at Balaclava.'

'Tell me what happened.'

He glanced over at Mrs Turner, as though reluctant to speak of it or remember the day.

'Please,' she whispered. 'I want to know.'

At last, he lowered his voice. 'Men were shot down around me, by the hundreds. Myself included.'

'You lived.'

'Only because I fell beneath Henry's body. When the

enemy soldiers stabbed their bayonets into the dead, they stabbed Henry. Not me.'

The desolation and bitterness in his voice made her reach out to take his hand. Though both of them wore gloves, she tried to offer him the comfort of touch.

'He was already dead, wasn't he?'

'Yes. But I should be the one dead, not him.' He shook his head in disgust.

'It wasn't your fault that he died. Only God can determine who dies and who lives.' She reached out and took his hand in hers. 'Don't punish yourself for being one of the lucky few.'

He gripped her palm. 'Can't you understand? If I am proven to be the Prince, Reischor wants to place me upon the throne. Why would a man like me deserve a fate like that?'

'Perhaps it's an obligation. A chance for you to make changes that will help this country. What if you could protect others from dying at war?'

He looked away. 'I don't want it, Hannah. I'm not a man who can lead others. It's not in me.'

He exhaled, and the breath was filled with guilt. 'I couldn't even look after my own men, Hannah. How could anyone believe I could look after a country?'

'Because you care about others. And because you're bullheaded enough to do it.' She released his hand, leaning back against the coach.

The throbbing of her headache started to bother her again, and she reached for the vial of laudanum she had given to Mrs Turner.

'Are you having another of your headaches?' Michael asked suddenly.

She shook her head. 'I hope not. Sometimes if I take

the laudanum soon enough, it keeps the headache from becoming too bad.'

After she measured out two drops, she closed her eyes, resting her head against the side of the coach. When the bouncing of the wheels made her clench her teeth, she lowered her head into her hands.

A moment later, she heard Michael removing his gloves. He reached over to her bonnet and untied it, lifting it away. She didn't protest, not wanting to wake Mrs Turner.

With his bare hands, Michael covered her hair, his thumbs massaging her temples. The gentleness of his touch, his desire to take away the pain, made her breath catch.

His thumbs were rough, his fingers slipping into her hair, framing her face. The effects of the laudanum, coupled with his gentle caress, made her relax.

The circling movement of his thumbs and the light pressure on her scalp helped her forget about the headache. She grew less restrained, leaning into his touch.

'I shouldn't let you do this,' she whispered. The more she allowed him liberties, the worse she would feel in a few days when he was gone.

He lifted her hand to his mouth, removing her glove before kissing her hand. 'Nor this.'

The languid heat of his mouth against her skin was tantalising. Seductive. She wanted to sit in his lap, as before, and pull his mouth down to hers.

'If you were a Prince,' she breathed, 'you wouldn't look twice at a woman like me, with all the scandalous things I've done.'

'If I were a Prince…' he nipped at her fingers, sliding the tip of her thumb into his mouth '…I would make you a Princess.'

He caressed her palm, adding, 'I'd lock you up in a tower

and come to you at night.' A dark smile crossed his face. 'I'd forbid you to wear anything at all, except your hair.'

She jerked her hand away as if it were on fire. Her skin certainly was. His evocative images made her body ache and her mind imagine things that weren't going to be.

They would never be together, no matter what the future held. The words were part of a game, nothing more.

Michael reached for her hand again, his long fingers twining in hers, almost as if he drew comfort from her presence.

Hannah stared at the door to the coach, knowing she needed to break free of him. Last night, she had allowed him intimacies that only a husband should know. The pleasure could not eradicate her guilt.

'I'll be arriving at my cousins' house tonight,' she said, unable to keep the sadness from her voice. Gently, she pulled her hand away and put on her glove. 'I shouldn't see you again.'

'You're right.' He rested his forearms on his knees, glancing outside at the clouded scenery.

The evening light was fading, night slipping soundlessly over the land. Barren fields overshadowed the greenery, ploughed in preparation for planting. The dismal landscape darkened her mood even more.

What had she hoped? That he would ask her to stay with him? He wouldn't. Not ever, for she doubted if she meant anything more to him than a distraction.

The tiny space inside the coach was starting to close in on her, as though the bars of her exile were shutting out the rest of the world.

Michael didn't look at her again, and Hannah closed her eyes so she wouldn't dwell upon it. The anger and hurt brimmed up inside. Her headache was starting to fade, and she drifted into sleep.

Abruptly, the coach came to a stop. Hannah stared at Michael, wondering what had happened. 'Stay here,' Michael ordered. 'I'll find out what it is.'

'Did something happen to the Graf's coach?'

'I don't know. I'm going to find out.' He stared hard at her. 'But do not leave this coach.'

She forced herself to nod, though she could hear the edge in his tone. Fear penetrated her veins, and she rubbed her arms to warm them.

Hannah looked over at Mrs Turner, who hadn't woken up. That was good, for if there truly was a threat, the widow would only be more frightened.

She strained to hear the men talking. Perhaps the Graf's coach had gotten mired or a horse was having difficulty. It was likely nothing more than that.

But when she heard the sounds of gunfire, she ducked down below the window, grabbing Mrs Turner and pushing her against the seat. The widow opened her eyes briefly, but in her drugged haze, she wasn't aware of what was happening. Moments later, she started snoring again.

The men were shouting, and more gunfire erupted. Outside, Hannah heard the coachman abandoning his seat, joining in with the others.

Oh God, what was happening? It hurt to breathe, and Hannah closed her eyes, praying that no one would be hurt.

It was a foolish thought, for the fighting continued outside. She tried to glimpse the men from the window but could see nothing. When the shouting stopped and the voices grew low, she suspected the worst.

More minutes passed, but she didn't leave the coach. Michael had ordered her not to.

But what if he's dead? her mind offered. *Or wounded?*

What if they needed help, and she was doing nothing

but cowering inside the coach? Hannah took a deep breath, then another.

Her hands shook as she turned the door handle, climbing down from the coach. It was getting too dark to see, but from the whale-oil lamps she glimpsed the road. Thank goodness the laudanum had managed to keep her headache from transforming into a vicious illness, like before. But it made her unbearably tired, and she struggled to keep a clear head. Ahead, she heard the Graf issuing orders in Lohenisch.

'Peter, see if the women are safe. Gustav, take my coach and go to the nearest village with the other servants. Arrange for a doctor to meet us at the inn. *Schnelhurt!*'

Though his orders held the undeniable air of command, there was an edge of pain beneath them. As Hannah drew closer, she saw the Graf seated on the ground, with a panicked Estelle and a footman beside the fallen body of Michael. Two other men she didn't recognise lay dead, a few paces away.

'Is the Lieutenant all right?' She rushed to Michael's side, kneeling before him.

'You shouldn't have left the coach, Lady Hannah,' the ambassador argued. 'It's not safe here.' He nodded for the coachman to accompany her back, but Hannah refused to go.

'What happened?'

The Graf released a breath. 'I went with Gustav to investigate and saw that someone had blocked the road. I was shot.' His eyes closed as he fought off the pain. 'Lieutenant Thorpe and the coachman did most of the fighting, but the last one got away.'

Hannah wouldn't leave Michael's side, and once he was safely clear of the coach, Gustav drove away with the servants. She lifted Michael's head to rest in her lap, and he groaned at the movement. Thank God he was alive.

'Was Lieutenant Thorpe shot, as well?'

'A bullet grazed his arm, but nothing too serious. I'm more concerned about his head injury. His attacker struck him against the coach before Gustav shot him.' The Graf winced at the memory.

'I'm sorry...for endangering you,' he apologized, his voice breaking. 'Until now, I didn't believe it myself. But... there must be a connection to the royal family. Why else would anyone try to kill the Lieutenant?'

'Why indeed,' Hannah remarked, not speaking a word about the earlier attack on board the ship. Changing the subject, she asked, 'What about you? Where are you hurt?'

The Graf slipped back into Lohenisch, almost without realising it. 'I know of at least three bullet wounds.'

Hannah hid her fear, for she didn't know the first thing about tending such injuries. Her stomach tightened with queasiness. 'How bad is it?'

'I'm afraid I cannot walk at the moment.'

Thankful that it was dark, Hannah removed one of her petticoats. If she could stop some of the bleeding, perhaps that would help.

'I already tended to Lieutenant Thorpe's wounds,' the Graf murmured. Hannah leaned down to examine Michael's head, where she saw bruising and a swollen knot. His upper arm was partially wrapped with a man's cravat, blood staining the cloth.

She tore the petticoat in half, then in half again. 'Who do you believe the Lieutenant really is?'

While she wrapped the Graf's first wound, he answered, 'Most likely the Changeling Prince.'

Hannah tied another bandage around the Graf's knee, while he revealed the tale of the young Prince who disappeared on the night of All Hallows Eve, only to return the next morning.

'He looked slightly different, so the stories say. Not a great deal, but enough to make those around him wonder. He cried often, and he stopped speaking for nearly a year. His nurse thought he'd been bewitched. But the King put an end to the rumours, swearing that the boy was indeed his son.'

'If there was a switch, do you think the King had something to do with it?' Hannah suggested. She tightened the bandage around the Graf's leg, trying to stop the bleeding.

It was then that the Graf seemed to realise that they hadn't been speaking English. 'Exactly how many languages do you speak, Lady Hannah?'

'Five.' Her face flushed, for she didn't want him to think her an aberration. 'Including English.'

'That may prove useful to us,' the Graf mused. 'If you decide to stay with our travelling party.'

What was he suggesting? That she accompany them into Lohenberg? Her first instinct was to protest that, no, she couldn't possibly continue with them. But when she looked down at Michael's unconscious form, her heart shredded into pieces. She worried about him, far more than she should.

At that moment, Michael sat up slowly, clutching his temple. Hannah was saved from further discussion, and she helped to support him with both arms around his shoulders.

'Where are they?' he demanded, rubbing the back of his head.

'Gone, I'm afraid,' the Graf answered. 'Our men weren't fast enough to stop them.'

Michael released a curse and tried to rise. Hannah helped him to steady his balance. 'How badly are you hurt?'

'I'm fine.' He looked down at the Graf. 'What about him?'

'Both of you need to be tended by a doctor,' Hannah asserted. 'He's been shot several times, and I'm not sure if all of the bullets passed through.'

She didn't voice her fear that the Graf might not survive the injuries. She'd never seen a man die before, and she didn't want to think of it.

Turning to the Graf, she asked, 'How far are we from the village?'

'Too far,' he managed. 'Several hours, at least.'

Michael leaned down, and too late Hannah realised that he meant to pick the Graf up.

'Your arm—' she protested.

'It's nothing. Hannah.' Michael emitted a hiss of pain when he lifted the Graf up. The coachman, Peter, moved towards them and helped put the Graf inside the vehicle.

When the Graf was safely inside, Mrs Turner stirred. Her eyes flickered upon Michael and the Graf, and she let out a cry of alarm at the sight of their wounds.

'What's happened?' the widow demanded. 'You're bleeding.'

'Nothing serious.' Michael shrugged it off. 'A minor wound—no need to worry.' Nodding toward the Graf, he added, 'But Reischor suffered worse injuries. I need you to help Lady Hannah tend him while I drive us to the closest village.'

Mrs Turner covered her mouth, her eyes still glazed over from the effects of the laudanum. 'But what happened?'

Hannah cut off further questions, saying, 'I'll explain everything to you, on the way.'

Michael handed her one of the lamps to illuminate the interior of the coach. While the coachman checked the horses and started the carriage back on the journey, Hannah helped Mrs Turner with the Graf's wounds. The petticoats were soaked through with blood, and she blanched at the sight.

Mrs Turner didn't seem at all bothered by the injuries and took charge, offering him a dose of laudanum to dull the pain. The Graf took it gratefully.

As the widow helped tend him, Hannah's thoughts returned to Michael and the story of the Changeling Prince. Whoever believed he posed a threat wouldn't stop until the threat was eliminated.

She stared outside the window, the wretched fear gathering up inside. Though she couldn't grasp what her feelings were, she didn't want anything to happen to the Lieutenant.

Tomorrow, she was supposed to bid him farewell while he continued his journey to Lohenberg.

But she didn't want to leave him. Hannah felt as though she were stumbling blind, without a path to follow. They were at a crossroads, their lives taking different turns. Was it so wrong, wanting to walk with him a little further?

Though she didn't know what would happen, Hannah was certain of one thing. She was not about to be left behind, not when the man she cared about was in such danger.

CHAPTER FOURTEEN

MICHAEL KNEW HE was dreaming. And yet, he couldn't push away the strange visions. In the dream, he was a young boy again, holding his mother's hand.

It was a warm afternoon, the air sour with the odours of London. The buzzing of unfamiliar voices and sounds made him stay close to her side.

'It's all right, Michael. You'll be safe now.' She brushed a light kiss on his temple, murmuring words of comfort.

'I'm afraid.' He gripped her leg, burying his face into her side. 'She said they were going to hurt me if I wasn't good. If I didn't do what she said.'

Every stranger, every unfamiliar face, was a threat to him. His stomach gnawed at him with worry and hunger.

'We're going to take care of you now,' Mary whispered. 'No one will ever harm you again.'

'Michael,' he heard Lady Hannah murmuring. 'Wake up.'

He let out a breath, realising that he'd been given a few drops of laudanum. His head felt heavy, his eyes leaden. 'I will. I just need a moment.'

Her hand reached out to his face, her warm palm resting upon his cheek. It was nice. He wanted to stay here a little longer, feeling her hand upon his skin.

'Michael, I need you to open your eyes. Look at me.'

His vision flickered, then cleared as he saw Hannah. From her rumpled appearance, she probably hadn't slept at all. Her hair had been hastily repinned, her long-sleeved rose gown wrinkled. She'd discarded her bonnet on a chair nearby.

Had she stayed with him all night long? By the looks of it, they were inside a room at the inn. 'Where is Mrs Turner?'

'She is for, I mean *with*, Graf von Reischor.' Her face flushed, and she kept staring at him, a worried expression on her face. 'Estelle is helping her.'

'You shouldn't be here alone with me,' he warned. 'Think of what the others will say.'

'I told the innkeeper you were my husband.'

He raised an eyebrow at that, wondering why she would lie. 'And the Graf agreed to this?'

'He was sleeping permanently.'

He frowned, not knowing what she was saying. 'I beg your pardon?'

She flushed again. 'I mean, he was unconscious.' Her mouth pursed tightly, and he couldn't understand why she kept gaping at him.

'What's wrong?' He glanced at his right arm, but the bandage appeared clean. His wound ached a little, but it was bearable. The bullet had only nicked the skin. 'Why are you staring at me that way?'

'Don't you realise what you're doing?'

'I don't, no. Tell me.' He sat up carefully on the bed, swinging his legs over the side.

'Listen to yourself,' she said. 'You've been speaking Lohenisch in your sleep during the past hour, and just now. Another language, Michael. One you claimed you didn't know.'

'I haven't—' he started to say, but then he heard the unfamiliar words. It was as if his voice and his brain were disconnected somehow. He had spoken from instinct, without thinking.

And Hannah had also been speaking Lohenisch, he now realised. It was why she'd made a few mistakes, errors that she'd corrected.

The revelation was like a knife slicing through his throat, cutting away any further denials. There *was* a connection between him and Lohenberg, one he had long forgotten. Somehow, the country was a part of his heritage.

He struggled to speak the language again, but the words eluded him. The moment he tried to think about what he wanted to say, he couldn't grasp a single sentence.

Hannah placed both hands on his shoulders, regarding him. 'I think we both know that you are not merely a fishmonger's son.'

He didn't want to believe it. The idea of having another life, another family who hadn't wanted him, seemed to shift the ground beneath him.

'Then who am I, Hannah?'

'That's what we're going to find out.'

'We?'

She offered a hopeful smile. 'The Graf cannot possibly travel to Lohenberg in his condition. Not only that, but my cousins do not know exactly when I will arrive. A few days won't matter. I'll come with you.'

He stood up, pressing her hands away. 'No. It's inappropriate for you to travel with us.'

She stared down at her hands, her cheeks brightening. 'I want to help you. You'll need help remembering the Lohenisch language.' Squaring her shoulders, she added, 'After that, I'll leave. You needn't worry that this would be anything more than…than friendship.'

The embarrassment on her face increased his own feelings of awkwardness. He'd misinterpreted her offer, thinking she had changed her mind about being with him.

Damn it all, he didn't know what to do about Hannah. She wasn't a woman he could marry, nor could he become her lover. And yet, he couldn't quite bring himself to push her away, the way he should.

'I can act as your translator,' she offered. 'Without the Graf, we'll attract less attention, and Mrs Turner will be fine with him.'

Alone with her? Was she so naïve to think that no one would notice an unmarried woman and man travelling together? 'Others will speak poorly of you,' he warned.

'Not if they believe I am your wife.' She stood only an arm's length away from him. 'It's a travel arrangement, Michael. Nothing more than that.'

Looking at her innocent face, he saw that she truly thought they could travel together as friends, not lovers.

'Twice, someone has tried to kill me,' he argued. He wasn't going to put her into harm's way, no matter how she tried to convince him. 'It could happen again.'

'Not if we disguise ourselves.' She reached out and touched his coat. 'With the right attire, we could blend in with the others. No one would know we're any different, especially without the Graf to draw notice.' She pulled her hand away once more. 'And we'll find the answers you're looking for.'

He kept silent, pondering her idea. It wasn't sensible at all. To travel alone with Hannah, into a country he barely knew, was risking far too much.

Most of all, she risked her innocence. For if he had to remain at her side every hour of every day, he doubted if he could resist touching her again.

'It's not a good idea, Hannah. It's dangerous.'

She started to protest again, something about all the

reasons why he should uncover the past. He silenced her by kissing her.

With his mouth, he ravaged her lips, trying to show her how much he desired her. Her arms wound around his neck, whether for balance or whether in response to his kiss he didn't know. She smelled so good, the jasmine fragrance exotic and tempting. He softened the kiss, sliding his tongue inside her mouth. Coaxing and urging her to give him more, he used his good arm to draw her close.

'Do you feel how much I want you?' he whispered, bringing her hips to his. 'The danger you face is from me, not the assassins of Lohenberg.'

He lowered his mouth to the curve of her neck, whispering upon her skin, 'If you travel with me, pretending to be my wife, I can't promise not to touch you.'

She pulled away, composing herself. 'I'll take the risk.'

'THE GRAF VON REISCHOR isn't dead, is he?'

'No,' the servant apologised. 'He survived the assassins we hired. And as for the Prince—'

'Do not call him that. He is only a man with an unfortunate resemblance to the King. A bastard son.'

The servant cleared his throat. 'You are right, of course. But if he is only the King's by-blow, is there a need to kill him?'

'There can be no usurper. No reason to question the rightful heir to the throne. He bears too strong a resemblance to the King.'

'You are right, of course,' the servant confirmed. 'And it will be noticed, once he enters Lohenberg.'

'You cannot allow it. If you have to kill him yourself, ensure that this man poses no threat to the throne.'

The servant bowed. 'It will be as you wish.' Straightening, he inquired, 'Do you wish for me to remain in the

Graf's employ? I can continue to watch and inform you of his doings.'

'Yes. And return to me, as soon as it is done.'

'What about the Queen?'

A brief nod. 'See to it that she's kept quiet. Use your connections in the palace and tell no one of the Graf's doings. I don't want any more stories about the Changeling Prince.'

A bag of coins exchanged hands. The servant gave thanks, but hesitated before departing. 'What of the woman who is travelling with them? She was supposed to be sent to some cousins in Germany, but after the Graf was injured, they were delayed. If she witnesses anything—'

'Dispose of her, if you must.'

HANNAH'S BOTTOM FELT as though it had been beaten with wooden paddles. She clung to her horse, knowing the Graf's servants would pursue them. Reischor would be livid when he learned of her impulsive plan. Not only because they had 'borrowed' horses from his coach, but also because he would suspect they had discovered something about Michael's past.

Yet Michael faced more danger by travelling with the Graf than with her. It might not be the best of circumstances, but he could hide his identity easier if he didn't arrive in a grand coach with servants.

The cool morning air held a mist that clung to the forest tree trunks, an enchanted cloud hiding the green moss. Michael seemed not to notice their surroundings, keeping his gaze fixed ahead. He rode beside her, dressed in grey trousers, a white shirt, black waistcoat and matching jacket. The subdued colors were less conspicuous, and Hannah had chosen a faded blue long-sleeved gown that she'd borrowed from Estelle.

She worried that, by taking horses, they still might attract notice. Perhaps they should have walked or hired a wagon.

There was no time for it now. Though it was barely past dawn, Hannah feared they hadn't left soon enough.

There was only one road leading into Lohenberg, and as they crossed the border, Hannah saw that Michael kept glancing behind them. Like her, he appeared unsettled about what they had done.

'Is anyone following us?' Hannah asked.

'Not yet.'

Ahead, the road curved toward a small village. Vast fields encircled the farmhouses, ready for planting. Michael led them into the village, surprising her when he stopped the horse at a tavern. 'We'll eat breakfast here.'

His offer surprised her, for she hadn't expected to stop. It was only a few hours more until they reached the capital city of Vermisten. The royal *Schloss* lay on the outskirts, and Hannah was anxious to see it.

He helped her down, but didn't look at all eager to eat. 'Are you certain you wish to stop?' Hannah questioned. 'You don't have to on my behalf. I can wait until we reach Vermisten.'

'We're gathering information,' he said, taking her hand. 'Neither of us has been to the capital city before, and we need to know what we're facing.'

'Know your enemy?' she guessed, thinking of his military background.

'Precisely.'

He led their horses into one of the brick stables, giving a young lad a handful of coins to care for them.

'Those are Lohenberg coins,' Hannah remarked. 'Where did you get them?'

'Graf von Reischor provided me with a purse of coins

to spend upon my arrival.' He shot her a sidelong glance. 'I doubt if this was the way he intended for me to use them.'

'He puts a great deal of effort toward appearances.' Hannah took his arm as they approached the door. 'But since he cannot accompany us, I think he wouldn't mind.'

Michael took her hand in his. 'Are you ready?'

She nodded. He led her inside the tavern. A dining room was set aside for travelling guests, with several sturdy tables and clean tablecloths. The tables were full and only a few empty chairs remained.

'Good morning,' a thin-faced woman greeted them in Lohenisch. Her grey hair was pulled back from her face, and she wore a white apron over her black gown. When Hannah explained their desire for a meal, the woman answered, 'If you don't mind sharing, I can seat you beside some guests over there.' She nodded toward a table by the window.

'That will be fine,' Hannah answered in the same language. 'My husband and I have been travelling all morning.'

From the blank look on his face, Michael hadn't recognized the woman's words. He held Hannah's hand firmly as they joined the elderly couple at the far table.

A serving maid approached them after a few minutes. Before she could ask Michael any questions, Hannah interrupted, asking for them to be served breakfast.

Switching to English, she whispered to Michael, 'Do you remember the language any more?'

He shook his head slightly. 'I can't quite grasp it. I feel as though I *should* understand what she's saying.'

'I'll translate for you,' Hannah offered. She noticed that he still hadn't released her hand. Beneath the table, he continued to hold her fingers, his thumb caressing the top of her hand. A breathless ripple of feeling permeated her skin, and she admitted to herself that she wouldn't mind if he held her hand throughout the meal.

'This was a mistake,' he said. 'I shouldn't have let you talk me into this. If I can't even understand the damned language—'

'You will,' Hannah reassured him. 'I promise you, it'll come back to you.'

'It's of no use to me, if I can't recall a thing unless I'm drugged or half-asleep.'

'It's there. I'll help you to remember.' She gave his hand a squeeze, and just then their food arrived.

Hannah noticed the couple beside them had been watching their interaction. The man and woman were trying not to stare, but Michael had definitely caught their attention.

'Hello,' Hannah greeted them in Lohenisch. Though she was well aware that it was highly inappropriate for her to speak before Michael, she didn't see any other choice. They were here to gather information, and she was the only one who spoke the language. At least, right now.

She introduced Michael as Lieutenant Thorpe and herself as his wife. The older man returned the greeting, and Hannah learned that they were Helmut and Gerda Dorfer.

'You are from London?' Herr Dorfer asked in Lohenisch.

'We are.' Hannah took a bite of her sausage and added, 'I have cousins in Germany, and my husband has always wanted to visit Lohenberg.'

'If you don't mind my saying so,' Frau Dorfer spoke up, 'your husband looks very much like our König Sweyn.' Her face softened. 'When he was younger, that is.'

At the admission, the woman suddenly grew fearful, as if she'd said too much. Herr Dorfer sent his wife a warning look, and she fell silent.

Hannah wasn't about to lose the opportunity. Extending her hand to Michael, she sent him a silent signal for coins.

Thankfully, he placed a handful into her palm. Hannah slid the money toward Frau Dorfer. 'We are planning to visit the *Schloss* when we arrive in Vermisten. I would be grateful if you know someone who could answer our questions. We would like to seek an audience with the King.'

Frau Dorfer glanced at her husband, who offered a relenting nod. Her hand covered the coins. 'I can answer your questions. I used to work in the *Schloss* as one of the maids before I married Helmut.' Looking uncomfortable, she enquired, 'But why do you seek the King?' Her gaze travelled over Michael once more.

'Ask her if she has heard the story of the Changeling Prince,' Michael said.

Helmut exchanged glances with his wife after Hannah translated. Gerda's face paled, and the pair argued for a moment.

It seemed Frau Dorfer won the disagreement, for she suggested to Hannah, 'Go and speak to the master of the household, BurgGraf Castell. He can advise you and possibly arrange a private audience with the lord chamberlain, Herr Schliessing.' She blushed. 'The lord chamberlain would know what to do.'

After Hannah translated, Michael's face tightened with frustration. Whether from the information or from his inability to speak, she wasn't certain.

She thanked Frau Dorfer for the information, and the woman offered them the name of a respectable inn in Vermisten where they could stay.

'And,' Frau Dorfer added, 'you would be wise to keep your husband's appearance hidden, if possible, until you've been granted the audience. If anyone sees his resemblance to the King, his advisers may refuse to allow you entrance.'

Hannah nodded her thanks to Herr and Frau Dorfer before turning her attention back to her meal. Michael was eating while staring off into the distance, as if trying to recall the forgotten language.

Hannah kept their conversation in English to remain private. 'I don't believe you should seek a private audience with the lord chamberlain,' she admitted. 'It would be too easy for the King to brush you aside, pretending you don't exist. I think we should make use of your appearance.'

'What do you mean?'

'I believe you should confront them directly. Demand to see the King. Find out if you truly are the Prince.'

'Twice, someone has tried to kill me,' Michael pointed out.

'That's exactly why it must be true. Someone considers you a threat. And he wants you dead.'

CHAPTER FIFTEEN

THEY SPENT THE remainder of the afternoon in Michael's own personal version of Hades. Shopping.

He had allowed Hannah to drag him from one shop to the next, while she ordered clothes for him. He'd paid for them with the money the Graf had given him.

Hannah was adamant that he be clothed like a member of the royal household. From sports attire to formal evening wear, it seemed she hadn't missed a single thing. Not even hats, gloves or…undergarments. Michael shuddered at the last shop. Some things weren't meant to be measured or prodded.

'The Graf was right about this,' Hannah had explained. 'It's about appearances.'

'And we couldn't have ordered everything at the first shop?'

'Of course not!' She eyed him as though he'd suggested wearing rags to greet the monarch. 'You need to be seen by as many people as possible today. Then the King cannot ignore your presence. He'll have to help you discover the truth.'

It was also a much greater risk. Michael couldn't abandon his old habits of constantly looking over his shoulder. There had already been two attacks—a third was imminent, and he didn't want Hannah caught up in it. The threat would come—the only question was when, not if. By then, he hoped to have Hannah escorted back to her cousins' home.

Glancing at her, he saw her face bright with enthusiasm. She was enjoying the afternoon they'd spent together, though she hadn't bought a single thing for herself. It struck him as wrong, and he took her to one of the shops, hoping she could have a new dress made.

'There's no need,' Hannah protested. 'Don't waste a penny on me. I'll have plenty of gowns, once my trunks arrive with the Graf.'

But when he saw her eye drawn to the milliner's, he sent her to choose a new bonnet. While she was busy with the shopkeeper, he slipped next door to make another purchase.

The gift cost far more than he'd anticipated, but it was something he wanted Hannah to have. Michael used the last of his own savings, instead of money given by the Graf. He hid the gift inside his pocket, wrapped in brown paper, and made it back inside the milliner's before Hannah realised he'd left her.

HOURS LATER, AFTER dinner when they were back inside their room at the inn, Hannah sank down into a chair. 'My feet are exhausted,' she said, unfastening her shoes. 'I feel as though we walked twenty miles today.'

He ventured a smile, suddenly feeling anxious to give her the gift he'd purchased. He wanted to see her expression when she opened the parcel.

'Here.' He thrust the box at her without a word of explanation. 'This is for you.'

She set her stocking feet back on the carpet, accepting the box. 'Now when did you get this?' With a soft smile, she added, 'I hope it's something sweet.'

She tore open the brown paper, and lifted open the box. Inside rested a diamond-and-aquamarine ring.

Hannah didn't react, or say a word. She simply stared at the jewellery. He hadn't had but a few minutes this afternoon, but the moment he'd seen it in the shop, he'd known it was meant for her.

'Well, go on. See if it fits.'

He removed the ring from the box and slid it on the third finger of her left hand. 'I can have the jeweller adjust the size, if needed.'

Fate was on his side, for the ring fit beautifully. Hannah clutched the diamonds, staring at him. 'Michael, what have you done?'

'You've told everyone we're married. Don't you think they would wonder why you aren't wearing a ring?'

She shook her head, her face paling. 'You can't afford this. It's too much.'

Though that might be true, his pride bristled. If he wanted to spend his savings on her, that was his choice. And this was something he wanted her to have as a memento of their time together. Something to keep, that would make her think of him.

'Don't worry about the cost.'

She took the ring off, pressing it back into his hands. 'You shouldn't have done this. I can't accept it.'

The small bit of metal seemed to burn into his skin. Why couldn't she?

'Isn't it good enough for you?' The bitter words escaped him before he could stop them.

The stricken look on her face was worse than a slap. God knew he deserved it. He was behaving like a child, sulking because she didn't like the ring. But it was the first time he'd had any money at all to spend on her. And she didn't want the gift.

'You don't understand.' She spoke quietly, averting her gaze. 'I can't accept a ring from you. We aren't really married.'

'No. But it will keep others from talking.' He came and held out the ring in his palm. 'Take it.'

She shook her head slowly. 'This is too much. I can't take a ring made of diamonds.'

'Why not?' He'd expected her to love the jewellery, to be pleased with the setting. Not give him reasons why she couldn't wear it. 'I'm not the only man who's given you jewels, am I?'

'You're not my father or brother. It isn't suitable.'

'Everyone believes I am your husband.'

'Can't you understand?' she whispered, standing up. Her hands covered his. 'This ring means you're making a sacrifice for me. You're giving up too much. I'm not worth that to you.'

'I'll determine what you're worth. And I'll be damned if I give you a ring made of tin.'

She blinked hard, sitting back down again. Her palms rested on her gown, and she refused to look at him. 'I can't take it, Michael,' she whispered. 'Not only because of the cost…but because I would want it to mean something more.'

HANNAH HEARD MICHAEL leave their shared room after he'd shoved the ring back inside his pocket. After he'd gone, she released the harsh tears gathering in her throat.

It was a beautiful ring. A stunning cluster of diamonds and aquamarines that she would be honoured to wear, if it were a true wedding ring.

She drew her feet up beneath her skirts, her corset cutting into her ribs as the unwanted tears streamed down her face. Why had he done this? He knew their arrangement was only temporary. After he had the answers he sought, she would be out of his life. It had to be that way, and both of them knew it.

He'd been so angry when he left. Would he want her to leave now? The thought of travelling to Germany without knowing his fate was like a hand strangling her breath.

She was losing her heart to this man, whether he was a common soldier or a forgotten Prince. Somehow, he'd guessed at the hidden feelings inside her. Her secret, that she wanted to take every stolen moment she could with him, no matter how great the cost. She wanted him to touch her, to make her come alive the way he had upon the ship.

The bedroom seemed unexpectedly empty. Hannah stared at the bed, realising that she'd never truly thought about where they would sleep tonight. Did she dare rest beside him, the way a true wife would?

She sat down upon the coverlet, running her fingers over the worn quilt. Today there had been nothing untoward about his behaviour. He'd endured the shopping trip, letting her order purchases for him, though she could see that he didn't care for it at all.

He must have gone to the jeweller's while she was trying on bonnets. It had been such a short moment, but he'd seized it. For her.

Well done, Hannah. The man spent a fortune on you, and you cast it back in his face.

But she couldn't let him do it. Not even if he had a fortune to spend. A ring like that, so personal, so precious. It was something she would treasure for the rest of her life.

If she accepted it, the gift would haunt her, reminding her of the feelings she held for him.

She sat up, suddenly afraid of where he'd gone. Michael couldn't go out walking alone, not when it was such a risk. He'd been shot only two days ago. What if someone attacked him?

It was far too dangerous. Hannah pushed her feet back into her shoes, not even bothering to finish buttoning them. She flew down the stairs and pushed her way past the other guests who were enjoying their dinners downstairs.

She found the Lieutenant inside the stables, tending his

horse. With a sharp look towards the stable lad, she asked for a moment alone with her 'husband'. The boy tipped his cap and waited outside.

Standing behind Michael, she wondered what she could say. The acrid odour of the stalls surrounded them, not exactly the best place for an apology.

'Michael,' she murmured, 'will you come back inside?'

He didn't turn around at first, but kept brushing the horse's back in slow, even strokes.

'Go back to our room, Hannah. It's been a long day, and I know you're tired. I'll be up later.'

She couldn't bring herself to leave him. By refusing his gift, she'd wounded his pride. She touched the sleeve of his coat, resting her forehead against his shoulder. 'Don't be angry with me.' A thousand excuses tangled up in her mouth, but all of them were a mockery of what she was feeling right now.

'I'm not angry.' His clipped voice belied the words. 'It was an inappropriate gift. You were right.'

'It was a beautiful ring,' she said, stepping between him and the horse. Trapped in his arms, she gave him no choice but to look at her. 'And if circumstances were different, I would be proud to wear it.'

'But they aren't.' He set down the brush and let his hands rest on her waist. In his eyes, she saw disappointment, masked by duty. Didn't he understand why she had refused the ring? Didn't he know that she was trying to keep both of them from being hurt?

'Go back, Hannah. I want a moment to myself.'

She couldn't do it. If she left him right now, the breach would only widen. He'd sleep on the floor and within another day or two, she would be inside a coach, bound for Germany.

He's going to break my heart, she thought. *But there wasn't another choice, was there?*

She stood up on tiptoe and kissed him. Her arms wrapped around his neck, while she tried to show him what she felt. The desires she couldn't voice, the forbidden yearning to steal whatever moments she could.

At first, he didn't kiss her back. But as she pressed her mouth to his, slowly tempting him to yield, she felt his arms tighten.

His kiss was tentative at first, as though he weren't sure she truly wanted him. Hannah gripped his neck, hoping he would respond to her invitation.

'Don't hold back from me,' she whispered, when his mouth broke free from hers. 'Not tonight.'

Michael brought her against the door to one of the stalls, lifting her up while he kissed her hard. 'I'm no good for you, Hannah.'

'I don't care any more. I need you.' She held on tight, shuddering when his thigh slid between her legs. Hard and firm, he nudged her, making her ride him.

Though anyone who happened upon them would only see a husband and a wife caught in an embrace, beneath her skirts, he made her feel completely vulnerable.

'Take me back upstairs,' she whispered.

'In a moment.' He took her mouth roughly, his hands dragging through her hair. Pins fell everywhere while he kissed her, his tongue teasing in the intimate act she feared. Her mouth was numb, swollen from his kiss, while she ached between her legs. When he pressed his thigh between her legs again, she couldn't stop the shattered gasp that escaped. It was like the night upon the ship, only this time, the impact was far greater.

That night, she'd suspected they would not become lovers. But now, she wasn't certain how far she would let him go.

Michael slid her down, touching his head to hers. 'What are you doing, Hannah?'

She shivered, fighting to catch her breath. 'I think you know.'

He grabbed her hand and pulled her outside the stable. Hannah knew the stable lad could have guessed what happened to her, for her hair was falling about her shoulders, her face flushed with unfulfilled need.

When they reached the doors to the inn, Michael stopped short. 'Go up to our room and wait for me there. I'll only be a moment.'

She fled up the stairs, not looking at any of the guests and praying they weren't staring at her dishevelled appearance. When she reached her room, she took off her shoes again, blindly pulling at the remainder of pins that held up her hair.

Oh, heaven. What was she about to do?

She stared at the solitary bed and the flickering candle illuminating the small space. Everything about this room was primed for a seduction. One she wasn't ready for.

It was too easy, falling into his arms within the stable. Now that he'd given her a moment alone to think, her mind was screaming out every lecture her mother had ever given.

Never let a man touch you, unless he is your husband. Not even a kiss. And especially never let him see so much as a bared ankle.

The door opened, and Michael stood with something hidden behind his back. Hannah craned her neck to see what it was, and then spied a covered plate.

Michael removed the cover and revealed a thick slice of cake with buttercream icing.

Hannah didn't smile, though it appeared mouth-watering. Glancing at the dessert, she mentioned, 'You…forgot to bring a fork or a spoon.'

'No, I didn't.'

She didn't know what he meant by that, but sensual images of him feeding her from his fingertips suddenly erupted in her mind.

Michael set the plate down upon the dresser and closed the distance. He moved behind her, his hands upon the buttons of her gown. Though Hannah tried to relax, her skin had gone cold. It was easier to imagine surrendering to him when he was kissing her, not allowing her to think.

Instead, his hands flicked over the buttons of her gown, one by one. Her mind was raging that she should stop him and hold fast to her innocence. Her body tensed as more and more skin was revealed.

'I know you're afraid,' he whispered, dropping a kiss on her nape, 'but you have no maid, and you cannot sleep in your corset.'

He was offering her the choice, she realised. He would not ask for more than she was willing to give.

'If you'd prefer, I could ask one of the maids downstairs to come up and assist you.'

She let out a shaky breath. That would be the easiest course of action, but it would also raise unnecessary questions about why she wasn't allowing her husband to unfasten her gown.

'It's all right,' she managed. 'You can help me.' Her heartbeat clamoured in her chest, punctuating the indecision building up inside her.

'Will you turn down the lamp?' she whispered. 'I don't want you to see me.'

He didn't answer. Instead, he came around to face her. He made no further move to undress her, but the gown sagged about her shoulders. 'Do you want me to sleep somewhere else?'

'No. You can't.' Not only was it too expensive to hire out a second room, it wasn't safe to be apart.

He stepped back, waiting for her command. Hannah clutched the edges of her gown, as if trying to hold together the last remnants of her upbringing.

Michael seemed to be weighing his own decision. In the end, he walked towards the hearth and sat down in one of the chairs, his gaze averted from her.

It was like she'd already lost him. And it hurt, worse than anything she could imagine. This man had taken care of her when she'd needed him most. He didn't live by the rules, but by his judgement. And she knew there would never be another man like him in her life.

If she did marry, it would be to a titled lord who would expect her to bear his children. She'd met dozens of them over the last year, and not a single one would come close to the intense feeling she held for Michael Thorpe.

She wanted to know him intimately. To feel his skin upon hers and to know that he cherished her. There was not a doubt in her mind that if she let him make love to her, it would be the worst sort of rule to break. It would also be wonderful.

Her moments of freedom were slipping away, with every hour. This might be their only night together. And she wanted it, no matter that it was wrong. No matter that he could never be hers.

Hannah let her gown slide down, baring her corset and chemise. She untied the petticoats, stepping free of them.

The long walk across the room was the most frightening she'd ever taken. But in her heart, she knew she would hold regrets if she did not reach out to him now.

In the candlelight, he would see every part of her body. Right now, shivers prickled over her skin as she walked in front of him. Wearing only her undergarments, she laid herself bare, offering herself.

And still Michael didn't move. His eyes stared into hers, as though he didn't know what to think of her actions. Kneeling down before him, Hannah reached out to remove his coat. Her fingers shook as she untied his cravat and unbuttoned his waistcoat. Abruptly, Michael's hands suddenly closed over hers.

'You don't want this, Hannah. I can see your fear.'

She'd never been so bold in all her life, but more than anything else was the fear that he would turn her away.

'I am afraid, yes. And I know that I should ask you for help with my corset and sleep far away from you.'

He waited, and she touched her hand to his heart. Despite the calm mien he presented, his pulse was racing. 'I know what I should do,' she repeated again. 'But I want this night. Give me a memory I'll always have.'

CHAPTER SIXTEEN

HER BODY TENSED when Michael reached the laces that tightened her corset. He loosened the stays, and his fingertips caressed the thin fabric of her chemise. Almost instantly, her nipples puckered. As he helped her remove the corset, the stiff panel brushed against her breasts. A pang of arousal echoed within her core, and the awakening of desire began to silence the voices of her mother's warnings and her conscience.

Layers of clothing fell away until she wore only the thin chemise and drawers. Michael had removed his shirt, and in the firelight, his bare skin was golden. She reached out to his wounded upper arm and saw that the angry skin was healing. The abrasions on his neck were also fading.

'Does it hurt?'

'Sweet, there's only one thing I'm feeling right now. And it's not the kind of pain you're thinking of.' He glanced up at the mantel. 'The candlestick is there, if you need it to bash my head.'

She almost smiled, but the overwhelming nerves were gathering strength. 'How do you want to…do this?' Perhaps if she had an idea of what was expected, she could calm the anxiety boiling inside her. 'I don't know what I am supposed to do.'

'I'll start by kissing you.' His voice rumbled against her ear as he slid her chemise and drawers away. Before she could comprehend that she was no longer wearing anything at all, his mouth came down on hers.

Hot, feverish feelings permeated her, sending flames of desire over every part of her body. Michael picked her up in his arms, laying her down upon the bed. Her hair fell across the pillow, and he caressed the length. A moment later, he turned around and removed his trousers and undergarments. She caught a glimpse of his taut backside, the rigid curve of his hip. When he turned around, he was holding the plate of cake and there was a wicked gleam in his eye.

He wanted to eat, now? Confusion caught her sensibilities, making her wonder what he intended.

Michael walked towards her naked, his erect manhood jutting forward. A flash of panic flew through her mind, for she couldn't imagine him joining with her. He sat down beside her on the bed, setting the plate down.

'Open your mouth,' he ordered, breaking off a morsel of cake.

A distraction. That's what this was, she realised. Something to calm her down.

She tasted the sweet creamy icing, but it did nothing to alleviate her apprehensions. Michael kissed her again, devouring the traces of buttercream from her lips. She clung to him, startled by the feeling of his bare skin upon hers. Her breathing quickened as he ran his palms down her spine and over the curve of her bottom.

'I know I shouldn't do this,' he murmured, lowering his mouth to her shoulder, drifting downwards to her breast. 'But I've given up trying to resist you.' He dipped his finger into the cake icing and touched it to her nipple. 'It's too late now, sweet. I intend to spend the rest of the night taking you apart.'

With that, he covered her nipple with his mouth, swirling against her skin with his tongue. He licked the icing off, sucking hard while she shuddered at the sensation. She was bending to him, growing moist between her legs.

Michael turned his attention to the other breast, kissing it with the same attention while he flicked the erect bud of the first nipple with his fingers. Tormented by his touch, she fought to catch her breath.

'You're more delicious to me than any cake,' he murmured. 'I could taste you all day.' His mouth drifted lower, down her stomach toward the soft hair covering her mound.

His cheeks were smooth against her thighs, and she clamped her legs tight, afraid of what he might do next.

He lifted his head up, staring at her. In the dim light, his hazel eyes held the warmth of chocolate, with green flecks. 'I'm going to give you a night to remember, Hannah. Trust me.'

He pressed a kiss upon her stomach, his hands reaching beneath her spine to her hips. He drew his palms over her bottom, pressing her close to his face.

Oh, sweet God. He wouldn't taste her there, would he?

He dipped his finger into the icing, brushing a small amount upon her cleft. A moment later, her hands dug into the sheets, a keening cry erupting from her throat as he covered her intimate flesh with his mouth.

He nibbled at her delicate skin, arousing her until she arched deeply, shaking with the ferocity of his wicked tongue.

The rising crescendo of need burst forth in a release that made her cry out. She tried to sit up, but he held her down, her legs splayed as he worked her again with his mouth.

'I can't. Michael, I can't do this. It's too much.'

In answer, he slid two fingers inside her wetness, stretching her. It sent her over the edge once more as he entered and withdrew.

'Touch me,' he urged, pulling her hand to his shaft. She

had never felt a man's flesh before and had never realised how soft and smooth it was. Her thumb caressed the tip, and she felt moisture there.

As she dragged her hand along the length, she watched him hiss with pleasure. He let her explore him, feeling the change in skin texture, and the way he grew even harder in reaction to her touch. When she began to glide her hand up and down, he caught her wrist and pushed it aside. 'Not tonight. This night is for you.'

Michael turned her on to her side, while he came up behind her. Raising her leg over his, he placed his manhood between her thighs. 'When you're ready for me, I'm going to be inside you.'

He cupped both of her breasts, nipping at her shoulder with his mouth. His thick erection nudged an inch within her, and Hannah trembled at the feeling. As he continued to caress her nipples, rolling the tips while he teased her wetness, she pleaded with him, 'Michael, I need…something. But I don't know what it is.'

He moved his length between her legs. 'Sweet, don't rush. I want this to be good for you.' Slowly, gently, he eased himself into her body. He didn't force her, or hurt her. Just a gentle sliding, back and forth. The thickness of him was like a caress inside her body, each time going a little deeper. His thumb moved to the ridge at the top of her womanhood, stroking her while he sheathed himself partway inside her. 'I want to see you come apart again,' he murmured, coaxing the wet heat.

Her body ached, squeezing him while he rubbed the small hooded opening. She felt herself rising up again, reaching for the intense pleasure. He held back from her, slowing his pace. Tears escaped her eyes, and she shivered violently against his hand.

'Come for me,' he commanded. And with another stroke

of his hand, she soared. He pushed the rest of the way inside her, filling her up until they were fully joined. Though the fit was tight, she held him close, shocked at the wonder of it.

Her hips arched as he pulled back and slid home once again. The tenderness of his penetration made her heart weep for this act of love.

But she sensed he was holding back, trying not to hurt her. The position of being on her side felt too cautious, and she wanted him to know the same fulfillment.

She eased away from him, lying on her back and bringing him atop her. With her hand, she guided him inside once more, raising her knees. 'Take what you need from me, Michael.'

His face turned to stone, his body growing harder within her. He plunged inside, quickening his pace. She gripped him, holding tight as he rode her hard.

A moment later, he pulled her hips to the edge of the bed. He stood up, lifting her legs high while he filled her. His face transformed with his own pleasure, tight with suppressed need. She met each stroke with her hips, offering a counterpressure. It wasn't enough. Michael gripped her hard, thrusting his body inside her until at last, his face tightened, and he let out a low groan.

He collapsed on top of her, their bodies still joined. Hannah felt a wetness from his warm seed, and she reached down to run her hands over his backside. She wrapped her legs around him, squeezing him in a different sort of embrace.

No wonder men and women never talked about this. She'd never dreamed that the intimacy would be this wild, this pleasurable.

'How are you feeling?' he asked, his voice husky.

'I feel beautiful.' And she did. Languid and relaxed, as

though it were the most natural thing in the world to be naked with a man.

'Hungry?' he prompted, withdrawing from her.

'A little.' She let him feed her cake from his fingertips, and she licked the icing, watching his eyes grow dark with desire once again.

'You're going to kill me if you keep looking at me like that.' He ran his hands over her flesh. 'I won't be able to get enough of you.'

Hannah locked her arms around his neck. 'I don't mind.'

LATER THAT NIGHT, after he'd made love to her twice more, he straightened the bed sheets. 'Time to sleep.' She was about to curl up next to him when he dropped a pillow on top of her.

'What is that for?' She tried to move the pillow away, but he laid it in the centre of the bed. When she reached out, she felt the presence of the two pillows set lengthwise down the middle of the bed.

'I'm setting up a barricade on the bed. You'll sleep on your side, and I on mine.'

A pillow barricade? What on earth?

'You don't want to sleep beside me?' she asked, confused at the gesture. 'Is something the matter?'

'Sweet, if you come anywhere near me again, I won't be responsible for what happens.' His body weight settled on his side of the bed. 'I'd suggest you stay over there, if you want any sleep at all.'

She smiled in the darkness and huddled beneath the coverlet. Was he truly serious about being unable to resist her?

A moment later, a hand nudged at her cheek. 'You're on my side,' he said.

'I'm on the edge of the bed! If I move any further, I'll fall off,' she protested.

His leg tangled up in hers, beneath the pillow barricade. 'You're still on my side.'

When she realised that his long leg was sprawled all the way across the bed, hanging off the end, she started to laugh. 'If you had your way, this entire bed would be your side.'

'It is. I'm just letting you borrow it.' He withdrew his leg, his hand reaching for hers.

Lying on her back with their palms entwined, Hannah released the laughter building up. 'You don't like to share, do you?'

'Not at all. And I'll never share you.' His hand moved up to caress her face with his knuckles. And when at last, she heard the quiet sounds of his breathing, her heartbeat wouldn't calm at all.

For this was the sort of marriage she'd dreamed of. A handsome husband, teasing her. Making her feel beloved. Lying beside him at night, whispering secrets in the dark.

Please don't let him be the Prince, she prayed. For if he was, he was as good as lost.

MICHAEL ROSE BEFORE the sun came up, letting Hannah sleep. She was curled up on her side, her palm slightly open. He dressed in silence, slipping outside the door. He reached into his pocket and found the ring, still there. At first, he'd planned to return it to the jeweller's. But after last night, he wasn't certain.

He didn't know what had come over Hannah, why she had given herself to him. She'd refused to accept a ring from him, telling him that she would want it to mean something else.

Was she saying she wanted to marry a man like him?

It was foolish to consider the possibility. He was better

off living on his own. He couldn't take care of her in the manner she deserved.

Grimly, he thought of their impending visit to the *Schloss*. The cynical side to him didn't believe it would accomplish anything. A man like him…becoming a Prince? He simply couldn't believe it could ever be true. They would take one look at him and toss him out.

But if he were a Prince, he'd have the means to take care of Hannah. He could make her a Princess.

You're not capable of protecting a wife. Don't even consider such a thing.

Being with Hannah last night had changed everything. He'd become her lover, and it had been better than anything he'd ever imagined.

Sweet, fiery and passionate, she'd swept him away. He'd been conscious of her every move, her every sigh.

He fingered the ring in his pocket, and continued towards the innkeeper. He thought of hiring a maid to help Hannah dress, but in truth, he wanted another excuse to touch her again. Instead, he ordered a tray of food to be sent up for their breakfast.

While the innkeeper's wife went to prepare the food, the innkeeper paused. In halting English, he offered, 'Lieutenant Thorpe, some men arrived last night. They were searching the inn for a man of your description. I thought you should know.'

He suspected it was the Graf's men. But it could also be the men who had attacked their coaches. There was no way to be sure. Nonetheless, it was not safe for them to remain here any longer. Michael thanked the innkeeper and went upstairs with the tray of food.

Hannah was already awake and struggling to dress herself. 'Good morning,' she said, offering a hesitant smile. 'Could you help me with this?'

'Of course.' He set down the tray and came up behind her, his hands grazing her shoulders. With both hands gripping the corset strings, he tightened her stays.

'Why in the name of God do women torture themselves this way?' he grumbled. He'd worried about hurting her, but Hannah had only laughed and told him to pull it tighter.

He'd much rather have unlaced her, baring her soft, pale skin. As it was, he stole another kiss, trying to quench the need for her body. Her mouth moulded to his, her arms wrapping around his neck.

The dark desire to have her again took control without warning. He wanted to strip her down, making love to her until she trembled with pleasure.

But Hannah broke away from him, her face crimson with embarrassment. 'Michael, I've been thinking. Last night when we…were together, well… I don't think we should… do that any more.'

Her sudden refusal bruised his pride. He reached into his pocket, touching the ring. *This was her choice,* he reminded himself. And perhaps it was better that way.

'You're right.' He shrugged as if he didn't care one way or the other. But he knew he'd become too tangled up with thoughts of her. Their time together would be short enough, and the more they became involved with one another, the worse it would be to say goodbye. 'Last night was a bad decision for both of us.'

She paled, but nodded her head in agreement. 'I had no regrets at the time. But what if…there's a baby?'

He lost his breath at the very thought. He'd been caught defenceless by her, unable to think beyond the staggering desire. A baby. An innocent child, who would look to him as a father, a provider.

Harsh visions struck him down, of a child crying out for food. Of Hannah wearing a threadbare dress, her hands worn from scrubbing floors. Would that be their lives, if he remained a soldier? He couldn't let that happen.

'If there is a child, I'll take care of you.' He voiced the words she expected to hear, though the idea of giving her anything less than the life she had was horrifying. He prayed that there would be no child, no lasting consequences of their forbidden night together.

'All right.' But she didn't look overjoyed by the prospect either.

Michael turned his back, gathering up the edges of his thoughts. 'I received word that men are looking for me. We shouldn't stay here tonight.'

'Where do you want to go?' Hannah moved in front of him for assistance with the buttons running down the back of her dress. Though he fastened them for her, the feel of her skin beneath his hands only re-ignited his hunger.

'The *Schloss*. For now, at least. We'll decide where to stay afterwards.' Michael offered her the tray of food, choosing a scone for himself.

Hannah picked at the food, as though she didn't like that idea. 'We have to speak to the King. There's no other choice. But I can't shake the feeling that something terrible will happen if we do.'

She pushed her plate aside and donned her pelisse. After putting on her bonnet, she tied the ribbon beneath her chin.

'It's a risk, yes.' But a necessary one. Michael wanted the answers, if for no other reason than to close this part of his life away. More than ever, he felt on the verge of unlocking the secrets of his past. Perhaps just by visiting the *Schloss*, he would sense something.

Hannah finished putting on her gloves and regarded him. 'Should we wait for the Graf to arrive after all? He knows more than we do about the royal family.'

'True. But at the moment, we have the element of surprise,' he murmured. Finishing his breakfast, he rose and picked up his hat. 'We'll do as Gerda suggested. I'll ask to speak to the master of the household, or possibly the lord chamberlain.'

'Should I request an audience with the Queen, while you do that?' she suggested. 'I might be able to find out more.'

'No. We should remain together. Especially if others believe we're married.' His gaze fell upon her hand.

Hannah saw the direction of his gaze. She let out a shuddering breath and removed her glove. 'All right. I'll wear the ring, but only for a few days. After that, I'm returning it to you.'

Michael withdrew the ring from his pocket and slid it on her finger. He held her hand a moment longer than he should have, but she refused to look at him.

In her eyes he saw the self-flagellation, the anger at herself for breaking so many rules. He wanted to say something to make her feel better. But what could he say? He'd been selfish, indulging in the night he'd spent in her arms. Even afterwards, with the shield of pillows between them, he'd needed to know she was close.

Hannah had fallen asleep holding his hand. It had felt nice, watching over her while she dreamed. She was far too good for the likes of him, but it was too late to undo what had transpired between them.

She adjusted the ring on her finger. 'I hope you find what you're looking for today, Michael.'

So do I.

With her hand in his, he led her down the hallway and towards the stairs. Below, he heard the din of voices gathering. It sounded as if someone important was here. Instinct made him keep Hannah behind him.

When he reached the bottom of the stairs, people seemed to swarm from every angle. A group of soldiers came forward, armed with muskets. They cleared through the crowd, forming a line at the bottom of the stairs.

'His Royal Highness has asked to see you,' the Captain of the Guard announced.

Not the King. The Prince.

Michael glanced back at Hannah. He reached back to take her hand, bringing her beside him. 'I suppose we're going to get our audience after all.'

CHAPTER SEVENTEEN

'NOT HER,' THE Captain corrected, in halting English. 'Only you.'

Of course, Michael thought. It didn't surprise him that the Prince wanted to address him alone. It was the easiest way to eliminate the threat.

When the Captain started to argue, Michael cut him off. 'My *wife* comes with me.'

All around, he heard the buzz of voices. Though he couldn't understand all of the Lohenisch words, he overheard them discussing the Changeling Prince. He tried to shield Hannah from the throng, but several of the men and women crowded too close.

That was it. Michael stopped walking with the soldiers, levelling the crowd with his anger. 'You do not touch her. Ever.'

He guided Hannah to walk in front of him. The soldiers eyed him with distrust, as if they thought he would try to escape. Not at all. He had every intention of accompanying them to get his answers. It didn't bother him that he was about to face the Prince of this country, the man who stood to lose the most.

His immediate concern was Hannah's safety. And though a part of him feared that it could be a trap, these men didn't have the look of executioners. He'd seen soldiers who had been commanded to kill a man. The emptiness in their eyes and the grim reluctance were evident. No, this was duty. And so he kept Hannah close to him and kept another eye upon their weapons.

The soldiers escorted both of them towards a cart drawn by horses. The primitive transportation would have insulted anyone of true noble birth. Hannah eyed it with the greatest reluctance. Even so, she said nothing as Michael lifted her up. In English, she whispered, 'Why did they come for you? Do you think your enemies have found us?'

'More likely word has spread of our arrival, after yesterday.'

'I don't like this.' Hannah shook her head, her gaze focused upon their muskets. 'One of them said it was for our protection, but it doesn't feel right.'

'I agree.' At the moment, he didn't want her to leave his side. 'If they try to separate us, send word to the Graf immediately.'

'I'm not worried about myself,' Hannah whispered. 'I'm worried about you.' She gripped his hand, and he traced the ring upon her finger. Though she'd sworn she would only wear it for a few days, he didn't want it to leave her hand. The delicate jewel was a means of keeping other men away from her.

'I can take care of myself, Hannah.'

She still didn't look convinced.

WHEN THEY ARRIVED at the *Schloss*, she craned her neck to study it. The stone walls gleamed in the light, the pointed towers reminding Michael of a fairy-tale castle. A sudden memory took hold, of walking through a flower garden, and a dark-haired woman smiling at him.

He'd been here before. There was no doubt of it in his mind.

'Do you suppose they'll lock you inside one of those?' Hannah pointed to one of the towers, only half-teasing.

He didn't smile. Truthfully, he had no idea what to expect from this audience. The soldiers helped them disembark from the wagon, and they were led to a private entrance.

The stone exterior of the *Schloss* had an older foundation that was built centuries ago, while newer grey stones formed the upper levels. Glass windows reflected the morning sunlight while wild roses formed a pink-and-green hedge against the side. Six large chimneys rose from the topmost towers, reminding him that this was a modern *Schloss* and not an ancient crumbling castle from hundreds of years ago.

'Lieutenant Thorpe and Mrs Thorpe, please follow me.' The Captain escorted them through the back entrance and down a long hallway.

A winding stone staircase led to the upper levels, and when they reached the first floor, the Captain stopped and opened the door leading to a small parlour. Motioning a female servant forward, he said, 'Mrs Thorpe, you may await your husband here.'

Hannah eyed the small sitting room, her gaze searching Michael's.

'She stays with me.' He wasn't going to be separated from her until he knew what to expect.

'I am sorry, Lieutenant Thorpe. Fürst Karl wished to speak with you alone. We must obey his orders.'

Michael stared at the Captain. 'I am not subject to his rule. And Lady Hannah remains at my side.'

He was well aware of the insult from the way the Captain stiffened.

'Michael, I think you should go with them,' Hannah interrupted. Leaning close to his ear, she added, 'I may learn more about your circumstances if we are apart.'

'Not this time. Not until we've met them.'

For long moments, the Captain seemed hesitant to disobey, but at long last he signalled for them both to follow. He led them up another flight of stairs to a large room with a set of four Gothic windows. Light spilled into the chamber, illuminating a grand piano flanked by delicate French chairs. Long blue curtains hung around the windows, giving the room a touch of warmth.

But there was no warmth coming from the man seated in a leather armchair at the far end of the room. His expression was grim, a man who radiated anger and hostility.

Michael kept Hannah's hand in his as he stared at the man. Though the dark hair was slightly lighter, the Prince's face was nearly a mirror image of his own.

'I SUPPOSE YOU'VE come here, hoping the King will acknowledge you.' Fürst Karl stared at the man and woman who sat down before him. The gossip in Vermisten had risen to a fever pitch, the people wondering who the Lieutenant really was. The old stories of the Changeling Prince were resurfacing, and Karl sensed his grasp upon the throne slipping.

The legends and stories were just that—fictional tales born of superstitions. He refused to believe that anyone else could ever usurp his place as the Crown Prince of Lohenberg. All his life he'd devoted himself to Lohenberg, his beloved country. But his kingdom was drifting toward chaos if he didn't settle this problem.

The man seated across from him was, without a doubt, a half-brother. Michael Thorpe, a lieutenant in the British Army, and most likely his father's bastard son.

Whether or not his ailing father had heard of the man's arrival, he couldn't be sure. But Karl would go to any lengths necessary to protect his mother. The Queen didn't need to know about her husband's indiscretions. She'd endured enough punishment over the years, from her own weak mind.

Mad Queen Astri, locked away from the world for her own good. Few people dared to talk to her any more, for it only provoked another bad spell. Even his father avoided his wife, behaving as though he'd been widowed years ago. And as far as Karl was aware, only the Graf von Reischor had met with the Queen.

Now this.

'What is it you want?' Karl demanded, continuing to speak English to the couple. 'Money?' The idea of paying a single *pfennig* to this man, to keep him away from Lohenberg, was repulsive.

'I came here for answers.'

The Lieutenant stared back, as though making a comparison between them. Karl tensed, for this man looked more like his father than he did. It unnerved him.

'How old are you?' Karl asked.

'Twenty-six.'

The same age, then. Karl bit back a curse, furious with his father. How could Sweyn have done such a thing? He might have understood it, if the Lieutenant were a younger man. Astri's madness had cast an unforgivable shadow over the *Schloss*. It would have been understandable, if his father had sought comfort in another woman's arms.

But the presence of this man suggested something else. Perhaps Astri had known of her husband's infidelity. Perhaps that had pushed her past the brink of reason.

It made him sick to think of it. Karl leaned forward slightly, staring harder at the Lieutenant. There was no doubting the resemblance between them. It only fuelled his anger toward the King.

'We share the same father, obviously,' the Lieutenant

said, 'but I wonder about our mothers. Which of us was truly born of the Queen? Should we ask her?'

Never. The idea of forcing Astri to endure this man's presence was unthinkable.

'The Queen will not see you.' Prince Karl stood and went to stand by the window. 'She sees no one.' Not even him. His mother had barely acknowledged him during his entire childhood. That wasn't about to change.

'What if I spoke to her?' the woman spoke up suddenly. 'Surely Her Majesty would not feel uneasy about my presence. I am no threat.'

Karl hadn't given the Lieutenant's wife much thought. She'd remained quiet throughout their discussion, but from the confident way she held herself, he suspected there was more to her than he'd first suspected. She was beautiful, certainly. But there was something uncommon about her, too. An air of quality, as though she belonged here.

Even so, he could not let anyone see the Queen.

'No one,' he repeated. Right now, he wanted to be rid of both of them. Though Karl loathed the idea of bribery, he didn't see that he had much of a choice. 'Return to London, and do not set foot in Lohenberg again. I'll see to it that you receive compensation.'

'We're not leaving,' the Lieutenant argued. 'Not until I've spoken with the King and Queen.'

Karl raised his hand in a silent signal to one of his guards. 'Show the Lieutenant and his wife out. Be sure they reach the borders safely.'

He wanted them gone from the *Schloss*. Out of Vermisten, out of his life. The sooner they were back in England, the better. If he had to use force, he wouldn't hesitate. This was about protecting his family.

The couple didn't argue, but the Lieutenant stood, facing him. His gaze held the promise of a threat. In Lohenisch, he said calmly, 'I didn't ask for this. But I swear to you, I'll have my answers. And so will you, whether you want to hear them or not.'

MICHAEL COULDN'T SEEM to catch hold of the thousand-and-one thoughts racing through his mind. Confronting the Crown Prince had been like having his face smashed against a mirror. He'd seen traces of himself in the man's features. His half-brother. But which of them was illegitimate?

His thoughts returned to his parents. They had lied to him, letting him believe that he was their flesh-and-blood son. Had it been out of love, to protect him from harm? Or had they stolen him away?

His earliest memories of Mary Thorpe were of a woman who had soothed him, rocking him to sleep. Ever patient and loving, he'd never had any reason to doubt her. He still didn't want to.

He held fast to Hannah's hand, for she was his only constant presence in this ever-changing chaos. She grounded him, keeping him from losing his mind.

God in heaven, he didn't know what to do. It was clear that his life was a missing piece in this strange puzzle. But did he possess a birthright? Could he make the transition from pauper to Prince, if it were true?

The soldiers escorted them to the front of the *Schloss* just as Graf von Reischor arrived with his servants. The ambassador's face was nearly grey with exertion, and his footmen carried him towards them.

'Coming here alone was a mistake,' the Graf said without prelude. 'You have no idea the threats you could face.'

'Twice, men have tried to kill me,' Michael retaliated. 'I know precisely what we face.' With a hint of satisfaction, he added, 'And yet there hasn't been an attempt on my life since we left your side. Why do you suppose that is?'

'You should have waited for me,' the Graf insisted. His footmen eased the ambassador to a standing position. A moment later, Reischor motioned the servants away and lowered his voice. 'What happened?'

Was I right? he seemed to be asking.

'The Prince ordered us to leave,' Michael answered. 'His guards are escorting us to the borders.'

His reply fuelled the Graf's indignation. 'I didn't tell you to speak with the Fürst. Of course *he* wouldn't want you in the *Schloss*.'

'We weren't given a choice,' Hannah interrupted, her hand squeezing Michael's in an attempt to calm him. 'This morning the Prince sent men to the inn, and we were brought before him.' Keeping her voice just above a whisper, she added, 'He feels threatened by Michael.'

'Well, of course he would.' The Graf straightened, sending a thoughtful glance toward the *Schloss*. 'It seems we will need to alter our strategy.'

He spoke quietly to his own men, ordering them to escort Michael and Hannah to his hunting lodge. 'I will join you there this evening, after I have spoken with Her Majesty.'

'The Prince says the Queen will see no one.'

'He means they won't allow it.' The Graf's face hardened with frustration. 'They accused her of madness and locked her up. No one wants to admit that she was right, all along.'

'Right about what?'

'About you being stolen away.' The Graf cleared his throat. 'But this is not the place to discuss it.'

He signalled to the Prince's guards. 'My servants will drive Lieutenant Thorpe and his…companion to the border. You may return to your duties.'

The Captain looked suspicious, but he obeyed. Within seconds, the Graf's servants surrounded them, and they continued walking towards his coach.

'My driver will bring you to my hunting lodge after he's certain you aren't followed out of Vermisten,' the Graf told them.

Hannah wasn't convinced. 'The Prince will order us out of the country, if he discovers we're still here.'

The Graf appeared irritated at her concern. 'Your presence is not required, Lady Hannah. If it bothers you, my men can escort you to your cousins' house in Germany, even now.'

She looked uncomfortable and turned to Michael, her eyes searching his. He didn't want her to leave, not yet.

'I need someone I can trust, to be my translator.' Michael took her hand in his. He didn't mention that he was starting to remember the language. Best to let others believe he couldn't speak a word.

When they reached the coach, the Graf's gaze flickered toward their joined hands. Michael saw the instant the Graf noticed the ring upon Hannah's hand.

'Have you gone and done something foolish?'

Hannah blushed, covering the ring with her hand. 'Not really. It was a gift. If others believed we were married—'

The Graf's face tightened with disgust. 'I hope, for the sake of the Lieutenant's future, that not too many people believe it.'

Her face paled, and Michael tightened his hand on hers. This wasn't her fault, and he'd not let the Graf lay the blame upon her. He held up the ring. 'I've protected her reputation with this.'

'You shouldn't have brought her here,' the Graf protested. 'Her cousins are probably already wondering where we are.'

'We've been gone only two days,' Michael pointed out.

'And do you intend to keep her with you, as your—?'

'Don't say it.' Michael was about to move towards him when Hannah stepped between them.

'It's all right,' she said slowly. Looking the Graf squarely in the eye, she said, 'I have no intention of interfering with the Lieutenant's future. I will return to my cousins' house soon enough.' She released his hand, taking a step away. Her face was perfectly composed, showing no trace that she felt anything.

She was right, of course. That was the proper thing to do, and Michael should never have allowed her to come with him. But the idea of her leaving him, returning to a house of strangers who would help her marry a foreigner, made him want to take her hand back again.

After he helped Hannah into the coach, Michael asked, 'Where is Mrs Turner now?' He'd believed she would be safe, remaining with the Graf.

'She is staying at an inn with Lady Hannah's maid and the other servants.' The Graf visibly winced. 'She was not pleased about the journey here.'

Michael didn't doubt that. 'Bring her to the lodge, if you would. I want to speak with her as soon as possible.' Abigail Turner had known his mother since he was a small boy. She might be able to shed light on whether or not Mary Thorpe had ever been to Lohenberg.

The Graf nodded, though he didn't appear enthused about the idea. 'As you wish.'

Inside the coach, Hannah appeared shaken by the interaction. From the way she wouldn't meet his gaze, Michael suspected she was considering leaving.

Did he want to be a part of this royal family, though he was undoubtedly the black sheep? Instinct made him consider leaving it behind. They didn't want him—of that he had no doubt. But if he turned his back upon them, he would not see Hannah again. He was torn between a life he didn't want and a woman he did.

THE JOURNEY TOWARDS the border was a jarring, rough ride. The miles passed, and still he didn't speak to Hannah. She was twisting the ring around her finger, deep in thought. When the afternoon sun began to drift lower in the sky, she turned to him and asked, 'What did you think of the Prince?'

'I think he's afraid.' As any man would be, when faced with an unexpected piece of the past.

'What about you? Are you afraid of what will happen?'

He shook his head. 'I'm not the one with a kingdom to lose, sweet.'

'He's your brother, isn't he?' She looked troubled by the prediction, as though she didn't want it to be true.

He nodded. 'I'm probably a bastard son. They'll want to be rid of me, for appearance's sake.'

She shook her head, meeting his eyes with her own. 'I don't believe that, Michael. I saw the portrait of the King in the library. You are the very image of your father.' Deep green eyes stared into his. 'If anyone is a bastard son, it's the Prince.'

CHAPTER EIGHTEEN

HANNAH STARED OUT the window of the coach, feeling more and more uneasy about their circumstances. Now that Fürst Karl and Michael had met, she didn't doubt that the threats would worsen.

Michael rested his wrists upon his knees, glancing outside at the forest. 'I don't think there can be a good outcome for me, Hannah. There's too much at stake.'

'But if the Kingdom rightfully belongs to you…'

'I don't want it,' he admitted, shaking his head. 'I know nothing about Lohenberg. I was brought up in England as a fishmonger's son. I couldn't be a Prince, even if I wanted to.'

He'd already discarded the idea; she could see it on his face. He didn't believe he was capable of governing the people. But he was the sort of man who had seen the darker side of poverty. He would know, better than anyone, how to help those who were less fortunate.

She rested her hands upon her skirts, leaning towards him. He needed to put aside his doubts and reach for the future he deserved. 'You could. And I think you were meant for this.' Thinking a moment, she asked him, 'If it weren't for you, how many more men would have died at Balaclava?'

'I didn't save enough.'

'But many more lived.' She reached out to touch his cheek. 'You're a man who takes care of others. Your men. Mrs Turner.' She forced him to look at her. 'Me.'

'I'm no good at it, Hannah.' He glanced at the lavish gilt interior of the coach. 'I don't belong in a *Schloss* like that.'

'And what if they are your real family? You'll simply turn your back on them?'

A harsh laugh escaped him. 'They turned their back on me.'

'You don't know that. There are a thousand things that might have happened. Give it a chance. Find out the truth.'

'And what about you?' he asked quietly. 'What will you do if we find out I'm the Prince of this country?'

She stared at the ring on her hand, turning it over to hide the diamond-and-aquamarine cluster. 'I suppose I'll go to Germany.'

He took her hand and turned the ring back to reveal the stones. Shrugging, he said, 'I need you to translate for me. After that, it's your choice.'

There was no mention of wanting her there. She had hoped he would ask her to stay, to tell her that she meant something to him. But he didn't appear to care whether or not she stayed. It battered her foolish dreams, and she berated herself for even thinking of it.

Crestfallen, she chose her words carefully. 'You're remembering more of the language every day. You were born knowing it; it's only a matter of time before you remember everything. You don't need me.'

Tell me you do, she pleaded silently. *Let me believe that last night was important to you.*

But he said nothing.

Hannah glanced outside so he couldn't see her eyes brimming with tears. 'The Graf was right. We shouldn't have pretended to be married.' Her face felt brittle, and her throat tightened in a struggle for control.

'You want to leave,' Michael murmured softly.

'I want you to ask me to stay.' The words slipped out,

and she longed to take them back. 'I know I shouldn't have come with you here. It was wrong.' One of the tears slipped free against her will. 'But… I didn't want to leave you.'

Blood rushed to her face, as she laid her confession bare before him. 'I wanted to be with you, for however long that would be. And I don't regret letting you share my bed.'

He moved across the coach to sit beside her. With his thumbs, he brushed the tears away. 'If I were a better man, one who could take care of you, I wouldn't let you go. I'd damn the consequences and force you to stay with me.' He held her gloved hand to his face. 'But there are people who want me dead. It might be best if you stayed with your cousins, where you can be safe.'

She shivered, rubbing her arms, though the air was still warm. 'Is that what you want?'

He leaned in, touching his forehead to hers. She could feel the warmth of his mouth against her cheek, the hushed breath between them. The feverish burn of desire crept over her, the need to feel his body pressed close.

'You know what I want. And there's nothing honourable about it.'

Spirals of need threaded through her, and Hannah softened beneath the onslaught of Michael's kiss. The sensual pressure of his mouth and tongue loosened her doubts. Without words, he was coaxing her, silencing the warnings in her head.

When he broke away, it took a moment to steady her breathing. Every memory of last night came crashing through her mind. The touch of his hands, the feeling of his body joining with hers.

She needed to be with him, even if it meant being his mistress and not his wife. And though she knew he would break her heart in the end, she would take whatever moments she could.

MICHAEL COULDN'T SLEEP. Though he'd been given the best room in the Graf's hunting lodge, the soft featherbed offered nothing in the way of true comfort.

When he heard the door creaking open in the middle of the night, he reached under his pillow for the knife he'd hidden. Slowly, the footsteps drew closer. He held his breath, waiting. It was a risk, for he didn't know who was approaching or why. It might be someone trying to kill him, or it might be a servant who'd forgotten something. But then, a servant would have knocked first.

It was risky to wait, if the assailant had a gun. He held his position for as long as he dared, while the footsteps came even nearer. There was a faint scent of faded herbs, like a lavender sachet that had been trapped in a drawer for too long. A familiar perfume, but one he couldn't quite place.

When he sensed the person standing by his bed, he charged forward, with the knife drawn. 'Who's there?' he demanded.

A woman gasped, and he reached out to turn up the lamp. The dim glow illuminated the room, revealing the presence of Abigail Turner.

'Mrs Turner, what are you doing here?' he demanded.

She trembled, her face white with fear. He realised he was still holding the knife, and he set it down.

'I wanted to talk with you.' She sat down in a nearby chair, her voice quaking. 'Since you didn't heed my warning, I wanted you to understand. They're going to find me, and then I can't say what will happen.'

She spoke as though she'd done something wrong. He half-wondered if she was having one of her spells again. 'Find you?'

Raising her chin, she nodded. 'I was supposed to give you to them.' Her lower lip trembled, and she shook her head, her face tight with unshed tears. 'But how could I let them kill you? You were a boy…just a boy.'

He was having trouble understanding what she meant. 'Are you saying, you are from Lohenberg?' he ventured. 'This is your country?'

She glanced away. 'I haven't been back in over twenty-three years. I never wanted to return…after…what I did.' She gripped her arms, her voice fading softer. 'They took my husband, you see. They said if I didn't give you over to them, they were going to kill Sebastian.'

He stared hard at her curling grey hair and her soft brown eyes, but could not tell if it was the truth she spoke. She reached out and cupped his cheeks with her hands. The tears did spill over now, and she wept openly for her loss. Michael held her hands, trying to offer her comfort, though his mind was reeling from her revelation.

Though he didn't want to cause her more emotional pain, he needed to understand. 'You abducted me from my family,' he said slowly. 'Because these men took your husband.'

She nodded. 'I was in the Queen's service and was one of a few women who could get close to you.'

'Who were these men? Who hired them?'

'I don't know,' she wept. 'They came to me on All Hallows Eve. There was a masked ball that night, and everyone, even the guards, had masks.'

She wiped her tears, adding, 'I imagine that's how they were able to get inside the palace without anyone noticing. I was supposed to take you away from your nurse and bring you to a coach that was waiting outside. With all the other carriages for the ballroom guests, no one would notice it.'

'How did you get past the guards?'

'I told them I was taking you outside, to the gardens where the Queen was waiting. They believed my story and let me pass.' She lowered her head in self-loathing. 'They trusted me. I didn't know until later that the hired men had put another child in your place.'

Michael didn't allow a single emotion to be revealed. He struggled to keep back the surge of resentment. Mrs Turner had known about his past, all these years, and had never once said a word about it. She'd known that his parents were not his own.

But if he revealed any of his frustration now, she might slip into a fit of madness, and he'd never hear the entire truth.

Carefully, he asked, 'What happened after you took me from my nurse?'

She continued weeping, clutching her hands together. 'I almost gave you over to them, God forgive me. You were asleep in my arms when I got inside the coach.' Her hand went to her middle. 'But I had recently learned that I was expecting a child of my own. Henry.' A mournful smile crept through her tears. 'And I thought about how I would feel if anyone harmed my own child. I couldn't bring myself to do it. Even if it meant losing Sebastian.'

She dried her eyes, seeming to pull her thoughts together. 'I stopped the coachman and bribed him to drive me home instead.' Her gaze turned solemn with regret. 'I suppose we were both having regrets.'

'I gathered up all the money and jewels that I could, and I used it to buy our passage to London,' she continued. 'I kept you for a few months until I was about to give birth. It was then that I met Paul and Mary Thorpe. They were childless and they promised to take care of you and help me with my own baby.'

Mrs Turner let out a heavy sigh. 'I was afraid of anyone finding us. I also knew I would have to live in poverty for the rest of my days. It was the only way to avoid notice.'

He'd often wondered how Mrs Turner had managed to

survive, without a husband to support her. He'd always believed it was his parents' charity.

'Did my parents know about my past?'

She shook her head. 'It would have made them uncomfortable to know you were a Prince. They'd have treated you like a bit of glass, and then what sort of man would you have grown into?'

She took a deep breath, blowing her nose in the handkerchief he gave her. 'I told them you were orphaned in Lohenberg, and that I'd promised to find a home for you. I let them raise you as they chose. But the one thing I insisted on was your education. Dear heaven, how I pestered Mary about that. I told her that you might be a fishmonger's son, but you deserved a chance for a better future.'

'How could they possibly have afforded my schooling?' Michael voiced aloud. 'I never understood it.'

'I sold some jewels I'd kept from Lohenberg.' She dabbed at her eyes. 'Mary let Paul believe that she'd inherited a small sum from an aunt who died.' She patted his cheek. 'You needed it more than I did.'

'What happened to your husband?'

Silent tears rolled down her face. 'I've never known. I haven't seen Sebastian since that night.' She shivered at the memory. 'I hoped that somehow he managed to survive. But I couldn't write to him or ever learn what happened; otherwise they might have found you.'

The burden of her secret seemed to grow lighter, now that she had laid it before him. But Michael felt its weight suffocating him. He didn't want a royal life, or the difficulties it would bring.

'I sent the last of my funds to bring you back from Malta, after I learned you were wounded,' she admitted. 'I had hoped that both you and Henry would return.'

Michael embraced her while she wept for her son. With

Abigail Turner's confession, he could no longer deny the truth staring him in the face. He would have to confront the impostor Prince Karl, as well as the King and Queen. God help him.

Mrs Turner leaned her head on his shoulder, patting his back. 'I am sorry for keeping this from you, Michael. I thought the only way to save your life was to keep it a secret.'

She was asking for his forgiveness, but right now he was having trouble thinking clearly. He forced himself to give her a light squeeze, but inside, his thoughts were churning.

Mrs Turner pulled back from him. Her face still held the melancholy, but it was soon replaced by stubbornness. 'I will go to Queen Astri in the morning and tell her everything.'

He wasn't so certain that was a good idea. 'We've already been forbidden to see the Queen. I don't think—'

'I was one of her ladies-in-waiting for over five years. The Queen will see me.'

'Not if she believes you stole her only son.'

Mrs Turner's face crumpled up with tears, as though he'd struck her across the face. But she needed to understand that any contact with the *Schloss* would mean her own imprisonment, possibly death.

'If you try to speak with her, you'll face punishment for what you did. The men who took your husband might find you again; they know I'm still alive. It's too grave a risk.'

'I have to atone for what I did. I have to bring you back to her, so she knows that I never meant to betray her.'

'In time. I will face her first, before you.' He crossed his arms in front of him. 'But even if she does agree to see me, she might not believe it. There's no proof that I am her son, except for my resemblance to the King.'

The corners of Mrs Turner's mouth turned up. 'You're wrong, lad. There is proof that you are the Prince.'

He waited for her to continue, and she came up behind him. 'You have a scar here.' She pointed to his left leg. 'On the back of your calf.'

Michael had seen the scar before, but he'd never remembered how he'd received it.

'When you were two years old,' Mrs Turner said, 'you loved climbing up on tables, no matter how your nurse tried to stop you. One day, you fell backwards and cut yourself on one of your toys. You cried and your mother held you while they stitched up the wound.' Mrs Turner stretched her thumb and forefinger to show the size. 'It's naught more than this large. But only a few members in the palace knew about it.'

She grew solemn. 'You're going to get your throne back, Michael Thorpe. I promise you that.'

MICHAEL SPENT THE last few hours of the night pacing. Mrs Turner's confession made it impossible to deny his past any longer. Now he had to decide whether or not to seek the Kingdom he'd lost.

He threw on a pair of trousers and a shirt, not bothering with a waistcoat. Tiptoeing outside his room, he moved down the corridor and towards the back stairway. The Graf's lodge was not large, though it was luxurious.

He didn't know what drew him towards Hannah's bedchamber. It wasn't the desire to intrude, but a deeper need. If he could sleep beside her, he sensed he could calm the tangled state of his mind.

The Graf had given her a room on the opposite side of the house. Although they had kept up their ruse of marriage to the outside world, Heinrich von Reischor intended to uphold Hannah's virtue as best he could.

Quietly, Michael opened the door to her room and moved inside. Though he doubted if she'd hidden a knife under her pillow the way he had, he whispered, 'It's Michael. Are you asleep?'

'I was,' Hannah replied, rolling over and blinking at him. 'What is it?'

He closed the door behind him, thankful to find that she was alone. Without another word, he crossed the room and lay down beside her in the bed.

She wore a thin cotton nightgown, and her body was warm from sleep. A light fragrance of jasmine clung to her hair. Michael curled around her, holding her close.

She didn't ask for explanations, but softly ran her fingers over his arm. A reassuring touch, one that helped to calm his troubled spirits.

'Stay with me tonight,' she whispered.

He kissed her temple in answer. Though his body was already responding to her nearness, he forced the desire away. Right now, he just wanted to sleep beside her.

'You can tell me, you know,' she whispered. 'Whatever is bothering you.'

'In the morning,' he promised. 'Right now, I've the need to hold you.'

She rolled over on to her side, propping up her head on her hand. 'Tell me.'

He explained Mrs Turner's confession, all the while finding an excuse to touch Hannah. He ran his fingers over her shoulder, down to the curve of her hip. 'I hardly know what to do any more. The throne isn't something I want.'

Her hand came up to his face, and she pressed her lips to his in a soft kiss. 'If Queen Astri is your true mother, she'll want to know what happened to you.' She pressed closer to him, stroking his spine. The gesture made him grow hard, and he fought to gain control over his body's instincts.

'They're strangers to me,' he admitted. 'I know nothing of the way they live or how I should act.'

'I'll help you.' Hannah ran her fingers through his hair. 'I'll come with you to the *Schloss* for a few days.'

He pulled her on top of him, holding her close. The edges of her nightgown slid up around her legs, and when he reached down to correct the hem, he realised she was naked beneath it.

His palms moved over her bare bottom, and his manhood swelled against the soft spot between her thighs. She tensed, and he felt the prickle of gooseflesh on her skin.

'Michael,' she breathed. It was neither a protest, nor an invitation. He sensed that she desired him, too, but was trying to resist him.

He cupped her face, drawing her in for a kiss. His frustrations, his uncertain future, were making it impossible to think clearly. And right now, if she was willing, he wanted to forget.

She kissed him back, her mouth warm and wet. He rocked her hips against his, and she shuddered at the contact. His palms squeezed her soft bottom, while his shaft strained to break free.

'I want to be inside you,' he murmured against her mouth, sliding his hands beneath her nightgown to cup her bare breasts. The fierce need burned inside him, and if she allowed it, he wanted nothing more than to turn her over and fill her body with his own.

She stilled, and her hands captured his wrists, pulling them away. 'Michael, no. I can't.' Hannah extricated herself from his embrace, and he noticed that her fingers were bare, unlike a few hours ago. She must have removed the wedding ring he'd given her.

His desire was instantly replaced with wariness. 'I didn't

come here to seduce you. I'm not going to force you into anything you don't want.'

She sat up and drew her nightgown over her knees. In the fragile garment, she looked like an innocent maiden about to be sacrificed to a dragon.

'I was wrong. I thought I could be your mistress.' She gathered up the bed sheets like a shield.

He took several deep breaths, feeling as though he were walking upon a precipice. 'I told you. If there's a child, I will provide for both of you.'

She shook her head slowly. 'We made the mistake once. Not again. If I bore a child, you would resent me.'

He couldn't understand what she meant. 'I would never resent you.'

'I thought that if we were together, even if I were nothing but your mistress, you might eventually want to marry me.' She lowered her head. 'It was a foolish thought. As the Crown Prince, there is no chance of it.'

'I don't live by the decisions of others.'

She ignored him. 'You could marry a Princess. Or a duchess. Anyone you please.'

His anger ignited. 'Do you think I give a damn about social status?' He stood, his shadow falling over her. 'Are you demanding that I marry you? Because I don't think that's what you really want.'

His fury erupted. 'You want a man with a title and several estates. You want a respectable name and separate bedrooms with an adjoining door. When you sit at your dinner table, you want a man at your side whom others admire. Not a man like me. A soldier, responsible for the deaths of hundreds of men.'

She spoke not a word, and he realised he'd been hoping for her argument. He'd hoped she would deny it. But he suspected he'd been her temptation, a sinful indulgence that she didn't want forever.

'If I thought you wanted me, I'd find a minister right now,' he murmured, sitting down. 'I would make you a Princess. But you wouldn't say yes, would you?'

Because she knew where he came from. She knew who he truly was—a man from the streets.

For the longest moment, Michael stared into her bleak face. Waiting for her to tell him he was wrong. Waiting for her to embrace him or offer words of reassurance.

'No, I wouldn't,' she said at last. Her face was pale, but determined. 'I'll help you acclimate to the *Schloss*. And after that, I'm leaving for Germany.'

THE DOOR CLOSED behind Michael, and Hannah buried her face in the pillow, weeping hot tears. The wretched pain of forcing him to leave her was more than she could bear.

His idle remark, that he'd make her a Princess, made her shudder. He didn't know what it was like to live in a gilded cage, the way she did.

Hannah understood exactly what it was to have her appearance inspected every few hours, her food selected based on what would keep her figure slender, and her life ordered to a stringent set of rules.

For a Princess, it would be far worse.

The hot tears caught up in her throat, for it had taken every bit of her willpower to hold firm on the decision. She had fallen in love with Michael Thorpe, but not once had he spoken of his feelings toward her. And the thought of living in a *Schloss*, hoping for a scrap of affection or a night in his arms, was too much to bear.

She'd rather be the wife of a nobleman or a commoner. Someone who would let her have a taste of the freedom she'd never possessed.

Michael's life would be controlled by the strings of politics, his future no longer under his control. If he were the Crown Prince, he couldn't avoid his fate.

But she could.

And though it broke her heart into a thousand pieces, she couldn't endure life as a Princess unless he loved her back.

CHAPTER NINETEEN

THOUGH HE WAS healing from his bullet wounds, the Graf von Reischor was still unable to walk. While Michael waited in the coach with Lady Hannah, the older man's servants used a wheeled chair to push him into the *Schloss*.

'Do you think he'll manage an audience with the Queen?' Hannah asked, watching as they disappeared inside.

'I have no doubt of it.'

'What about the royal guards? The Prince ordered us to leave the country. Surely, they won't allow it.'

'They haven't seen us yet. For now, they believe the ambassador is paying his respects to the Queen.'

THEY WAITED FOR nearly two hours before the Graf returned to the coach. The man looked exhausted, but satisfied. To Michael, he said, 'I've arranged an audience. The King has agreed to meet with us, overruling Fürst Karl's orders.'

'What about the Queen?' Hannah asked. 'Will she see us?'

The Graf nodded. 'We will see her first, before our audience with the King. But we must be careful, because Her Majesty is confined to one of the towers. Visitors are rare, and I would caution you not to upset her.'

Would the Queen be like Abigail Turner, with fleeting moments of clarity? Michael wondered. Or had she crossed past the point of rational behaviour?

The Graf took assistance from the footmen, who helped him back into the chair. Michael adjusted his gloves, while his doubts and apprehensions rose higher.

Hannah closed the door to the coach for a moment, keeping her voice low. 'When you encounter anyone at the *Schloss*, do not allow them to touch you,' she said. 'Royalty may never be touched without permission to do so.'

He gave a nod, trying to memorise her instructions.

'Wait for a footman to ask permission to take your coat,' she continued. 'You must stand and allow him to take it off you.'

He stared at her. 'Do you mean to say I am not allowed to remove my own coat?'

'Others will be responsible for dressing you and undressing you,' she answered. 'A valet will be assigned to you, and you must permit him to carry out his duties.'

'As if I were nothing more than a child?'

'No. Because it is your right to be waited on by others.'

'What if I refuse?'

'You mustn't.' She glanced back at the *Schloss*. 'Already there will be those who doubt your right to be Prince.' She took his hand and pleaded, 'Trust what I say. It will be easier if you obey the rules that are expected.'

He glanced down at their joined hands. Hannah tried to jerk her fingers back, but he held them in his grip. Beneath the glove, she still wasn't wearing the ring he'd given her.

'Should I tell them that you are my translator, my mistress or my wife?' he demanded.

For an infinite moment, she looked into his eyes as though he were crushing her heart. He'd expected a firm refusal, as well as a reminder that she would only stay for a few days. Clear green eyes watched him with an unnamed emotion.

'Tell them whatever you want,' she said.

Why in God's name couldn't women simply state what they desired instead of hiding their true thoughts behind a set of good manners?

A servant opened the door to the coach, and a chill swept over Michael at the thought of meeting the Queen. He disembarked and reached up to help Hannah down.

'Don't do that again,' she murmured. 'You're royalty. Let a footman help me down.'

He couldn't believe what he was hearing. Did she expect him to behave as though he owned the earth and everyone else was privileged to be in his presence? From the way she followed, a discreet distance behind him, it seemed that was exactly the case.

Servants carried the Graf up two flights of stairs, to a private drawing room within one of the towers while they followed behind. When Michael waited for Hannah, she shook her head. 'This is your audience, not mine. I will await you here.' She pointed to a wooden high-backed chair.

'Do as you please.' He turned his back on her, unable to conceal his anger. What was the matter with her? He couldn't understand why she was behaving like his subject instead of his equal.

Before he could think upon it further, he was led into a private room. The Graf's men seated him in a chair, and the ambassador was pale from overexertion.

'Lieutenant Thorpe.' The Graf struggled to rise to his feet. 'May I present to you Her Majesty, Queen Astri of Lohenberg?'

At the Graf's bidding, the servant opened another door, leading to a room Michael hadn't noticed before. After a moment, he moved forward without making a sound.

A woman was seated, staring out the window. Iron bars had been fastened in front of them, and a lady-in-waiting sat nearby, embroidering the hem of a gown.

Michael didn't know what to say. He'd never been in the presence of a queen before, much less one who was possibly his true mother. In the end, he knocked softly upon the door frame.

'Your Majesty…' he began.

Her head turned at the sound of his voice. When she saw him, her hands began to shake. Her eyes welled up, and she pointed to him.

'Come closer,' she murmured. And he saw that she was not at all mad. Her hazel eyes were the same as his own, and he saw similarities between their facial features.

'Graf von Reischor told me that he'd found you. I didn't believe him.' She beckoned for him to draw nearer, and Michael forced himself to come and sit beside her.

The Queen's dark hair held no traces of grey. It was braided and wound into an elaborate coiffeur, adorned with jewelled hairpins. She wore a black moiré gown trimmed with black velvet.

'They told me I was mad, when I said that the boy they gave me was not my son. No one would believe me.' She stared at him. 'You look a great deal like the child I lost. Are you he?'

'I don't know.' But something about the Queen's voice, the soft tones of it, was familiar. 'I thought I was Michael Thorpe. I don't remember anything about this country or anyone else.'

She reached out to him. 'May I?' He gave a nod and she touched his cheek, studying his face closer. 'How did you end up in London?'

'Abigail Turner claimed she took me away, when men were trying to kill her husband. She hid me in London these past twenty-three years.'

'Abigail Turner.' The Queen's face darkened with rage. 'She deserves to be put to death for what she did.'

'She saved my life,' Michael countered. He explained what Mrs Turner had told him, and all the while, the Queen listened with an unreadable expression.

When he'd finished, he said, 'I wouldn't blame you if you didn't believe a word I said. Why should you? I'm a stranger claiming that I could be your son.'

'You don't want this throne, do you?' the Queen said slowly.

'No.' He strode away from her, even knowing that it was rude. 'I wanted to believe that Mary Thorpe was my mother. I wanted to go back to my life as a lieutenant in the British Army.' He folded his arms across his chest, switching to Lohenisch. 'But I can't deny the memories I have. Nor this language.'

When he turned back to face the Queen, her gaze met his.

'You're not a lieutenant, are you?' With her posture ramrod straight, she rose and walked towards him. 'Show me your left calf.' He raised the leg of his trousers, lowering his sock until he bared the scar.

Her hazel eyes glistened, and Queen Astri covered her mouth with her hands. 'You're the son I lost. Fürst Karl.'

'My name is not Karl,' he protested. 'I am Michael.'

'Yes. Karl Peter Michael Henry, Fürst of Lohenberg.' She drew closer, staring at the scar. 'It was in the wrong place, you see. The scar on the boy they gave me. *His* scar was just above his ankle. Yours was below the knee. But the King wouldn't believe me. He told me that the boy was our son. The scar was enough to convince him. He had me locked away, believing I'd gone mad when I said the child wasn't ours.

'May I?' she asked, and once again he realised that she was treating him like royalty, requesting permission before she touched him.

Her arms went around him in an embrace, and awkwardly, he stood still, not sure of what to do. When she moved away, her eyes were wet. 'You don't know me. I'm aware of that, but it's been so very long.'

Another tear rolled down her cheek, combined with a laugh. 'I was right, you see. They didn't believe me, but I was right. The boy they gave me wasn't you.' She removed a handkerchief and wiped her eyes. 'I thank God you're alive.'

The door to the Queen's antechamber opened, and Fürst Karl entered. He strode forward, bowing to the Queen, but his eyes blazed with fury.

'Your Majesty,' he greeted her. To Michael, he said nothing.

'Get out,' she ordered Karl, pointing at the door. 'I've no wish to see you.'

'My lady Mother, I—'

'Out!' she shrieked. 'Leave my presence! I am not your mother, and you are not my son!' Her face filled with loathing, and Michael glimpsed the Prince's shuttered expression.

'If you have need of me—'

'I would never call you, if I had the need. You are nothing to me but an impostor! Lying traitor!'

The Prince sent Michael another dark look, bowing as he made his way out of the chamber.

The Queen apologised as soon as the door closed. 'Tonight, I will order a welcoming feast for you, my son. And the world will know the truth of who is the real Prince.' Her face curved in a smile. 'They have only to look upon your face to see it for themselves.'

But despite her happiness, Michael hadn't missed the hatred upon Karl's face. He'd just deposed a man who had been born and bred for the throne. And he had no doubt that Karl would fight for his kingdom.

HANNAH DUCKED BEHIND the tall wooden chair when Fürst Karl exited the chamber. Anyone could have heard the Queen's rejection, and from the iciness on the Prince's face, it was clear he was furious.

He stopped in front of the chair. 'You may as well come out, Mrs Thorpe. Your gown gives you away.'

Hannah straightened, realising he was right. 'I didn't mean to pry. I was simply waiting upon my…that is, the… Lieutenant.' She didn't say Prince, for it would only fuel the Prince's rage.

Fürst Karl stepped forward, his eyes burning. 'I ordered both of you to leave my country.'

Hannah drew upon every facet of her training to respond. 'I understand how angry you must be with us. But—'

'You understand nothing.' The coldness in his voice was lined with pain.

Hannah prayed she could somehow ease the Prince's anger and reassure him. But this was a man who was about to lose everything. His home, his title…even his family. No words would take away the loss.

'You didn't live here your entire life, did you?' she began. 'Do you remember what it was like before the palace?'

The Prince seemed taken aback by her questions. Rightfully so, she supposed. Royalty was never meant to be interrogated.

'I never lived anywhere else.'

'You might not remember it,' she offered, changing tactics. 'But surely, if you think back to your earliest memory, you know of a time when you were frightened.' She stepped closer to him, her own fears quaking inside. 'When you were but a small child, pushed into a world you didn't understand.'

Careful, Hannah. Don't make him angrier.

But his face remained blank, as though she hadn't spoken at all.

'I can understand why you might resent Lieutenant Thorpe,' she said gently. 'To find out that your life was not what you thought it was…anyone would be angry at the changes.'

'Nothing has changed,' the Fürst insisted. 'And I won't let him do anything to upset the Queen.'

The Prince's protective nature over his mother made Hannah's heart ache. She doubted if Queen Astri had ever accepted Fürst Karl as her son. In her mind, Hannah imagined a lonely boy, trying to win his mother's love. And never succeeding.

'Lieutenant Thorpe came to find out the truth. Not to hurt anyone, especially not the Queen.' She could see the pain in his eyes, of a man whose life was crumbling at his feet. 'Talk to him, I beg of you. If the two of you would come to an understanding, there might be a way to compromise.'

Her words made the Fürst stiffen. He crossed the hallway, coming to stand directly in front of her. 'There cannot be a compromise, Mrs Thorpe. Lohenberg is my homeland, and I will die before handing my throne over to a stranger who knows nothing of our country.'

'He is your brother, by blood,' Hannah said quietly. 'And regardless of the conspiracies that happened years ago, the two of you should put your differences aside. Try to work together.'

The Prince shook his head. 'It's not possible.'

Hannah looked into his eyes, noting the trapped frustration. 'Lieutenant Thorpe is a good man. And I believe you are, as well.'

'I care little about what anyone thinks of me. Least of all, the wife of a lieutenant.'

Her expression grew strained. 'I am the daughter of a Marquess. Not the wife of a lieutenant.' Steeling herself, she admitted, 'I lied about being married. It was merely a way to stay with him.'

'You're in love with him, aren't you?'

She didn't answer, trying to keep the bottled-up emotions from spilling over. 'I want him to be happy. Whether he is a soldier or a Prince.'

The Prince's expression grew taut. 'You want to become a Princess.'

'No.' She took a deep breath. 'Actually, I'd rather be a soldier's wife.' Glancing toward the Queen's chambers, she added, 'I know what it is to be imprisoned in a life like this. To be measured and inspected. And still never be good enough.'

The Prince's gaze met hers, and she thought she detected a softening. For a moment, she saw herself mirrored in him, and wondered if he, too, craved his freedom.

'You will always be a Prince here,' she ventured, touching her own heart. 'A man who loves Lohenberg as you do would make a strong adviser.'

'I'd make a better king,' the Prince responded. His chin raised up, and he added, 'Your days in Lohenberg are coming to an end. Rest assured, Lady Hannah, I'll let no one take what belongs to me.'

HANNAH WAITED THE remainder of the morning for Michael, but when he finally emerged from the King's chambers, she caught only a glimpse of him before the servants led him away. After they disappeared down the corridor, the Graf hobbled out, sinking gratefully into the chair offered by his servants.

'They accepted him, then?' Hannah asked. 'Did the audience go well?'

'It did. And I should imagine they will formally acknowledge him as the Fürst within a day or so.' The Graf gave a relaxed smile. 'There's no need for you to stay any longer.'

Hannah didn't return his smile. 'I promised I would remain for a few days.'

'There are others who will help him to assimilate. He does not require your assistance.'

'Trusted servants?' She shook her head. 'Not yet. There were two attempts on his life already. He needs someone to watch out for him, to make sure he's safe.'

'He'll have guards for that.' The Graf motioned a servant forward. 'Escort Lady Hannah back to my coach.'

'Forgive me, Graf von Reischor…' the maidservant curtsied '…but the Queen has already ordered a bedchamber prepared for Lady Hannah.'

Hannah held back her sigh of relief. Her thoughts were so tangled, right now all she wanted was to rest in Michael's arms, to feel the warmth of his body beside her. But he hadn't spoken to her, nor even glanced in her direction when he'd left with the Queen. She tried to ignore the disappointment settling in her stomach.

As she followed the maidservant to one of the guest rooms, she was startled to cross paths with guests she'd met aboard the *Orpheus*.

'Why, Lord Brentford,' she greeted, surprised to see the Viscount. 'And Miss Nelson. This is a surprise.'

The Viscount beamed, returning the greeting. 'I was delighted that the König accepted my request for an audience,' he explained. 'And, of course, we simply *had* to bring Ophelia to meet the royal family. My wife insisted on it.'

Miss Nelson glanced at her father, clearly uncomfortable. She twisted her hands, not offering a greeting or any remark to Hannah.

'Where is Lady Brentford?' Hannah asked, curious as to why the Viscountess was not with them.

'Shopping.' The Viscount winced. 'She claims that Ophelia needs a more dramatic gown for tonight, and she's having a gown altered.'

'Perhaps I'll see all of you at dinner this evening,' Hannah offered.

'Perhaps,' Lord Brentford replied. 'We are hoping Ophelia will be presented to the Crown Prince. After all, he has not yet chosen a bride.'

Hannah wasn't certain how Lord Brentford had wormed his way into the *Schloss*, but it was clear he wanted an advantageous marriage for his daughter.

'Good afternoon to you both,' she bid them in parting. Lord Brentford's broad smile never faded as he continued down the corridor.

The maidservant, Johanna, showed her to a room decorated in shades of green and cream. Though it was small, each piece of furniture was exquisite, with warm shades of wood and shining brass handles.

Hannah gave instructions for her trunks to be delivered to the *Schloss*, along with her maid Estelle. Johanna promised to make the necessary arrangements.

AN HOUR LATER, when Johanna returned with Estelle and the trunks, Hannah asked her maid, 'Where is Mrs Turner?'

'She remained at the Graf's estate,' Estelle answered. 'On his orders.'

Likely to keep her safe, Hannah mused. Still, she wished for the woman's friendly presence.

Behind the two maidservants, a tall, elegant lady entered the room. Her grey hair was pulled into a neat coiffeur, and she wore a flounced maroon dress with draping sleeves.

'I am Lady Schmertach, head of the Queen's ladies-in-waiting,' the woman introduced herself. 'There are certain rules that all guests must abide by, and I am here to see to it that you understand them.'

Were all guests greeted this way? Hannah wondered. She felt rather like a child in the schoolroom, preparing to receive instructions.

After Lady Schmertach seated herself upon the velvet sofa, she cleared her throat. 'First and foremost, you are not to address the King or Queen under any circumstances. Should they choose to speak with you, they will send an attendant to fetch you.'

Rather like a pet dog, Hannah thought. While she listened, Estelle and Johanna began helping her to dress. She noticed that they had selected a rose damask gown flecked with silver threads. It had not been one of her favorites, and she interjected, 'I would prefer the violet tarlatan with the flowers embroidered on the overskirt.'

Lady Schmertach's expression hardened. 'I was not finished explaining matters to you, Lady Hannah. Please do not interrupt. Courtesy is another rule by which we abide here.'

Years of Hannah's own training in courtesy prevented her from snapping out her own retort at the Queen's lady. She bit her lip. 'You were saying?'

Estelle continued working with Johanna, fitting the rose dress over Hannah's corset. Hannah hid her displeasure, waiting for the older woman to finish her lecture.

'You will be seated at the end of the table, along with the other unmarried ladies.'

A little pang squeezed at her heart. So, Michael had not told anyone that they were married. She should have expected it, for it gave her a means of leaving the *Schloss* without anyone noticing.

Lady Schmertach continued her long diatribe, explaining that she should not expect to dance with Fürst Karl, nor to be introduced. 'Royal marriages are not fairy tales,' she insisted. 'They are political alliances that benefit both countries. So you must not allow yourself to fall into the common belief that he will notice you.'

Johanna picked up a hairbrush and began to comb Hannah's hair into a severe knot that pulled at her face. Hannah was beginning to feel like a doll, dressed up in ribbons and lace, unable to move without someone pushing her limbs into place.

'Do you understand all that I have instructed you?' Lady Schmertach asked. 'Have you any questions about how to conduct yourself this evening?'

'No.' She understood perfectly well that she was to remain exactly in her chair and to keep a full distance from the royal family.

'Good. Graf von Reischor has informed me that your cousins will arrive shortly to escort you back to Germany.' With a prim smile, she rose from her chair. 'I hope you enjoy the hospitality this evening.'

Hannah's temples ached from the tight hairpins, and she ordered Johanna and Estelle to leave her alone. When they had gone, she stripped away every pin until her hair hung down below her shoulders.

What is the matter with me? she wondered. *Why can't I tell them what it is I really want?* The words of protest seemed weighted down by years of obedience.

There was a soft knock on the door. Hannah called out, 'Enter', expecting one of the maids to return.

Instead, Michael stepped inside. He closed the door behind him, seemingly surprised to find her alone.

Hannah stood, wondering if she was supposed to curtsy before him. He hadn't changed his clothing from this morning, and his cravat hung crooked at his throat as if he'd tugged at it. She resisted the urge to correct it. 'Was there something you needed?'

His dark gaze fixed upon her. 'Yes. There's something I needed.'

All the blood seemed to rush to her face, and prickles rose up on her skin. Whether it was nerves or simply the intense awareness of Michael, she didn't know. She forced herself to sit down.

'The Graf gave you the chance to leave, earlier today,' he began. 'But you didn't take it. Why?'

She drew on one of her gloves. 'Because I promised I would stay here for a few days longer. To help you grow accustomed to your new life here.'

'Is that the only reason?'

No. I didn't want to leave you. 'What other reason would there be?'

His gaze swept over her gown, but he made no comment. 'I saw that Viscount Brentford and his family are here.'

'Yes, I spoke with him and Miss Nelson.' She grimaced. 'Though they don't know you're the real Prince. I suppose it doesn't matter whether it's you or Fürst Karl. And it won't be the last time you'll be pursued by eager fathers and daughters.'

'Does it bother you?' He folded his arms across his chest.

Of course it bothered her. But she couldn't do anything about it. 'What do you expect me to say? That I'm jealous?' Her shield of calm collapsed into pieces. It wasn't women like Miss Nelson who bothered her. No, it was the soldier's mask that never revealed a hint of Michael's feelings.

'No. You wouldn't be, would you?' he responded. 'I can see that you've made your decision already.'

She crossed the room and stood in front of him. 'What decision? What decision have I ever been allowed to make? You've already made up your mind about me and what you think I want. Just as Estelle and Johanna have decided what I'll wear and how my hair should be arranged. And Graf von Reischor has decided that I'll be returning home to my cousins.'

She rose from her chair and crossed towards him. With a not-so-gentle push, she said, 'My decisions don't seem to matter in the least, so why bother asking?'

He caught her in his arms. 'Because I don't believe what you told me this morning.' He tilted her face to his, their mouths the barest breath apart. 'I don't know which is worse…forcing you to live a life you don't want…or letting you go.'

His hazel eyes were full of desire, his mouth achingly close to kissing hers. God help her, she needed him so much. Being without him was going to rip her heart apart.

'Make your decision, Hannah.' He pressed the ring into her palm. 'Either become my Princess in truth. Or leave.'

He withdrew from her embrace, walking away. When the door closed behind him, she stared down at her rose gown. She didn't care for the colour, nor did she want to wear the pearls Estelle had chosen.

She hated herself and what she had become. And then her gaze fell upon a list Estelle had made, detailing everything Lady Schmertach had instructed.

Whether it was a list of reminders or a list of orders, Hannah didn't care. She tore the paper into tiny pieces, ripping apart all the expectations.

This was her life, was it not? If she wished to wear violet, she could. If she wanted to wear her hair down, who were the servants to tell her otherwise?

The years of fettered isolation were drowning her. She didn't know if she could stand living in this isolated, rigid palace of rules. But there was one thing she wanted more than anything in the world, one man worth fighting for.

She slid the aquamarine-and-diamond ring upon her finger and threw open the door to her room. Picking up her skirts, she raced down the hall. When she rounded the corner, she nearly crashed into Michael.

He caught her before she fell, his hazel eyes questioning. Hannah didn't speak a word, but took his hand in hers, leading him back to her bedchamber. Once they were inside, she turned the key in the lock.

'What do you want?' he asked. His eyes stared hard at the ring upon her hand.

'I don't want to wear this gown tonight,' she answered. 'Nor these pearls.' She reached behind her neck, fumbling with the clasp. Her hands were shaking, her heart pounding in her chest.

Michael came up behind her, his warm hands resting on her nape. With the flick of his thumb, he unfastened the necklace.

'Now the dress,' she ordered. 'Help me. Please.' She wanted his hands upon her, removing all the layers between them.

I don't care that this is wrong. I don't care, I don't care, I don't care.

But Michael took his time unfastening the dozens of buttons, his fingers touching her with unbearable slowness. With each release, her skin erupted with goose bumps. She was waiting for him to kiss her, but he held himself back.

Hannah removed her petticoats, standing before him in her corset and undergarments.

'Am I to play your lady's maid?' he murmured.

'No. You're going to play my husband.' She reached up to kiss him, and their mouths came together in a heated frenzy. He stripped off his coat, and she helped him with his waistcoat and shirt until his chest was bared to her. Hannah kissed his skin, moving her mouth over his pectoral muscles, the marbled skin that was everything she wanted.

He unfastened her corset, turning her to the wall as he unlaced her stays. His hands cupped her breasts, pushing away more clothing until both of them were naked. Her palms pressed against the wallpaper and behind her, he moved close so that his erect shaft slid between her open thighs.

With his fingertips, he teased her breasts. His mouth moved over her shoulders and down her spine until he eased the tip of himself inside her, from behind.

She bloomed with moisture, aching for him. As he slid deeper, he murmured, 'This isn't the proper way to make love to a lady.' With himself still inside her, he guided her to move towards the sofa, leaning over the side. She cried out with exquisite pleasure as he filled her from behind.

'I don't care about what's proper any more,' she breathed. 'Just be with me now.'

He withdrew, then penetrated her again. 'I am at your command.'

CHAPTER TWENTY

MICHAEL KISSED HANNAH's shoulder, her hair falling against his face as he plunged inside her. He couldn't stay away from her, no matter how hard he tried. When he was with Hannah, the emptiness of his life and his past failures all seemed to dissolve. She made him feel whole again.

No kingdom was worth being without her.

She was close to her release, and he pushed himself against the wetness, driving her nearer to the fulfillment she craved. Half-sobs were coming from her, but the long smooth strokes weren't giving her what she needed.

'Hold on,' he urged. Bracing her hands against the couch, he took her roughly. The increased tempo and pounding of his body inside hers made her breathing quicken.

His erection grew harder, and as her body tightened around him, squeezing him in her liquid depths, his control was splintering apart.

Michael pinched her nipples, coaxing her, 'Reach for it, Hannah.' He didn't care how long it took; he would be her slave if it meant bringing her the pleasure she needed.

He reached down to caress the fold of flesh that would help. The touch of his hand made her buck against him, and the counter-pressure of her hips sent his own release blasting through him. At last, she emitted a shuddering gasp, her body trembling wildly. Her inner walls climaxed around him, and he groaned, pulling her hips tight against his own.

For a moment, he rested his cheek against her back, no

longer certain he'd be able to walk. No woman had ever made him feel this way. He couldn't possibly let her go. She was his to protect, his to care for.

He withdrew from her, sweeping her into his arms and taking her to bed. They lay facing one another, skin to skin. He kissed her lips, apologising, 'I didn't hurt you, did I?'

Her cheeks were glowing, her green eyes luminous. 'I felt like a conquest of war.'

He lowered his forehead to hers. 'I'm sorry. I rather lost my head.'

She shivered, and he held her tighter, her bare breasts teasing his chest. 'I wasn't thinking clearly, either.'

His leg moved atop her hip. 'We could stay here. Scandalise all of them by remaining in bed.' He kissed her mouth. 'Then you'd have to marry me.'

She looked away, her face disconsolate. 'Michael, be serious. This is your future. It's where you belong, and you need to choose a wife who can endure a life such as this.'

He didn't like the tone in her voice. 'And that wife isn't you?'

She didn't answer, and he let her pull away from him. With only a sheet covering her, she looked fragile and uncertain. His frustration deepened, for he couldn't understand why she was so reluctant to become a Princess.

He ran his hand over the curve of her body, down to her bottom. 'I'm not a man who begs, Hannah. Either become my wife or don't. It's your choice.'

Without another word, he dressed and left her bedchamber.

'YOU HAVE NOT done as I asked,' the voice said. 'The Lieutenant must not be allowed to take the throne. I want him removed.'

'I am so sorry, my—'

'Apologies are unacceptable. Either dispose of him or you will not like the consequences. You have a wife of your own, I believe.'

'She is innocent,' the servant insisted. 'Please, I beg of you. Don't bring her into this.'

'You will not presume to tell me what to do. Take care of the Lieutenant and use any means necessary. Even Lady Hannah, if need be. Is that understood?'

'It is.'

'Good. The King must not recognise Michael Thorpe as his son.'

The servant bowed. 'I will see to it.'

IT TOOK ALL his restraint to allow another man to dress him. Michael stood while the valet helped him out of his afternoon attire and into the formal black cloth coat and white cravat. The Graf had arranged for his belongings to be sent to the *Schloss*, along with the clothing Hannah had ordered from the tailor.

When he saw the reddened skin on Michael's arm where the bullet had grazed it, the valet asked, 'Do you require a new bandage, my lord?'

'It's all right.' The minor wound had healed enough that he could put it from his mind. The neck abrasions could be hidden with his cravat. He preferred it this way. It was easier to blend in with the nobles, not drawing attention to himself.

He was going to face a battle of a different sort this evening, though he'd prefer not to do so in public. Tonight would be a test, and he suspected that his half-brother, Fürst Karl, would be in attendance.

But not the King.

Michael tensed at the thought of the audience, earlier in the afternoon. It had been brief, for the frail ruler was hardly able to receive guests. When the Graf had whispered to him about Michael, the ageing monarch had tried to sit up. With long grey hair and a short beard and mustache, his father appeared far older than he was. But the King's eyes had held intelligence and curiosity.

An unexpected memory had flashed through Michael. Of apples, strangely enough. Without asking permission to leave the King's side, Michael had gone over to a bowl of fruit in the corner, retrieving a single apple.

Holding it before the King, he said, 'You used to peel these for me. With a jewelled dagger.'

He kept speaking, not knowing if what he was saying made any sense at all. 'I used to sit on your lap and you would try to peel the entire fruit in one long piece. You promised that one day you would give me the dagger.'

The King's expression had paled at the story. And Michael had shown him the scar.

'She was right,' the King whispered, before his eyes closed. 'Tell the Queen…she was right.' The monarch gripped the sheets, and the palace physicians surrounded him, making further conversation impossible.

It bothered him, to have caused the older man further distress. Yet, there was nothing to be done about it. He now understood why the Graf had been so insistent on bringing him to Lohenberg with all haste. It was doubtful that the King would live much longer.

Graf von Reischor arrived at his door a few minutes later. Escorted by two servants, they pushed him in the wheeled chair.

'You should remain in your bed until you've healed,' Michael chided.

'Nonsense. This is a dinner, and I'll be seated most of the time. A man has to eat.'

And a man had to manipulate, Michael thought. As he

walked alongside the Graf, he couldn't suppress the sense of foreboding. This dinner was going to go very badly; he had no doubt.

They arrived just before the seating of the guests. Michael remained behind the others, despite the Graf's insistence that he stand near the front.

Michael watched the guests, nodding politely to Viscount Brentford and his daughter. He sensed their gazes upon him, and the light murmur of gossip.

Though he waited to catch a glimpse of Hannah, there was no sign of her. He was about to enter the banquet hall, when all of a sudden murmurs of surprise came from behind him.

The throng parted, with a sea of curtsies and bows as Queen Astri made her entrance. She wore a champagne-coloured silk gown trimmed with silver and gold embroidery, and two ladies-in-waiting helped manage her train. A moment later, the Queen approached him.

Michael remained standing while the women around him fell into curtsies. He gave an awkward bow to his mother.

'Will you join us, Fürst Michael?' she asked.

A hundred sets of eyes stared at him, agog at the Queen's announcement. Michael moved forward, unsure of where to stand, and not knowing whether to offer his arm or not. The Graf discreetly motioned for him to walk behind her.

Michael continued in the royal procession, still hoping to see Hannah. But once he had joined the Queen at the head of the table, he had to turn his attention to her. His mother's face was alight with happiness, as though her joy could not be contained. Throughout the meal, she peppered him with questions while he did his best to answer.

'Was the King all right after I left?' he asked her at last.

'I wouldn't know.' Astri's expression turned shadowed.

'He locked me in that tower for over twenty years. Tonight was the first time I was allowed to come and go as I pleased. I have the both of you to thank for it.' She cast a gaze at the Graf, and her face softened. Michael detected a faint blush behind the ambassador's countenance.

'The King has accepted you as his son,' the Queen said. 'And I am grateful that you have been returned to me at last.'

THROUGHOUT THE REMAINDER of the dinner, Michael waited for Hannah's arrival. When the hours dragged on, his concern sharpened. It was considered unforgivable to leave a monarch's side without prior permission, but he was beginning to see no alternative.

After the dishes had been cleared away, he stood and made his apologies, excusing himself. The Queen's expression faltered, but she gave him a wave of dismissal.

The people in the banquet hall stared at him, but he didn't care about being rude. Right now, he needed to find Hannah and learn what was going on.

When at last he reached her room, he threw open the door without knocking. Her room was empty, with no trunks, no belongings. The bed was made, and there was no sign that she'd even stayed in the room.

Something was wrong.

Michael strode down the hallway and when he caught sight of a maid, he cornered her. In Lohenisch, he demanded, 'Did you see Lady Hannah leave?'

'Y-yes, sir,' the maid stammered. 'Her cousins arrived, and she went to Germany with them an hour ago.'

He stepped backwards, cursing. He never thought Hannah would actually leave him, but it appeared she'd already done so. He had believed she would give him a chance, that a Marquess's daughter might let herself love a soldier.

It seemed he'd been wrong.

'Lieutenant Thorpe,' a matron's voice interrupted. 'Might I have a word with you?'

Michael turned and saw Lady Brentford waving at him. He had no desire to speak with the Viscountess, but perhaps he could excuse himself.

'Lady Brentford, I'm sorry, but this isn't a good time.'

Her gaze turned knowing, and she smiled. 'No, I suppose it isn't. You were rather close to Lady Hannah, weren't you? I know more about why she left. If you'd care to hear her reasons, why don't you join me for a few moments?' She began walking towards one of the sitting rooms.

He didn't at all believe Hannah would have confided in the Viscountess. However, he had so little information, perhaps she might have something to offer.

Once they were inside, she closed the door. Michael's gut warned him that Lady Brentford's intentions were not altruistic. Particularly since she had a stepdaughter of marriageable age.

'What is it you want, Lady Brentford?'

She gave him a serene smile. 'I want to see everything put back the way it should be. And we both know that after tonight's dinner, there will be rumours about you.'

'I hardly care about the gossiping tongues of women who don't have anything better to do.'

She flinched slightly. 'Well. Be that as it may, I think you will have an interest in this matter.'

He waited for her to go on. She walked around the edge of the salon, behaving with a familiarity that seemed out of place. 'This isn't the first time I've been in the palace, you know.'

He didn't respond. She traced her hand over a porcelain figure of a shepherdess. 'I was a long-time companion of König Sweyn. His mistress, you might say.'

Horror washed over him when he stared at her.

'No, I am not your mother,' she said, voicing his fears. 'But I think you know the man who *is* my son.'

'Karl,' he said slowly.

'Yes, Karl.' Lady Brentford walked towards the door, stopping before it. 'The King and I were lovers, even after he married Astri. When the Queen became pregnant, she denied him her bed. It was easy enough to coax him back into mine. But it was short-lived. Soon enough, he went back to her and sent me away.'

'Did he know about Karl?'

'I tried to tell him, but the Queen refused to let me into the *Schloss*. So, I decided that if I could not take my rightful place on the throne, my *son* would.'

Michael sensed a ruthlessness, a woman who would stop at nothing to get her desires. He edged his way towards the door, to prevent her from leaving.

'It took a great deal of planning to switch two children,' he said. 'I presume it was you who hired the men?'

A grim smile crossed her mouth. 'Yes. I had to marry the Viscount for his money and influence, a year after Karl was born. Brentford never knew anything about my son. I paid a woman to keep him in the village, far away from us. And my husband was so occupied with his beloved little girl, born from his first wife, he didn't care whether or not I gave him a child.'

'You waited years,' Michael said. 'I was three when you made the switch.'

She nodded. 'I had to wait until Brentford was traveling abroad, before I could come back to Lohenberg with Karl. It took time to choose the right men who could hide amongst the palace guards. And of course, every detail had to be right. Even the scar upon Karl's leg. I carved the wound myself, when he was two,' she said, with a note of pride.

Knowing that she'd hurt her own child made Michael even more tense. 'You want him to become the King.'

'If he is king, then my blood will be part of the royal line, just as it always should have been.'

Michael chose his next words carefully, for he knew it was too late for Karl to claim the throne. Not after the Queen had formally acknowledged him tonight. 'What do you want from me?'

Her icy smile grew thin. 'I want your life, in exchange for Lady Hannah's.' She opened the door, her eyes narrowed. 'Karl will not lose what I've worked so hard to gain.'

HANNAH'S THROAT WAS raw, and her eyes were burning. She didn't know what had happened, but one minute, she was preparing for the banquet, and the next, she was opening her eyes inside a darkened coach.

A man sat across from her, a revolver in his hand. 'So, you're awake, are you? Good.'

'Where are you taking me?'

He smirked. 'Away from the *Schloss*. Once Thorpe learns you've been taken, he'll come after you. I imagine he won't want anything to happen to a pretty one like you.' He tipped the revolver towards her.

Hannah's heart clamoured, realising that they meant to lure Michael to her and then kill him. She closed her mouth, not wanting to provoke her attacker by asking more questions. She wondered if he'd been sent by Fürst Karl.

Closing her eyes, she leaned her head against the side of the coach. Once again, she'd been taken captive by a man against her wishes. Only, with Belgrave, she'd relied upon Michael to save her. This time, she had to save herself.

Remain calm, she urged herself. *Think of your options.*

Her hands weren't bound, but jumping from a moving coach was dangerous. If she fell badly, she could break her neck. But then again, once she reached their destination, her escape options would be worse. They'd probably tie her up. And if Michael did come to rescue her, after they'd killed him no doubt they would take her life as well.

She stared down at her violet gown. The skirts were going to be a problem, hindering her escape. But perhaps if she removed the petticoats, the gown wouldn't billow out so much.

'How much further are we travelling?' she asked her guard.

The man shrugged. 'An hour, perhaps.'

There was a chance he would fire his gun at her, but more likely he needed her alive, in order to lure Michael. Her best chance of escape was now.

Hannah pretended to settle back against the seat, but she inched the back hem of her gown to rest above her hips, so that she was no longer seated upon it. The front of the gown covered the numerous petticoats, but now she could reach the ties that bound the skirts. With her fingers working quickly, she untied them. The man didn't seem to notice her efforts, since it was so dark.

When the last petticoat was unfastened, Hannah stared at the coach door. She would have to open it in one swift motion, stepping free from the petticoats and leaping from the moving coach.

Her common sense told her that this was not a good idea. She would probably tangle up in her skirts and fall on her face.

In her mind, she could almost imagine what her mother would say. 'A proper young lady would never dream of trying to escape. She would simply fold her hands in her lap and wait calmly to be killed.'

Hannah grimaced, and began easing the petticoats past her hips, keeping her lap covered with the dress.

Her pulse was pounding so hard, it was a wonder the man hadn't heard it. Her courage was waning with every second, while her brain screamed out all the things that could go wrong.

Before she could stop herself, she reached for the door handle and threw herself outside the moving carriage. Her body struck the ground hard, and a vicious pain rolled over her as she tumbled off the road. Every inch of her would have bruises, she was certain.

But she was alive.

The sound of male voices shouting made her aware that she couldn't stay for long. They would search for her, and she mustn't be found.

Without the petticoats, her gown hung down low, and she gathered up the hem with both hands. Thank heavens her dress was violet; it would keep them from seeing her clearly. Ignoring the pain, she held fast to her skirts and ran towards the forest. She didn't know where she was or how far she was from the palace.

Her chest ached from running so hard, but she forced herself to keep going. For this time, her life depended on it.

CHAPTER TWENTY-ONE

MICHAEL REACHED OUT and seized Lady Brentford's arm. He twisted it behind her back and forced her into the corridor. 'Where is she? By God, you're going to tell me or—'

The woman laughed at him, and when he looked into her eyes, he saw the true face of madness. 'If you kill me, you'll never find her.' Half-choking on her laughter, she didn't seem to care that she was caught. 'Never, never,' she sang.

At the end of the corridor, he saw Queen Astri approaching with her guards. The men came forward to surround them, and the Queen's face hardened at the sight of Lady Brentford. 'I forbade you to show your face here again.'

Lady Brentford's laughter ceased. With a sly smile, she attempted a curtsy, though Michael kept his grip firm. 'Queen Astri.' Disrespect coated her tone.

'She is the woman responsible for kidnapping me years ago,' Michael told the Queen. Though he didn't want to offend his mother, she needed to understand the Viscountess's actions. 'Karl is Lady Brentford's son. She had hoped he would take the throne.'

The Queen's expression didn't change. 'I've always known that Karl was the result of one of my husband's liaisons. It's the only reason others believed he was the King's son. They thought me mad when I claimed Karl was not my child.' She shivered as though from a sudden chill. 'But I always knew. The scar was wrong.'

Queen Astri turned to her men and commanded them,

'Chain the King's whore in the south-west tower. Let her know what it is to be a prisoner.'

Immediately, the royal guardsmen came and took Lady Brentford into custody. The Viscountess didn't look at all concerned by her fate; instead, she continued to laugh.

'Find her if you can, Lieutenant. Remember—your life, for hers.'

'Her men have taken Lady Hannah captive,' Michael explained to the Queen, after the guards took Lady Brentford away. 'With your permission, Your Majesty, I need men to help me find her.'

The Queen laid her hand on his. 'I will grant you my assistance.' Her hazel eyes hardened. 'But you must promise that afterwards you will assume your place as the Crown Prince.'

Though he understood the the Queen's desire, he didn't want to endanger Hannah. 'Not until Hannah is safe.'

The Queen's face tensed. 'This woman means a great deal to you, doesn't she?'

He met her gaze, leaving no room for disagreement. 'She is going to become my Princess.'

A soft smile touched her lips. 'Then you'd better find her.'

KARL FULLY INTENDED to get drunk. He'd nearly finished off one bottle of brandy and was intent on starting another when he'd overheard laughter in the hallway.

He'd stumbled to the door, intending to slam it shut. But then he'd seen Lieutenant Thorpe standing in the corridor, forcing a woman forward while guards approached them. The woman's face had haunted his nightmares.

Frozen, he'd stared at them, only half-hearing the revelation that the laughing woman was his mother, the King's mistress. He'd not seen her face in years, but the memory of her cruelty struck him to the bone.

For so long, he'd believed the visions were bad dreams. But they had been real.

The Viscountess had come to visit him, inspecting him and ordering him to stand up straight. When it wasn't enough to meet her standards, she'd locked him in a cupboard, screaming at him.

And the knife. Karl shut the door to the study, the vivid memory terrifying, even after so many years. She'd wielded a blade, cutting into the back of his leg while he'd screamed.

He reached for the bottle of brandy, draining it with one last swallow. He closed his eyes, recalling the night he'd been brought to the *Schloss*. He'd been taken from his nurse, crying. The Viscountess had warned him not to speak. And fear had silenced his tongue for nearly a year.

He set down the bottle, no longer knowing what to do.

I know what it is to be imprisoned in a life like this, Lady Hannah had said to him. *And still never be good enough.*

Damn her, she'd seen right through him. She'd tried, in her own way, to reassure him. But Karl knew it wasn't going to be all right. He wasn't the Crown Prince, only a bastard. The years of hard work and patriotism had meant nothing.

His fingers closed around the neck of the empty brandy bottle, the blunt pain clouding out everything. And suddenly, he crashed it into the hearth. Glass shattered everywhere, like the pieces of his life.

Without thinking, he strode out of his study and into the corridor. He found a servant and gave the order to prepare a horse and fetch his cloak.

He knew that Lieutenant Thorpe had taken a group of soldiers with him to find Lady Hannah and bring her back. They didn't need his help, and Karl wasn't nearly drunk enough to join his half-brother in the search.

But perhaps, though he'd lost his birthright, he could prove his worth in another way. Perhaps being a Prince didn't have to be by blood.

But by actions.

HANNAH CONTINUED WALKING through the forest for the next hour, to hide from the men searching. Her entire body ached, and she had bruises up and down her arms and legs. The urge to cry kept rising up, but she reminded herself that tears weren't going to help her get back to Vermisten.

She kept away from the main road, knowing that the men would expect her to follow it. Several times, she stopped, waiting for the moonlight to illuminate her way.

But after another hour, the forest ended, and she had no choice but to venture out into the open. She waited, praying, *Dear God, don't let them find me.* As she walked parallel to the road, she tried to keep hidden.

But still, her thoughts were caught up in Michael.

This afternoon, when he'd returned to her, she'd disobeyed so many rules. Lying in his arms, letting herself be with him, had been one of the most glorious moments of her life. And though her courage had faltered, she now knew that she loved him, whether he was a common soldier or a Crown Prince.

It would break her heart if she never saw him again. She wanted him, more than anything else in the world. And though her feet were blistered and her body was bruised, her heart ached even more.

I don't want to live without him.

All her life, she'd been told what was right and proper. She'd been given rigid rules, expected to be a perfect lady at all times. For so long, she'd lived under that shadow, allowing others to make decisions for her.

She'd blamed everyone else for her lack of freedom,

when one simple word would have changed everything: no. A Princess lived under a rigid set of expectations, true. But she did not bow to the whims of anyone. A true Princess gave commands and decided which rules were meant to protect her and which were meant to control her.

Hannah sat down in the tall grass, resting her feet for a moment. She needed to stop being a lady. And start being a Princess.

Her eyes were blurred with tears when she stood up. In the distance, she heard the sound of a horse approaching. Hannah ducked into the underbrush, her heart thundering in her chest.

When the rider drew closer, she caught sight of his face in the moonlight, and her heart nearly stopped. He moved his horse off the roadside, directly towards her.

Hannah couldn't breathe, couldn't move. Then he stared at the very spot where she was hiding. At his side, she saw the gleam of a revolver.

His voice was cool and resolute. 'Did you lose your way, Lady Hannah?'

DESPITE HOURS OF searching, all they found along the main road was an abandoned coach and a pile of discarded petticoats, nearly twenty miles from the *Schloss*. The road was covered in ruts, made by the wheels of hundreds of coaches. There was no way to tell what had happened to Hannah.

Michael cursed, and wheeled his horse around, doubling back the way they had come. He must have missed something. But what?

The Captain of the Guard approached. 'Forgive me, Your Royal Highness. I believe we should spread out our search in a different direction.'

'She can't be much further from here. The clothes were hers; I'm certain of it. And I'm not leaving her alone.' He touched the revolver at his side, hoping he found Hannah before anyone else did.

The night had begun to fade with the rising of the sun. Amber rays slid over the horizon, the sky dipped in shades of violet.

Michael spurred his horse faster, searching along the edge of the road. He studied the carriage tracks for anything out of the ordinary, wishing to God that he could find something.

And then, it was as if the Almighty answered his prayer. He pulled his horse to a stop and saw it. There, in the dust, he saw the fragment of a violet gown. Just a small tear, but he knew without a doubt that it was hers. It lay near an open meadow, and he noticed tracks leading away from the road.

'This way,' he commanded the men.

As he tracked her through the field and east of the city, he kept the scrap of fabric clenched in his palm. *I'm going to find you,* he promised her. *And God help the man who took you.*

Michael increased the punishing pace, relying upon the bent grasses to guide him. Then, only a few miles east of Vermisten, he sighted a single horse carrying two people. The woman wore a violet gown, leaving no doubt it was Lady Hannah.

Michael rode as fast as he dared, the palace guards joining behind him. With the company of these men, he was certain they could intercept the rider.

But something made him pause. His soldier instincts told him that this was too easy. A trap, perhaps.

He decreased the pace, only slightly, and the palace guards joined him on either side.

The first bullet struck a guard on the outer perimeter, dropping him from his horse. Michael spied the glint of a rifle from behind them. A small group of six men flanked them on both sides, and his own soldiers were within range of the gunfire. Michael charged his mount faster, and the guards followed.

It reminded him of Balaclava, in that fatal moment when he'd tried unsuccessfully to lead his men out of harm's way. And right now, their opponents were gaining on them.

He wasn't going to reach Hannah in time.

If he didn't get these men away safely, all of them would die. And he'd sworn he'd never let anything happen to her.

The leadership of these men was on his shoulders, all of their lives dependent upon the decision he would make. And though doubts rose up, strangling his confidence, a sudden clarity emerged from his fear. He couldn't control the outcome, but he could give an order that might save them.

One of the men turned and tried to fire back, but his shot flew wide. Time to act before anyone else was shot.

Michael signalled them closer. 'Four of you go to the left and take cover near those rocks. The rest of you go to the right and leave me here. I am their target, and it will give you a better chance of picking them off.'

'We can't leave you unguarded,' the Captain argued. 'Our orders are to protect your life.'

'I won't remain on horseback,' Michael countered. 'If we fire from three directions, we'll get them. If we try to outrun them, Hannah will be caught in the crossfire.'

'Your Royal Highness, I'm not certain—'

'Do it,' Michael commanded. 'If you don't, we die.'

With a quick nod of his head, the Captain gestured for half of the men to follow. The other four went right, and Michael wheeled his horse around, reining the animal to a stop. He dismounted, taking cover on the ground.

In this position, he was reminded of the battleground again, surrounded by the enemy. It was familiar, and yet different, for *he* had given the orders this time. Not for the glory of war or the honour of a country—but to save the men.

No longer was he afraid of failing them, of being responsible for their deaths. Instead, he'd given them the chance to save themselves. Their fate lay in God's hands and in their skill.

His guards fired from both directions, and Michael took careful aim at the centre rider. His first shot was out of range, but the second struck its target. They kept up a steady stream of gunfire, but in the meantime, he was losing Hannah while the rider was taking her further and further away. With a glance behind him, Michael saw her disappearing on the horizon.

He expelled a curse, forcing himself to concentrate. The attackers attempted to scatter, but three more shots ended the battle.

Afterwards, the men rejoined him. The Captain looked shaken, but thankful for his life. 'Your Royal Highness, are you all right?'

Michael nodded. 'Send two men to retrieve our fallen man. The rest of you, follow me. We still have to rescue Lady Hannah.'

He mounted his horse, and reloaded his weapon with ammunition given over by the Captain. Urging his steed faster, he rode as fast as the animal would take him. With each mile, his dread intensified.

He couldn't lose her. Hannah belonged to him as surely as she held his heart. And though she had voiced arguments, trying to convince him that she wasn't worthy of being a Princess, he wasn't going to accept them. He would keep her at his side, both to protect her and to love her.

At the crest of a hill, he saw the pair of them near the city borders of Vermisten. The rider had stopped, and he held Hannah captive.

Michael drew his weapon. Right now he couldn't risk firing it, for fear of striking Hannah. He kept up the unyielding pace until at last he reached them.

And when he saw that it was Fürst Karl who held her, a suffocating rage came over him.

His guards joined him, surrounding the pair with weapons drawn. The impostor Prince had his own weapon, but did not reach for it. Instead, he lifted Lady Hannah down from the horse. Hannah raced to his side, and Michael turned to his guards, signalling. 'Take him away. He is guilty of kidnapping Lady Hannah.'

He dismounted and crushed Hannah into his embrace. Gripping her hard, he couldn't calm the racing of his heart. Her dress was ragged, the hemline dragging on the ground. Tangled brown hair hung across her shoulders, and her arms were reddened and bruised.

'Michael, no. The Prince didn't—'

He shushed her, covering her mouth with his. 'He's going to answer for every bruise I see.'

She drew back, not allowing him to kiss her fully. 'Let him go. He was keeping me away from the gunfire, not running from you.'

In her eyes, he saw unyielding stubbornness. And though he had trouble believing that Karl would lift a finger to help them, Hannah stepped back from him and turned to the former Prince. 'Thank you, Your Highness.'

The Prince's mouth tightened, but he nodded. Just as he was about to leave, Michael called out to him. Karl turned, his expression taut and unreadable.

'You have my gratitude.'

The former Prince met his gaze, then turned away. Though Michael still didn't trust him, Hannah was right. Karl had found her, keeping her away from the gunfire. He owed the man for that.

'You came for me,' Hannah whispered. She kissed him, winding her arms around his neck. The simple touch of her lips made him forget about everything but her. He didn't care about anyone around them, nor what they might think. He was simply glad she was safe.

When Michael pulled back, he cupped her face, examining Hannah to be sure she was all right. 'I'm sorry that you had to endure such a terrible night. I should have made sure you had better protection.'

'I don't blame you for it.' She stifled a yawn, leaning her head against his chest. 'I'm just glad you found me.'

'Hannah, I was angry, and I said things I didn't mean.' His fingers traced the line of her jaw. 'I love you, and I'm offering you a choice. I want you to marry me, whether you want to be a Princess or merely a lieutenant's wife.'

She stood up on tiptoes, lifting her mouth to his. 'I love you, Michael. And wherever you go, I will go.'

'Even if it means having to endure this life, with all the trappings of royalty?'

She sent him a mysterious smile. 'Oh, I don't intend for it to be a trap. Not any more.'

CHAPTER TWENTY-TWO

Three days later

'LADY HANNAH, YOU simply must wear white,' her maid Estelle argued, holding up one of her mother's lists. 'Lady Rothburne specifically listed this gown in her instructions, should you attend a formal occasion.'

'No, I disagree. White would make her brown hair stand out too much,' Lady Schmertach argued. 'She needs something softer, more feminine.'

The two ladies were battling between an embroidered ivory silk gown and a pale sea-green gown trimmed with antique lace. Tonight, the King was planning to formally acknowledge Michael as the Crown Prince to the people of Vermisten. In turn, Michael intended to announce their betrothal. The entire palace was buzzing with the news.

Hannah ignored the two bickering ladies and opened the door to her wardrobe. Staring at her choices, she selected a crimson silk gown trimmed with ribbons and pearls. It would bare her shoulders, with only slight wisps of fabric as sleeves on her upper arms. With long white gloves, the gown would be vibrant, commanding everyone's attention.

'I will wear this.'

Both women gaped at her. 'But, Lady Hannah, that colour is too scandalous,' Estelle burst in.

'It's the sort of dress a courtesan would wear,' Lady Schmertach interjected. 'Not a Princess.'

No, it wasn't at all the dress a Princess would wear. At least, not a Princess who would be subservient to the wishes of those around her. Not a Princess who would hide behind lists and rules, wondering if she was behaving like a proper lady.

No, it was the gown that a confident woman would wear. A woman who was making her own rules.

Hannah's smile was serene. 'I have made my decision.'

'But, my lady, you can't possibly—'

'You will abide by my wishes, or you will both find yourselves in another post.' Hannah sent them a cool, commanding look, and her message was clear. After exchanging looks, both women dropped into curtsies.

My goodness, that felt good. Liberating, actually. She'd never given orders before, always letting others dictate her decisions.

'Do you...wish to wear the diamonds or the rubies, my lady?' Estelle ventured.

'The rubies,' Hannah pronounced.

She held out her arms, waiting for them to finish dressing her. Estelle clamped her mouth shut and obeyed. Though Lady Schmertach appeared horrified, she, too, assisted the maid. When they had finished, a soft knock resounded at the door.

Lady Schmertach answered it at Hannah's bidding, and a footman came forth with a message. 'The King has requested your presence, Lady Hannah. He wishes to speak with you about your betrothal.' The servant bowed and stepped back into the hall, waiting to escort her. She couldn't exactly keep the King waiting, so she followed the footman, with Lady Schmertach trailing as a silent chaperone.

Hannah felt more than conspicuous in her red gown, particularly for a royal summons. It was one thing to wear a shocking dress for a court ball; it was another to wear such a garment in front of a dying king.

The footman led her into the King's chambers, where she saw the monarch seated in a high-backed, upholstered chair.

Hannah fell into a deep curtsy. 'Your Majesty, I received your summons.' It was the first time she had ever been in the presence of a king. Her nerves grew rattled, and she was afraid of somehow saying the wrong thing.

The King was not old, but illness had drawn away his strength. His grey hair hung at his shoulders, deep wrinkles set within his eyes. Yet she sensed a ruthless air of authority. His gaze passed over her gown with disapproval. 'I understand that my son wishes to marry you. And that you are the daughter of an English Marquess.'

'Yes, Your Majesty.'

'Why would you believe that you could possibly understand the role of a Princess? Do you think yourself capable of ruling at his side?'

No, she didn't know anything about ruling a country, any more than Michael did. But beneath his pointed questions, she saw a man who was trying to intimidate her.

Be polite, she warned herself. 'I can learn what I need to know.'

The King regarded her with dismissal. 'You haven't any idea what the life of a Princess is like. I suppose you believe that Princesses sit around all day wearing diamonds and choosing new gowns.'

His callous remark sent all of her years of good manners and training up in flames. Hannah counted silently to five, then ten.

'No, that's not what I believe at all.'

'You want to marry my son because you want to become royalty, isn't that right?'

'I am going to marry Michael Thorpe,' she said firmly.

'Not a Prince or Fürst, or whatever else you want to call him. I am going to marry the *man* I love, not his title.'

Before the King could add another sardonic remark, she plunged forward. 'And, yes, I know exactly what the life of a Princess is like. She has rules to obey, expectations to live up to and countless advisers telling her what she should and shouldn't do.'

Hannah picked up her skirts and stood directly in front of the King. 'And I would likely be the worst sort of Princess you'd ever have. Do you want to know why?'

The King shook his head, but she spied a gleam in his eyes.

'Because I refuse to live like that. I don't care at all whether I should be wearing a white gown or pearls or a crown. Or whether I should host a garden party or an evening soirée.' Her hands clenched into fists at her side.

'I care about whether the man I love is safe at night. I care about a widowed woman, Mrs Turner, who risked her own life to save his. And I care about a man who is about to lose not only his kingdom tonight, but his own father. Just because he was born on the wrong side of the sheets.'

When she was finished, her lungs were burning. But Hannah met the King's enigmatic gaze with no regrets.

'You're wrong, Lady Hannah,' the King said. 'You wouldn't be at all the worst sort of Princess. You'd be the kind of Princess I would want my son to marry.'

The King reached out for her hand, and smiled. 'After the ceremony, I have no doubt you will tell me all the changes I need to make to my kingdom.' He coughed, signalling to a servant for his medicine. Then he leaned back against the chair to rest.

Hannah's face turned the same shade as her dress. 'My mother would be appalled at what I've just said to you.'

'I prefer a woman who speaks her mind. And—' the King's smile turned wicked '—that is a fetching gown, I must say.'

For the ceremony, Michael had ordered thirty guards to surround them, with more men disguised as townspeople to infiltrate the crowds for the greatest protection.

'We don't need an army,' Hannah protested, taking his hand in hers. 'It's only a ceremony and a blessing. The King will acknowledge you as his son, and there will be a ball tonight. You're behaving as though we're about to go to war.'

'I'm going to keep you safe.' Michael studied every angle of the men, ensuring that each one was in his place. Stealing a glance toward Hannah, he added, 'As beautiful as you look tonight, I wouldn't be surprised if someone else tried to take you away from me. And I'd rather not murder a man in the midst of the ceremony, all things considered.'

'I'm so glad you decided to take your place as Prince.' Hannah leaned in and pressed a kiss upon his cheek. The diamond-and-aquamarine ring sparkled upon her hand. Though the Queen had tried to get her to wear an heirloom betrothal ring that belonged to one of his great-grandmothers, Hannah had refused.

'I don't have a choice,' Michael admitted, 'but it's the right thing to do.'

Though he had not been raised to a life of privilege, he could use his past experience to help the people. He could be a better Prince, precisely because he understood their hardships and could relate to them. The guardsmen, in particular, had already begun treating him as their ruler. Word had spread about how he had led them against Lady Brentford's men and saved their lives.

'You should consider Karl as one of your advisers,' Hannah suggested, with a smile. 'I've never met a man so devoted to his country.'

'I don't entirely trust him.' Michael still felt a lingering resentment that Karl had found Hannah first. And despite her claims that the Fürst had been honourable, Michael couldn't believe the man's motives were selfless.

'I hope you don't mind, but I asked a guardsman to check on Lady Brentford,' Hannah said. 'Even though the King sent away the Viscount and his daughter, I have a bad feeling about her imprisonment.'

'There were three men guarding her,' Michael insisted. What he didn't tell her was that he, too, had gone to ensure Lady Brentford remained imprisoned. The Viscountess had laughed at him again, swearing that he would never become king.

'Nothing will happen,' Michael promised.

'I hope not.'

They could not engage in further conversation, because it was time to join the King and Queen on the dais. Hours of political speeches preceded the King's formal announcement. Though König Sweyn had to lean upon his servants to stand before the people, his proclamation was clear and undeniable. Michael was his true son and would inherit the throne.

Michael hardly heard a word of the King's speech. His gaze studied each and every member of the crowd, for fear of someone threatening Hannah. But when the archbishop approached to give the blessing, Michael had no choice but to leave her side.

A flicker of motion caught his attention. He saw Karl, standing amid the crowd, only a few feet away. There was a look of determination in the former Prince's eyes, just as he raised his revolver.

Michael threw himself towards Hannah and the gun exploded.

CHAPTER TWENTY-THREE

A SERVANT WHO'D been close to Michael dropped forward upon the dais, a knife clenched in his hands. Blood pooled from his chest, and Hannah recognised him as one of Reischor's footmen. He'd been sent to assassinate Michael.

She covered her mouth with her hands, while Michael pulled her tightly to him. Her hands were shaking, and she couldn't let go.

Chaos erupted below them in the crowd, guards surrounding Karl. But Hannah couldn't dwell upon it, for her mind was centred on the danger. Michael could have been killed just now, and she couldn't bear the thought of losing him.

'Are you all right?' she asked, gripping him tightly.

Michael shook his head. 'Stay here with the guards. I need to speak with Karl.'

'He saved your life, Michael,' she reminded him. Though the shot had been risky, if Karl hadn't taken it just now, Michael would be dead. Hannah shuddered to think of it.

He touched her cheek. 'I won't let him be harmed.'

Michael walked back on the dais, shielded by the King's men. Karl held his ground, meeting Michael's gaze with a steadfast look of his own. It was the look of a man satisfied with the outcome.

The crowd studied the two men, both sons of the King. Murmurs of the Changeling legend were whispered. Every last citizen of Vermisten stared at the pair, shocked and fascinated by the mirrored faces.

Karl attempted a bow, but Michael stopped him. Instead, he crossed forward and offered his hand to his half-brother. In doing so, he acknowledged Karl as an equal, granting him the highest honour.

'It seems I owe you my thanks a second time,' Michael said, his voice loud enough for all to hear. 'Brother.'

One month later

'YOU AREN'T SUPPOSED to be here,' Hannah chided, when Michael slipped inside her chamber. 'If my mother finds you, she'll beat you across the head with her parasol.'

'I doubt it. She's too eager to have you marry into royalty.' He lifted her hand, where the diamond-and-aquamarine engagement ring sparkled.

'She's going to send me into an asylum,' Hannah groaned, just thinking of her mother's excitement over the past few weeks.

'Don't worry. Mrs Turner will keep your mother occupied.'

Hannah ventured a smile. Abigail Turner had been granted a full pardon by the King and Queen, and had rejoined the Queen's ladies. The castle staff was aware of her condition, and Mrs Turner had a servant of her own to tend her, when necessary.

The remainder of the time, she was under the care of her husband, Sebastian, who had escaped his captors and had hidden in Denmark the past twenty-three years. Hannah still smiled to think of their reunion, the elderly couple embracing as though it was their wedding day.

Michael kissed her deeply, and a secret thrill heated her

blood. She couldn't believe this man was going to be her husband tomorrow.

When he pulled back, he offered, 'I spoke to Karl this morning. He seemed surprised at the estates and land I granted to him. But I thought it was only fitting, since he is to be an adviser.'

'It wasn't his fault that he was caught in the middle of this,' Hannah said.

'I agree. Queen Astri isn't pleased, but the King is acknowledging him as his illegitimate son and granting him an honorary title.'

Michael's hands moved down the silk of her gown, and he nipped at her chin. 'Do you want to be late for dinner tonight?'

Before she could answer, the door burst open. Lady Rothburne clapped a hand over her mouth. 'Hannah! What on earth are you thinking, being alone with a man in your room?'

'Michael is going to be my husband tomorrow,' she pointed out.

'Well, he isn't right now.' Lady Rothburne made a shooing motion with her hands. 'And I'm certain that His Royal Highness *can wait.*'

Michael sent her a secret wink, nodding to the women as he made his exit. His palace guards followed him, once he was in the hallway.

Lady Rothburne began discussing the wedding flowers and decorations, arguing in favour of roses instead of lilies. Hannah ignored the conversation, for she didn't really care what kind of flowers there were at the ceremony.

'And, Hannah, you really should change the gown you're wearing. That amethyst colour...why, it's scandalous. No decent woman would wear such a thing to dinner.'

Hannah simply ignored her mother's chiding. She had

livened up the colours of her wardrobe, after Michael had sent her shopping for her wedding trousseau. Afterwards, many of the ladies of the court had followed her example. 'This particular gown was a gift from the Queen, Mother,' Hannah added, enjoying the look of astonishment on her mother's face.

'Well. I suppose it must be perfectly appropriate, then.' Lady Rothburne touched her heart and gave a happy sigh. 'I can hardly believe that my little girl is going to be a Princess. It's what I've always dreamed of.'

Hannah would have wed Michael if he were a beggar, but didn't say so.

'And your cousins, Dietrich and Ingeborg, were surprised beyond belief to hear about your engagement. I cannot believe you never once visited their estate in Germany.' Her mother fanned herself, her cheeks flaming. 'Oh, the scandals you've caused.'

'It was never my intention to worry anyone, Mother.' She hadn't revealed any of the attempts on their lives, not wanting to make her mother any more agitated than she already was. 'And everything is going to be fine. No one cares about the past.' Particularly herself.

'I must admit, this is all so unfamiliar to me,' Christine blustered. 'I hardly speak the language well enough, and the customs are so different. Why, I'm not even certain how I should behave at the simplest of society functions!'

Hannah drew her mother into an embrace, hiding her laugh. 'Don't worry, Mother,' she said, drawing back with a broad smile. 'I'll make you a list.'

'YOU WERE MEANT to be a Princess,' Michael said, as he knelt before Hannah, gently massaging her sore feet. 'Queen Astri was quite proud of you.'

Hannah's ladies-in-waiting had helped her to remove

the wedding finery, and his new wife wore a simple nightgown trimmed with lace. He didn't intend for Hannah to wear it much longer.

Their wedding day had been nothing short of a fairy tale, with a horse-drawn carriage, the ceremony itself held inside St Mark's Cathedral in Vermisten. He'd been spellbound at the sight of Hannah in her cream silk wedding gown and the diamond crown the Queen had insisted that she wear.

Around her neck, Hannah had worn the diamond necklace from that night at the ball, so many months ago. Just seeing it nestled against her throat brought back so many memories of the time when he had rescued her from Belgrave. And he understood that she'd worn it as a reminder of that night when they'd spent hours together.

'Are you disappointed not to be a soldier any more?' she asked, helping him to remove his shirt.

'I can help the troops more as a Prince,' he admitted. 'I've arranged to send fifty men from Lohenberg, to deliver supplies to the front. The general was most grateful, even if he did grant me an honourable discharge from the British Army.'

Hannah's palms slid over his bare skin, and he leaned in to kiss her throat. The heady fragrance of jasmine swept over him. 'What about you?' he murmured, lifting the hem of her nightgown, sliding the silk up her thighs. 'I've imprisoned you in this life, as my Princess. Any regrets?'

'None at all.' She inhaled with a gasp when he lifted the nightgown away. 'I was wrong to think this would be a prison. It's only a prison if you let others command you.'

'Princess, I am at your command.' Michael knelt at her feet, touching her long legs, kissing her soft skin. He caressed a path up to her breasts, teasing and tasting her until her hands dug into his hair. 'What are your orders?'

'Take off your clothes.'

Though her tone was teasing, he obeyed. When he was naked, Hannah's arms encircled his neck, and he kissed her deeply. Skin to skin, he possessed her, letting her feel how very much he loved her.

Michael lifted her into his arms and strode over to the bed. Dropping her on to the coverlet, he reached for her discarded crown. With a teasing smile, he laid it upon her head. Like a pagan princess, she captivated him.

'What are your orders now?' Michael covered her body with his, enjoying the way she trembled with desire.

'Love me,' she whispered, reaching up to kiss him. The warmth of her mouth evoked a searing desire and the need to join their bodies together.

Michael lowered his mouth to her skin, marvelling that she belonged to him now. His Princess and his beloved wife.

'Always,' he promised.

EPILOGUE

HANNAH SAT UPON the floor of the drawing room, serving tea to a stuffed bear. Emily Chesterfield, the Countess of Whitmore, had her own skirts tucked over her feet while their daughters offered chocolates to the other doll guests. Diamonds and priceless jewels hung from the little girls' necks, while heirloom tiaras rested on their heads.

'I don't know about you, but I'm not going in,' the Earl of Whitmore announced, nodding at Michael, who stood in the doorway with him. 'They might make us wear a crown.'

Hannah smiled and rose to her feet. 'Michael already has to wear one on formal occasions,' she told her brother, as she drew closer to the men. 'It's the price of being a Prince.'

Michael kissed her hand in greeting. 'May we join you for tea?'

The Countess got up from the carpet, holding the hand of his daughter, Charlotte.

At the age of four, Charlotte wore her hair in two braids, one with a pink ribbon and one with purple. She'd inherited her mother's beauty, but her stubbornness was a trait of her grandfather.

'Papa, you have to sit by me.'

Michael allowed Charlotte to take him by the hand, leading him to a chair. His daughter chose a chocolate biscuit from the tea tray and stuffed it into his mouth. 'I made these, with Aunt Emily's help,' she explained.

He brought her up to sit on his knee. 'They are delicious.'

Charlotte sent him a sunny smile and wound her arms around him. Her sapphire-and-diamond crown dipped below her forehead, and he adjusted it on her head. Pride and contentment filled him up inside, along with the gratitude that he could now give his wife and daughter everything they would ever need.

Hannah came up beside them, and Michael took her hand in his. As their daughter chattered with her cousin Victoria and the Countess, he met his wife's gaze. Love shone from Hannah's smile, along with silent amusement.

Charlotte jumped down from his lap to serve tea to the dolls, and Michael turned to Hannah with a wicked gaze. He glanced down at his lap and whispered, 'There's room.'

'No, you wretch.' Hannah rested her hands on his shoulders, laughing in his ear. 'That would be improper.'

'I like being improper,' he whispered back. 'We could be quite improper later.'

'Yes, later,' she promised.

He stood up from the chair and reached out to adjust her crown. Hannah's smile transformed at the touch of his hands. In his eyes, he let her see all the desire he held, and how much she meant to him. How much he loved her.

Taking his hand in hers, Hannah sent him a soft smile of her own. 'Or sooner.'

* * * * *

Fleeing an unwanted betrothal, Lady Carice's days are numbered. So when she meets Norman soldier Raine de Garenne she longs to experience one night of passion...

Read on for a sneak preview of WARRIOR OF FIRE, a powerful new book from
Michelle Willingham,
the second in her ***WARRIORS OF IRELAND*** *duet.*

In the darkness, she reached up to Raine's face, touching his cheek. She explored the smooth surface, fascinated by him. He caught her hand and drew her fingers back to her lips in a warning to be still and silent.

The risk of being discovered was far too high. She knew that—and yet, she was tempted to seize a moment to herself. He was only going to push her away as soon as they were out of hiding. She wanted to embrace every last chance to live, even if it was pushing beyond what was right. Raine would never understand her need to reach out for all the moments remaining.

This man intrigued her, for he was a living contradiction. He was both fierce and benevolent, like a warrior priest. And though he claimed to be a Norman loyal to King Henry, she knew he was a man of secrets.

His skin was warm beneath her fingertips, his face revealing hard planes. A sudden heat rushed through her as she explored his features. During her life, she'd never had the opportunity to be courted by a man, and her illness had shut her away from the world. Her father had isolated her until it seemed that only the hand of Death was waiting in her future.

Perhaps it was the lack of time that made her act with boldness. Or perhaps it was her sudden sense of unfairness. There was a handsome man beside her, one who attracted her in ways she didn't understand. Being so near to him was forbidden…and undeniably exciting. Why shouldn't she seize the opportunity that was before her?

Her pulse was racing, and the proximity of his body against hers was a very different kind of risk.

He leaned down and, against her lips, he murmured, "Don't move." The heat of his breath and the danger of discovery only heightened the blood racing through her. She was aware of every line of his body, of his warm hands around her, and the feeling of his hips pressed to her own.

Her imagination revelled in what it would be like to be kissed by this man. His mouth was so close to hers…and if she lifted her lips, they would be upon his.

HHEXP1115

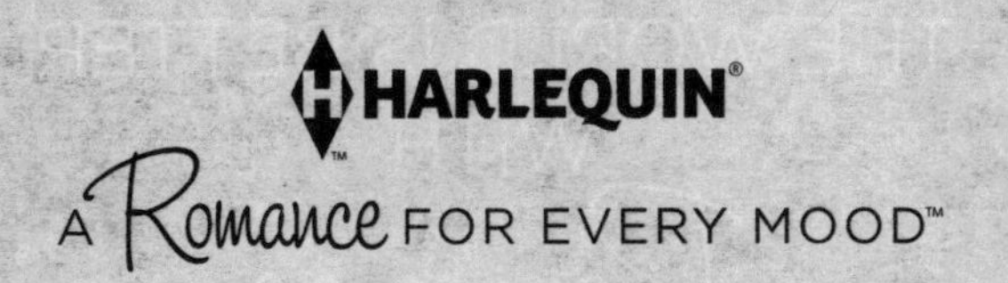

JUST CAN'T GET ENOUGH?

Join our social communities and talk to us online.

You will have access to the latest news on upcoming titles and special promotions, but most importantly, you can talk to other fans about your favorite Harlequin reads.

Harlequin.com/Community

Facebook.com/HarlequinBooks

Twitter.com/HarlequinBooks

Pinterest.com/HarlequinBooks